Cottages

~

A Chesapeake Bay Novel

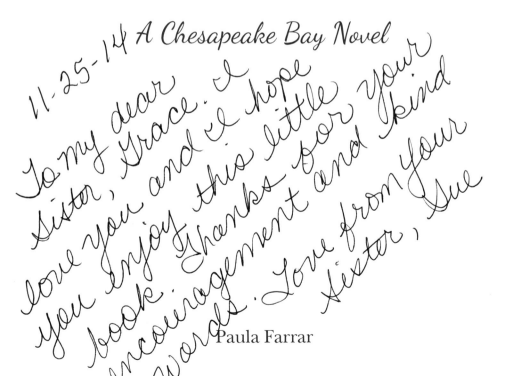

11-25-14

To my dear Sister, Grace. I love you and I hope you enjoy this little book. Thanks for your encouragement and kind words. Love from your Sister, Sue

Paula Farrar

Grace Brown

ISBN: 1497324637
ISBN 13: 978-1497324633

Chapter 1

Angry

The Chesapeake Bay was angry again. But it was a different kind of anger this time. The old folks, who remembered the hurricane of 1940, quietly sat in their weatherworn rockers, snug behind a rusted screen porch, appraising the bay for ominous signs. The bay churned up white foam, blowing it over the rock revetment and onto the hibiscus, the large hot-pink flowers bending their heads with each assault. The sky, a dark gray canopy hanging low, seemed to pull the gulls and osprey under it as they scurried, wings beating against the unbalanced current air.

Brown pelicans were diving for their quota of feed fish, much closer inland than in recent memory, and small craft were missing from the usual areas out front, except for a crab boat bobbing side to side, its diesel engines blowing black smoke. Sure-footed workers hurried to haul up every crab pot, emptying the catch quickly and stacking the empty pots on top of one another. As the captain steered the boat on to the next pot, the wind blew the smells of the Chesapeake up and down the cottage road, diesel fuel and brine mixed together.

Instinct had overtaken speculation from those creatures who knew from some primordial knowledge that, indeed, the bay was angry again. But I had no such instinct. There I was, alone in an old cottage that was missing a few roof shingles and a small amount of worn-out siding, not knowing or caring about what was in store for me that day—the day that changed everything. I listened to the heavy wind gust and wished it would blow into my cottage; into my head, blowing away my nightmare along with my messed-up mind.

Someone told me once; a previous counselor, that I needed to take control of my dreams. She said I only needed to try. Of course I tried, but I was sleepless again, drinking coffee to stay awake, while yearning for sleep. My counselor also advised me that I just needed to think "happy thoughts." I tried that too, but inside I felt like a wreck most days. Now a new day was about to begin and I wondered if I would be able to make it through. I didn't even have the strength to be angry about my situation. But then, the bay looked like it was angry enough as I stood watching, wondering if I would ever feel in control of anything.

So that's the shape I was in that day in the summer of 1995, and that was the shape most of the circa 1920s cottages were in on our road at the end of nowhere. I fit right in. In our tiny community we liked our unassuming and imperfect cottages; a refuge from that Joneses sort of life. The bay was the main point, and most of us were content with its ever-changing personality, and the freedom of not having to appear one way or another. There was not a lot of drama going on between neighbors either. You could keep to yourself, or you could be friendly. I liked keeping to myself as much as possible.

"Rainey," or "Ms. Grant," neighbors would often ask me, "Come over for a visit or a cup of coffee soon." But I gave excuses, faking it with a smile and a promise to take them up on their invitations.

To someone from the city, our little places probably looked ragtag and disheveled. Built in the 1920s, they were only meant to be weekend getaway places. Each cottage was no more than twelve by fourteen feet originally, but over the years various owners would add a porch, an outdoor shower, or a deck, and then they'd close the addition in as part of the interior. As a result, the patchwork of underpinnings would separate, sag, and give the general appearance of being dilapidated fishing huts. Those of us who loved the neighborhood considered our look to be more eclectic than shabby, but "shabby chic" might be stretching it a bit.

In summer everyone piled onto the pier on the creek, behind the pink cottage. The owner, Mrs. Finch, always welcomed the neighbors, who enjoyed crabbing or fishing from her pier, allowing anyone on who could find a spot—along with their children, dogs, crab nets, fishing poles, and bloodworms. Oftentimes Mrs. Finch would bring a wooden folding chair out for herself. She loved to watch everyone enjoying life as much as she loved Motown music, which she often played on her tape deck through an open window. The Four Tops singing "Sugar Pie Honey Bunch," her favorite song, was an open invitation to come on over.

Her pier often wobbled when neighbors crowded onto it, and on more than one occasion, someone ended up in the muddy-bottomed creek. We all knew better than to dive in from the Finch pier or swim or wade in the creek, even on the most humid of summer days. If we wanted to swim, we would head for the little private beach on the bay side of the road. Falling off of the pier was not a pleasant experience; however, the crabs seemed to like the mud. There they would hide in the shallows until tempted out by a chicken neck tied to a long piece of twine and dragged overhead.

Eventually a small channel was dredged so that people could take their boats out of the creek and into the bay. The salty bay waters entered the creek where the wildlife estuary harboring osprey, mute swan, bald eagles and brown pelicans coexisted with loud boats speeding by the marsh, and where the blue crab visited in and out of the creek along with the tides.

There were others besides the pink cottage. A shingle that read MUD MANOR sat in the yard of a gray clapboard cottage next to the pink one. The name was appropriate as it was the lowest-sitting cottage and was always flooding after a nor'easter. Cleanup was a frequent chore, but the owners didn't seem to worry about it. Every weekend there would be cars there with many young and not-so-young adults, playing card games and drinking sweet teas and sodas from behind a screened porch.

At the beginning of our road sat Short's Beachfront Resort. It had been a popular weekend place in the early 1920s, but by the 1940s erosion had taken away the last remnants of the fishing pier, and the land as well. The last owner, "Shorty," had done everything he could to stop the erosion, but he'd finally resorted to dumping old tires and even junkyard cars into the water as a sort of man-made barricade against the hungry bay tides.

The roof had a multitude of leaks, and customers had to negotiate their way to the bar to order a crab cake, but the one thing that was certain about Shorty, who was actually over six feet tall and seemed nearly as wide, was that nobody in Southern Maryland knew how to cook a better crab cake. Shorty was always yelling at his wife, his customers, his dog, and himself, but that only added to the charm of the place. Ornery from birth, he never surprised anyone with a caring word. His wife used to say to him, "Shorty, one of these days you are just going to drop dead of a heart attack," and that's exactly how it happened. One day he was yelling at his dog for getting into his crab cake batter and died right on the spot. His wife and his dog lived another life after that. With no one to yell at them, Shorty's wife got bored, sold the place, and moved away with the dog.

We were a mixed lot of individuals, young and old, educated and not, business owners and laborers. I was somewhere in between—forty, partially college educated, and out of work as a bookkeeper for a small contractor. I was laid off temporarily due to another tax on small businesses which made times lean for my boss. I felt expendable. My boss was a terrible bookkeeper, but he had no other options.

"I promise you, Rainey," he had assured me, "that I will get you back here before October begins. Besides, don't you think you could use a little vacation time? I think you sure could." I guess he thought that he was encouraging me. That's what really bothered me the most. Being laid off for business reasons was understandable, but I knew what he was getting at.

I had thought my private life was my own business and not a company matter. The overheard and muffled conversations about what I needed to do with my life, and often from people who should have listened to their own advice, were hard to ignore. But I knew that gossip was the one constant thing in the office. I just wished the gossip hadn't been about me.

It had been a rough year, and I had gone to my cottage for solace and recovery. I had just buried my parents' ashes in a plot that I had paid for out of my inheritance. Though they had died years apart, I had their ashes shipped to me from Washington State so I could have them near me again. I ached for something to care about; ashes would have to do.

Their ashes were the only family I had left, so while I was laid off, I planned to spend some time doing historical research in the area near my cottage. I had nothing else to do. Visiting my parents' gravesite every day wouldn't bring them back. I just wished I had flown home to visit them more often. Why do regrets always come too late?

The crisp, salty breeze picked up, and my sheer white window drapes blew horizontally into my small living area. I wished for a storm. Storms could be a good thing. Anything that could bring a cool breeze to a home lacking air conditioning was a welcome relief from the oppressive and humid August air.

Opening the front door, I went out to retrieve a fold-out metal chair from the front yard. As I was folding it up, I was hit in the face with foamy spray, which woke me from my solitude, and then I tripped over the chair legs and fell to the ground face-first. At least there was no one outside who could have seen me fall again. Why was I always falling on my face?

I remained still, allowing the wind to send the soaking rain all over my body. I had wanted a storm. A storm was a reason to come outside when everyone else hurried indoors, a perfect excuse to be my usual unsociable self. Was this a nor'easter? I removed a piece of crabgrass from my chin and stood up.

Everything looked gray, even the waves until they were lifted up by the wind and changing tide, exposing the lightest green color I had ever seen. I could almost see through to the other side. The transparency was beautiful, but the gray color matched my mood and somehow was more comforting to me.

Looking out, I could see that the water level was very high upon the rocks out front, but then as luck would have it, another wave blew over the wall, sending the burning salt water into my eyes and nearly knocking me over again. I hurried into my cottage, slamming the door shut behind me. There I stood, water dripping onto the sloping marine-blue painted wood floor.

For some reason it seemed logical to change my clothes, but instead I plopped my drenched body into my old blue armchair and cried. I always cry at the oddest times. But my tearful solitude was interrupted by a gentle knock on my door. I sat low in the sun-faded armchair and tried to ignore the knock, remaining still and silent. I wasn't in the mood for people. The knocking continued. I thought, *why can't people figure out that I don't want to be bothered and just leave me alone?*

"Ms. Grant, are you doing all right in there? Mrs. Manny and I saw the wave knock you down and thought I'd better come see if you need some help preparing for the nor'easter coming in. You may need to plywood your windows."

I wiped my face with my wet hands and called out, "Yes, I'm fine. Just a minute please." *Maybe he'll see how wet I am and think nothing of my red, tear-streaked face,* I thought. Opening the door, I motioned for him to come inside. I put on my biggest fake smile for this man with the genuine face.

"I see you were hit pretty hard with one of those waves," he said kindly. There's nothing like salt in the eyes. Could I help you batten down the hatches?"

Mr. Manny, as we in the neighborhood fondly called him, had to be in his eighties. His hair was solid white, and he walked favoring one thin leg over the other, rolling his bent back in uneven sways. But his gentle and loving smile gave no indication of pain.

He was a gentleman from Virginia, and it didn't seem right to call him anything but "Mr. Manny." Even here in this remote spot, he dressed in a nice, though worn, plaid cotton shirt, with to-the-knee shorts, long socks, and comfortable-looking black shoes. Atop his white hair sat a straw hat, which he always wore when outdoors. When he took it off, I was amazed at how much hair he had. I was nearly forty with straight, thin hair, but this man had a mound of hair under that straw hat. Would I be so lucky at eighty? Finding a small scatter rug, he stood still as his wet clothing dripped.

"Thank you," I answered. "I'm just going to close up the windows and sit it out. I'm fine, really."

The old man stood smiling and nodding his head in understanding as he listened to my refusal for help. Then he ignored everything I had said. Had he even heard me?

"The missus and I were wondering if you'd like to come and sit out the storm with us. She's going to put a nice tomato pie in the oven, and as long as the storm doesn't knock out the electric, we're planning to sit and enjoy a bite. She's made up some of her good sweet tea also."

Jill, my closest friend, told me that I had become a hermit, preferring to spend my weekends at the cottage while avoiding contact with those who cared about me in town. My answer was always the same: "I'm busy doing research. How does that make me a hermit?"

Wishing to be left alone, I would pretend that I was upbeat and together, and Jill would always allow me to do that. It was a blessing to me that she would back off and leave me alone for a week or two, but then I would get a call and she would bring my condition to my attention again. I hated that.

"You know, Rainey," she would begin, "you need to talk about it."

"No, I don't need to talk about it," I would cut in. "Why do you insist that I do? Not everyone is the same. Please don't categorize me with all of humanity."

"Oh, so Rainey Grant is no longer a part of humanity? I didn't know that."

Jill made me think about things, even when I didn't want to, so I would joke with her and get off of the phone as quickly as I politely could. But I couldn't politely refuse Mr. Manny. His kind face would not let me.

"Sure," I answered. "Let me just get some dry clothes on, and I'll walk over." Then after he left, I chided myself for not having the courage to just be honest and say, "No, thank you." In fact, most of my life I had always done what others expected of me. Here I was doing exactly that. I disliked that about myself, along with other things. Why did I always choose peace over honesty?

My parents grew to hate one another, no matter how I tried to talk and make peace between them. Their drinking finally got them drunk enough to not care about each other, but I cared, so I finally moved away, thinking I could find someone else to make happy. That brings me to my own marriage. I couldn't fix that either. Now being alone seemed the only sure remedy for peace. So there I was, agreeing with a smile, to go to a neighbor's cottage where I would be forced to chitchat. Talking is so overrated.

Mr. and Mrs. Manny lived a few cottages down from me alongside another cottage, which took all the beatings from the wind and spray blowing over the seawall. Being blocked by another house, the screened-in porch did not allow a full view of the bay. But like a smaller child hidden behind a protective brother, it was the only cottage on the narrow gravel road that sat back enough to offer it some protection when nor 'easterly winds blew.

As old folks go, these two brought a sense of community to the end-of-the-road cottages. I often wondered how two people could live together in such harmony. How did they stay married to one another for so long when the entire world was abandoning matrimony in favor of divorce frenzy? At last count about forty percent of marriages ended in divorce. Mine was no exception. In fact, that was the one area where I did fit in. Would divorce be my only legacy?

On stormy days I always thought of Patrick. We'd enjoyed many good times here together. We were young and beautifully in love and spent most of our summers with his family in their small cottage. I had never loved anyone before Patrick. To me he was the answer to my vision of a perfect man—handsome, sure, and devoted to his parents and me. We got married, and then everything started to go wrong. Patrick told me that I needed to do something more with my life. He was bored with me and my quiet ways, and seemed to always have the urge to push me to be like other women he admired. I tried to comply with his wishes, but I just could never measure up. The harder I tried, the more he criticized me. Still, I loved him.

His mother and father passed away after a car accident, and their place had to be sold so that the inheritance could be settled between Patrick and his sister. So we bought our own little cottage, one that his parents had owned as a rental property, just down the road. I loved the cottage, and still do, but that didn't make things better for us, though I had hoped somehow it would. Patrick grew more interested in work than he was with me and with other people when he wasn't at work. I didn't seem to be the antidote for his grief, and it left me feeling helpless.

I suppose I could have joined a community singles group after the divorce, but then it has always been my opinion that most of those people are confident and social; skills I seem to lack. Then of course, there are all of those matching and dating things on television, where lonely people lie about their height, weight, age, hair, and personality. *Why bother?* I wondered. *Love isn't what it's supposed to be anyway. Love is an illusion and a cruel joke.*

Personalities change, and so does love. About the only thing I got out of fifteen years of marriage was the cottage. We had no children. Patrick never wanted them. We didn't even own a dog together. He didn't want a dog scuffing up our hardwood floors. He took the house in town, and I opted for an apartment near work and the little cottage. And now here I was, jobless and afraid to go outside unless it was storming, and then only if everyone else had fled to their cottages, closing their storm shutters behind them. Not me. The bay did for me what I didn't have the courage to do for myself.

Did I have to go to the Manny cottage? I thought about not going for well over an hour, but I figured that a few minutes with them might keep Mr. Manny from showing up at my door again. After dropping my wet clothes on the bedroom floor, I changed into my shorts, T-shirt, Sperry flip-flops, and orange rain parka. Then I put my hair back into a ponytail, pulled up the parka hood, and started walking the gravel road to the Manny cottage.

There I found Mr. Manny in his rocker on the porch. He had not closed the plywood shutter down to block out the wind and spray, and he seemed perfectly dry and content. When he saw me approach, he came to the screen door and opened it wide. "Come on in, young lady," he said with a grin. "Mrs. Manny is thrilled that you want to try out her tomato pie, despite coming out in a storm."

I thanked him and entered the screened porch area, hoping that I wouldn't have to endure chitchat. I was no good at it. Here on their little cinder block porch sat three high-backed wooden chairs. The Adirondack chairs looked as though they had been there for generations. I guessed that Mrs. Manny had sewn beautiful pillows for the backs and seats. The fading fabric was a blue-and-cream stripe with a little gray cord of piping all around the edges. The cushions were held on with gray ribbons tied in bows, which were frayed but hung on to the chair backs with a good grip.

A ceiling fan circulated the breeze coming from the bay, and I found it comfortably cool. There beside the three chairs stood little fold-out tin tray tables with painted flowers on top, each holding tall glasses of iced tea.

"Is this for me?" I asked. Mr. Manny nodded and motioned for me to sit. Maybe my wish would come true and we could just sit there without me having to force conversation out of myself.

"Yes, please drink your sweet tea," answered Mrs. Manny as she pushed open the screened door from the house and joined us on the porch. She was carrying an old metal tray on which three pieces of red tomato pie sat on little white plates.

"Here you are," she said as she held the tray in front of me, offering a piece of the red pie. I looked into her deep blue eyes and thanked her. In her eighties, she displayed a poise and lightness that seemed age-defying to me. *Surely this woman had never been rejected*, I thought. *She has always had the love of a devoted husband as well as his praise. Who wouldn't radiate with that kind of treatment?* She handed me a fork and a paper napkin.

"Thank you so much," I said. "This is my first taste of tomato pie, and it looks great. What are the ingredients?" For some reason I felt that I needed to make small talk, but I was a failure at that and felt my face getting red. She didn't seem aware of my nervousness, but then I was always nervous. Why couldn't I just take the pie and keep quiet?

"Oh, it's simple enough," she answered. "There are about five large sliced heirloom tomatoes, some basil leaves, some mozzarella and cheddar cheese, a little Old Bay seasoning, salt and pepper, and homemade pie crust. Then I just bake it in the oven until the crust is golden brown and the pie just starts to bubble, and there you have it." She nodded her head for Mr. Manny to bless the pie, and afterward I tasted the concoction.

My fork slid through the flaky crust and then through a layer of cheese and tomatoes. As I lifted it to my mouth, I could see that they were both waiting for my reaction. The crust was still warm from the oven, and I could not believe the flavor.

"This is wonderful and tastes sweet, like a dessert pie." Wasn't I expected to say that?

"No one can match Mrs. Manny's cooking," Mr. Manny said with pride. Mrs. Manny smiled as though she had never heard her husband say those words, but I thought differently. A woman doesn't have her kind of confidence unless she has first been lavished with praise.

We gulped down the tea and ate another small piece of pie before we noticed that the storm was worsening. "I may have to close us all in with the plywood shutters," warned Mr. Manny. "I think maybe you should ride this out right here with us."

I nodded in agreement but planned to leave as soon as possible. Then I helped Mr. Manny lower the huge window shutter that enclosed the porch. The wind beat hard against the shutter and slapped it against the screen before we could slow it down. A few yard items blew into the oak tree out front. Mr. Manny led the way, and we all retreated to the interior of the little cottage.

I had never been inside their house before. Patrick had never seemed interested in joining them for iced tea, always citing some excuse. The thought of doing something friendly or changing what he wanted to do for the benefit of being neighborly, seemed to escape him. Had I become like him?

There I was, doing it again. Why couldn't I stop this negative thinking? Why did thoughts of Patrick enter every conversation, every circumstance, and every friendship? Lost in chiding myself again, I barely noticed that Mrs. Manny was asking me a question. "I'm sorry," I said, "I guess I was listening to the wind and didn't hear you."

"Oh, that's fine, dear," she said. "I was just asking about how your history research is coming along."

"Oh, it's coming along just fine. I've recently spent some time at the Maryland State Archives, where I found out a bit more about our little area here during the Civil War period. Point Lookout Prison Camp for Confederates, which is right up the road from us, is a subject that intrigues me. The little museum near the old camp also offered up some interesting facts and…" I was doing the usual; going from silence into nonstop banter, while suddenly forgetting what I was going to say.

"I agree with you. It is a very interesting subject," said Mrs. Manny. "That place brings a particular sadness to some folks in our area, a sort of haunting of the souls of the descendants of those who died there. Some have claimed that their ghosts haunt Monument Park. Many others refuse to acknowledge what took place there. Maybe you'll share with us what you've found?"

I assumed that she had not noticed my hand wringing so I went on. "Well, let me see," I said. "There are some bits and pieces of history that I've found. Some of it seems a bit speculative, and there are some old stories that might be fables as well. I actually got my hands on a few letters that were written by prisoners at the war camp during the Civil War, plus some other records and recollections of prison life there. Of course there are always new stories to discover, and I find myself trying to imagine what happened to some of the prisoners."

"Well," said Mr. Manny, "I don't mind a little imagination mixed in. It looks like the storm will keep us indoors for a time. Why not enjoy a story or two?" Mrs. Manny nodded her head.

Not knowing how long the storm would last, I reasoned that I may as well tell a story or two. Telling stories kept things less personal anyway. I began to tell Mr. and Mrs. Manny the story of a man who wrote to his wife while he was a Civil War prisoner at Point Lookout.

Chapter 2

Blue Crabs and Sea Nettles

Virgil E. Cummings had a business going for himself, and the business was the blue crab. He knew how to fish crabs out the water and steam them in a can with very little effort. While the others fished from the ramshackle pier, he would wade out into the bay to catch his crabs.

He cooked them with salt stolen from the meat-curing shed. Some of the salt had not yet been removed from the hams that were hung to cure, and while scraping the salt from the ham, Virgil would also quickly bite off and devour a chunk of the ham to reward himself for his daring escapade. Virgil could get into any building, locked or open, even in this godforsaken place, and the pork-flavored salt was an ingredient that kept his boiled crab meat in demand, making the risk worth taking. Virgil was sure that that nobody would ever be able to figure out his recipe.

By the time the blue claws had turned an orange-red color in his tin steamers, made from large pans he had bartered for, the crabs were ready to be sold, bartered, or bargained for. He could bargain away the succulent blue crabs for nearly anything he wanted. Prisoners were always willing to trade with him, but he made it a point never to trade with the guards, as some prisoners had a habit of doing.

Virgil was one of the few Confederate prisoners who could stand the sting of a sea nettle without being deterred from his livelihood. It was sort of a painful bliss knowing that he had a crab on his trotline while sometimes having a sea nettle wrapped around his leg. What he didn't know was that the crab he was now looking at had been eyeing him back for quite some time. Looking up from below the piling of the wooden pier, an enormous crab saw the blurry form and human eyes looking down on him, and considered some inherent options.

The male crab knew he could sink slowly to the bottom and hide in the murky brown water. But basic instinct told him that the option of sinking down had many drawbacks. He could try to float away on the next big wave, but that too seemed very risky, and there was no motivation to let go of the pier piling. Finally, he opted to stay put. The crab had not finished busting out, which was a slow process. In his helpless state, he went with the camouflage tactic by clinging to the piling with weakened claws.

After the process of busting out of his old shell, he would need several days for his soft skin to begin to harden. Only then would his claws become useful and his swim paddles powerful enough to head for the deeper parts of the bay, where the feed fish were careless and humans scarce. For now, everything about him was weak.

The old crab had gone through the process of shedding many times in his long lifetime. He had escaped death for countless years as he ate whatever came his way, dead or alive. He had feasted on an abundance of food in his years of existence, everything from live minnows to dead terrapin. He had even tasted human flesh, though this was not preferred. The image of this particular human, blurred by water and bright sunlight above, was clear enough.

The human's eyes were intense as he offered the crab a chicken back with only slivers of meat attached. He dangled it close to the crab on a piece of string. The crab would have had his claws on the meat by now had his claws not become useless. As it was, just clinging to the pier was an effort.

The human found a stick and began to push it against the piling in the direct path of the crab. Letting go, the crab allowed himself to sink lower into the brine, but before he reached the darker, more camouflaged recesses under the pier, a stick with netting surrounded his entire body. Before he could sink farther down, he felt himself being pulled up to the surface. As he came up out of the water, he could see his captor clearly.

"I got him! Look at the size of this buster!" Virgil held the defenseless crab up for all to see before jumping up onto the shaky pier. "This will be a nice soft crab in a couple hours. Give me that bucket of water over there," he yelled to Gus, a fellow prisoner and hired man in Virgil's crabbing enterprise.

Gus pulled up his trotline and began dancing a jig, making the pier wobble even more. He was already thinking about the plug of tobacco that Virgil would share with him after bartering off the enormous crab, or even better, the extra portion of meat that could be bartered from the prison cooks. Gus fetched the bucket, and Virgil tossed in the crab. Now the crab could see four eyes through the briny water. Instinct did not tell the crab which direction to go. Sinking to the bottom of the wooden bucket, the crab had never experienced anything quite like this and so thought little more about it.

Later, much to Gus's disgust, Virgil traded his prize blue crab for a few sheets of writing paper, some writing instruments, and some potato scraps, which Virgil had been known to magically turn into potato skin soup. Normally Virgil traded for things Gus could get a piece of. When Gus saw that there was nothing in this trade for him, he protested loudly, but Virgil shot back quickly.

"Get your own crab. I'm sick of fetching for you. You're lazy and always have your hand out for something that I've worked for. When you get off your lazy backside and do something that helps others instead of just yourself, maybe then I'll deal with you again. But for now you're on your own." Virgil had been supplying Gus with enough goods and was feeling rather tired of his frequent protests. There were others who would work in Virgil's business without so much complaining.

Gus, wanting to choke the life out of Virgil, made a quick decision to remain calm. After all, the potato skin soup would be ready soon, and if he played his cards right, he'd get a spoonful or two. Gus could be very patient, and maybe Virgil would settle down after a while and hire him back. If not, well, there were other options. Virgil wouldn't always be telling him what to do.

Doing a quick about-face, Gus picked up the trotline with the nearly meatless chicken bone attached to it and found a spot on the crowded pier. "Maybe that granddaddy crab has a brother," he encouraged himself. He scratched his head, questioning if he had gotten rid of the lice that had been bothering him recently, and then threw the trotline back into the bay. A great blue heron flew just above the water, followed by a squawking seagull.

If Gus had a gun, he would have shot anything that could fill up his stomach, including that seagull. He'd like to shoot Virgil as well, but then, he reasoned, he had no gun to shoot him with. Besides, he was hungry, and if he was careful enough, he might get Virgil to change his mind and maybe get some soup. Then he thought too that if he got his own business going, he wouldn't have to put up with Virgil. Maybe Virgil would get himself shot and killed by a guard, and Gus could just take over Virgil's business. It had happened to other prisoners.

Back in camp, Virgil pulled up the flap over the door of his canvas tent, which was enforced several feet high with wooden cracker boxes around the perimeter. A splintered sign above the highest box said, "Virgil's Blue Crabs and Fish." It was his home and his business as well, and he didn't do badly at his business unless the crabs stopped running and he was forced to get by with little to trade. Enduring the winter in the cold was something he tried not to think about. There were other prisoners who had their little businesses too, but Virgil had a keenness for operating his enterprise and often helped other prisoners by giving them jobs. September and October were still working months, but wintertime was coming soon.

This day the heat inside Virgil's tent was overwhelming. It had to be ninety degrees, with at least that much humidity. He left the flap open and then untied the corded seam on the other side of the hut to allow some kind of air to pass through. Trouble was there was no breeze. Virgil rationalized that at least there was some shade from the sun. A large horsefly made itself at home on Virgil's leg until he knocked it senseless to the ground and then promptly stomped on it. In no time, a string of ants surrounded the dead fly, ready to pick it apart.

Virgil took the wooden vegetable crate that he had traded for recently, along with his other traded items, and placed it on the dirt floor in front of his cot. Then arranging a flat scrap of wood on top of the crate, he placed the precious sheets of paper down, removed the writing instrument from his deep pocket, and began to write.

August 1, 1864
My dearest Joanna,

Well, here I am in this place without you. The days are getting shorter, but the heat is near to killing me off. There are no trees at all, just rows and rows of tents full of prisoners like me. I'd love the pleasure of sitting under the trees with you like we used to do. I miss you so.

I obtained this nice paper by trading off the largest blue crab that I have ever seen. It was a buster that had almost completely shed his old shell. Wish you could have seen the look in his eyes as he sank helpless to the bottom of a bucket. I also wish I hadn't had to catch him. That old crab has got to be the granddaddy of all crabs. He'll make a good meal for somebody though, and bartering crabs is a little business I have going here in this rat hole of a prison camp.

Speaking of rats, it has become a game around here with those critters, and even the black guards get into the amusement. What we do is chase the rats out of their hiding spots and try to steer them toward a particular hole in the stock-ade wall. We pick out a certain hole and then take sticks and chase them to the hole that we have bet on. The winner gets a prize of some kind. I don't like to tell you all the bad things that go on in here without telling you a bit about what we do for amusement. I have won a time or two.

The sad thing is that some of the men catch the rats and cook them for food. I would rather starve, but I can't really blame them. They have nothing to barter with as I do, and some of them are just boys from farther down south with no knowledge of how to survive.

I've hired some boys to crab for me, and I share the profits with them. They are pretty good at crabbing for me, but when they get stung all day by those sea nettles with their long tentacles and their jelly slime all over them, the younger boys holler and don't want to crab much after that. Today I fired a lazy worker who just doesn't care about anything but taking advantage of others, but I won't be putting up with him any longer. I have made several enemies of those I have let go and have even been threatened by a few of them. Life is cheap here, and threats come often from men who are ready to pick a fight over anything.

I guess you know that a lot of these Southern boys end up dead in the prisoner hospital. It isn't a hospital, only a couple of large tents—just a place to die. Hammond Hospital filled up so quick with injured Yankee men, our injured men are put in a large over-crowded tent. The only thing good about the hospital is that when you're there you sometimes get a little food and some fresh water. Most of the time the water outside the hospital is tainted with salt water, and that makes a person sick as a dog. And the sewer is nothing more than some deep trenches right out along the camp road. The mosquitoes are so bad and the smell so revolting that it's enough to make you want to die.

After a while, I think some of the younger men just give up. I often hear them crying at night as a few of them don't appear to be more than thirteen years old. When this summer ends and the cold winter sets up again, I pray that there will be enough wood to keep everyone warm. A couple of boys froze to death last winter as we had only enough wood to burn every other day when I first got here. That's why some of the younger boys died of exposure, though I bet their families will never find that out.

Here I am telling you awful things again. You are such a lady, and I shouldn't be writing to you about things you don't need to know, much less hear about from your own husband. I'm sorry, Joanna, but I need you, and I want you to know that thinking of you helps me survive in this prison. I need you to write to me and to pray for me. Why are you not writing to me?

Oh, how I wish I could get out of this place. I miss you so awfully much. Could you send me another picture of yourself? The one I have is beginning to fade more and more, and looking at your angelic face keeps me going. I've only been here six months, but it feels like a lifetime without my beloved wife. I need to get out of here and home to you.

When I look across the Potomac River and realize that you are just on the other side of it, it makes me crazy sometimes. I picture you over there at Walnut Oak, together with my mama and papa and everyone, and it's hard on me. I dream of my release and my homecoming. I think often of our last night together at the farm. You looked so beautiful. What we shared was beautiful too. Do you remember?

Is there no way out of this dreadful place? I hate Maryland and this government camp, and I long for the Northern Neck of my beloved Virginia. There have only been a few escapes from this place. There were some small Virginia rowboats coming across the river by night to look for anyone who may have escaped to the shoreline, but now the Union has put those gunboats all over the bay, and the river is no longer safe. I have often dreamed of you coming over with a boat to bring me home. When is this war going to end?

We are trapped here until General Lee wins some battles and comes to our rescue. I heard tell that Lee has busted into Maryland near a place called Antietam. I heard too that Lee is sending a regiment to break us out, but it just never gets here. Maybe I should keep my head and not listen to these false hopes. Oh, but if only it were true. If I had not been captured and sent to this place, I would still be fighting for our cause, knowing the South would win and I would soon be home in your arms. I dream of that moment every night and of your kisses and caresses. It is painful to think that I cannot hold you except for in my dreams.

I will close now. You are still staying with my parents, aren't you? Kiss Mama for me when you see her next and Papa too, and please write to me. You must be writing me and the guards are throwing out your letters or something. So far I've only received a few letters, and those I received after I was first brought to this place. It has been some time now since I was captured and put here at Point Lookout. You are writing me, aren't you? Your letters will help me survive. Please write to me, Joanna.

Things are very difficult to cope with in here. I have to be careful what I write to you, and I dare not tell you some of the things that go on, but I will tell you that these black prison guards think that they are real powerful. They have rifles and blue Union uniforms, and they stand up on the guard walk like they were all General Grant himself. I best not say anything else, or I could find myself fired upon. There have been a few times when some shots have been fired, and one or two prisoners have been shot for no good reason whatsoever. I have no dealings with those guards, and I do not intend to do so, ever.

Please remember, my dearest, that I love you and that I will be home soon. This war has got to end. Pray that it ends soon.

Your beloved husband,
Private Virgil E. Cummings
Company G, Fifty-Ninth Virginia
Point Lookout Camp for Confederates

Chapter 3

A Hurricane

When I realized that I had been talking nonstop and that Mr. and Mrs. Manny were listening intently, I became self-conscious and stopped. Suddenly I couldn't remember the other information that had interested me at the Maryland State Archives.

"This is a wonderful story so far. Keep going," encouraged Mr. Manny.

"Well, I want to save a little for later on," I answered. The sudden urge to run out of their cottage was overwhelming. Was this feeling of sudden panic ever going to stop? Had Mr. and Mrs. Manny noticed?

"I guess this would be a good time to pause," agreed Mr. Manny. "Just listen to that wind pick up. You know, this is going to go on for at least three days. They always do when they start up like this."

I knew that he was right. The combination of several hurricanes in the thirties and forties, along with the usual frequent nor 'easterly storms, had collapsed the wooden bridges, sinking the old road. One by one the cottages began to fall into the bay. Our road was the last thin line between the bay and the creek, and only a handful of cottages remained, mine included. This day the bay seemed hungry to take the rest.

A gale of wind abruptly picked up and blew the plywood storm shutter away from the commercial-sized hook-and-eye latch that had held it to the window. The strain of the constant pounding of wind and rain had loosened some of the eyes on one side. The eyes let go, and off flew the plywood. It fell hard to the ground, resting from its duty. Mr. Manny got up from his chair and opened the door to the porch, surveying the lost shutter.

"This is beginning to look more like a hurricane then a nor'easter," he said. "The shutter has blown off along with a good bit of roof shingles. Maybe I should go next door and see how the Wilderman folks are holding up." I could hear the concern in his voice.

"Well, if you think it is safe enough, then maybe that's a good idea," answered Mrs. Manny, apprehensive but supportive.

"No, I'll run next door," I blurted out. I may have been a recluse up to now, but there was no way I was going to let an old man go out in that wind and rain. "I'll be back in a minute." I pulled my rain jacket over my head and quickly bolted out the door before Mr. Manny could protest.

The wind slammed me in the face and blew the rain jacket off of my head, and I was drenched by the time I had reached the neighbors' door just twenty feet away. I pounded on the storm door, and immediately it was opened as the Wilderman family crowded together behind the screened porch door. All seven of them looked at my rain-soaked hair and dripping raincoat and seemed stunned to see me.

"Well come on in before you catch your death of cold!" ordered Mrs. Wilderman. She ushered me through the kitchen door and closed it tight behind me. "Why on earth are you out in this mess? I know I've invited you over for tea many times, but what a day you've chosen to take me up on it!" She laughed, and soon the whole room of little eyes joined in. I've always hated being the center of attention.

"Here," she said, "let me hang up your raincoat, and then I'll get a clean towel for you to dry your hair with." Mrs. Wilderman had a heavy British accent, which she had not lost in all the years since World War II. She was a war bride who came over on one of the bride ships shortly after the war was over and England had been left in ruins.

They met at a hospital in London after Mr. Wilderman was wounded at the Battle of the Bulge. She had been part of an entertainment troupe that performed for the injured soldiers. Oftentimes now she would sing to her family, her voice floating up so that the neighbors on our little street could hear her. Everyone said that she sang like a bird and that her voice was soft and soothing. I guessed that Mr. Wilderman fell in love with that voice.

Her brood of five grandchildren, once satisfied that I was not totally insane, sat back down around a crowded little table. They were playing cards with their Grandfather Wilderman, who nodded a surprised hello to me as I accepted a small dish towel from Mrs. Wilderman. I dried my hair and looked around the room.

"I know that my place is a big mess," said Mrs. Wilderman, "but with five of my grandchildren being cooped up inside here, I have little reason to clean now." I thanked her for the towel and began to tell them the purpose for my visit.

"The Mannys just wanted to know if everyone here is all right," I said. "The storm seems to be stronger in force than the usual nor'easter."

"This may not be just a nor'easter but the outer bands of a forming hurricane," said Mr. Wilderman. "Have you been listening to the emergency band radio?"

"No," I answered. "I've been boarded up next door with Mr. and Mrs. Manny. I don't think they have a television, and I didn't see an emergency band radio over there either."

Actually, I didn't have a television or emergency radio at my cottage either. To me, not hearing anything but the sounds of the bay, the wind, and the call of the great blue heron was enough. Patrick, however, needed to keep in touch with everyone he knew at all times, and so I had given in to installing the phone. After Patrick left me, I replaced the house phone with a cell phone, and the radio went as well. Now I saw the folly of being out of touch, especially with a possible hurricane upon us.

"Well then," said Mr. Wilderman, "if it gets any worse or a warning comes to evacuate, I'll be sure to come over and let you all know. In the meantime, you need to stay indoors and keep the storm shutters closed up over the windows."

"Yes, we're doing that," I answered, "but the wind just blew a shutter off of the porch. It's lying on the ground between their cottage and yours." I took a quick glance around the one open room and saw that the children were not fazed by the possibility of gale-force winds, flooding, or even losing the cottage. I wanted to sit down with them, play cards, and just relax with no worries.

"The children all seem very calm," I blurted out.

"Yes, they're calm when they aren't running around like banshees," said Mrs. Wilderman. "This is our favorite way to spend a week with the children, and they love being together," she said fondly. "Why don't you sit down and let me make you a nice cup of tea?"

For some reason I really wanted to do that. There was a feeling of safety there in that cramped room full of children. Ordinarily I would have felt claustrophobic. "I think I had better go back to warn Mr. and Mrs. Manny of the possible hurricane or evacuation, but thank you," I replied. Then I thought how odd it was to be asked to have tea with a hurricane hastening to blow our cottages down or worse. *Is this British resolve?* I wondered. *When the Germans are bombing and the queen is in hiding, why not enjoy a cup of tea?*

Mr. Wilderman spoke up. "I'll go next door and bring Mr. and Mrs. Manny here. Those old folks shouldn't be alone over there. Let's just pray that the seawall will keep us all from floating away." Mr. Wilderman got up from his card game and walked over to the storm door. "Look at those waves coming over the seawall now," he said. The children quickly ran over to the door to peer out. I could see for myself that the situation did not look promising.

The water level was now nearly to the top of the stone seawall. As the salt water was pushed up and over the top, it fell powerfully onto the small grassy lot with each breaking wave. "Do you think we'll have to evacuate?" I asked feebly.

"I don't know," he answered. "It looks bad. Remember it is high tide right now but nearly time for the tide to recede. We'll see what happens then. The hurricane might not get all the way up to our portion of the bay." Out the door he went, leaving the storm door to slam behind him. Mrs. Wilderman quickly latched it closed. *He certainly knows a lot about storms,* I thought as I tried hard to keep my mind away from impending doom.

Within five minutes, the three came hurrying into the cottage. Mrs. Manny held on to both her husband and to Mr. Wilderman. Mr. Wilderman also carted a huge picnic basket on his free arm, and Mr. Manny carried a thermos. Mrs. Wilderman met them at the porch door, quickly opening it.

"Thank you for having us over in this terrible storm," said Mrs. Manny, clearly out of breath. "We've brought food to share. Who knows how long we'll all be indoors."

"Yes," said her husband, "we thought maybe we had lost our storyteller to you good folks." He was followed by Mr. Wilderman, who closed and latched the storm door. Mr. Manny removed his straw hat and nodded a warm hello to everyone before placing it down on a little stool. How he had kept that hat on his head I'll never know.

Paula, the youngest of the Wilderman grandchildren, perked up. "What story is she telling you?" Paula came over and stood directly in front of me. "Will you tell us a story too?" she asked.

She was a cute little thing. Dressed in blue gingham shorts with a white cotton eyelet top, she pulled herself closer to me with an inquisitive look on her face. She had a kid-sized Baltimore Orioles baseball cap on backward to keep the strawberry-red hair out of her face, but nothing could cover her freckles or her excitement. Before I knew it, I was surrounded by little children, not to mention the four adults standing in the kitchen area.

"Maybe I'll tell you a little story later," I offered, but I was thinking that I would like to go back to my cottage and had no plans to tell stories. "I think we're going to get a bite to eat right now." Then I looked down at Paula and wished that she were my little girl. If Patrick had wanted children, I would have had one or two about her age by now. Paula pulled me over to the table, and Mrs. Manny invited everyone to have some of the snacks she had brought.

Mrs. Manny opened the basket and set the contents on the well-worn plastic tablecloth, placing cold crab cakes beside the leftover tomato pie. Next to that was a glass container filled with sugar cookies. "I made those cookies yesterday. "I hope they're still fresh. And I made the crab cakes this morning before the storm came in. I like cold crab cakes on toast, but if you like, you can warm them in a pan."

Next to the crab cakes was a container of some sort of cold noodle salad with black olives, feta cheese, and assorted julienne vegetable throughout. Mr. Manny placed a large thermos near the food as Mrs. Manny continued. "I brought you some nice hot tea too. Maybe we'll have tea and sugar cookies later. I had just made a pot of tea when your kind husband came over to save us." Mrs. Manny was clearly as nervous as I was, yet she had chosen to be sociable.

"Wonderful," Mrs. Wilderman said. "This will all go nicely with the leftover ham I have in the icebox. I may have some slaw in here as well, along with a three-bean salad. The electric is bound to go off at any moment, so we may as well enjoy a feast in the meantime." Together the women surveyed their wares on the small table.

Why are they making this out to be a safe little picnic? Why don't I just leave now and let them chat and picnic away? I thought.

"What a nice meal we'll have to share," said Mr. Manny.

I couldn't believe the calm manner of these people. I figured that they must be just as anxious as I was, but they were covering their anxiety with eating and gabbing about nothing. Anxiety was always a good reason to eat a meal. I had gained a little weight from that very thing. Only at that particular moment I would have rather been up the road at a restaurant enjoying togetherness with total strangers. But instead there I was, risking being washed away along with hot tea and cold noodle salad.

"A good meal indeed," Mrs. Wilderman added. "Everyone, please come over and hold hands so that Mr. Wilderman may ask the blessing."

I listened but kept my eyes open as Mr. Wilderman gave thanks and a request to God. The thanks were for the food and the provisions that were on the table, and the request was that we would all live to enjoy the meal. Everyone chuckled during the prayer, except for me. *What makes them think that God cares?* I asked myself. *And what's so funny about the situation anyway?*

When the prayer was finished, we each dished up a plate of food and found a place to sit. The meal was eaten with everyone talking at once. I sat nervously listening to things banging around in the yard as the banter continued on for some time, and then Mrs. Wilderman asked me a question.

"What's this I hear about a story?" Mrs. Wilderman looked at me curiously as she began to collect the paper plates, tossing them into a metal outdoor garbage can next to the stove.

"I really don't know a lot of stories," I explained, "just a few things that I've picked up along the way about our area and the old Point Lookout prison camp. Really, I'm just now starting to piece a bit of it together. It isn't really all that interesting at this point, just a lot of stories." *And let that be a hint that I don't want to talk.* I wondered why nobody could see that I was nervous to the point of running out the door.

"Oh, but what you've shared with us has been very interesting," insisted Mrs. Manny.

"Well, I don't know if I have anything to share right now." I thought hard, wanting to leave, but I could hear the wind picking up and the sounds of metal lawn furniture being toppled, and thought it better to stay awhile. "I could share a few things about the man who developed our community back in the 1920s, but again, some of the facts may be just bits and pieces of inaccurate information. You know, I did meet the daughter of the land developer once. She's in her seventies now and very friendly, and she shared a story about her father with me once." Nervous prattle was coming from my mouth as I started to wring my hands together.

"Oh, that would be interesting for all of us to hear," added Mr. Manny. "I've met that dear lady a time or two while Mrs. Manny and I were taking our daily walk."

"Please do go on," encouraged Mrs. Wilderman. "The children are all ears."

Normally I don't do well under pressure, but I finally realized that they wouldn't allow me to just sit there with a frightened expression on my face. I began to tell them a story about how our cottages were built by a developer who couldn't keep buried some infamous events that had taken place at Point Lookout near the end of the Civil War.

Chapter 4

Steamboats and Old Hotels

The steamboat *Rue Purchase* made its way down the Potomac River and around the southern tip of St. Mary's County, where the point separates the Potomac River and the bay and where both the Patuxent and Potomac Rivers empty their fresh waters into the briny waters of the mid-Chesapeake. There on the Patuxent side, a man stood on a large wooden wharf where he could see the steamer on its way toward his hotel. It had been sixty years since the end of the Civil War, and the man had his mind set on a better future for himself and for the county. This after all was nearly the begging of the 1920s and a return to normalcy, as touted by presidential campaigner, Warren G. Harding.

Lewis Chambers anticipated that he had a possible gold mine or two traveling on that steamer as it churned the waters in his direction. The boat was on its way from Washington, DC, dropping passengers off in Leonardtown and then swinging down and around the point and up the Patuxent side of the bay to bring others to their destinations. He prayed that at least two very wealthy persons would shortly be stepping off of the passenger boat. Nearly broke from restoring the old hotel he knew he had to be positive about the possibilities.

The steamer would make a quick stop at his wharf, and if luck had it, these wealthy debarking guests would be very interested in his new development. He prayed too that the lure of the fishing, crabbing, swimming, dining, dancing, and special drinks that could be had in this secluded area of Maryland would further entice them to buy a lot, a cottage, or both.

It was early June, and the heat, mosquitoes, jellyfish, and sand fleas had not yet made their annual appearance. Gentle breezes and warm sun, minus the impending humidity, made the day perfect for visitors. Lewis looked back at the hotel he had paid to have lovingly restored, and took pride in the fact that he, so far as he knew, was the sole investor in this area of Southern Maryland. No other wealthy individuals had yet discovered this pristine area, often called "God's Country" by locals. Nor, he comforted himself, had land speculators arrived in these parts of St. Mary's County. He did not favor competition at this point in his well-laid plans.

In fact, few Marylanders even knew where St. Mary's County was located, even though Maryland history began just a few miles up the road from the hotel. It was a well-kept secret, and Lewis Chambers planned to keep it that way, at least for now.

Annapolis, the second capitol of Maryland, had replaced the first capitol and statehouse—along with any notoriety that St. Mary's City had once enjoyed. Little thought was given to the actual region where Maryland had first distinguished itself as an English settlement where freedom of religion—a right denied to Englishmen—would be established for both Catholic and Protestant believers. Eventually religious and political differences caused the Protestant revolution of 1689, which ended the rule of Lord Baltimore's dream of religious toleration, making it difficult for Catholics to hold office or practice their religion.

Annapolis became the capitol in 1694, and St. Mary's City became a rural and agricultural city in the years after. Annapolis, with its beautiful and accessible harbors, its new State House, and its political as well as business opportunities, left St. Mary's City to be almost forgotten as the original capital of Maryland.

Lewis Chambers felt it a privilege to share this history with his guests, and this he did each evening seated at the large dining room table. His plan was to put St. Mary's County back on the map with his beach resort and cottages by the bay. For this he needed wealthy investors.

Pulling out a silver pocket watch from his waistcoat, Lewis smiled. The steamer was on time, and his hotel kitchen crew, headed by Gerdie Wilkes, had been cooking and picking crabs for nearly four hours in preparation for the arrival of these potential investors. Today the view was clear, the sun was shining, the people were coming, and Lewis Chambers had faith that God was going to answer his prayers.

Chambers was aware that this endeavor had been attempted by an investor before that fateful day in 1861 when the first shot was fired and the Civil War began. After that investor had spent a fortune on his resort, he sold the land and buildings to the US government, and his resort quickly became a Union hospital and shortly after a prisoner of war camp for Confederates captured by the Union during the war. That investor had made very little profit for all of his efforts and dreams.

Whatever may have happened then, Chambers felt that the right time for a resort was now, but he made it a point to never discuss the previous resort or the prison camp with his guests. He found it strange though that not a single guest had ever asked about the Confederate prison, but then there was little written or known about it outside of Southern Maryland.

Only those who had lived it could know what an awful scar it had left on this beautiful part of Maryland. Few locals ever discussed it either. Life was hard enough without ruminating over what had been.

His own father, Jacob Chambers, had died in that prison and Lewis planned to claim and develop the land as a monument to his father rather than a sorrowful graveyard where thousands of men had died.

Over sixty years later, a fresh coat of warm yellow paint, with creamy white for the trim work, had been selected for the hotel. Though it was not a new building, the repair work had been finished in record time thanks to Jeremiah Wilkes and his son. During its days as a prison, the building had housed a brigadier general in style. Lewis Chambers had bought the tract of land along with the large structure, which had fallen into disrepair and ruin. Now it stood proudly, with fresh paint covering up the cracks in the plaster walls, white trim framing window boxes full of new spring flowers, new white oak wooden floors covered with a variety of Oriental rugs, beautiful drapes sewn by local women, and plenty of antiques purchased at various auctions in the area.

Each guest room had been painted in hues of greens and soft blues and creams, and each room had a view of the bay. The back of the hotel, near the dirt driveway, was reserved for the kitchen staff, the laundry rooms, and tool and equipment rooms. Food was delivered and garbage removed via the back of the hotel, where the staff entered and exited as well.

In the center of the hotel was the dining hall, where there were tables enough for at least twenty-five hungry guests, with more chairs available on the covered front porch for those who preferred romantic candlelit dining. Rockers were also lined up where guests could catch an afternoon breeze or watch steamboats run up the bay toward points north, such as Baltimore and Annapolis. Sailing vessels and white wooden boats dotted the blue waters as well, scurrying up and down the bay harvesting precious oysters.

The aroma of crab cakes and Chesapeake Bay oysters being roasted in the kitchen had just been picked up by the gentle breezes and carried past Lewis Chambers, who had confidence that his kitchen staff would deliver their part. Now as he watched the steamer approach, he could see that many passengers had made the journey. Captain Woodburn blew the steam whistle three short blasts, and the *Rue Purchase* came to rest beside the wharf, where the boat crew securely fastened it to huge piling rings.

Five ladies from the kitchen and three maids hurried to the front porch of the hotel lining up in neat rows to either side of the entrance, poised to welcome the guests as they disembarked. The guests were led down the steamer's plank walkway and onto the new boat landing, making their way toward the Point Lookout Hotel.

Gerdie Wilkes was the only worker who did not present herself at the greeting, feeling it wasn't her duty to make an appearance. She had been in the middle of shaping the delicate white crab meat into tin molds of various patterns to be served on beds of fresh field greens, accompanied with buttered red potatoes and spoon bread fresh from the brick oven. All the fresh spring vegetables came right from the farm that she and Jeremiah ran, and all of the recipes were her very own.

The prepared dishes would be brought to the dining room in fine white porcelain bowls dotted with blue flowers. Roasted oysters were brought in on silver platters. Today's welcoming lunch would not be complete without Gerdie presenting her homemade peach cobbler, served with fresh cream drizzled on top. Her famous sweet tea would chase it all down.

Mr. Chambers had often told her that she was the best black cook for miles around, but she knew she was the best cook, period. "Good food is good food," she'd always say. Most of the time though she just did her work without commenting about the goings-on. She knew a few things that Mr. Chambers had not even thought about, and one of them was that this old hotel would have fallen down by now if not for her husband, Jeremiah, and son, Tiberius, working almost a year restoring it. They were both hardworking men who never dwelt on the negative things in life, except for that morning when her son brought her news that was now threatening her peace of mind.

Usually Gerdie complained of nothing outwardly, but inwardly she did plenty of thinking and agreeing and disagreeing with people and their ways. At seventy-nine years old, Gerdie's hands were gnarled with arthritis, but she was still strong enough to do kitchen labor. This day she noticed that her hands were aching more than usual, and her mind was racing and not as peaceful as the Good Book urged. Tiberius had reported to her that some strangers from Virginia were stopping off at farms in the area, asking questions about the Civil War camp that had once stood around the hotel site. They were looking for someone, and that was news she did not want to hear.

Soon Gerdie heard the steam whistle blowing a long farewell. That meant that the guests were making their way into the hotel. Some would probably poke their noses into her kitchen to see if things were proper, but she didn't mind that at all. In her mind, nobody had a more proper kitchen than Gerdie Wilkes. She put her thoughts behind her and said a little prayer request to God. He would bring the peace she needed.

As she heard the steamer puffing its way back down the bay, Gerdie took a small bag from her white cotton apron pocket, broke off a plug of chewing tobacco, and placed it under her lower lip. The earthy tobacco was a daily pleasure for Gerdie, one that she had been treating herself to since she was a child, working tobacco with her older siblings. Tobacco was still the cash crop of Southern Maryland and a calming balm to her thoughts, when needed.

Jeremiah, Gerdie's husband, was eighty-three years old, but nobody would guess that. He was the overseer of the best tobacco farm in these parts. Together, Gerdie and Jeremiah farmed tobacco for Mr. Lewis Chambers. With their five adult children and their fifteen grandchildren, they managed to farm the tobacco crops as well as a few acres of corn and vegetable gardens that they owned. Jeremiah sold produce to Mr. Chambers as needed for the hotel and to others in the community as well. His family also did cooking for Mr. Chambers and other odd jobs that needed a competent hand. For this Mr. Chambers paid them well and sold to them a small portion of land in Leonardtown. Someday Jeremiah hoped to build a nice house for Gerdie there.

Gerdie let the pungent tobacco slowly dissolve in her mouth, occasionally spitting the brown-green fluid into a little tin bucket near the kitchen door. Then wiping her mouth with a white handkerchief, she washed her hands with lye soap and went about the business of picking meat from the rest of the steamed crabs.

As her kitchen staff returned from greeting the new guests, Gerdie quickly assigned their tasks and set them to their duties. There was no resistance from the five middle-aged women, who were grateful for the work and respected Gerdie's authority. There was laughter in the kitchen as the staff spoke about "the rich white people and their tons of luggage for one little old weekend stay." A few guests strolling by the kitchen were overheard as they commented on the beautiful hotel building, but Gerdie could not stop thinking about what her son had told her.

∾

Bennett Cummings was delighted with his accommodations at the hotel and found Mr. Chambers to be a charming host. Bennett had arrived not on the steamboat with his fellow weekenders but in his own mode of transportation, which he had parked behind the hotel next to the only other automobile.

His car was an ocean-blue 1920 Packard Twin Six. It had black trim around the hood and engine, complete with a black grille and white-wall tires. A blue running board ensured smooth stepping from the car to the road, and it had comfortably carried Mr. Cummings and his two companions from the Northern Neck of Virginia to the southern tip of Maryland.

Lewis Chambers's car was equally impressive, though not as detailed. It was a 1921 black Dodge Brothers Touring Sedan. In this car Chambers traveled back and forth from his four hundred–acre tobacco farm just north of Bayside to his hotel on the bay.

Bennett Cummings had wired a reservation for three rooms in advance, and Chambers was certain that this gentleman and his two companions had come to invest in his beachside development of summer cottages. Why else would they have driven so far when a steamer could have cut the travel time in half? To Lewis Chambers's mind, these men meant business, and he was ready to sell.

"My, my, this is some of the best home cooking I have enjoyed in these parts," said Cummings as he lifted another forkful of delicate crabmeat to his mouth. "What secret ingredient has this crab meat been graced with?"

"That would be a secret that only my cook knows, and at last word it's going to stay that way. She won't tell anyone, not even me." Chambers could tell by his dress and by the car he had driven over from Virginia that this man was very wealthy. The accent seemed to be from the northern part, he thought. "I do believe that my black cook, Gerdie, could beat anyone in the county with her cooking skills."

"Well, you know the Negroes and how they like to cook for us," said Cummings. "In fact, every kitchen should have one. Don't you agree?" He smiled at Lewis Chambers, who did not return the smile. "I enjoyed your informative history talk at the dinner table, Mr. Chambers," he added.

"I believe every kitchen would appreciate the skills of my *black* cook," Chambers said. "I enjoy sharing the history of our little part of the world with our guests and whoever may find the subject interesting."

"I too know a little history from around these parts," Bennett boasted, "such as some of the history about your *black* people, as you call them. In fact, many of them served the Union government very gratefully during the war."

"Yes, that's correct," said Lewis. "Some were forced to do so, and some volunteered."

"Some even worked in that old infamous Point Lookout prison camp just down the road from here. Of course there isn't much left of it now on account of the US government tearing it down and hiding all the important evidence of their atrocities, but there are a few buildings left—this fine hotel of yours, in fact."

Lewis Chambers was not enjoying the way this conversation was going. The conversation had not started out this way, and he could scarcely figure out how it had gone from conversing about Southern Maryland history and his plans for a summer cottage development, to a conversation about the still-unpleasant tensions of days gone by. The former prison camp did not make for good conversation in his opinion, and he was not in the mood for it.

He had studied human behavior all of his life. It was essential in the hotel and land development business. Now he sat across from a man who was intent on discussing the old prison camp. Lewis looked to both sides of Mr. Cummings and noted that the two men who were with him had not joined in the conversation, but seemed attentive to every word spoken.

"And just what is it in this part of Maryland that you fine gentlemen would be interested in learning more about?" asked Chambers. "I take it that you're not here for investment purposes?" He lit a cigar for himself and then offered one to Mr. Cummings and the two gentlemen seated beside him. Mr. Cummings accepted the cigar, and the man to his right quickly lit it for him.

"This is a very fine cigar." Mr. Cummings took a few more puffs and fingered the light brown tobacco leaves. "Would this be tobacco from your own plantation just up the road in Bayside? I understand that only premium tobacco products come from your fine farm, but I have not yet had the pleasure until now."

Chambers slowly nodded his appreciation. "Yes, that would be my tobacco that you're enjoying. You seem to know a lot about my undertakings," he said with a half smile, "and not a little about the people of the area and some history as well. Are you a historian? Or perhaps you're doing research for the sheer enjoyment of it?"

"Enjoyment would not be my reason for this particular visit, and no, I am not a historian. But I do read a lot and am interested in history. Individual people are the most interesting of all," Cummings said.

"Yes, I agree with that," said Chambers. "We have a very interesting mix of people down here in Southern Maryland. Many are direct descendants of the original settlers down the road at St. Mary's City. Have you studied much about the settlement here in the county before today? I am always amused by how little Maryland history is known by people who live in and around this beautiful state."

Cummings nodded his head and took a long puff from his cigar. "It is true that Maryland has a very rich heritage from that era of first settlements, for example the landing of the *Ark* and the *Dove*, but I am particularly interested in the era of the Civil War. It wasn't all that long ago you know, and yes, I have heard that there are still many Negros, or rather *blacks* from that era who remain to this day and are just full of stories about that time period."

Bennett took another slow puff and blew the smoke out over the table. "I find it fascinating that any of them would want to stay in this section of the state after all the slavery that went on here. Of course that isn't a well-known fact. But Maryland was a border state whose citizens couldn't seem to make up their minds whether they were for the Blue or for the Gray, slavery or emancipation. In fact, many of your Maryland boys found their way right over the Potomac River to Virginia's shore and fought very bravely for the South." Cummings paused and lowered his voice.

"There were even some blacks who fought for our side, but then I can see that many freed blacks find a sympathetic employer in you, Mr. Chambers, and maybe they stay in this area out of gratitude to the Union for setting them free and giving them jobs. You might say that they too are direct descendants of history in these parts, and some of them like to talk about it. I have had a few good conversations with some of your local people."

Lewis thought about the conversation and the two men who were staring at him, and he remembered hearing a few rumors about some inquisitive visitors from out of town.

Bennett Cummings put his cigar down on the silver ashtray. "I am sure that you are aware that many of your black people from this area were even given military pay and fancy uniforms provided by the Union government so that they could stand guard over the Southern prisoners; a fact that is hard to imagine."

"How right you are," said Lewis. "But surely with your exhaustive research you must also know that most of the local blacks were assigned duties that were, shall I say, less dignified? They were assigned to burial detail and grave digging, along with ditch and sewer digging, food and mail delivery, and transporting fuel into the camp. I think if you do a little more research, you will find that many of the black prison guards were not from around here at all, most being freedmen from farther up north such as the Fifth Massachusetts Colored Cavalry or the Thirteenth Ohio Infantry Regiment from out west. But yes, there were some local black guards in the camp." Lewis Chambers calmed his voice, thinking it best to be somewhat agreeable for now, unsure of where the conversation would lead.

Again Lewis looked over at the other two men and then back to Cummings. "You still haven't told me what it is you do over in Virginia, Mr. Cummings. Or are you and your rather quiet friends just interested in the study of Civil War history here in Southern Maryland?"

"How gracious you are to ask, Mr. Chambers. As I said, I do enjoy history, although by trade I am a lawyer. You might say I am currently enjoying a brief hiatus. And you are correct about research. I have done my research and have found that some of your local boys round about these parts were indeed guards at the prison camp, just as you have stated." Bennett paused and waited for a reply, but Chambers said nothing.

"These two gentlemen seated beside me are my researchers. In fact, they are what you would call detectives. Not Pinkerton detectives or anything like that," he said, "but I have hired them to help with my investigation, so there is really no need to give introductions here, though I suppose that would be the proper thing to do. However, you only need converse with me. As you can see, these two gentlemen have serious things on their minds."

Chambers was becoming extremely annoyed with the conversation. He sat back in his chair and slowly eyed Bennett Cummings. The three men were not revealing their true reason for visiting. In fact, he thought, Bennett Cummings seemed to be speaking in a challenging tone, not the friendly tone he'd used when they first sat down.

"Tell me, Mr. Cummings, just what information do you and your two detectives hope to glean from your stay at my establishment? I had rather hoped to show you fine gentlemen a great investment opportunity. As a matter of fact, the largest and best lots, which of course are situated with pristine views of the Chesapeake, are still available."

"Well, that's a real nice idea," said Cummings. "I do rather prefer to be near the water. I own waterfront properties just across the Potomac from here in Virginia—more than I need, in fact. However, I'll be visiting this area often and would consider reviewing your properties. Unfortunately, I will have to save that for another visit. I hope to make many visits to your little retreat here. I find it quite pleasant. Oh, and as for why I am here, I'm looking for a former guard—a local boy, my researchers have deduced—who was stationed at Point Lookout."

Chambers usually didn't allow anyone to upset him, yet now he could not help tapping his heel against the chair. "The war has been over for sixty years. I doubt that you will find that guard, no matter what kind of research your two detectives have conducted. Most are dead and buried or have moved on."

"I only want to find one guard," replied Cummings. "What could be so difficult about that? Sixty years is a very short time as history continues to live on in the lives of those who experienced that dreaded war. Besides, I'm not looking for just any guard, as I told you, but a particular guard."

"And which guard would that be?" Lewis asked.

"That would be the black guard who shot through the tent of a defenseless Southern prisoner, murdering him as he lay sleeping."

Lewis Chambers sat back in his chair and forced calmness into his voice. "Have you been engaged as a lawyer to find this person? And if not, may I inquire how it is that you are so connected with this prisoner that you would look for this particular guard after all these years?"

Bennett Cummings leaned forward. "That prisoner's name is Virgil Cummings. He was my father."

Chapter 5

Evacuation

Something slammed into the Wilderman cottage, and everyone bolted upright. The children said nothing but looked over toward their grandfather for a word of explanation. Their once-unconcerned faces were now showing signs of fright.

"Sounds like the wind blew something onto the porch roof," Mr. Wilderman said, evenly controlled. He approached the door and opened it. There hanging down from the roof, partially bent and stuck through the screened porch, was Mrs. Wilderman's British flag, still attached to the metal flagpole.

"Not my flag! Get my flag down from there!" she yelled to her husband. "I thought we had taken the flag down!"

I felt bad for her. Obviously that flag meant more to Mrs. Wilderman then I realized.

Paula, looking sad but hopeful, put her little hand in mine. "My granddaddy can save that flag."

"It must be a very special flag to your grandmother," I said.

"Grandma brought that flag here all the way from England, and we get to help her put it up every time we come here."

"Oh, I see," I said, squeezing her hand gently and smiling down at her.

Mr. Wilderman struggled to push the pole out of the screen and into the yard, the wind and wake fighting him. Finally he untied the fasteners holding the flag, left the metal pole where it was, and brought the flag into the cottage.

"I don't think we're just in the outer fringes of a hurricane. It looks like we're smack-dab in the middle of one. I had better turn the radio on and see if we need to evacuate. We might be in for quite a flood." He handed the flag to Mrs. Wilderman and went straight to the emergency band radio.

"Evacuate." I wasn't prepared to evacuate or leave my little cottage to the elements. "I need to go lock up my cottage," I said.

Mrs. Wilderman smoothed the wet flag and began to put it up in a doorway to dry. "That's not really a good idea right now, dear." Mr. and Mrs. Manny waited for my response, but Paula let go of my hand and confronted me.

"You can't go outside now!" Paula said.

"Now just hold on a minute, everyone," said Mr. Wilderman. "Let me check the weather on the radio, and we'll see what this is all about." He turned the crank on the side of the emergency radio. We could barely understand the broadcast because of the static, but Mr. Wilderman seemed to understand exactly what was being reported.

"OK," he said. "This is a category one hurricane, and they're warning people to evacuate. I should have kept the emergency radio out. The tide will change any minute now and that should help with the high water coming over the seawall. Our trouble isn't going to be what's coming over the wall though, but what's going to slowly rise from the creek behind us. Outside there I could see water seeping onto the road from the creek. Just to be safe, I think we should all drive up the road a bit, maybe to Bud's Country Store. We'll take you over in the van to get your car, Ms. Grant, and then we can all drive up to Bud's and wait to see what happens. Mr. and Mrs. Manny, let me drive your car out, and Mrs. Wilderman will drive the van with the children."

Everything he was saying made sense to me, but the thought of abandoning my cottage left me sick inside. This wouldn't be the first unexpected hurricane to do damage to my cottage. The last one put a foot of water and mud—along with lawn furniture and even a crab pot—through my sliding door. Patrick, his sister, Darla, and our good friends Warren and Joan worked from early morning into the next day, scraping the walls and bleaching the floors in order to prevent mold from taking the drywall. The flood had ruined most of our furniture and appliances, along with all of our lower cabinets. It took months to repair the damage, but the cottage was saved.

I knew that I had to leave though, so once to my car I followed the van and the Mannys' vehicle up the road, knowing that we had done the right thing. Water was now inching its way up the tires of my car, and I was feeling a little worried as I took a last glance in my rearview mirror at my little home on the bay. Looking ahead, I could see that the rest of the neighbors were all in the process of packing up their cars and trucks as well. As we passed by the pink cottage, we could see Mrs. Finch closing up her home.

"Hey there," said Mrs. Finch with a wave. Mrs. Finch was one of those ladies who never showed anything but calm dignity. If any tragedy occurred on our road, even the loss of a pet, Mrs. Finch always brought an apple pie to her grieving neighbor. Never one to show pity for herself, she frequently found ways to cheer others up instead.

She had lost her husband in the Vietnam War; he was a pilot shot down over some obscure jungle area early in the war. Since his body had never been found, Mrs. Finch always displayed her POW flag, which she flew atop her flagpole. Some flags carry deeply personal memories.

We all stopped to make sure that Mrs. Finch would soon be following us out. "Yes, I'll be right behind you," she yelled above the noise of the wind.

The next cottage on our way out was Mud Manor. The owners had already left, but in their yard we could see their lawn mower, covered with water up to the motor, as well as their rowboat, which had been sitting on a couple of saw horses on the side of the cottage. It was now floating free in the little yard as the sawhorses had been blown over by the wind gusts.

The Carey family's cottage was next. They spent their weekends at the cottage along with their special-needs child, a daughter by the name of Billie. Often Mr. Carey would take Billie, a young woman of twenty, from cottage to cottage, visiting and talking about the bay and the beautiful swans that had recently come to settle in the creek along with a new family of osprey. Billie's love of nature was second only to her love for her stepfather, who made sure that Billie had every picture book that he could find about the habitat of the bay.

They were still inside their cottage when Mrs. Wilderman pulled her van to a stop and honked the horn. Mr. Carey forced opened his screen door against the strong winds and stuck his head out. "We're just finishing up, and we'll be along in a minute. Don't worry about us," he yelled as he waved for her to continue. I could see Billie through the window looking back at me. She was not scared in the least and smiled and waved as we started up the road again.

Most of the other cottages had already been boarded up with shutters and latches, their owners having gone to higher ground. We followed each other for about three miles, slowly entering the only state road out of our area. Campers, trailers, and vans packed with would-be fishermen from the campground joined us as we evacuated the lower parts of the bay. It was slow merging into the camper traffic, but we managed. Finally, as we approached Bud's Country Store, we could see that we were not alone in our efforts to find a nearby refuge.

Bud's store wasn't my favorite place to frequent. It was always a joke with Patrick and me that I was the only one in Bayside who could cause Chester, the owner's Saint Bernard, to get up from his spot on the porch. He was normally sedate, almost dead looking, but he'd immediately go into a barking rampage when he saw me. He didn't like me, and for some reason neither did his offspring, Chesterfield. At any rate, here I was again with Chesterfield, barking and following me into the store, which was now filled with storm refugees.

Bud couldn't have been happier about the storm. He had an old-fashioned soda fountain that he had found somewhere containing Bud's homemade beer. The bar was made of hickory and was crowded with people who were enjoying his brew and food. The bill of fare offered grilled hot dogs, chili dogs, cheese dogs, and his own concoction, "hot, hot dogs." These were made with his own hot sauce. Few mouths could tolerate the heat, so some of his customers bought and drank his soda fountain beer to cool their tongues.

Those in our small caravan managed to grab some seats near the rear of the store, and the children gathered together in a back room where an antique pinball machine and a few other games could be found. An old jukebox filled with songs from the fifties blared out "Lucille," which didn't quite calm the panic in my shaking body. Little Richard's voice came screeching out of the speaker just the same. Why couldn't someone play a more soothing record?

But despite the fact that we were all worried about our homes, there was a feeling of sturdy survival in the store. Though we had been displaced, most people were quickly caught up in the loud talk and camaraderie that helped to dissipate the hurricane fears shared by all. It reminded me of the first time Patrick had brought me down to this hidden little part of Maryland.

His family had always owned a little cottage just across the street from the one that we later bought. Their place was sitting only a few feet back from the seawall. Before the seawall was constructed, the water would actually go right under their cottage and slap against the fireplace bricks. Patrick said that if it had not been for the fireplace anchoring the house down, the cottage would have been another casualty to the fierceness of the bay. At high tide we often jumped off the back porch into the water below. How the house survived so long I'll never understand. But despite the precarious condition of that house, I had always felt safe there. His parents never seemed to worry about it being destroyed.

I often thought about how much Patrick had suffered over their deaths. I suffered over the loss of them too, but somewhere inside me I believe that Patrick could not overcome his loss. I couldn't help his grief, and he couldn't visit our cottage without becoming depressed. Oftentimes I would go without Patrick just to mow the grass or take care of other small jobs that I could do without him. Sometimes I would spend a night or two by myself. That may have been a big mistake on my part. It took him no time at all to find someone to fill my place on those few weekend nights. It took him even less time to divorce me. Though I tried to work things out with him, he said that I just didn't understand him and that he wasn't happy.

"God wants me to be happy," he would tell me, "and I'm not happy in this marriage."

I always wondered why my life had to be shattered so that God could make Patrick happy. Was God playing games with my life? Where was the justice in that? Now Patrick was gone, and so was his parents' cottage. A group of lawyers invested in the property, tore the cottage down, and built a two-story beach house. Somehow the house seemed an intrusion to our small community.

Over the crowded room, a phone rang. Bud, the store owner, answered it and asked everyone in the room to quiet down so he could hear the caller. "Hey, everyone," Bud called out, "it's Mr. Carey down the road. He says his car won't start, and water is already up to his bumper. He's got one of them little cars, and the engine is probably full of water. We've got to get some help out to them. Does anybody have a four-wheel drive vehicle? We may even need a boat to get them out, or maybe a fire truck."

A tall man stepped up to the bar and offered to help. "I've just put my boat on my trailer outside. My truck has four-wheel drive, and if I can't get them out in my truck, I'll use the boat. I'll have to see how deep the water has gotten. How many people are stranded, Bud?" he asked.

"Three are there," I answered, "Mr. and Mrs. Carey and their adult daughter, Billie." Usually I'm the last to speak, but I kept picturing Billie innocently waving from the cottage window, and now I was worried about her.

"Now that I think about it, the hurricane looks to be intensifying, so maybe I should call the fire department or the Coast Guard, David," Bud said.

"Bud, I think that the Coast Guard has their hands full about now, don't you? You can call the fire department, but I still should go and see what can be done. There may not be time to wait for the fire department."

"Yeah, maybe…I guess you're right, David, but don't you need to take someone with you to help get the Carey family out?"

"I'll go!" I offered. *What am I thinking?* I asked myself.

"OK, come on, let's get going," David said. I followed behind him through the crowd of people.

Mr. and Mrs. Manny looked at me with great concern. "Please be careful, young lady," Mr. Manny said. "I'm sure that David is a great boater, but the elements are going to make it difficult."

Mrs. Manny touched my shoulder lightly as I sped by her. Mrs. Finch smiled her encouraging smile, and I walked past everyone else without looking.

Little Paula ran up and threw her arms around my legs. "Do you have to go?" I nodded and then told her that I would be back soon.

Several people came out onto the covered porch to watch as we climbed up into the high-rise pickup truck. David gave me the plan of action. "When we get into the boat, I want you to stay in the bow so that you can tell me how to maneuver in all of the garbage that will be float-ing in the creek. Do you think you can do that for me? It will be hard to hold on up there because the boat is going to be taking on some pretty sizable waves." I nodded as he started the truck and drove away from the store. As people waved from the porch, I started to panic.

"If we get the boat close to the Carey cottage, then you'll change places with me. You will need to keep the boat as steady as you can, and I'll help the Carey family onboard. You got that?" The driving rain pummeled the window, and I could see trees bending like feathers. I nodded, but my fear level was rising. What did he mean by "if"?

Already the water had filled up the runoff areas on both sides of the road. We hydroplaned a few times, but David knew how to keep his truck on the road quite well. As we got nearer to the creek, I could see the damage that had already occurred in my absence. Trees were down, the wind had blown some of the power lines over, and much farmland had flooded.

David maneuvered the truck and boat with slow, careful turns. As we approached the only area where we could launch the boat, the truck managed to stay on the road. David backed the truck as close to the deeper water as he could while keeping the tires on the watery road. Then he looked over and saw my face.

"Don't worry," he said. "This truck is heavy, and it'll be here when we get back here with the Carey family." I was not comforted in the least.

The boat slid off the trailer and into the water without effort, but I had trouble just opening up my door while stepping into water above my ankles. I thought about a huge water snake that I had encountered once while out canoeing on the creek. I'd never forgotten the size of it or the way it thrashed past me, undaunted by my paddle as I tried to frighten it away.

The wind was still driving in gusts and stinging my eyes as I looked up. "OK, come over here," David called, "and I'll help you into the boat." The boat was a good size with two inboard motors. On the side of the boat near the identifying registration numbers was a name in cursive letters: *Evelyn*. David gave me his arm to balance and then flipped me inside the boat bottom before he climbed in and started the inboard motor. "Sorry about that," he apologized. Then he helped me climb to the bow, tossed me an orange life vest, and showed me what to hang on to for balance. The loud engines smoked as the inboard propellers churned up the muddy water. I hurriedly put the life jacket on and hung on for dear life.

Slowly we made our way to the other side of the creek, where we could eventually see the Carey family holding on to each other, perched on top of their small vehicle. They yelled out to us over the gusts of wind, too afraid to let go of each other, their voices sounding miles away.

Behind them I could see the bay. I had never seen anything so awesome and powerful. It was impossible for me to know if the wind was controlling the waters or the waters controlling the wind. Off and on I felt panic rearing its head, but seeing the Carey family on top of their car, I tried to remain hopeful as my heart continued to pound in my chest.

David motioned for me to take the wheel, and we slowly traded places with David holding on to me as I crawled past him. The boat fought the waves and wind, going forward only when a gust of wind subsided. When the boat came near the stranded family, David gave me directions by pointing left and right with his arms so that I wouldn't steer into the larger debris. The waves were higher on the creek than I had ever seen. We passed an oil tank followed by a shiny slick of fuel, a picnic table and assorted lawn furniture, a few umbrellas, and what looked like siding from my cottage. Debris hit the boat on all sides as I followed David's directions, slowing the boat to a crawl. The wind was blowing the rain so hard now that I had trouble looking up, but we finally got within range of the Carey family.

The boat swayed back and forth, and holding it steady was nearly impossible. When we finally neared the car, David reached over and secured a rope around the open car door window frame. The stranded family then took turns holding on to David's outstretched arms, finding their way into the boat. I felt we would capsize, but eventually all were safely aboard. Billie was first into the boat, and crawled back to where I was balancing myself at the wheel, sitting down close to me. "I like big waves," she said innocently. Mr. and Mrs. Carey, both clearly shaken, quickly sat down without a word being spoken.

"Hold on right here," I shouted to Billy above the noise. She did as I asked and put her hand on the boat rail. I took my life jacket off and put it on Billie. David tossed life jackets to Mr. and Mrs. Carey, their faces displaying shock. The boat tilted with each wave, and again I was certain that we'd all end up overboard, but before I could say anything, David motioned for me to move out of the way as he cut the rope loose from the car window and made his way back to the wheel. Turning the boat back in the direction of his truck across the creek, he quickly removed his life jacket and tossed it to me.

No one said a word as David, sitting down next to Billie, told me to hang on to the railing next to her. Balancing myself by putting my knees on the boat bottom, I held on to the railing as David carefully maneuvered the boat, its engines resisting the force of the heavy winds. Now there was no avoiding the floating debris as more smashed into the side of the boat.

David fought again to turn the boat away from the sting of the bay water, and I began to feel queasy looking back at the small car that had been the Carey refuge as it bobbed and swayed up and down in the water, following David's boat into the creek until it was totally submerged.

As we slowly made our way to the area where we'd left the truck and trailer, we could see that the local fire department had sent the big engine truck out to assist us. With lights flashing and blaring horns giving us a signal, they had found David's truck and were waiting for us to return. I'd never been more grateful to see a fire truck in my life.

When we approached the yellow fire engine, a fireman tossed a rope to David, who quickly secured it to the bow of the boat. The men on the other end attached the rope to their rig and hauled the *Evelyn* in so that we could all be safely removed from the boat and helped into the fire truck cabin.

Next they lifted the boat back onto the boat trailer and secured it, and both the boat and the truck were fastened to the fire engine tow.

After all of that was done, David climbed into the fire truck with the rest of us for the ride back to Bud's Country Store. We were wet, exhausted, and in a daze as the fire engine slowly made its way onto higher ground. Only Billie spoke, commenting randomly about the big waves.

One of the rescuers, an EMT, checked us for signs of hypothermia or shock, but he eventually declared that we would not need hospital attention. He distributed warming blankets, and we took them gratefully, but all I could think about was getting as far away from the bay as possible.

When we got back to the store, we were greeted by many of the local people who had come out to help those of us who had sought refuge. There was less than standing room now. When the Carey family came through the door, followed by David, me, and our rescuers, loud applause broke out.

"David, you're the man," said one of his friends.

He was treated to a few cheers and multiple pats on the back, but David held my hand up like a prizefighter referee and said, "And here is a very brave lady. She did the hard work." With that, everyone applauded me.

With my lips quivering, I said a quick thank-you, and then, ducking my head down, I went to the area where the Wilderman and Manny families were still applauding.

The Wilderman children all came up and hugged me. Paula wouldn't let go. "I knew you could save them," she said. "You tell good stories, and you're brave too."

"Thank you, Paula," I said, "but I'm not brave." Trying to look calm and casual, I turned to my neighbors and asked if there was any news about the hurricane. I also tried to hide my chattering teeth.

Mr. Manny took his dry jacket off and put it over my shoulders, giving me a look of grateful appreciation. Bud brought some old towels from the back of the store and rolls of paper towels to help us sop the water from our clothing, and his wife brought hot coffee in Styrofoam cups for each of the rescuers and for those who had been rescued.

"What you did for that family will never be forgotten young lady," Bud said quietly to me. Then he spoke to the crowd. "The announcement on the radio stated that the fast-moving hurricane is weakening already and should be out of our area in another hour or so. In the meantime, you all will have to either stay here and wait for word as to when you can get back into your cottages, or else go on to higher ground and come back down in a couple of days to survey the damages. You're welcome to stay here as long as you want today. I'll keep the place open all night if I have to. I got lots of hot dogs left, and we're in a pretty well protected area here."

"I think we'll try to find a motel up in Lexington Park for the night and then drive down when the waters recede," Mr. Manny said to me. "I want to get into the cottage and clean it up before mold and mildew set in."

"That's a good idea," said Mrs. Wilderman. "We'll probably do the same. How about you, Rainey, what will you do?"

"I don't know what I'm going to do," I answered. "I may just try to find a place in Leonardtown somewhere near the library. I heard from the librarian at my last visit that some rare books had been loaned to the library. Maybe I'll find out something more about our area. It seems as though I'll have plenty of time for that. Actually, there's a nice B&B there where I might stay for a night or two. I'll try to get back here as soon as I can, though I don't know what I'll find left of my place."

I tried to sound unaffected by the trauma, explaining things of no importance, but my body was starting to shake over the fact that my little cottage might have been totally demolished, that I was soaked to the bone and cold, and that I very nearly could have ended up staying in my cottage had it not been for Mr. Manny's invitation to enjoy some tomato pie.

"If we hear that we can all return to our cottages, we'll call up to Leonardtown and let you know," offered Mr. Manny. "The missus and I have stayed there at that B&B. It's the only one in Leonardtown. Maybe when we all get back together you can continue with your story?"

"What story is that?" Bud asked.

"Oh, we have our very own storyteller right here with us," answered Mr. Manny, "and she has really done some good research about our little area."

"I'd be interested in hearing some of that," Bud said. "How about you letting some of the rest of us in on whatever you know?"

"I'd like that," I lied, "but I really don't know so much. I read a lot, but I'm sure that you probably know more about the area then I do." Why couldn't I have just agreed to share what I had? Bud continued to wait for me to agree. *Why are these people chitchatting during a hurricane?* I asked myself.

"So I guess we'll see each other back here in a few days, or whenever they allow us in. I can assume from the high water that we'll be cleaning up for quite a while this time." I hoped that my enthusiasm sounded genuine, but I felt like crying. My body was shaking, and I wanted to get somewhere and take a nice hot shower.

After saying good-bye to my neighbors and the fire crew, I stepped out onto the covered porch and down the steps to my car. The strong wind was blowing cigarette smoke into my eyes as people gathered on the porch. There was plenty of smoking and beer drinking going on in the parking lot to distract the dog, but Chesterfield immediately got up off of the porch and followed after me, barking all the way to my car door.

"He really likes you, doesn't he?" It was David Woods. He had just unhitched his boat trailer from his truck where he kept it stored behind a chain-link fence and where Bud stored everything from boats to portable toilets.

"Yeah, really," I said. "I think I must be very special to get so much attention from a dog."

David laughed. Standing against the truck door, he spoke to me. "You know, I have to tell you that anyone would have been frightened to do what you did today. But I didn't see any fear in you at all. Are you always so calm?"

"Are you kidding?" I asked. "I was so frightened that I almost went numb! I'm still shaking."

"I am too," said David. "I really didn't think we would make it back a few times. I did a lot of praying."

David smiled warmly and waited for my reply, but I had nothing to add. Since when do men ever admit such a thing as being frightened, or for that matter praying?

"Well," I said, "I better be going. I need to find a place for the night or for whatever length of time it takes for the authorities to declare the area safe again."

David nodded, and I walked to my car without another word. As I drove away, it dawned on me that I had just left a kind man standing by his truck without thanking him for everything that he had done. I thought about it all the way to Leonardtown. I also thought about his soft brown eyes. I always get my first impressions about people from their eyes. There was thinking going on behind those eyes of his, but about what?

There was one room left at the B&B just off of Leonardtown Road. After I checked in and closed the door to my room, I allowed the full extent of my exhaustion to hit me. I took a quick shower and then put on the bathrobe provided for guests; I washed out my shorts, top, and tennis shoes. Once I had twisted the water out and hung them over the shower pole, I fell onto the bed as deep sleep finally overtook my thoughts.

∾

It was almost ten the next morning before I was able to get out of the bed. My clothes, though damp, were at least clean. I used the B&B blow-dryer to help with the dampness before putting them on, and then I went downstairs to the dining area. There I saw a lady about my age, busy dusting furniture.

"Good morning," said the woman. "You had quite a day from what you told my husband when you checked in. My name is Linda Raley, and my husband and I own the B&B."

"I'm Rainey Grant," I answered, "and yes, it was quite an ordeal yesterday, but I survived." I looked around the beautiful room. "I don't know if my cottage has survived though. I'm hoping that I can get in to see it in a couple of days. The cottage was built in the 1920s, and I'm not sure that it could have held together in such a tough storm." It hit me again that I just might have lost my little home by the bay, and here I was chatting away nervously.

"Well, if your cottage has been on the bay for that many years, it may still be standing. There have been many devastating storms here over the years," said Linda. "I'm always amazed by how fierce the bay can be. So far I haven't heard of anyone with major damage here in town, even though the wind and rains were fierce here as well, but I'll pray that your home isn't lost."

"Thank you," I said. "In the meantime, I plan to spend a little time across the street at the library, where I ordered some books about local history." *Here is another prayer,* I thought to myself. *I'm surrounded by religious people. What good does prayer do?*

"This area has a lot of interesting history for sure. Some of it's hilarious as opposed to devastating floods and hurricanes. If you get time during your stay with us, I would love to share some of it with you—that is, if you'd like that." Linda seemed eager to share, and I was eager to leave, but I didn't want to appear rude. I wanted to be alone more than anything, but I was still too exhausted to even walk across the street to retrieve the books.

By now my stomach was growling, and I wondered where to go get a quick breakfast in the area. "Could you tell me where there is a restaurant that would still be serving breakfast near here?"

"Come on into the dining room and I'll fix you up something to eat." She smiled. "No charge for late risers, and if you have time, I'll tell you a little story to brighten your day. You'll have plenty of time for the library, and I may know some stories that you won't find in a book."

She brought me a breakfast that was sure to please anyone. Local sausage, hash browns with yellow summer squash and zucchini bits, as well as onions and red peppers, thick slices of scrapple and buttered homemade biscuits, all brought out on a large platter. I hadn't realized how hungry I was until I ate the last bite of biscuit and washed it down with coffee. When the table was finally cleared, Linda sat down and began to tell a story.

Chapter 6

Temperance

*T*emperance. Walter Graves had come to loathe that word. His wife, Greta, used it every chance she could to warn Walter of the dangers of alcohol. It had been preached at church too often as well, and lately it had become an annoying word associated with the St. Mary's County Women's Temperance League, in which his wife proudly boasted membership in the Leonardtown chapter. Walter found that Greta had become less then "temperate" toward him.

That's what bothered him so much. Lately Greta had been strutting herself around the farmhouse as though she had forgotten who was boss. He was sure that the children had gotten wind of her new-found attitude, and he wasn't about to allow much more of this display of hers. Oh, she was still keeping up with her chores and such. She took care of feeding the kids and Walter, the cows and chickens, tending the vegetable garden, and canning everything that could be canned. She also kept up the washing and ironing and darning the clothing that had all but worn out. But this attitude of hers wasn't justified in his mind.

Walter thought about everything for a few minutes before deciding to let it go. He'd have a chat with the pastor the next Sunday and suggest that he preach from the Good Book the verses about wives submitting to their husbands and showing proper respect. A good sermon would surely turn things around. Besides that, if he came down too hard on Greta tonight, she might just catch on to his little business enterprise that he had going on with Peaches, his friend and fellow farmer next door. The two farmers had been friends since childhood, and they always helped each other. These days a man could use all the help he could get just to survive.

Walter was glad that Peaches owned the farm next door, just down the road a bit, because Peaches was known as a good and honest man by most folks. Besides that, Peaches knew a lot more about farming than Walter. He knew about the latest crops and how to get the seeds before anyone else did. He figured out that crops needed rotating, a fact that made Walter wonder why his daddy had never taught him anything but tobacco growing. A person needed food these days, and because of Peaches, Walter had enough vegetables for Greta to put up for the family. But lately the heat and drought was causing trouble with the crops, as well as years of tobacco farming, which had all but ruined the soil, or so Peaches had told him.

Peaches had been given his nickname because whenever anyone ever asked him how he was doing, he would always reply, "Just peachy!" Hardly anyone knew his legal name, but Walter and Peaches had history together, at least in Walter's mind, so he never felt it necessary to ask Peaches about his name. He was content to just listen to Peaches go on about hopeful things, like the end of times and things that awaited good people in heaven, like golden crowns and a big supper with the Lord.

Walter often wondered why his wife, Greta, couldn't be more like Peaches's wife, Betsy. Betsy was always kind and real nice to Walter. But Greta was not someone to pick a fight with, and whenever she was in the same room with Walter, he felt himself walking on eggshells. Besides, he reasoned, Greta would probably be in a bad mood again when she got home from her temperance meeting tonight, and that would set him off. He needed to take command the moment she set foot in the door, but he'd be careful not to set her over the edge.

But if he mentioned to her about the Bible saying that it was her duty to submit to Walter's authority, it could backfire. It had before. What was that verse in the Bible about it being better to live on the roof of the house then in one room with a scornful woman? It went something like that. Anyway, he would have to ask the preacher about that too. Was that kind of woman called "scornful" or "contentious"? No matter, the preacher would know what Walter was asking him about. If Greta came home in that mood again, he best not pick a fight. He would let the preacher straighten Greta out when the time was right.

Besides that, Walter was wanting to go out a bit that night and thought he best not pick on her at all, at least not until he found out the location of the exact verses in the Bible about submission. Greta always confused him when he tried to quote from the Good Book. She would say things like, "Walter, that isn't in the Bible!" She was always making him feel stupid. He would have to take some time and look up those verses so she wouldn't be able to scorn him again. Trouble was that she had taken the family Bible with her to her meeting.

At eight o'clock, Greta swung open the kitchen door and glided in. She didn't look at Walter or offer him a how-do-you-do. She just took the long silver pins out of her hat and laid them purposely on the wooden table. Walter looked at her tiny waist and her beautiful brown hair falling out of her hat and started thinking thoughts of romance again. His legs started to tingle, and he forgot about what he was going to say to her. But after removing her rather large black hat, she turned to where Walter was sitting and looked down her nose at him.

"Hello dear." Walter nodded respectfully. "How was your little meeting?" He did his best to sound interested. Greta was not impressed.

"If you knew the evils of alcohol, you wouldn't need to ask me questions like that. Our meetings are not weak *little meetings*, Walter, they are meetings with purpose and power."

Walter was beginning to drift already. He had heard this same argument until he was blue in the face. "Dear," he said, "I don't disagree about that. Alcohol is a bad thing. Why, I suppose you think I don't know how important you women are in trying to keep this county sober." He pounded the table a little for emphasis. "I'm just proud that you're so, so—"

"Never mind, Walter," Greta snapped. "I know that you drink alcohol. Nothing you can swish in your mouth can cover up that awful odor. Not mint or parsley or any of that other stuff that you put in your mouth and spit out. It's all disgusting. All it does is turn your deceitful tongue green!"

For a little woman, his wife was pretty spunky. What she lacked in size, she had coming out of her mouth in big buckets. Walter had the urge to put her in her place, but instead he just gave her a weak nod before heading out the kitchen door and onto the side porch, which needed repair and was leaning on one side.

"Walter! Where do you think you're going?"

"I'm going for a walk, dear," he said as he looked back over his shoulder.

He wondered for a moment if his little wife had eyes in the back of her head or the nose of a bloodhound. Her eyes were always on him, and she was always sniffing around. Her attitude gave him the urge to pack his stuff and hit the road on more than one occasion. Instead, he let himself out of the front gate and leaving it open, proceeded down the road to meet Peaches. He had always thought that chewing on fresh mint leaves could cover any of his little nips of alcohol, but Greta never let anything escape her.

The sun was just starting to sink behind the hillside, and Walter walked along the narrow dirt road, watching the glowworms dance in the grassy fields between his farm and the next one. He always liked to watch them as they skipped around just above the grass. Their light was an amazing thing to him. It seemed that the hotter the night and the more humid the air, the more the little bugs glittered about.

Often he would take his children out into the fields at night to chase them. Then he would let them fill up canning jars and take them home to put beside their beds. The children would fall asleep to the blinking lights, but Walter would always set the creatures free after the children had finally closed their eyes. He saw no purpose in letting the little glowers die, held captive in a canning jar. It was what he had done as a boy himself on the same farm on the same road. He always let them go.

Once he took his children out for a treat, telling them to cover their eyes and to hold on to him as he led them into the field where an ancient oak tree stood. Its trunk was enormous, and Walter guessed it to be a couple hundred years old. Once he had the children positioned in front of the old tree, he told them to uncover their eyes. As they did, they beheld a miraculous sight. Every branch of the old tree was covered with glowworms, and it looked like someone had placed thousands of tiny blinking candles in the tree. It was a sight that Walter had never forgotten—his children and their wide-open mouths and glowing eyes reflecting the tiny lights, and that old oak standing proud and displaying itself like some great statue all lit up.

The farm had been much larger at one time. His father had inherited the farm from his father and back in the family as far as the beginnings of Maryland. Walter had been told that one of his ancestors had actually come over on the *Dove*. Of course they had not started farming tobacco originally, but after being shown the wonderful effects of the tobacco plant by the Indians, it had not taken long before the leafy crop had become a staple in this small area of the new world and a way of living for the Graves family.

The land that lay between the Potomac River and the Chesapeake Bay proved to be excellent land for tobacco, corn, and assorted vegetable farming. Before long, huge tobacco plantations appeared, and the farmers began sending their tobacco as far away as Europe. The first settlers had used indentured servants to help harvest their crops, but as these servants eventually gained their freedom and a right to their own property, the need for cheap labor began to outgrow local availability. Importing slaves seemed to be the answer to this problem.

At one time Walter's grandfather had boasted a holding of fifty slaves, most purchased at a slave auction in Prince George's County. They were an expensive investment. Hearing the stories about the slaves often upset Walter, but he reasoned that they were better off here then in some jungle without anyone to take care of them. That's what he had heard his father's friends say about it. Wouldn't they have to fight off wild animals, and wasn't there no one to teach them the Good Book over there? He had picked up bits and pieces about them, but it was all very confusing to him, so he usually just avoided the subject altogether.

Peaches had been his friend and neighbor since childhood, but it had never occurred to Walter that Peaches would have liked to attend the white schools or socialize with the other boys or dine at restaurants where only white folks were served or maybe even drink from the same water fountain. That was the way it was, and Walter never gave it much thought until he and Peaches had become young men. One day Peaches let Walter know that he resented the fact that blacks had been slaves.

"Your granddaddy was a mean old cuss," Peaches said out of the blue one day.

"You have no call to say that about my grandpa," said Walter, "and you never even knew him, so why are you saying this?"

"I'm saying it because he owned slaves, and he didn't treat them well. One of them was my great-grandmother."

This was news that Walter didn't want to hear, but try as he might, he couldn't dispute it. "Peaches, I don't know anything about all of that. Why do you want to go and talk about that now? You never said nothing about that before."

"Hey," said Peaches, "for all I know we could be related. How would you like to start telling everyone that you're related to a Negro?"

"Peaches, I don't know what's gotten into you, but I'll thank you to stop this nonsense. We're not related. We're friends."

Walter decided to walk off toward his farmhouse and tried not to think about what Peaches had told him. He didn't have any answers, and he was feeling confused by the things Peaches had said. By the time he arrived, he had so many questions on his mind that he walked to the tobacco barn to confront his father, something he had never done before. He found his father sitting on a stool inspecting tobacco leaves. A jug sat near him.

Walter Graves Sr. was normally not accustomed to answering questions. He spoke when he had something to say and didn't feel it his duty to answer his wife or children when they asked him unimportant questions. Usually he walked off or gave them a look that let them know not to be asking him anything. Every once in a while, though, he would give a yes or a no, but rarely did he discuss what he didn't feel like discussing. He paid no attention to young Walter as he stood waiting for his father to acknowledge him.

"Pa, I need to ask you something. I need you to tell me if my great-grandpa was a mean old cuss who treated his slaves bad and got Negro women pregnant." His father gave him no acknowledgment at all but continued to string tobacco leaves on a long pole.

"I'm thinking that it must be true. Is that why you never answer no questions anybody asks you?" Young Walter was confronting his father for the first time in his life. "Do we got something to hide in our family?"

His father sat up straighter on his stool, dropped the tobacco pole, and turned toward his son. "You better keep that fat mouth of yours shut, boy."

Young Walter felt that getting some response from his daddy was better than none, so he continued on.

"Peaches told me that we might be related. Could that be true? Peaches never lies, and he's my best friend and—"

Before young Walter could ask another question, he found himself flat on the dirt floor of the tobacco barn. His nose was bleeding, and his teeth hurt. When he felt his mouth, he could feel that one of his front teeth had been knocked sideways. He looked up from the ground and saw hatred in his father's eyes. His whole face hurt, but he was afraid to get up off the ground, so he stayed put as his father walked away with the jug in his hand. Tears of pain mingled with the blood splattered on the ground beside him.

It took him a long time to be able to face his father again, and when he did, it was always with his head hanging low to avoid eye contact. Walter's mother took care of his bleeding mouth and kissed his cheeks. She was a quiet woman who had no time to give individual attention to her children unless the situation was critical. She was too busy most days. Walter never remembered seeing his father hug her or talk to her. Most of the time, his father was out in the barn messing with his tobacco leaves or off somewhere with the other farmers doing whatever it was they were doing.

Walter didn't forget the tenderness he received from his mother that day, but he never had a conversation with his father again. If his father told him to do something, then Walter would do it without a word.

Walter missed his mother and often spoke to her over her grave. On her birthday each year, he would place some sweet bay magnolia blossoms on her grave near the little cross. But he placed nothing on his father's grave, and he never spoke of him again or the way his drinking and cruelty had brought the family shame.

It no longer mattered to Walter that his father had died and left them all nothing but the farm. His mother had survived a few more years, but soon she too had passed away. They were both buried with the rest of the Graves family on a hillside near their church, a few miles outside of Leonardtown.

Walter had thought to visit his mother's gravesite more often, but he had other things to do like taking care of his younger brothers, keeping the farm going, and seeing to it that the farm would be able to feed them all. One by one they would all grow up and leave the farm. When they had all gone off, Walter stayed on the farm and tried his best to support his own little family. Now with tobacco prices down again and the drought causing the other crops trouble, it had come to this.

Turning the last bend, Walter could see beams of light shining through the small farmhouse windows where Peaches lived. There was always light shining from that house, Walter mused. Peaches had a nice wife and some great children, and they all seemed to be happy.

In Walter's house, there was always some kind of turmoil going on. The children mainly took after their mother and often talked down to Walter. It was a relief to him just to go over to visit Peaches for a little while. He wasn't treated with much respect in his own home, but then he was going to talk to the preacher about that on Sunday—maybe.

Walter knocked on the screen door of the farmhouse. "Come on in," said Betsy.

He entered the main room, and Betsy smiled as she put a plate of chicken and buttermilk biscuits down in front of Peaches. "Sit and have a bite to eat, Walter," she offered.

"No, thank you, Betsy, I just ate a bit at home, but you go ahead and finish. I'll just wait out on the porch." Walter hadn't really had much to eat for dinner, and his stomach began to growl as he smelled the chicken, but he never did like imposing on people.

"Suit yourself," replied Betsy, "but I hear that stomach growling, Walter Graves. You sit yourself down here and have some of my good fried chicken." But Walter had other things on his mind, and putting his hands deep into his overall pockets, he shyly slipped out onto the porch.

Half an hour later, Peaches opened the door and joined Walter outside. Though it was getting darker, Walter could see that Betsy had a way with flowers. Black-eyed Susans were sitting up close to the house, just under the windows. All along the walkway there were yellow and orange mums. Walter loved flowers and wished that he had a knack for growing pretty things, but his farming revolved around tobacco, and he had little time for fixing up a flower garden. Greta was always complaining about it, but she had not bothered to garden flowers herself. Walter watched as glowworms danced just above the mums.

Peaches approached Walter and motioned for him to follow him to the barn beside the house. Both men walked together as they looked back to make sure they wouldn't be overheard or followed by one of Peaches's children.

"You ready for this?" asked Peaches.

"Yep, I'm as ready as rain," replied Walter. "This is it. We're either going to get rich or get shot at."

"Don't jinx us like that!" whispered Peaches. "You know better then to say things like that." Walter could see that Peaches was clearly nervous.

"I'm sorry," said Walter. "I was just making a joke with you."

"Yeah, I know it, but you don't seem to take this as seriously as I do. Those revenuers have been all up and down the road from Leonardtown to Bayside, and they mean business. I guess you heard they made Cyrus Posey a revenue agent?"

"I heard that," said Walter, "but that guy won't go after his old school chums, friends, or neighbors."

"Who you kidding?" asked Peaches. "He has a job, and he gets paid. Do you think he's goanna get caught giving his friends and neighbors a break? Just last week I heard that Cyrus arrested Garner Tibbs even after Garner offered to destroy his own still. He pleaded with Cyrus to give him a break, but Cyrus wouldn't back down. I tell you, that Cyrus is a Judas as far as I'm concerned."

Peaches opened the barn door and grabbed two lanterns from a couple of nails, handing them to Walter. Then Peaches took a shotgun down from a tall shelf and some shells from a box next to the gun.

"What's the shotgun for?" asked Walter.

"I told Betsy we were going to hunt for some possum tonight. I told her I set some traps and would go see what I got, but I didn't tell her the rest. That's a lie you know, and I just hate to tell Betsy lies. She doesn't deserve for me to lie to her, but I told her I wouldn't come back empty-handed, so I may have to shoot something if the trap is empty."

"I know what you mean about that. It don't seem right to go to church on Sunday and then have to lie about doing something illegal just to support our families during the week. Then again, I never get away with telling Greta a lie. She just don't like me no matter what I do, and she's always letting me know what a failure I am. I'm her husband, but she don't like me." Walter looked to Peaches for comfort.

"No, she doesn't like you at all, I'm thinking," said Peaches. "Don't think she ever did." Peaches handed his dejected friend the box of shells and closed the barn door. Then he struck a match and lit both lanterns, taking one of the lanterns back from Walter. "Come on; cheer up, because she'll like you even less if she finds out about this."

Walter tried not to think about the wrath he would suffer if Greta ever found out, and he soon became somber. But as soon as he saw some glowworms near the edge of the woods, he began to feel good about the money that would soon find its way into his pocket. He had a feeling that the glowworms were a good omen for the new business venture he and Peaches were starting. Those bugs had a way of perking him up.

Chapter 7

Brew

Greta was certain that Walter and his friend were up to no good. She had always known that Walter could never get away with anything on his own because he lacked imagination. However, with his friend Peaches, anything was possible.

Peaches was a successful and capable farmer, and unlike her do-nothing husband, Peaches was a doer. This night, Greta waited for Walter to leave and then came up with a plan to find out just what was going on with the two men. If it was what she thought it was, she would put an end to it herself.

A few things had become obvious to Greta lately. For example, no matter how much she conserved her sugar, there seemed to be less and less in the containers. She had cut back on baking pies and other needless desserts and had even cut out sugar in her tea, yet her supply had seemed to dwindle rapidly over the past several weeks. The second thing that she noticed was that she was missing some of her gallon water jugs. She had made more trips to the water pump then she cared to think about and finally concluded that she had better count her jugs. Where once she had counted twenty jugs, she now counted only fifteen. Walter claimed that they had never owned twenty jugs, but she knew better.

Probably the last thing that she had noticed was that Walter's behavior had changed. Walter once had a habit of mocking her temperance meetings, but now seemed to encourage her to go. This was much too conciliatory to be authentic on Walter's part, Greta concluded, even though she couldn't remember a time when Walter didn't back down or cower over disagreements. He had no spine, as far as Greta was concerned, and probably never would.

Greta was also suspicious because the children had told her on more then one occasion that after she left for her meetings, their father would put them to bed way before their bedtime, and they often heard him going out the kitchen door. It also seemed strange to her that Walter was always sitting in the kitchen waiting for her to come home from her meetings, but where he had gone before she returned home was a mystery. His late-night hunting with Peaches was dubious to her as well since Walter wouldn't kill a deer if his family was starving. Tonight she would try to find out what Walter Graves was up to.

Greta put the sleeping children under their bedcovers, and without changing out of her black dress, which she only wore to the meetings, she left the house and walked along the dark road toward the neighbors' farmhouse. She wasn't surprised to see a light on as she knocked on the open front door. It was hot and humid, and now she had wished that she had taken time to put a lighter dress on, but she was on an important mission and would have to endure the temperature.

"Come on in," Betsy said. "Whoever it is, you are welcome." When Greta walked in with her fancy black dress, Betsy was shocked to see her. For a moment she wondered if Greta had come to invite her to the meeting. This would have been a huge honor for Betsy since the meetings were by invitation only, but to date Betsy had not been invited. Betsy assumed that Greta had not thought to invite her before but now had changed her mind, and had come to offer her a place in the group.

"I'm so happy that you stopped by for a visit. Could I get you a glass of cold tea or something else?" Betsy noticed that Greta's face was covered with perspiration and couldn't imagine wearing such an outfit on a night like this, even for a temperance meeting.

"Thank you, yes, I would love a cold glass of tea, but I have come on an urgent matter, not for a social visit. I know it's late in the evening, but I feel that what I have to say will be of utmost importance to you." Greta moved closer to Betsy and whispered, "Where have Walter and Peaches gone tonight?"

Betsy motioned for Greta to sit down. She decided that this must not be an invitation. "What is it? Is it something about my Peaches?" she asked, alarmed. "I know he and Walter have gone out hunting, they've been doing that a lot lately, but is Peaches in some kind of trouble?"

"Calm yourself," said Greta. "What I have to say concerns both of our husbands." Greta looked slowly around the room. "Are the children in bed?" she whispered.

"Yes, they are all in bed asleep. What in the world do you need to be telling me in secret, and why are you whispering?" Betsy was becoming more concerned and fearful. What had her Peaches gotten himself into? She excused herself and went to the icebox, removed some shaved ice and put it in a glass along with some freshly brewed tea and a mint leaf. Betsy handed the glass to Greta and took her seat again. "Well, what is this all about?"

"I think we need to go into town and speak to Cyrus Posey," said Greta quietly.

"Cyrus Posey?" Betsy shouted. "Why would I want to speak to that man?" Betsy did not attempt to hide her disdain for Cyrus Posey. He had caused a lot of trouble lately.

Greta shushed Betsy. "Because if we don't talk to Cyrus, our husbands may get caught by some trigger-happy revenuer. I heard that Cyrus has hired himself an agent from Virginia. Our men are going to be caught and maybe shot dead in the process. I have a plan that may save their foolish necks. They are up to no good!"

"Caught doing what? Are you trying to tell me that our men are moonshiners?" Betsy stopped her rocking chair and looked hard at Greta. "You don't know anything like that for sure because it just isn't so. My Peaches would never break the law like that. He doesn't even drink alcohol." Betsy was clearly offended.

"Well, he may not drink it, but he surely is making the stuff," replied Greta. "Let me ask you a thing or two. Have you happened to notice that your sugar is rapidly dwindling away but you haven't been baking any more than usual? Are you missing any jugs? Has Peaches been extra nice to you over the last several months?"

Betsy began to rock again, and her brain was working overtime. She thought about the sugar. Yes, her supply was down lower than usual, but Betsy had attributed that to all of the sweet tea she had made on this unusually hot summer. As far as jugs go, she did remember asking Peaches to look out in the barn for some as she had been missing a few. But the nice way husband had been treating her? Well, he had always been kind and affectionate.

"Well?" Greta asked.

Betsy put two and two together and thought about how many evenings Peaches and Walter had gone out for a stroll or a hunt together recently. Sometimes Peaches went out alone to hunt possum or squirrel, but then he could have met Walter someplace other then the house. It seemed odd to her that the two of them would take up hunting together. To her knowledge, Walter didn't like killing animals. Peaches often took Walter a fresh kill, but only after skinning and cleaning the thing. And it was Greta who accepted and cooked the meat and Greta who would bake a pie or two for Peaches, in appreciation.

"Well, I have been missing a few little things around here, like yeast." Greta stopped rocking and leaned forward. The two women looked at each other for a moment. Greta nodded her head.

"Maybe we better go see Cyrus Posey," Betsy reluctantly agreed, "but he isn't sympathetic with anybody. He would turn in his own flesh and blood these days. He's got a sick wife at home, everybody knows it, and he's counting on keeping his job for as long as he can, and that means we would be in real trouble if he doesn't like us or doesn't want to give Walter and Peaches a break. You must be thinking that he will, but I'm not so sure this is a good idea!"

"You need to stay calm, Betsy. I've come up with a plan, so don't you worry. I've always had a way with men, and I may have to get creative, but I'll manage to get my plans heard. If I can divert Cyrus in some way, he might just believe me." Greta patted Betsy's hand to reassure her.

"Well," said Betsy, "I don't know what you mean by the word *creative*, but I do know that you're a God-fearing Christian woman, so I'll have to put my eggs in your basket for now." She watched as Greta slowly drank the last of her iced tea, and then the two women spoke more about Greta's plan of action.

After Greta left, Betsy sat rocking in her chair. She had never known Peaches to break any law. He was always honest as the day was long. He never bribed anybody, and he was always reading the Bible to the children.

Yet prices were down again on tobacco, and it was getting to be very hard just to put food on the table. Things were not growing so well in her vegetable garden either. She often saw her husband pacing around the property or reading about the latest crop seeds. He had tried everything to keep their heads above water.

She loved her man, but she also feared what could happen if Greta was correct about the moonshine. On top of all that, Betsy also knew that most farmers were indeed giving the business of home brewing a try. The Depression was in full swing, and everyone she knew was suffering in some way.

"Dear Lord," she prayed, "please keep my Peaches safe from harm, and please do not let me say nothing to him that is accusing, just in case he isn't doing what Greta says. And Lord, if you don't think this Mr. Cyrus Posey is going to believe our little story, then tell me now. You know, Lord God that I don't tell lies, but even David's wife, Michal, had to lie to protect David from King Saul. Please tell me if what we women are about to do is wrong."

Betsy waited for a reply from the Lord, but having received none she got up off of her knees and began to pace the floor, waiting for Peaches to come home.

ॐ

By the time Walter and Peaches neared their handmade contraption at the bottom of a steep ravine, it had become a dark night. Briars and branches sheltered the still from the light of the moon and stars, so Peaches decided to turn up the flame of his oil lantern. Not watching where he was going, Walter slipped on a pile of cow manure before he could turn his flame up, and slid down the ravine and into the shallow creek at the bottom.

Peaches laughed uncontrollably. "What's the hurry Walter?"

"Oh no, Greta is going to see me all wet with cow manure on me and ask me a load of questions."

"Don't worry about it." Peaches laughed. "Just tell her we were after some possum and didn't know how deep into the dark woods we got ourselves. She knows that the cows come down here to drink. Tell her you slipped and tumbled all the way down the ravine. Maybe she'll feel sorry for you. I doubt it, but maybe you'll be lucky." Peaches gave a chuckle. "Man, you stink!"

Walter tried to brush off the cow dung but finally gave up. "Where's the still?"

"It's right in front of you. Turn up your flame."

Walter adjusted the flame on his lantern and immediately saw the masterpiece of a still that he and Peaches had painstakingly built over the last several weeks. What they couldn't find or buy they had made in the privacy of Peaches's barn. Once completed, the two men took each piece down to the woods at night and assembled it right on the creek.

"What a beauty of a still," Walter said.

"Are you ready to try it?" Peaches asked. "You know I don't like liquor, so you're going to have to give it a taste. First though let's get a cup of it and see if we can light it up. If there's a blue flame, it should be good enough and ready to drink."

Walter took the box of matches from Peaches, and Peaches put a little of the clear liquid into a tin cup that he had brought down to the creek for the first sampling. Then Walter lit a match and held it close to the cup. A blue flame burned, lighting up the eyeballs of the two jubilant business partners.

Walter blew out the flame and held the cup to his lips, sipping the liquid carefully. The alcohol was sharp and bit into his throat as it passed on down to his stomach. "We've done it!" Walter shouted.

"Hush up! Do you want anyone to find out what we're doing down here? What's the matter with your head?"

"Sorry," whispered Walter, "but I'm telling you, we are going to get rich selling this stuff!"

Peaches looked at Walter and then back at the still. Eventually the realization hit him, and he broke out into a half smile, which got Walter laughing. Walter took another swig and smacked his lips at Peaches, who slowly allowed himself to overcome his previous trepidation. Then, sitting down on the manure-covered slope, he began laughing and whispering with Walter about all the nice things they could eventually buy, but only Peaches mentioned buying something nice for his wife. Walter bought Greta a ring for their wedding and had regretted it ever since.

After talking about what they were going to do with their future fortunes, a thought came to Peaches's mind. "We had best get over to the traps I've set and see if we've cornered a possum or some other critter. Betsy is expecting some fresh meat this time. We'll come back with some jars in a couple of nights and some more jugs and bottle this stuff up for sale."

Walter smiled at his friend wide enough to display his sideways tooth, and then he finished off the contents of the cup. Immediately he began to look around to see if he could find any mint leaves. He knew that Greta would figure out what he was doing though, so he gave that idea up. He was feeling a little dizzy but figured it was from sheer jubilation at their pending fortune. Peaches motioned for Walter to put the cup down and follow him back up the hill.

Luckily they found one of the largest possums that Peaches had ever managed to trap, but the possum was still alive. Peaches handed his lantern to Walter and, taking his shotgun in his hand, proceeded to let the barrel go off straight into the possum's head. "I just wanted Betsy to hear the sound because it makes things more authentic."

Walter looked at the poor dead possum and wanted to cry. "He was a pretty little possum."

"This will make a fine meal and satisfy my woman for a couple of days," said Peaches, ignoring his sensitive friend. The two men were happy but exhausted as they made their way up the hillside and over the farmyard to the road. Walter said good-bye near Peaches's barn, and the two parted company for the night, but Walter kept picturing the little eyes of that poor possum and wished he had turned his head away from the awful scene.

Arriving home, Walter stripped off his filthy overalls. Then he threw them out onto the back porch and washed up as best he could with some old rags lying on the porch floor, and a little water from a jug. He hurried up the steps and slipped under the bedcovers next to Greta, being careful to turn his face away from her.

"You stink!" Greta said. "Get out of this bed and go wash yourself good, or you you're not welcome here!"

Sheepishly Walter got out of the bed, but being too tired to wash up again, went directly to the barn where he eventually fell asleep on some hay, wondering why Greta could never think of anything nice to say to him.

Chapter 8

Agents

Cyrus Posey had an office in the back corner of the Leonardtown Farmers Bank in the very room that once hosted a group of Southern sympathizers during the Civil War. The men had met there often, trying to devise plans for breaking their fellow townsmen out of that godforsaken Point Lookout prison camp. Cyrus's own father had been one of them. Caught himself, Albert Posey had died a horrible death from consumption before he could be pardoned and freed. Several other civilians met untimely deaths there as well, yet little had ever been posted about it in the paper. The Union had taken over the entire town.

The editor of the *Leonardtown Herald* had been warned several times not to print anything "anti-Union," and fear had set in once a few reporters had been tossed into the town jail. Other citizens had been sent to Point Lookout; two had died there. The Union government kept facts about prison deaths in special files that were not let out to the general public. But there were leaks in the bucket, and the newspaper printed what leaked out.

Cyrus may have been working for the federal government as a revenue agent, but deep in his blood the rebellion continued. He would take any job he could get, even if it meant turning in a neighbor or two, but he wouldn't arrest everyone, and at his own discretion, he would sometimes allow a moonshiner to go free. He had ways of alerting citizens before a raid without ever implicating himself.

Cyrus didn't approve of what the Feds had done in the county during the Civil War, and he certainly had disdain for their interference in local affairs now. He had nothing against people making a living off of home brew, but he had the job busting moonshiners and bootleggers, and it was the only job he could find.

Many innocent civilians had died in that Confederate prison, and as far as Cyrus was concerned, he often prayed that the South would one day rise again. But the war was over, he was broke, and he had a sick wife at home. Sometimes a man had to do what a man had to do, and all that he had to do right now was this job.

When there was a knock on the window of his office door, he was taken aback. He had no friends in town, and his newest and only current employee was out on a job. He knew that everyone in town hated and avoided him, so he brushed up his jacket as best he could and sat up straight in his office chair. He feared that an agent from Washington was there to check up on him again. "Door's open," he called, unable to see through the frosted glass. The door swung open.

Standing there in the doorway was an attractive woman in a black dress and hat. At her side was a black woman in a simple summer dress. Cyrus wondered if the woman dressed in black was a widow. Why else would she wear a black dress in this oppressive heat? He thought that he recognized Betsy. She seemed to be a peaceful woman. Everyone knew who her husband was. Peaches had a reputation for getting along with everyone.

Cyrus stood up to show his respects to the ladies and noticed that Betsy wore a frightened look on her face and seemed very nervous as she entered the room behind the white woman. There was only one chair for visitors, and before he could offer it, Greta strolled over and sat down.

Betsy took a place near the window overlooking the town square and stood still. Silently she began to pray for Greta.

Greta seated herself and then calmly folded her hands together, placing them gently on her lap. She looked up and smiled at Cyrus Posey as she turned her chin strategically toward him. Greta knew that she looked attractive. She had taken extra pains to be sure of that. Her beautiful brown eyes did not go unnoticed by Cyrus, and he found himself staring at her.

"How may I help you today?" Cyrus thought he had seen this lady before, and on closer inspection, her dress told him that she was not a widow at all but more likely one of the temperance ladies. His wife had worn a dress just like this one when she used to go to her meetings. That was before the illness had come over her.

"Well, I hope that you may be able to help me, sir, or perhaps I may be able to help you in some way," Greta said. "I am a member of the Leonardtown chapter of the St. Mary's County Women's Temperance League. As you know, we respect your position in this county, and we wish to do everything possible to show our support for your most difficult profession. We also know that some people have taken to talking about you in a disparaging way, and the newspaper has been unkind to you as well. That is very unfortunate behavior on their part, I do believe." Greta paused. "And of course, I would also like to offer my thoughts and prayers for your dear wife. She had been attending our meetings for some time before she took ill."

"Thank you, Mrs.…?"

"Oh, I'm sorry. My name is Greta Graves. My husband, Walter, and I own a tobacco and vegetable farm just outside of town here. The farm has been in our family since the *Ark* and the *Dove*."

Cyrus knew who Walter Graves was. He had gone to school with him as a boy. He couldn't remember ever meeting his wife though. But as far as Mrs. Graves staking a claim in the origins of the county, Cyrus was not impressed. Cyrus knew that most of his fellow townsmen and women had staked a claim in that very bright piece of St. Mary's County history, and he wasn't interested in hearing about the subject from this woman. No other family could boast more about ancestry than his.

"Well, I see that you're from a very old family here in these parts then. I'm sure that whatever you and your lady friend have to say will be important indeed." Cyrus took his seat behind his desk and continued waiting to hear why these two ladies had come to his office, since it couldn't be a visit just to flatter him. Or was it? He looked again into Greta's brown eyes, wondering if he saw a hint of flirtation.

"And this is my neighbor, Betsy Wilkes."

Cyrus gave a glance over to Betsy and tipped his head slightly. "Mrs. Wilkes."

"Sir, I'll get right to the point, as we know that you are a very important person to the cause, and we don't wish to take up your time with idle chitchat." Greta waited for Cyrus's nod before continuing.

"We have come to bring to your attention the possibility that we may have moonshiners who have staked out a little spot between my property and Betsy Wilkes's." Greta paused to catch a reaction from Cyrus, but he gave away nothing.

"To make matters worse, we believe that whoever these moonshiners are, they may be doing this in our back fields, the fields between Mrs. Wilkes's farm and my own, trying to give the appearance that we innocent farmers are involved in that disgusting business."

Cyrus could see where this conversation was leading. "So you believe that unbeknownst to your husbands, someone or several persons are secretly building stills between your two properties?"

"Yes, that is what I am saying, sir," answered Greta. "We believe that our husbands have no knowledge of this, as we know our husbands to be good, God-fearing men as well as law-abiding citizens."

"My husband doesn't even drink alcohol," said Betsy.

Greta shot her a stern look. "Nor does my husband," Greta added quickly.

Cyrus studied the two women for a moment. "I see," he said. "What this means then is that you would like for me and my man to investigate this? You do realize, don't you, that some men have gone to jail for doing this very thing? You might even know some of them or read about them in the paper."

"Of course we do," Greta answered, "and that is precisely why we are here. We believe that some very unlawful men are hiding out on our property, just ready to place blame, should they be caught, directly upon our husbands."

Cyrus looked at Greta and smiled. "What is it that you would like me to do for you, Mrs. Graves?"

"What we would like you to do is come out tomorrow at about five in the morning and catch them in the act. That's when I have heard noises coming from deep down in the gully on the lower field. I've heard all kinds of banging and noise, such as metal being hammered together. If you could come out in the morning, I'd be happy to show you which direction these noises are coming from."

Betsy was proud of her friend. She was closely following the fool-proof plan that they had devised. Betsy knew that their husbands had been going out only at night to visit and do whatever it was they were doing out in the woods. If Cyrus could go down and destroy the still in the morning, Walter and Peaches would never know what hit them, and Cyrus wouldn't catch their husbands in the act. It seemed a fool-proof plan to Betsy, and watching Greta perform like a silly woman almost brought her to laughter. Greta was no silly woman, but Cyrus surely was being taken in by her, Betsy observed.

"Ladies," Cyrus said, "I can't tell you how much I appreciate your concern for the drinking problem that we have in this county. I can assure you that I will be paying your farms a visit first thing in the morning."

Greta nodded a thank-you to Cyrus and then rose from her chair as slowly as she had sat herself down earlier. Then smiling at Cyrus Posey, she turned, faced the door, and slowly moved toward it. She waited for Cyrus to come over and open the door for her. "Mrs. Graves, Mrs. Wilkes." Cyrus walked over to the door and opened it for the two ladies. "I have just one more question for you. Have you brought all of these observations to your husbands' attention?"

Greta turned back toward Cyrus and lowered her voice slightly. "Mr. Posey that is the last thing that Betsy and I would do. We wouldn't like either of our husbands to surprise any of those dreadful alcohol producers down in the woods only to have one of our husbands, or both, shot to death. Besides, my husband doesn't even own a weapon. Surely he would be shot and killed." Greta thanked him again, and then taking Betsy by the arm, turned back toward the exit, where the two women calmly walked away.

Once Cyrus had closed the door, he shook his head and laughed to himself. Not one moonshiner had ever been stupid enough to be banging metal together at five in the morning. They were called "moonshiners" for one good reason. Their work was done under the cover of the moon, not the morning sun. As for the noise not alarming their husbands, well, he had just about heard it all. She was good though, he thought to himself, and pretty too.

Once outside, Betsy grabbed Greta's hand and squeezed it tightly. "You may have just saved our husbands' lives, you know, and I want to thank you for all that you said to Cyrus Posey. He is sure to believe every word you said. You came up with an answer almost as fast as the question came out of his mouth! We had not even thought that he would ask if we had told our husbands!"

"I don't even know what I said in response to that last question," Greta said. Then grabbing a hold of Betsy, they both hurried out of the building.

Chapter 9

Reconstruction

I was thoroughly engrossed in Linda's story when I noticed a young couple enter the B&B's front hallway. Linda excused herself to greet her guests, so I poured myself another cup of coffee, forgetting altogether about the library across the street, my cottage, and all other concerns of the day. It was a restful afternoon, and I didn't want to think about anything other then what had happened to Walter and Peaches. When Linda finally returned, I was glad to see her take a seat on the sofa to resume her story.

"Those are the sweetest two young people," Linda said. "They were just married and booked the Victorian Room here for their first night together as husband and wife. It makes me believe that marriage is still a beautiful and sacred event, even these days."

I could see that Linda believed in marriage and honeymoons and all of those events that women get emotional about, but I only thought of what happens after a woman has spoken her vows. *Men are only into honeymoons*, I thought. *When the honeymoon is over, the real man magically appears.* Not wanting Linda to continue on about love and marriage, I changed the subject.

"Thanks for sharing the story about Walter and Peaches with me," I said. "But I'm a little curious as to how you came by this story. You tell it so well, it's almost as though you knew Walter and Peaches—almost as though you lived it."

"Well, in a sense you might say that I did live it. My maiden name is Graves, Linda Graves Raley now. Walter and Greta Graves were my grandparents. This B&B was the home of their youngest son, Wesley. Wesley was the only child of Walter and Greta who went on to receive an education. He became a lawyer and practiced for many years, right here in Leonardtown. When my father retired from practicing law, he made the family home into a B&B and let me and my husband takes it over."

"Where is your father now?" I asked.

"Where every retiree goes, I guess," she answered. "Florida. My husband and I have been running this old house as a B&B for about a year now, but Daddy still travels up here when he can pull himself away from his retirement activities, and he seems to always have a new story to tell. And then there is his journal, which I found in the attic one day. Now that's a book of secrets."

"I bet that you could tell some wonderful stories from that journal alone," I said.

"Yes, I really could, but some things are best kept in the family. I will tell you one thing. It was the oyster money that provided the education for Wesley Graves."

"Oyster money?" I asked. "I thought that making alcohol was what got them through the hard times. Did they sell their brew, or were they caught?"

She winked at me and then offered to continue the story. A phone rang in the other room, and she excused herself momentarily. In a minute she was back.

"The phone call is for you, Ms. Grant. It seems to be a concerned neighbor of yours."

I rose from the chair and made my way to the phone. "Hello?"

"Rainey, I'm so glad I found you. Mr. Manny told me you were up at the B&B there in Leonardtown. This is Mrs. Wilderman. We've just gotten word that the damage to the cottages is quite severe. We're on our way back there right now. Oh, I hate to tell you this, dear one, but both of those wonderful old oak trees have come down in your yard. I know how you must have loved them, but they're both destroyed. The good news is that neither tree hit your cottage. Other then some roof damage, some flooding, and a little siding missing, I think you came out of this very well compared to most."

"No one else escaped major damage?" I asked.

"No, I'm afraid not. Mr. and Mrs. Manny's cottage was hit very hard. They're taking it well though, and they asked about you too. The county is letting us all back onto the road, and there are crews of men ready to help anyone in need. David Woods has a crew down there already, and he seems to be the most reasonably priced contractor. Will you be going down yourself soon?"

I remembered then that David's truck had displayed the name of a home repair business. I think it said WOODS'S CONSTRUCTION AND HOME REPAIR, but at the time of the rescue I was too nervous to ask him about it.

"Yes, I'll be leaving here shortly and will be there within the hour. Are the Mannys there with you?"

"No, dear, they're at Bud's Country Store right now resting on the porch with some iced tea. They're a bit too old to help out with all of the debris, and it really isn't safe for them to be on the street from what

I hear. Things are a mess, but David Woods's crew is working on the Manny place right now, so I hope that the dear couple go on up the road to their place in Virginia until things are cleaned up a bit more."

"And how did your cottage hold up?" I asked.

"Not well, but we'll repair it as best we can. We spent the night in a hotel, but we still have the children with us. Their parents went out of town before the storm struck and are on their way back to pick the children up. You would never know anything happened as far as the children are concerned though, and they're looking forward to finding washed-up treasures on the beach."

I told Mrs. Wilderman that I would be leaving soon, and after saying good-bye, I hung up the phone and explained the situation to Linda. She said that I could hear the rest of the story after I returned later in the evening. Then I hastily retrieved my purse and car keys from my room, climbed into my car, drove around the town square, and then headed straight south.

As I neared Bud's Country Store about an hour later, I could see that there were many neighbors crowded onto the old wooden porch. I pulled into the parking lot and was immediately greeted by Chesterfield. He barked and began to circle around me, but this time I ignored him until he growled and found a cat in the parking lot to chase.

"I've never seen that dog bark at anyone like that," a man said, laughing at me.

There on the porch I found Mr. and Mrs. Manny, both drinking iced teas and rocking in chairs provided by Bud. Bud hadn't had this much business since the hurricane of 1965, and he was enjoying the frequent visits of those who were without electricity. He had enough hot dogs in his freezer to keep everyone happy for at least a week, and his microwave oven was also busy cooking frozen pizza slices that he had purchased from the local grocery store.

The Mannys seemed happy to see me. Mr. Manny rose and tipped his straw hat. "There you are, young lady. We were beginning to think that our storyteller had found her way home and we would have to wait until next season to hear the rest."

"I'm not sure that I have a lot more to tell," I said, "but I'll tell you what I do know after things are back to normal. I'm on my way down to inspect the damage to my cottage. I hear that yours suffered a lot of damage?"

"Yes, yes it did. But we already have someone down there working on it. He's going to get the mud out, treat the walls, and do the repairs that are most important." Mrs. Manny seemed satisfied that the necessary repairs would be completed.

"It's that nice man, David Woods, the one who helped you rescue the Carey family. He was down there first thing this morning offering his help. He is such a nice young man. He has suffered loss of his own lately, poor fellow, but that doesn't stop him from helping others."

"What loss is that?" I asked.

"Well, Bud told us that David's wife, Evelyn, passed away about this time last year. Bud said that David never gave up hope that she would live, clear up to the end. She received every cancer treatment that was offered to her, but to no avail. She was up at Johns Hopkins too, and under the best possible care, but Bud told us that she passed away after fighting it for a year. David told Bud that he had faith that God would answer his prayers and save Evelyn, but it didn't seem to be part of God's plan for her."

I had heard enough about faith and God's plans, and I didn't care to hear any more. It seemed to me that God had good plans for some and bad plans for others. God's plans made no sense, and I preferred to remain indifferent to the subject. After all, he hadn't bothered to answer my prayers. I loved my husband, and he loved someone else. Where was God then? Sleeping?

I had to stop myself from saying anything negative to the Mannys about God, but I thought to myself that if I had lost Patrick to death, it would have been less crushing then to have him tell me that I couldn't make him happy. At least David's wife had spared him that kind of agony.

"I hope that David will be able to give me a good price on the repair of my cottage." The Mannys politely allowed me to skip over their remarks, though I could see surprise in Mrs. Manny's eyes.

"Yes, why don't you go ahead on down and see what David says about it? I think we've held you up long enough, and I'm sure that you're concerned about the shape of your place. We may be going home to Virginia soon, but we'll be back to check on you and the others in a few days." Mrs. Manny smiled at me with her usual warmth and encouragement.

I said good-bye again and drove off, wishing that I could be as gracious as Mr. and Mrs. Manny. When would I ever learn?

Chapter 10

Aftermath

I arrived to see that my little community was looking much more like a war zone then a peaceful little cluster of cottages. Most of my neighbors had come back and were hard at work mucking out mud and moving ruined furnishings out to the street, where huge green trash barrels were filling up. Mud-covered debris was scattered everywhere as I slowed my car to a crawl, unseen objects crunching beneath my tires.

The Carey family waved as I went by, and so did the Wildermans. The people at Mud Manor were hoisting a tarp over their roof damage, and once again their rowboat had been retrieved from the creek and placed back on the sawhorses. Water sprayed up with every step as workers and owners moved back and forth across adjoining yards, trying to stay ahead of potential mold and mildew, which could set in without delay. Ruined furniture destined for the dump was piled near the road.

As I parked at a spot in my yard and got out of my car, I found two men operating huge chain saws that were noisily chewing up my two ancient oak trees. Tears came to my eyes as I watched their beautiful branches being cut into manageable pieces. Those trees had provided shade from the hot sun in the morning, and their leaves always caught a breeze. Now they were gone. The noise of the chain saws continued on as my tears fell on a pile of sawdust.

"I'm sorry that you lost your trees!" shouted a voice over the drone of the saws. Startled, I jumped. It was David Woods. It took me a few seconds to recover, and then I took a tissue from my pocket and blew my nose.

"Thanks," I finally said. "It looks like my cottage will survive, but it's so odd sitting out in the open without the trees on either side." I had to yell above the noise for David Woods to hear me.

"I hope you don't mind that I put a couple of my crew here to cut the trees up, but at least you'll be able to park your car next to the house now. It's amazing, isn't it, that though each tree dropped close to your place, your cottage wasn't hurt in the least, even by those enormous branches lying over here. You are really very fortunate."

"Yes, I guess that I'm fortunate indeed," I said halfheartedly, "but I'm really going to miss those trees." I blew my nose again, and David gave me a look of concern.

"I'm really sorry. Those trees were really very beautiful."

I appreciated his concern, but I wasn't used to that sort of sympathy from a man, especially from one that I hardly knew, so it seemed a bit overdone. All I knew about him was that he was a widower, a carpenter, and a rescuer of stranded people. I figured that I didn't really need to know any more than that about him. I had repair bills to worry about and was stressing about what his estimate for repairs would be, and I wanted to get down to business. Besides that, he was standing in my personal space, and I didn't like it. The noise of the chain saws continued.

David gave a signal to the men with the chain saws, and they powered down the equipment. "Go ahead a take a break," David said to them. "There are some cold sodas in my truck." The men nodded their thanks and went off to find the sodas.

"Hey," David said, "I know a wood carver who might want to buy some of this wood from you. He does small furniture and other creative things with wood, even sculptures. I'll give you his number if you're interested. He might be able to make some furniture for you. It would be a shame to sell this wood off without keeping some of it."

"That would be a comfort," I said as I backed away from him. "I just don't want it all hauled off and used for firewood. That would really break my heart." David nodded in understanding and stood without saying anything for a minute.

"This wood won't be used for firewood. It's too valuable for that," he said. "I've had a chance to survey your damages, and I don't think that you're in bad shape. You're missing a few roof shingles, part of your side deck, some siding, and unfortunately your above ground oil tank. It's probably floating out there in the creek somewhere. There's some water damage to the walls in your cottage and a fair amount of mud, but my crew managed to muck out a lot of it. I could get my crew back on it in a few days, unless you have someone else who can do it sooner. My men really just need to concentrate on the worst-hit homes for now."

"What will the repairs cost?" I asked. For me lately the bottom line was cost. Any amount to fix my cottage would be too much. I was after all, nearly broke.

"I'll tell you what," David said. "If you let me go ahead and sell some of the oak wood to a friend and the rest to the local mill, I think that will just about cover any repairs that you need. If there's a balance left over, I'll give you the cash back."

"Are you kidding me? Is the wood that valuable?"

"Yes, the wood is very valuable when there is this much of it. This is some of the finest white oak that I've seen for some time. I'm sure its value will more than cover your repair costs. If you want to use some of the wood for beams or furniture, my friend Bobby might be able to come up with something for you." David wrote the number down on one of his own business cards and handed it to me.

"That would be wonderful," I said. Then I noticed that he had invaded my space again.

"It's a deal then," he said, shaking my hand. "Until then, you might want to get one of the flat shovels out of my truck and start getting some more of the mud out of your cottage. I have some concentrated bleach to spray on the drywall also, and that should hold down on the mold and mildew, at least until we get in here to replace some of the drywall. Oh, and help yourself to the package of masks in the front seat while you're at it. Mold and mildew can cause a lot of respiratory problems."

"Thanks," I said. He nodded and walked away, his tool belt hanging low on his hips. I thought about what Mrs. Manny had told me about his wife's death and wondered if he was still struggling with the pain. Pain—is there ever escape?

After speaking with David, my hope felt restored. Maybe I wouldn't lose my cottage as a result of this hurricane or for that matter, the repair costs. Relief overwhelmed me as I looked at the bay where the gulls and osprey, out in force having gone without prey for the duration of the hurricane, were now diving after feed fish.

The pelicans had not returned, but out in the creek I could see that a family of tundra swan had come out of hiding and were paddling around in the reeds near the shore. The creek itself was full of debris, and I could see the unrecognizable tops of things bobbing up and down in the water, but the osprey went about their business as they always had, oblivious to the work going on below them.

Two of the young Wilderman grandchildren walked by on their way to the beach, and Paula gave me an enthusiastic wave as she held up her red plastic bucket and shovel. This was a custom that we all used to participate in after a nor'easter. Patrick and I had once found an old Civil War bullet in the sand as well as a shard of pottery from that era, both after nor'easters.

Looking closer at the damage, I could see that many of the huge boulders that made up our seawall had actually been carried up into my front and side yard. The enormous damage that the wind and waves did to the wall could only be repaired by the Army Corps of Engineers. The breaches in the wall made me nervous. What if another hurricane came up the bay? Would my cottage be taken out? Anxiety started to replace the tranquil peace I had experienced just moments earlier. *This cottage is all that I have left,* I reasoned.

Nervously I went to work dragging my damaged, wet furniture from the cottage, placing each piece out in the front yard. Deep down inside I hoped that everything would dry out and that I would be able to salvage at least my old worn armchair, but the damage was obvious. I worked for hours before the heat finally stopped me.

By late afternoon, exhausted and hungry, I had shoveled the mud from my main room and had also mopped and sprayed bleach as much as I could. My clothes were dirty and faded in spots where the bleach had taken away the color, and I just wanted to go back to the B&B. Closing the door behind me, I got into my car and drove slowly away.

I gave a wave to the Wildermans, who were also hauling out damaged furniture from their cottage. I didn't have much physical strength to help anyone else, much less myself, so I ignored everyone and continued on. Mold could still be forming, I thought, but spray as I might, I felt that the battle would be lost if I didn't get some help. I drove carefully away from the cottages, feeling rather defeated.

I hadn't driven far when David Woods signaled for me to stop a minute. Leaving the crew that he had started on the Manny cottage, he walked over to me. I rolled the window down, releasing my air conditioning onto his sweat-beaded face. "That feels nice," he said. He asked if the heat was too much for me.

"Yes," I said. "I can handle it while I'm just sitting in the cottage with the ceiling fans blasting full-force, but working in the heat and humidity with no power and without fans is a whole other story."

"I should have come over to help," he said. "I'm sorry about that. We have so many cottages that are in worse shape, that I unfortunately had to let yours go for a couple of days."

Again he seemed very concerned about me, but I said nothing.

"Will you be back later today?" he asked.

"I don't think so. I'm going back to the B&B in Leonardtown. There really isn't much else that I can do with my cottage today. I've thrown out my rugs, my furniture, and also some of my kitchen things that were on the lower open shelves. They were ruined too, so out it all went. I think I'm going to have to start all over again inside. But compared to most, I guess I'm lucky." I tried to sound positive.

"Yes," he said, "if you believe in luck, then I guess that makes you very lucky."

"I think luck happens every now and then," I said, "and I do prefer it to disaster."

David gave me a hesitant look. "You know, I want to ask you something while you're still here. I'm going to be in Leonardtown later this afternoon, and since you'll be up there, I was hoping that you'd allow me to take you to get a bite to eat this evening. Would you like to do that, or are you going to be resting?"

What on earth is he asking me? I thought.

"I just wanted to thank you for helping out with the Carey family rescue, and since I know a little about the history around this area, I was hoping to share some of it with you," he explained. Then he leaned over closer to the window to feel the air conditioner again. "The Wildermans tell me that you're quite the history buff."

I fixed my eyes on the steering wheel and then on his brown eyes. "I'm not sure. I mean, that sounds really nice of you, but…"

"Hey, don't worry about it," he said kindly. "I'm going up that way to the lumber store later and just thought I'd ask. I know you're busy with your research. Maybe some other time then?"

"That would be OK, I guess," I answered. David smiled and backed up. I rolled up the window and nodded good-bye, and he did the same. I watched him walk away in my rearview mirror until I turned the corner at the end of the road. Had he just asked me for a date? But then I told myself that he was just a businessman trying to drum up more business. Why make anything out of it?

Returning to the B&B, I stole past the sitting room and headed straight for the shower. The last thing I remember is waking up halfway across the bed, famished and sore. Later I went downstairs to find the owners eating a late breakfast in dining room. Seeing me, they invited me to join them. I didn't refuse. No other guests were at the table.

After breakfast was finished, I insisted that I help Linda with the dishes. Then I asked her if she would like to hear a story, from me this time, about an event that I had researched while at the library across the street on my last visit. It was the continuation of the story I had started in the Manny cottage before the storm had forced us out.

"Yes, absolutely," Linda said.

"Yes for me too," said her husband. "Things are calm here right now, so please tell us the story."

I caught them up with what I had told my cottage neighbors and then began to tell them more about Virgil Cummings.

Chapter 11

Virgil, October 1864

Virgil figured that he might have to give up on his wife, Joanna, and life altogether for that matter. She was life to him, and though they were newlyweds married less than a year, he felt that his beautiful young wife had forgotten about him. It appeared that she had. Having been a prisoner for months at Point Lookout, and having received only a few letters, being forgotten seemed a worse consideration then facing the winter to come. He knew he couldn't survive another winter by his wits alone. He needed hope, and that was a commodity he was growing short on.

Did she know how bitter cold it was in this camp in winter? There were only a few scrub pines to break the cold wind. The only life in those pines seemed to be birds of prey impatiently looking down from dead crooked branches, awaiting death's scent from one of the hundreds of tents housing prisoners. The past winter, winds off the Chesapeake Bay were colder than anything he had ever experienced in his short twenty-two years of life.

Several men had died in their sleep last winter from exposure, but Virgil knew there were blankets in storage that were not given out, just as he knew that there were food supplies and medicines locked up in storage. His skill at stealing salt from the ham shed had led him to other off-limit places in the camp. But men died of dysentery, typhoid fever, the pox, pneumonia, and only God knows what else. He could get used to fleas and lice but not the smell of death caused by the viciousness of the Union and their hoarding of those supplies.

Virgil hated the Union and everything it stood for. He didn't feel like a young man of twenty-two but much older. If the chill of winter cutting through the flimsy tents wasn't enough, the heat of the summer, the mosquitoes, the horseflies, the ants invading everything, the rats hiding everywhere, the stench of the open sewer, and the lack of clean water were enough to kill even the fittest. And it often did. The Union, so he was told, was keeping the Confederate prisoners in misery so as to force the Confederate troops at Andersonville to feed and clothe the Union prisoners of war. It had become a contest of cruelty between the North and South, he thought, and everyone was suffering, just like him.

Holding a piece of a glass mirror up to his face he couldn't believe that it was really his face looking back. His brown hair was stringy and long. His once neatly trimmed goatee was matted and shaggy. His face was looking leathery and hard due to the extreme heat and frequent burns from crabbing and fishing. His hazel eyes were dull looking, and his eyelids sagged, giving him a look of mourning.

Virgil was beginning to feel like a person in mourning too. He knew there wouldn't be much to trade for in the winter months. The male crabs would burrow down in the mud for the winter, and the females would head down to the lower bay area. Fish were hard to catch, and rations were shorter in the winter months. If the Union had anything for the prisoners to eat, it was probably being shipped farther south, where Sherman was busy setting fire to everything with his huge, hungry army of murderers. The guards were always laughing about it and saying cruel things to the prisoners.

"Want some heat this winter?" one of the guards would say. "If you do, I'll ask General Sherman to bring some of his fire up here and warm you're butts up!" Then the whole guard detail would laugh and spit and get a real charge out of it. No prisoner ever said anything back for fear of retribution. But hatred was growing, and with that came anger and infighting.

Virgil thought about taking his chances by swimming away from the prison out into the bay and across the Potomac River to Virginia by night, but there were gunboats out there. He also knew that the Potomac had undercurrents that couldn't be seen with the eye. Twelve men had drowned trying to do what Virgil was thinking of doing, and soon the water would be too cold for an attempt.

He often wondered what it must be like to drown. Maybe he could make it across the river, but he had seen bodies of escapees all bloated or picked over by fish or crab or God knows what. Then, almost as soon as the thought of death started to overwhelm him, he forced himself to think about Joanna. He had to see her, or at least hear from her.

Taking his bushel basket and his string, he thought that he would try his luck crabbing again. He was almost out of seafood, his most successful bartering chip, and he longed to get some information about why letters were not getting to the prisoners. He crabbed for nearly three hours, capturing a basket full of large blue crabs, yet again his mind thought of death. His headache started up again, and holding his head between his hands, he began to wish that he could die. It would be a good death, he thought. Somehow his death would be with honor.

I've got to stop thinking this way, he told himself. As he stood up and looked over between the hundreds of other prison tents, he imagined that he had a clear view of Virginia. Just to see Virginia across the Potomac River would help him clear his mind of this depression. He pictured his wife waiting on the other side of the river. She was waving to him and begging him to come home. Virgil went back to his cot and lay down, thinking and dreaming of her.

Joanna had the prettiest red hair and milky white skin, and she was always so soft when he touched her. He started to dream of her. He was holding her, and she was surrounding him with her arms, kissing him and loving on him as she whispered words in his ear…

"Hey, get yourself up!" It was Gus Pruitt, hanging over Virgil's bed and breathing on him. Then Gus shook the bed, and Virgil sat up.

"Get the hell out of here!" Virgil hollered. "You got no business at all being in my tent! Get out of here!"

"I got something to tell you! I got some news," said Gus as he backed away toward the tent flap.

Gus hated having to play the one always backing off, but Virgil knew how to get by in this place, and Gus knew that he lacked a few essential skills that only Virgil could supply. Besides, if he played his cards right, Virgil might just hire him back into his crabbing business. He didn't like having to scrap for himself. "You got to listen to me, Virgil. I got some news you been wanting to hear!"

Virgil rubbed his head. Putting up with Gus was more then he could take at times. His head was pounding now, and he had lost his dream visions of Joanna and her whispers and her skin against his. Besides that, Gus often spread news that turned out to be a figment of his own imagination. "What news?" Virgil snapped.

"It's about some new prisoners. They got some doctors and lawyers and people of that persuasion coming in to be kept, a whole wagon full of them. I heard tell that they was a bunch of them caught trying to plan a breakout for their friends who been in this here prison. They was all meeting over in Leonardtown where the Union set up their command, and the bunch of them got caught by the Union soldiers for what they called sedition. Most of them is locals from down these parts of Maryland, and I hear they was meeting in a bank and got caught in a back room or something." Gus waited for Virgil to say something.

"If that ain't enough," Gus continued, "some of them is newspaper writers. They been printing anti-Union stuff in their newspaper, and the Union government people closed them down. After they got closed down, they went underground and kept printing in secret. They was printing letters of complaint from the wives and families of us men imprisoned in this place. They wrote things exposing the awful cruel things going on in here too. So they closed down the paper, and the government is holding our letters for punishment. They threw the guilty citizens in here so they could repent of what they was doing."

For once Gus had some news. Virgil stopped rubbing his forehead and looked over at Gus. He tried to figure out what was truth and what was exaggerated lies. "Where did you get this news?" he asked.

"From one of my black guards out there on the wall," answered Gus. "I do a little trading with some here and there. Lately one of them don't have nothing to trade me for, so he gives me a little information when he hears something new, and I give him whatever I got in exchange."

"What guard?" Virgil asked.

"He's one of the local boys I trade with, and he's likely to keep me supplied with important information. The other guards don't like him much." Gus looked to Virgil for some acknowledgment of the valuable information he had offered. Then he peered over to the corner where Virgil's freshly caught crabs were still making their clawing noise in a wicker basket.

"How do you know he's even giving you true information? How do you know that he isn't leading you on for whatever you can give him?

It's just like you to believe anything you hear. You're just trying to act like you know something. Leave."

Gus thought for a minute that he could do what he often thought of doing; choke the life out of Virgil with his bare hands, but he made an effort to control himself again. "I got lots more information I can get from my guard, but I'll be needing something to give him, like some of them crabs you got over in that basket."

Gus thought a little while and then made a bold statement. "I ain't had much to eat today, and I sure could use me some boiled crab meat. I guess if you wanted to find out more from my Negro guard friend, I could ask him for more news. But I'm goanna need some of them crabs to barter with for the information. My guard has a taste for boiled crab." Gus looked over at the basket and then back at Virgil.

"If I want information, I'll get it myself. I don't need to pay you for it." Virgil motioned for Gus to leave the small tent. "Get out," he ordered.

"I give you good information, and you can't even be grateful?" Gus stood his ground, glaring at Virgil.

"I said to get out of my tent!" Virgil yelled. "I'm sick of the sight of you. I don't need your help, and you're not getting any more handouts from me!" Virgil's head felt like it was going to explode.

Gus's neck started to prickle, and he wanted to kill Virgil. "You can just get yourself to hell!" he shot back. "You think you know everything and that you can fire anyone you want, but you don't know nothing. I know why we ain't been getting our mail, and I got information I could sell to anybody, but I ain't selling it to you. You ain't worth nothing to me or anyone else in here. Nobody likes you, and I'm telling you now that you better wise up, or you might find yourself floating lower then a dead crab!"

Gus kicked the side of Virgil's bed, threw back the tent flap, and stomped out. He felt empowered now. No longer would he lick Virgil's boots. He would make his way in his own business. He would sell information.

Virgil watched Gus stomp off, wondering if Gus would make plans to kill him. He had seen that anger in Gus before but had ignored it. The thought bothered him, but for now Virgil was more interested in thinking about the information Gus had just given him, and so put his fears aside.

He thought about the letters Gus had told him about; there could be a dozen or more from his family by now. If he could just find out from a guard where the letters were being kept, he might be able to find them and read loving words from his parents and Joanna. The dilemma was that he hated doing anything that involved the guards. Could he really trust any of them? Soon his mood was lowered again by the prospect of danger.

Some of the prisoners traded with the guards for tobacco or a little food in exchange for some fresh fish or crab meat, but he never thought that he could buy information from any of them. Virgil had avoided contact with them for many reasons up to this point, but this new information was different. He knew by observation that the guards could never be trusted. He thought about the times when some guards had fired at random into the prison yard. One man had died when a bullet struck him as he was walking to his tent.

But this was a different situation, and this time Virgil knew that Gus was probably telling some truth, and the truth might bring him closer to knowing where his wife's letters were being kept. And if he could find her letters, he would find the will to keep surviving. The war had to end soon, or every man in this prison would starve to death or freeze in the winter. Virgil did not intend to die a death like that.

First though he would have to figure out which guard was bartering with Gus. Virgil considered a few things. Word was that the guards
got fed some pretty awful food and received less pay for watching
over the prisoners. They probably had little to trade with these days
and might be willing to trade information as Gus had said. But what
if Virgil spoke to the wrong guard? It could cost him his life, and he
knew that for a fact.

Virgil knew that there were a couple of different regiments of
black guards in the camp who'd been brought down from up north,
but some of the guards were from around these parts, men from the
local towns who had been forced to join the Union army. Gus had
said that his guard was a local, and what if Gus had told the truth for
once? Still, there was something about Gus that seemed unstable and
untrustworthy. Virgil didn't like threats from anyone, especially Gus,
but dealing with Gus would have to wait.

Virgil began to formulate a plan, knowing that he had to contact
the right prison guard or his life could be in peril. He would wait for
a dark, cloudy night to search for answers, carefully making his way
toward the guard platform and away from those fellow prisoners who
had become hostile to him. Taking a pencil and a piece of scrap paper
from under his bed, Virgil drew a picture of the route he would take
when he was ready to make his move.

"Well," I said, "that's about all the information I have for now. I plan to
get back to the library or up to Annapolis and do some more research
after I get the cottage repairs going."

"What an interesting story," said Linda. "You know, there is a
group here in Leonardtown that meets each year for the purpose of
putting articles together for publication. Their goal is to teach the true
history of what went on at Point Lookout. They have been protesting

each year on the grounds of the monument erected at the burial site for the prisoners who died in the camp. They meet at the monument and fly the Confederate flag as they read the names of the men who died there, or the missing men who were never accounted for. It may be something that you'd want to attend, and you might find someone there who could shed more light on prison life at Point Lookout."

"Yes, I've attended that before," I told her. "The Confederate flag has caused a lot of turmoil to those who visit the monument, especially African Americans. It is a symbol of oppression and slavery to them. But the flag is also a protest of sorts for the descendants of the Confederate prisoners, who still want answers as to what went on there.

"That's probably true, but history is an open book, and I guess anyone who fought in the Civil War would feel the same way if they had been on the Union side. Andersonville was a cruel place, as well as Point Lookout," Linda said.

"Yes, I agree with you there. I heard recently that there are plans to build another monument on privately owned land near the other monument. I believe that the descendants of those who died at Pt. Lookout are raising funds for it now."

Linda's husband got up and excused himself as a new guest entered the B&B. "Great story," he said as he left the room.

I thanked him for listening and turned back to Linda. "Is there any way that you could continue your story about Walter and Peaches sometime?" I asked Linda.

"Yes, of course. When I've finished my chores for the day, I would like nothing better than to tell you more about them."

I went across the street to the library and picked up the books that I had ordered. When I returned, Linda was ready to continue her story.

Chapter 12

Cyrus Posey, Revenue Agent

Cyrus Posey was a conflicted man. With his wife sick and in pain every day and with two small children to feed, he felt fortunate to have steady work. Yet on the other hand, he found that he'd become alienated from many of the town's citizens, especially those who were in the Leonardtown jail. His time at home was becoming more infrequent due to the demands of the job, and he recently had to hire a woman to come in and help him care for his wife and young children. His pay wasn't good enough to sustain the costs, and he knew that he would have to find another job on the side. Lately he felt as though he would never get out from under his burdens. And then there was the fact that he had to fulfill a quota of arrests, hauling St. Mary's citizens off to the jailhouse.

One or two of the recently released men had been friends of his at one time. These men had lost the time and money that it took to build their stills. Tobacco crops were failing due to a lack of cheap labor, and people had to feed their families. Many broke tobacco farmers had turned to alcohol production to survive.

Most people no longer figured it was a bad thing to brew and sell alcohol in order to feed the little ones. Not even Cyrus. But some of the would-be moonshiners had been making bad brew out of anything that they could find, including wood chips, and a nefarious few were even brewing the alcohol using old car radiators as cookers for the brew, leading to several deaths due to poisoning.

Cyrus had assembled a few men under him to do the dirty work of finding and destroying stills in the backwoods of St. Mary's County. Only the most reprehensible of moonshiners had been caught, and most of them were appalled that Cyrus would actually haul them off to jail. None of them ever stayed there long, however, as the local judges were often some of the biggest consumers of the home brew. Though he was just doing his job, his standing in the community had taken a turn for the worse.

The problem was that the local officials were taking their chances by letting moonshiners out of jail after just a couple of nights. From time to time federal agents from DC would find their way down to Leonardtown to inquire about the lack of arrests, and Cyrus Posey had to prove his worth by numbers. It was time to bust another moonshiner, and it looked as though Walter Graves and his friend Peaches were unfortunately about to go down.

Last month Cyrus had been forced to fire two agents due to a general lack of performance, and he'd recently hired a man from Westmorland County in Virginia as a replacement. He'd advertised in the local paper, but no one responded. It soon became apparent to Cyrus that the citizens of St. Mary's County refused to work for someone they considered a "Judas."

Cyrus had finally advertised in the Virginia papers. The St. Mary's County paper often printed details of the arrests and made sure that the name "Cyrus Posey" was mentioned in bold print as the villainous arresting agent, which further hurt his reputation with the locals. Only the Women's Temperance League posted flyers around town pointing out the dangers of alcohol. To Cyrus, a little support was better than none.

Danville Clarke was an expert in the illegal trade of home brew. After making a decent living shipping moonshine up and down the Cone River, where it eventually found its way to the Potomac River, then to points all over the East Coast, his family experienced the loss of Danville's uncle. His uncle had not only become an alcoholic by drinking more then he could handle, but he'd lost his family in the process. After they had left him, his uncle eventually drank himself to death. Danville knew that alcoholic husbands brought heartache to wives and children, making entire families victims of the very profits that had put bread on their tables.

When Danville heard the gospel for the first time, he'd taken a look at his own life. He didn't like what he saw. From that point on, he turned his life around. He not only gave up brewing alcohol, but he also refused to help his father ship the brew from the Northern Neck to all destinations.

After quitting the family business, he became a better husband and father in the process. He had a heart for people caught up in the bootlegging business and tried to reach them with the gospel, but he took the job as a revenue agent to save lives and maybe even save a soul from alcohol poisoning; a job that took him across the river and away from his disappointed family. When Danville moved across the Potomac River into Maryland, his family did everything to persuade him to come back, but since there were no legal jobs available, he had to look elsewhere for employment. He had a lot in common with Cyrus Posey. Answering the ad to become a revenue agent was a blessing.

Danville entered Cyrus Posey's office and took a seat. He noticed that Cyrus was downcast. "How is Mrs. Posey doing this week?"

"Not so well. I've had to hire someone to care for her." Cyrus fingered some papers on his desk. "The doctor says that I could lose her, and I'm not prepared for that."

"I don't think a man can ever be ready to lose his wife," Danville said. "Death is hard to take, no matter what the circumstances. But you never know, with the help of the Lord, she could pull through."

Cyrus had never really opened up to anyone about his religion or about his private feelings, but he found a quality in Danville Clarke that seemed to loosen his tongue.

"You know," said Cyrus, "my wife gave me her approval when I took this job, but all it has brought her and our children is grief. Many of her friends stopped coming to see her when she took ill, and the children are often teased and chided at school for what their father does."

Danville stood up and walked to the narrow window of the bank building and looked down at the crowded town square, where the flag had no breeze to lift it and people sat under the shade of trees fanning themselves. He pulled a handkerchief from his pocket and wiped his forehead.

"It sounds like things are getting you down today," Danville said. "I'm sure your wife will get better. It takes time to heal." After a pause he added, "Are we going to look for that still you mentioned? We could put it off for another night, if you'd rather."

"No, we'll go tonight as planned," answered Cyrus, shaking off his mood.

"Are these farmers old acquaintances of yours?"

"I went to school with one of the men for years."

"How did you find out about this still?"

"Believe it or not, their wives came in this morning, attempting to save their husbands' necks. They claim that their innocent husbands have no idea about what's being done on their property. They say that some moonshiners have been building a still down on the creek, and they want us to go out in the early morning to capture the guilty perpetrators."

"Capture them in the morning?" asked Danville. "Well, you have to admit that this is a different approach. Why would they suggest such a plan?"

"The wives have offered for us to come out first thing in the morning, probably knowing that their husbands would still be in bed after their moon shining activities. I told them that I'd check things out, but I didn't tell them that I plan to apprehend the men in the act by going tonight." Cyrus stood up and walked over to the window near Danville.

"I've got a lot of pressure on me. My quota for the month is way down, according to the agency. I had to fire the last two agents, and I don't want to have to do that again."

"Well, I hope you won't have to either," Danville said, "but you don't sound enthusiastic about this raid."

"No, I'm not enthusiastic, and I don't really think I'm going to be able to keep this up. People don't want one of their own arresting them. Do you know how hard it was to get someone to look after my wife and children? When I was interviewing women for the job, as soon as they found out that I was Cyrus Posey, they turned it down. I finally had to hire a black woman off of one of the larger farms. She's charging me an arm and a leg, but I hear that she's worth it."

"Well, she may enjoy city life here in Leonardtown. It's hard for some blacks to get off of the plantations and farms around here, even though the war was over long ago. There are no jobs. At least it's still that way in Virginia. There aren't enough jobs to go around, so a lot of former slave owners are in the same broken condition. Wealth kept the races together before the war, and now poverty keeps them together after the war."

"I only hope that this woman won't leave us before we get to taste the first meal," Cyrus said.

Cyrus walked over to the coat rack, placed his jacket over his arm, and pointed toward the door. "It's getting darker out now. Let's get a bite to eat over at Fenwick's Restaurant. After dinner we'll come back to the office and wait a spell. When it's much later, we'll get our lanterns and guns together and take a drive over to the Wilkes and Graves farms. Unless I get another tip by the time we finish our dinners, we'll have to arrest both men."

"That is if we catch them in the act," said Danville.

"Right—only if we catch them in the act."

Chapter 13

Collaboration

It was getting late in the day, and I realized that Linda's husband had politely excused himself a few times, asking her where the clean guest towels were, if she had picked up the dry cleaning, and if she'd bought more waffle batter from the store. Eventually Linda said, "I'm going to have to go help him. He's being patient, but we're fully booked. Could we continue this another time?"

"Yes, of course," I said. "I need to get back to the Maryland State Archives today anyway. There are some other materials I need to go through and also some records from the War Department about prisoners, patients in Hammond Hospital during the Civil War, and burial details. And then there are the books and memoirs that I picked up from the library."

My trip back to the archives was uneventful and slow. It was Friday afternoon and already Route 50 was filled with late-season beachgoers. I wished that I had a car full of children, heading out for some adventure, and even a dog or two. Instead I sat in the traffic, wishing for things that would never be a part of my life. Eventually traffic started to move so I took the Rowe Boulevard exit and continued on to the archives.

Once there, I quickly became engrossed in study as I rummaged through the microfiche reels. I found some information on one reel about some physicians who had been in charge of caring for Confederate prisoners at Point Lookout. Carefully scrolling my way through the documents I found a list of Confederate prisoners who had either died while in the camp, or had been released with physical conditions severe enough to keep them from rejoining their detachments. These men were allowed to go home as long as their homes were behind Union lines of occupation. The dead were buried near the camp.

There were no records about Virgil Cummings. Not a death warrant or discharge papers. Thinking this strange, I looked through the micro-fiche records for newspaper printings for the time during the Civil War and found archived events leading up to the closing of the *Leonardtown Herald.* Scanning I found some of the letters that I'd read about previously; they were from the wives of the prisoners, and one of the letters was written by Joanna Cummings.

August 14, 1864
To the editor of the Leonardtown Herald,

I am the wife of a Confederate prisoner of war who is now being held at Point Lookout, and it is to you that I make my plea, for I do not know to this day if my husband lives or is deceased. There has been little correspondence from my husband since he was taken to Point Lookout. I have written to those officers who are in charge of the camp demanding an explanation, but as yet I have not received a reply.

It is with great sadness that I have received news of the horrible conditions at that war camp from some who have been released or have escaped, and I fear every day that my husband is being mistreated or worse yet, harmed or disabled in some way as to no longer be able to write to me. Some of the women in my town have heard too that men are dying in that awful camp in numbers too dreadful to imagine.

There have been civilian prisoners there who have been quick to expose the atrocities as well, yet the Union commanders have turned a blind eye and a deaf ear to our pleas. One atrocity in particular is that men have died for lack of warmth in the winter months. One woman told me that her son died over the winter, found frozen to death outside of his tent. She received no word as to the circumstances of his death and has not been allowed to see any records pertaining to his death. She received notice two months after her son had passed. His body was buried there at the camp, and she knows not where. He was but eighteen years old and her only son.

As for me, my husband is not even aware that he has a son. Our son was born after my husband was taken away. The Union government swooped down on our little neck of Virginia and took away our men and boys. I am desperate to find out anything about my husband. His name is Private Virgil E. Cummings, being attached to Company G, Fifty-Ninth Virginia. He was captured while recovering from a severe head wound here at our home in Walnut Oak, Virginia, after the battle at Gettysburg.

Has my husband been sent to another Union prison? I am begging you for any information that you may be able to ascertain. My husband is an honorable man, and I know that he has written letters to me, provided that he has not been harmed in some way. This leads me to believe that my husband has come to a cruel end, and the pain of not knowing what has become of him has made life unbearable for me and for his parents. Again, I beg your help in this matter.

I am forever grateful, and may God bless you.

Joanna Cummings
Willow Branch Farm
Walnut Oak, Virginia

After reading the letter, I began to realize that Virgil's wife had no idea of her husband's fate after he was captured, and had received few of his letters explaining the conditions he had lived through. Did she know her husband had written her many letters? Evidently she had not received them, nor had her husband learned of his wife's pregnancy or about the birth of their child.

Having read other accounts of prison life at Point Lookout, I started to formulate what might have happened to Virgil Cummings. Since there was no record of him being buried at the mass grave near my cottage, I suspected that his was one of the many deaths that had gone unrecorded by the Union government. I had read a letter of Virgil's that mentioned he had enemies among his fellow Southern prisoners, not to mention the cruel punishment of the prison guards. Any number of scenarios could have played out. But my main concern was that to date I had found no record of what had happened to Virgil.

I tried to imagine what could have happened to him, remembering some of the concerns he had for his own life, as well as what I read of other prisoners' letters describing some of the things they had to do just to survive. One of my recent library books, a compilation of prison letters, seemed to offer a scenario. *Is it wrong to speculate as much as I do?* I wondered.

Chapter 14

The Only Game to Play

V irgil knew that the only game to play in prison now was the information game, and for that a man had to have goods to trade. Gus may have had a little information, but Virgil had goods, and Virgil wanted more then what a few cooked crabs could buy. Going against his own better judgment, he carefully took inventory of what he had to trade, avoiding the eyes of fellow prisoners.

At certain locations around the camp, Virgil had buried items that could be used for bartering. Among the items were tobacco plugs, writing instruments, Union army rations, candy, and some Union writing paper, all buried under scrub pine trees just off of the bay. The trouble was that his stash was getting lower, and winter was approaching. He would need to barter what he had left for some blankets to keep from freezing.

Virgil's most important cash crop, however, was seafood, and he could still catch anything from blue crab to blue fish clear up until winter set in. Now that the summer was nearly over, Virgil thought it best to find the guard who had bartered with Gus.

The possibility of getting at those letters or finding out information from that guard kept Virgil going, and he couldn't sleep for thinking of what he needed to do. He still had a basket of live crabs in his tent, and if he could find the guard who'd spoken with Gus, he might be able to cash those in for what he wanted. It would be worth the risk, and he really couldn't wait for a perfectly dark evening to try.

In the darkness of the evening, Virgil got up from his cot and pulled the flap back on his tent, listening and watching as he walked out into the night, following the route he had carefully mapped out. He could hear a few men talking in their tents and a muffled cry coming from another. He'd heard a lot of crying going on here at the prison camp. Some of the younger men couldn't bear being away from their families, especially in the evenings. Without any mail coming to them, and with the scant information they received about the war, most surmised that it wasn't going well for the South and had given in to despair.

Some feared that they would be executed if the war was lost. Rumors were going through the camp that the old Point Lookout lighthouse was being used to torture prisoners into giving up information about Confederate activity. Hope was a rare commodity in the tents, and information was almost nonexistent, yet the prisoners continued to pass on whatever they heard from one another.

Virgil tried his best not to listen to rumors, but there were currently more than twenty thousand prisoners all crowded into tents that offered little but thin shelter from the elements. Prisoners spent their days milling around the prison yard, some hungry, some despondent, some angry, some hopeless, and some spreading rumors of death and destruction.

Virgil had bartered for the materials to make his own tent. He was able to avoid the overcrowded tents where disease spread quickly, especially the coughing death, which arrived with the cold weather. A man could be put out of his tent by other prisoners if they suspected he had influenza. Tonight there was no coughing, but winter wasn't here yet, and Virgil knew that when the cold weather came, men could die of almost anything, even despair.

Several prisoners who couldn't take the harsh conditions had tried to escape, but they were caught and punished. Others gave up on life altogether, refusing to eat. The worst of the lot would sink to taking the oath of the Union government, but in Virgil's mind, those men should be hunted down and hanged. Being a traitor was worse than death to him.

Most men survived any way they could, even by playing with homemade cards and betting for food, but these card games often ended with fighting and accusations of cheating. Some of the prisoners fought with each other; pent-up frustration overflowing. Some died that way too. There were many ways to die, no matter the reason.

As Virgil carefully approached the prison yard, the guards were already responding. "What you doing, boy?" asked one guard, pointing his rifle down at Virgil.

"Yeah, what are you doing down there?" asked another guard as he looked down from the high walkway. "You get back in your tent, or I may just have to take a shot at you."

Virgil pretended to go back in the direction of his tent, but once out of sight in the shadows under the raised walk, he continued cautiously under the wood perimeter. Looking up between the cracks in the wood walkway, he tried to surmise which guards were tired and not paying much attention and which guards were standing alone. Eventually he came to one who was standing off from the others.

"Who's there?" the guard whispered down at Virgil.

"Name's, Virgil Cummings."

"What do you want?"

"Oh, I was just hoping for some trading is all." Virgil looked around to see if any other guards could see or hear them. "I have a few things that you might be interested in, and I heard the local guards were willing to trade a little."

"Trade for what?" the guard whispered.

"Well, for information I guess."

"What do you have?"

Virgil took this as a good sign. "I have tobacco, writing paper, and some seafood," he answered. "Are you a local boy or one of those soldiers from up north?"

"Why do you want to know? And what did you say your name is?"

"Virgil Cummings, from the Northern Neck of Virginia."

"Yeah, I've heard of you and your business down there in the yard. What do you want to know?"

"Did you join up, or were you forced into being a guard?"

"Mind your business."

"You're right. You've said a lot, and I'm grateful, but I want to know about those local folks who were brought in here. I figured if you were local, then you would know some of them. I hear that most of them are civilians from right around these parts." Virgil waited.

"What about it?"

Virgil was sure that this guard was the one trading information with Gus. "Do you have any contact with any of them? And can you find out why our mail isn't being delivered to us? I heard that it had something to do with the newspaper."

"Some of the Southern women were sending information to the Leonardtown paper about the conditions in this place." The guard looked around to make sure that the other guards weren't too close.

"I need to get hold of those letters. Where are they now?" Virgil asked.

"Locked up somewhere," he replied. "The officers here don't want information about the camp getting out to the public."

"Can you try to get me one of the papers?"

"No."

"Can you get me in touch with someone from the newspaper, or get a message to one of them for me?"

"Don't know. What's the message?"

"Ask one of the newspapermen if they ever received a letter from my wife. Her name is Joanna Cummings."

"I'll take that seafood first."

"I got some nice crabs today, and I can boil some for you and meet you somewhere in the morning when you get off the wall."

"How many you got?"

"Will a dozen be enough, sir?" He had never before called a black man sir, but he knew he had to show respect.

"That will be all right for now. Now you get on back to your tent," the guard whispered.

Virgil couldn't believe his luck. He would give the guard a dozen cooked crabs and still have enough to barter with around the camp. Feeling jubilant and proud he hurried back through the maze of tents, which were quiet now. He thought about his beautiful wife, and their last night together. It was what he would dream about all night, if his headaches would leave him alone.

The maze of tents passed him by, and he felt that he had wings on his feet as he soon arrived at his tent. He lifted the flap to his dark tent and entered, but a feeling of uneasiness came over him as he remembered that he had left the tent flap open.

"Where you been?" a voice from the direction of the cot asked.

"Who's there?" There was silence. "Answer me!" Virgil demanded. "Who's there?"

"You been messing with my guard, haven't you?" Gus wasn't budging from his place in the shadow of a corner.

Virgil, remembering the threat that Gus had made earlier, reached for his heavy stick. But it wasn't where he always kept it.

"Looks like your toy gun is gone," said Gus, "and now you'll find out that you been snooping with the wrong guard."

"What makes you think that guard is your guard?"

"I think you got warned about being so careless around here. You been trying to cut into my business by getting information from my Negro guards. I know 'cause I seen you over there. He's my guard, and you broke into my business that I've got going."

"You don't have any business going. Get out of my tent!" Virgil hollered, hoping someone would hear.

Virgil could see Gus's shadow move toward him before he felt the heavy stick strike his knees. As his knees buckled from the pain, the two went down in a heap with Gus on top. Frantically, Virgil fingered the dirt floor, trying to grab a weapon or a stick or anything that he could grasp, but Gus squeezed his large hands around Virgil's neck, holding him to the dirt floor until the pain in his legs caused him to stop struggling.

"Sleep well," said Gus. "This might be your last breath." Then after pounding Virgil's head against the hard ground repeatedly, Gus stood up and kicked Virgil's face. As Virgil cried out in pain, Gus lifted the tent flap, looked around the prison yard, then seeing no witnesses slipped out of the tent and into the darkness.

Virgil's head felt like it had been split open. When he put his hand on his face, he felt warm blood oozing from his mouth and his nose and ears. Virgil knew that Gus had inflicted some serious injuries. He rolled over and tried to get to his feet, but the pain from his knees prevented him from getting up. On his side he slowly dragged himself over to his cot, avoiding putting pressure on his knees. He was sure that he had broken bones, maybe even broken knees, and with the pain in his face and head, he knew also that his wounds could be fatal.

The room started spinning rapidly around him, so Virgil forced himself to think of anything but dying. He thought about what the guard had told him. The guard knew about the letters and why they were being held. What else had that guard said? Virgil again tried to think. This time he pictured Joanna. He could get her letters now...

Virgil's head was seized with pain, and his thoughts started to drift. Again he thought of the guard and how he would cook up the crabs in the morning and somehow get them to that guard. Then he would get some more information; maybe even get a note to one of the civilian prisoners.

Leaning on his cot, holding his head with both hands, he forced himself to stay awake. He'd had a concussion once before, and his recent wound at Gettysburg had multiplied the intensity of that pain, seven-fold. He remembered the accident he had as a young boy in the Northern Neck. He'd been building a tree fort when a friend accidentally dropped a hammer from above him. It hit his head, and he fell out of the tree. *What was that friend's name... Tom? I think it was Tom, but...*

Virgil's thoughts were broken as he drifted, startled only for a moment as he heard a muffled sound followed by rifles going off in every direction. The noise was deafening, but for some reason his head stopped pounding, and he lay peaceful and relaxed. Now he remembered. Yes, his friend's name was Tom, but it was an accident. Tom didn't mean to hit him with that hammer. He wished he could see Tom again.

Relaxed and without pain, Virgil drifted off thinking about his beloved wife. Joanna was walking in a field of flowers. Were they daffodils? Was it time for daffodils? Wasn't this the fall season? Those flowers don't grow in the fall. But they were beautiful, and maybe this was spring and he'd just forgotten.

The moon was full and bright, and it lit up a clear pathway leading to Joanna. At last he rose from his cot and ran toward his wife. She was smiling and holding her arms out. "Virgil, hurry," she said. "I have a boat, and I've come for you." But try as he might, he couldn't reach her, and eventually the moon was gone and so was Joanna. Somehow though the path shone bright and clear all on its own, even without a moon. Virgil found himself running on the path without any effort. He couldn't tell what was lighting the path, but he didn't have any worries as he ran toward light, which was brighter still, and soon he was bathed in light.

❧

The archive box held books of firsthand accounts of some of the prisoners' ordeals, memoirs written long after the end of the Civil War. The common thread that I could see was that many of them had reached the breaking point and had often turned on one another. They also wrote about the heartache of returning to their families only to find their homes burned, the crops destroyed, and their wives and children destitute. One mentioned a fatal shooting by a guard who had killed an innocent prisoner, but the prisoner's name had been blackened out. Could that man have been Virgil?

According to some medical entries, prisoners often hallucinated about being rescued. Was that also Virgil's fate before he died? I looked for a death certificate but couldn't find one for Virgil. In fact, other than his letter, I couldn't find his name on any documents. Several guards had been questioned in the death of a prisoner, and one of the guards questioned was Jeremiah Wilkes. The prisoner's name was not given in the report.

I left the archives and drove straight back to the B&B. When I got there, I found Linda finishing up the room next to mine.

"Hi," she said. "Did you find what you were looking for at the archives today?"

"Yes and no," I answered. "I'm beginning to wonder why I feel so driven to do this. I guess my life revolves around reading about other people's lives. I usually end up wishing that I hadn't started, but then I go right back to it again. Something is seriously flawed about me."

Linda laughed and sat down on the freshly made bed. "Why don't you sit down a minute?" she offered. "There's a nice comfy chair right over there."

"Thanks," I said.

"Did you find out something upsetting?" she asked. I guess she could tell that I wasn't my usual self.

"Well," I said, "it wouldn't be upsetting to most people, but then again, I guess I'm a little odd. I just read the documentation on the shooting of a prisoner, and I'm wondering if it could be the man I've been researching. He was that prisoner at Point Lookout during the Civil War that I told you a little about. I've been following his life through letters and other documents, but I've come to a dead end."

"It sounds to me like you're making headway though," Linda said.

"Yes, but nothing I've found so far completes the story of this prisoner. I mean I could go there and spend hours reading everything from personal diary entries to newspaper articles, but trying to get a clear picture of what happened in the prison camp has caused me to have a thousand more questions. There are so many varying accounts that I find my mind inventing scenarios."

"What scenarios have you invented? Can you share one?" Linda asked.

"The guard in question about the murder might somehow be involved in the story about the developer of the cottages on my little road. I read that Jeremiah Wilkes was a guard at Pt. Lookout and that he was questioned in the murder of a prisoner who may be the man I've researched, Virgil Cummings."

"Really? So does that mean that your little cottage may have been built by a suspected murderer?"

"I don't know for sure, but Jeremiah Wilkes was one of several black guards who were interviewed at Point Lookout, and he could be a suspect in the murder of Virgil Cummings. Records show that he was also employed by a man named Lewis Chambers after the war, so if he was still alive years after the Civil War, then he couldn't have been tried for the murder at the camp. It must have been one of the other guards who had fired the shot, killing Virgil Cummings."

"So if Jeremiah Wilkes wasn't tried and convicted for the murder of Virgil Cummings, are you going to look elsewhere to find out who the murderer was, or do you think that Jeremiah Wilkes got away with it? After all, there were several murders at that camp and shootings by the guards, but I have never read accounts of actual postwar trials. There are plenty of records about the Civil War and postwar proceedings at the National Archives in DC though." Linda seemed very interested in my investigation, and I appreciated her comments.

"I may have to go there soon," I said. "There must be more records about Point Lookout there then what I've found in Annapolis."

"Yes," said Linda, "they have documentation about all of the wars there. Maybe you'll find something about prison guards who served at Point Lookout or some other information about the guard who may have murdered that prisoner. It may not be Jeremiah Wilkes at all."

"That would be nice," I said, "but finding the records that I need could take me years and I'm too tired to even think about getting started."

"Well, if you think it would be relaxing, how about I tell you a little more about Walter and Peaches? I could go into the kitchen and get a nice snack for us and something cold to drink, and then I'll go on with the story."

"Thank you," I said. *Why are all of these people being so nice to me?* I wondered.

The phone rang, and I heard Linda say, "Yes, she's right here. Let me put her on the phone." Linda came over to me and said with a smile, "You never told me that your contractor was David Woods. He's on the phone to discuss something with you about your cottage." Linda motioned for me to pick up the phone in the hallway.

"Hello, this is Rainey," I said.

"Rainey, this is David Woods. I'm going to start finishing the cleanup at your cottage tomorrow and was wondering if you'd like to come and give my crew direction about what furniture you want tossed and what you want to keep. I know that you put most of it out in your yard, but there are a few pieces that could be cleaned up and restored."

"I hope you're right about the furniture," I said. "And yes, I'll come down first thing. Thank you for the call."

"No problem," he said. "See you tomorrow."

Linda came around the corner when she heard me hang the phone up. "Are you ready, or do you need to take care of something?"

"I'm ready," I said. "I'm too tired to go anywhere right now, so please continue your story."

Chapter 15

The Revenuers

Cyrus and Danville had enjoyed a nice steak at Fenwick's and settled into a serious conversation about the pending raid as they walked back to the office. The night air had become extremely humid, and the wind had all but stopped. Back at the office, both men took their weapons from the wall mount and loaded up.

Recently a farmer and local townsman had fired a warning shot in Cyrus' direction just before his still was found. The farmer got away, and though Cyrus expected no trouble tonight, he reasoned that desperate people making moonshine didn't like anyone sneaking up on them, especially agents. The sound of loading a shotgun could deter most sensible men, and so far Cyrus had not had to empty a shell, but he had chased a few men off into the woods and Cyrus was not about to have his luck change.

The short trip to the Graves and Wilkes farms was done at slow speed and with dimmed lights as the agents drove up the dirt road to the top of a hill. They went a little past the Graves farm and pulled off of the road just shy of the Wilkes farm. A distant dog began to bark but stopped as the men slowly eased out of their seats. Then with shotguns and unlit lanterns in tow, they carefully made their way over a split-rail fence, maneuvering through rows of maturing tobacco plants.

They could see the barn that belonged to Peaches Wilkes and quickly slipped inside, lighting their lanterns to a dim flame as they looked for anything that might be used in making brew. There they found clean glass five-gallon jugs lined up close to the door. Each jug was empty, and no other signs of contraband could be found. Cyrus signaled Danville and whispered that they should search behind the barn and down near the creek.

Cyrus was familiar with the Wilkes farm. As a boy, he had often gone there to join other boys for a swim in the dammed-up creek in the woods. He had surmised that if there was a still, it would probably be somewhere near the creek behind the farm. Shining his lantern back and forth, he found the same old well-worn path that had once led to the swimming hole.

The smell of cow manure and humid earth mingled together brought out the mosquitoes and horseflies. With lanterns and shot-guns in tow, the men had to put up with bites and stings. A copperhead snake resting its body across the path jumped at the infringement and quickly slithered away. It was particularly long, and Danville thanked God that he had not stepped on it. He had a deathly fear of snakes.

When the men got farther down into the woods, they turned the lanterns off and set them down near some undergrowth. Sitting several yards off of the trail, behind some thickets, they waited for the sounds of moonshiners at work. Crickets and tree frogs disturbed the night air, but an hour or so passed before the crack of branches and other noises were heard. The agents stood up and readied themselves to move in.

Cyrus picked up his shotgun and signaled for Danville to follow him. Carefully and slowly, the men worked their way down the steep hill closer the creek where they heard sounds of an unidentifiable nature. Stopping and listening again, Danville thought that it was a muskrat or possum, but muskrat and possum didn't make those sounds.

"That sounds like a cow," whispered Danville.

"No," said Cyrus, "cows don't sound like that."

"They do when they're sick or giving birth," explained Danville. "I've heard something like that before."

"I've never heard a cow sound like that," Cyrus whispered back.

The men stopped and listened again for another several minutes or so, but they heard nothing more. "I don't think there's anything going on down here, or we would hear voices," said Cyrus. "Let's light up the lanterns and look for the still. I hear the creek over here a couple of yards. We'll go up and down until we find the still."

Turning up the lantern flames, the men found their way down to the creek. The smell of alcohol was hanging in the dead, humid air as they neared the homemade contraption. The men turned their lanterns up and held them high in the air for a larger view of the area. They heard branches breaking and the awful sound once more.

Looking down the creek, they could see a movement. Danville prepared his weapon, and Cyrus, holding both lanterns, followed the sound. There in the creek lay the ruins of what was once a still. Metal pieces reflected the lamplight as the men approached. On some of the pieces was the unmistakable imprint of cow hooves. Other metal pieces were lying bent and strewn here and there. A copper coil was lying in the narrow creek.

Holding the lantern high, Cyrus was startled by a huge white face just inch from his own, glazed black eyes staring directly at him. Nearly dropping the lanterns, Cyrus jumped back. The cow turned around slowly, and then walking at a tipped angle, hung its head down and began to lap up the water. After a few laps, the cow began to bawl again.

"That cow is drunk," said Danville. "Look, it's lapping up the mash from the still." Cyrus put the flame up as high as it would go and scoped the situation out.

There lining the creek bed on both sides were several cows. One cow stood in the middle of the creek. None were standing upright, nor were they reacting to the light from the lanterns shinning on their eyes. They seemed somewhat oblivious, in fact, and continued to lap up the mash, occasionally letting out noises that sounded both mournful and unnatural. The agents stood dumbfounded.

"Those cows are stone drunk," said Danville. Both men stood for several minutes before finally climbing back up the steep trail, making their way up to Peaches's house. Finding him home with his wife, Cyrus proceeded to conduct a thorough interview. Danville took notes.

The same interrogation was carried out at Walter's house. Both agents hoped that one of the men would turn the spotlight on the other and tell the truth about the still. But after listening to the two farmers' explanations, and checking both barns again, the agents surmised that the men were keeping to their obviously rehearsed stories and gave up their questioning.

Cyrus thought to himself how hilarious it was that drunken cows had managed to take out a still without the help of revenue agents, and in the process had saved the necks of the two guilty farmers. But what could he write in a report about this? Who would believe it?

On the way back to the office, Danville began to laugh. "Maybe the agency should hire cows to do their dirty work."

Soon Cyrus joined in. "Yes, they should take out employment ads for cows by offering free moonshine to them. Just think of the stills they could destroy for us. They would have a real b-a-w-l as agents."

The two men laughed. "Seriously though, we've got to get back to the office and write this up," Cyrus said.

"Did we really want to arrest those two farmers anyway? "Their poor wives were frightened to death to see us show up when we did. But how are we going to account for our time, Cyrus?"

"I'll just report the truth as it happened." The report read:

August 8, 1930

A thorough search of the area in question was conducted by me and my deputy agent, Danville Clarke. We searched the area for several hours, and upon finding the still, we found no moonshiner activity in progress. However, we did find a still that may have been destroyed by some very inebriated cows. Hoof prints were found on the destroyed still and elsewhere around the scene of the brewery, located on Simm's Creek between the farms of Mr. Wilkes and Mr. Graves.

After reaching the home and properties of Mr. Wilkes, we found his entire family at home. When speaking with Mr. Wilkes, it was evident that he had not been involved with still manufacturing as he seemed relieved that the still had been found and destroyed. He did, however, state that some of his cows had not come up for their hay that afternoon and stated that he was about to conduct a search for them.

Agent Clarke and I also questioned the owners of the farm located adjacent to the Wilkes farm. Mr. and Mrs. Walter Graves were able to answer our questions to the satisfaction of both agents. Mrs. Graves reported that her husband had been home with her and could vouch for her husband, stating that her husband did not drink alcohol and that he was a God-fearing man who would never break the law.

After having inspected both barns belonging to Mr. Wilkes and Mr. Graves, we found no indication of still materials or alcohol of any kind on the premises of either farmer. It is our conclusion that Mr. Wilkes and Mr. Graves are not involved in the illegal manufacturing or delivery of alcohol. This office is pre-pared to continue inspecting that particular area for any activity along with other areas farther to the south in an effort to find and arrest those responsible for the building of the still on Simm's Creek.

Cyrus Posey, Revenue Agent
Leonardtown, Maryland

∾

The next morning, Peaches and Walter met to discuss their close call and their distress over what could have been their chance at wealth and fortune. The meeting was depressing and short as Walter blamed the miserable cows that should have come up to the barn for grain instead of drinking their precious liquor and ruining their new still.

"Them darn cows destroyed our beautiful still before we could make our first sale," Walter whined, "and I just can't figure why Cyrus Posey ended up in our neck of the woods."

"My cow's milk is going to be soured for who knows how long," Peaches lamented, ignoring Walter's comments. "Those are my best milking cows."

"Our still is broken to pieces," said Walter, "and that was the way we were going to get rich. Now what do we do?"

But Peaches didn't answer and appeared more downhearted then Walter could ever remember. "Don't you worry, Peaches. We'll think of some way to grow some better tobacco or something that will do good at the market. The great thing is that our wives never even suspected we'd do something like build a still."

"How am I going to feed my family?" Peaches could not be con-soled. "We never have grown anything that makes money except for tobacco, and you know those prices aren't going up. There's a depression going on, in case you hadn't noticed."

"Well then, we're going to have to come up with some way of making our tobacco special. We'll have to find out some way to cure it that helps make Maryland tobacco the best tobacco in the country. In the meantime, I guess we better think about corn and hay. Maybe we can grow some of them new soy beans too. Perk up, Peaches, our people go way back in this county, and not one of them ever gave up on the land. We'll get by." But Walter could see that Peaches wasn't listening to him.

Walter walked home after the depressing meeting with Peaches and realized that this was the first time he could remember ever having to console his friend. It was usually the other way around. But Walter liked the feeling of coming up with an idea or two, and he walked home feeling proud.

Nearing his house, Walter noticed that an automobile was parked on the side of the road out front. Not giving much thought to whom it could be, he opened the door to the kitchen and walked in. There seated at the kitchen table was Cyrus Posey.

It seemed odd to Walter that after all of these years of never giving Walter the time of day, and especially after Cyrus had gone snooping around on the property, probably trying to catch Walter to throw him in the Leonardtown jail, that the man would have the nerve to sit in his kitchen drinking his coffee and chatting with Greta. And for some reason, Cyrus seemed pleased to see him.

"Cyrus," Walter said.

"Walter, I'm sorry to barge in like this, but I just came by to say hello, and your wife invited me in to wait for you."

Walter hesitated slightly before receiving Cyrus's outstretched hand and taking a seat at the table where he was promptly served a cup of coffee by an unusually perky Greta. Walter didn't like it.

"Cyrus is here to talk to you about work," she chirped.

Walter looked at his wife and then back at Cyrus Posey. Greta was acting sort of silly and attentive, and Walter wondered why the two of them seemed so friendly and sociable. Walter noticed there were cake crumbs on a plate in front of Cyrus and glared over at Cyrus before lifting his coffee cup to take a drink.

After Walter sipped his coffee, Greta promptly brought him a large slice of rather nice-looking cake. He quickly dug his fork into it and brought an ample bite to his mouth. Walter had worked himself into hunger pains, and this was a cake to beat all cakes. Walter relished each bite. This tasted like that apple spicy cake that Greta used to make for him when they were first married, he recalled.

Walter began to think things out. It was true that they never did have much company and that he hadn't been served cake for a very long time. Maybe it was fine that she served Cyrus a little piece. Greta smiled at Walter as she took the empty plates from the table. Walter gulped his coffee down. Maybe she'd just been lonely for company.

Walter thought back and realized that this was the first time since their wedding day that Greta actually seemed to like him. She was looking very pretty now, and Walter was feeling good. Walter smiled at Greta and pointed to the empty cup sitting before him. Before he could say a word, she took the cup to the stove and filled it to the rim with rich, black coffee. As she placed the cup down a smile came from Greta's pretty lips, and Walter began to feel that tingling feeling all over.

"Would you like anything else, *dear?*" Greta asked.

"No," replied Walter. Though the word *dear* seemed foreign to Walter, he found himself sitting taller in his chair and wondering what *anything else* meant. Was this respect he was getting after all of these years? He pondered this idea for a moment or two. Then, thinking very deeply, he reasoned that Greta might just be showing off for Cyrus. He shrugged his shoulders and looked over at Greta. She was still smiling at him though, and it was one of those inviting smiles that he hadn't seen for years.

Does she want to be alone with me? She was, after all, a mighty good-looking woman. He wondered how he could get rid of his visitor. Otherwise, how could he and Greta take a little nap together? *Maybe now,* he thought, *I won't have to speak to the preacher about Greta.*

"Well, Walter," said Cyrus, "I've come to talk to you about work. Are you interested?" Walter could see Greta nodding her head up and down. Or was she reading his mind about that little nap?

"What kind of work?" Walter shook himself from his trance and looked Cyrus directly in the eye.

"Oysters," answered Cyrus Posey.

Chapter 16

Miss Biscoe

The story Linda told me made me think more about the people of Southern Maryland. Ever since Patrick and I bought our small cottage on the Chesapeake Bay, I had become enthusiastic about the history of the area. Now, with Patrick gone, I became interested in stories and legacies of people that had somehow become interwoven, bringing me to a closer understanding of this unique little area.

Another guest had arrived and Linda had to excuse herself to help her husband. I wondered again what kind of legacy I would leave behind. With no children and no prospect of a second marriage, I felt that my time thus far on the earth had been one of accidental events and structured insignificance. But I couldn't expect Linda to take all this time with me just because I was so needy for information.

After Linda left my room I thought of Cyrus, Peaches, Greta, and Betsy. Linda was helpful with information about her grandfather, Walter Graves, but I also wanted to know more about Peaches and his family. Later, when I asked Linda about Peaches, she gave me the name of an elderly woman, a friend of hers, who lived in Great Mills, not far from Leonardtown.

The woman was ninety-eight years old, and from what Linda said, "…had retained more information about the folks in the area then anything recorded in a journal." That was enough for me. With her name and phone number in hand, I called the number and was greeted by an energetic voice on the other end of the line.

"No, I'm not Miss Biscoe," said the voice, "I'm her caregiver, Miss Ellen. May I help you?"

"Yes," I answered. "I was given Miss Biscoe's phone number by Linda Raley. I'm staying at her B&B here in Leonardtown, and she has been gracious enough to share a little history of the area with me. Linda suggested that Miss Biscoe may be willing to share some of that history with me as well sometime. That is, if that would be something she would want to do."

"Oh," said Miss Ellen, "I'm sorry, but I'm afraid Miss Biscoe has retired for the evening. She does see visitors early in the morning hours though. Would you like to come for a visit tomorrow?"

"Yes, I'd like to do that."

"I'm just sure that Miss Biscoe would just love some company. Come by early though. She's an early riser, and if you want to come around eight or so that should catch Miss Biscoe before her ten o'clock nap. I'll make sure to put a nice pot of coffee on, and it'll be waiting for you when you get here."

"Thank you. That would be great. I'll see you at eight then."

"Bye-bye, Miss?"

"Oh, I'm sorry. My name is Rainey Grant."

"Well that's a pretty name. So Miss Rainey Grant, I'll see you first thing in the morning."

❧

The following morning after breakfast, I drove the few miles to Great Mills and turned onto an obscure dirt driveway that led deep into the woods. There were downed limbs and branches covering a great part of the driveway, but I managed to slowly drive over them, branches and limbs cracking and breaking under my tires.

On both sides of the driveway were overgrown trees and shaggy laurel bushes, and tucked between every other bush was a birdhouse of some kind. The houses looked as though they had been handmade and were decorated with painted flowers, which on closer inspection appeared to be decoupage. Some of the paper corners had pulled away from the birdhouses, exposing bare pine, but just the same eastern bluebirds, in numbers that I had never seen before, were hurrying in and out of the little houses.

Eventually I came to the home of Miss Biscoe, situated in an opening through the trees. It was a small house with a little lopsided screened-in porch, very much looking like it needed more than a little repair. The house displayed a faded blue color on the clapboard siding, and it looked as though some recent work had been done to the windows. Vinyl windows didn't seem to fit the old clapboard siding, but somehow the house was still charming.

I pulled up next to an early-model red Ford truck and reminded myself that a short visit would be best for a woman of ninety-eight years. I hoped Miss Biscoe would be able to recall some of the names of the people I wanted to know more about. As I got out of my car, Miss Ellen opened the screen door and greeted me. Then, entering the porch, I could smell pine cleaner and furniture polish. The wide heart-of-pine wood plank floors were shined to brilliance, and the sparse furniture was laid out with plenty of room for safe walking.

Miss Biscoe sat in a wicker rocking chair, wrapped up snug in what looked like an Indian blanket. She wore white toeless slippers on her feet, and I noticed that her toenails had been painted a deep red. "How do you like the way Miss Ellen keeps things around here?" she asked.

"I think that she keeps things wonderfully clean and bright," I said. "Hello, I'm Rainey Grant, and I really appreciate you taking time to see me."

"Gracious me," said Miss Biscoe. "I thank you for coming to visit. I guess some folks think that I'm getting too old to be social, but that's what keeps my mind sharp. I just love visitors. I used to get more folks visiting me then I do now, but I'm always so happy to have some company. Not that Miss Ellen isn't company enough, but you know she has a lot of cooking and cleaning and caring to do, and that keeps her very busy."

"Not that busy, Miss Biscoe," said Miss Ellen. "You aren't hard to take care of. You know that." She took Miss Biscoe by the hand and patted it. "You're a joy to be with and so full of stories to tell me. That's what keeps me coming back here every day."

"Oh," I said, "so you don't live here with Miss Biscoe?"

"Live here with Miss Biscoe? Why, no. Miss Biscoe would never allow that, honey. She says there's only room for one woman at a time in her house. I've offered to sleep over, but she loves her privacy too much to allow that." Miss Ellen left Miss Biscoe to her rocking chair, then excused herself and left the room.

"Miss Biscoe," I began, "a good source told me that you are a known historian for this area, and I'm intrigued by the local history. You see, I'm what you would call a storyteller. I research things that interest me, and then I find people who share my love of history, with the hope that they too will share their stories with me. I'm hoping that you may be willing this morning."

"Why, I think that is a wonderful thing to do," replied Miss Biscoe as she leaned toward me. "That makes us alike. We like to learn, but we like to tell even more. It is a socially acceptable way to gossip and a good excuse to do so. You could call what we do 'historical gossiping.' I think that's what makes life worth living; that and knowing the Lord, that is. I only hope that I know a little something about what you are interested in. You can ask me anything at all, and I will do my best to answer you honestly."

At this point I felt like I was with a kindred spirit. Miss Ellen emerged from the kitchen with two cups of coffee and asked what I took in mine. I poured a little cream into my cup with a sugar cube, and Miss Ellen put a lot of cream and two cubes of sugar in the cup for Miss Biscoe. We held our cups up and sipped the sweet, creamy brew.

"Do you have any of that good coconut cake left in the icebox?" Miss Biscoe asked Miss Ellen.

"Now you know that you're not to have a lot of sugar, and you already had a piece of cake for breakfast. What's that doctor going to say to me when your sugar goes through the roof?" Miss Ellen was making an attempt to do what was right, but when she saw the expression on Miss Biscoe's face, Miss Ellen backed down and returned to the kitchen.

"You might be ninety-eight, but you're still in charge," muttered Miss Ellen. In less than a few minutes, she brought out two little pieces of coconut cake with the frosting removed from Miss Biscoe's piece. I thanked her and held the plate of cake in my lap while Miss Biscoe made slow cuts into her slice. I couldn't help but notice how smooth her hands were for a woman of her age.

"What do you want to know about, dear?" Miss Biscoe asked me.

I took a bite of cake and licked some frosting from my lips.

"I'm wondering if you have any knowledge about a man who once lived in Leonardtown in the thirties by the name of Wilkes. I don't really know his first name, but his nickname was Peaches." Before I could continue, Miss Biscoe began to laugh.

"Did I know Peaches Wilkes? Yes, I knew him. Why, it wasn't even that long ago that he went to be with the Lord." She rocked in her chair and seemed to go into a little trance as she began to tell me the story of Peaches.

Chapter 17

Peaches Wilkes

When Peaches was eight years old, he was already big enough and strong enough to help his father and younger brothers roll a hogshead of tobacco down to the dock where a waiting steamer would bring aboard the best tobacco in Southern Maryland and take it off to points all over the globe. At least, that's what Peaches told everyone.

Even at eight he had an eye for business and knew the workings of tobacco, from the seed plants put into the ground to the curing of the full-grown weed in the barns at Calverton Plantation. He liked to tell the other workers on the plantation about the world and about how Maryland tobacco was in demand everywhere from China to European countries, like Spain and Italy.

He knew about such places because his daddy, Tiberius Wilkes, had taught him to read and had purchased a world atlas for him on his eighth birthday. He had buried his nose in that book every night since and had nearly memorized the major continents and many countries. He could spell them too. His daddy had learned about the world, but it was not because he had ever traveled far.

In fact, Tiberius Wilkes had never been any farther away from Southern Maryland then Washington, DC, and he hated that place with all his heart. It was there his parents had endured the awful experience of the slave auction where they were sold like livestock. But things got better for his family after many years.

His parents, Jeremiah and Gerdie Wilkes, had been born slaves and were sold in the slave market when they were but teenagers. They were purchased by an overseer of the Plain Farm, and then after emancipation came, they went to work at Calverton Plantation, eventually working for folks all around Southern Maryland.

Tiberius, their eldest son, was born on that plantation, but after the Civil War, many blacks lived hand-to-mouth as jobs were scarce, and they were often replaced by out-of-work white folks. Soon his parents moved farther down in the county, and both Jeremiah and his wife, Gerdie, took jobs doing whatever they could find. It was then that they found jobs working for Mr. Leonard Chambers.

After the war, when the slaves were all free to leave, some stayed on as hired men, but others, to survive the tough times, became tenant farmers. That was something that both blacks and whites had to do after the Civil War. They could live on or off the plantation. Many living outside the plantation often sold their wares and their skills back to the plantation owners. But if need be, other markets could be found as well. Tiberius's parents, Jeremiah and Gerdie, maintained a tobacco farm near Leonardtown after the war for Mr. Chambers. He also hired them to do building projects for him, and one year he rebuilt an old hotel and took in vacationers from all around.

Tiberius learned everything about building and farming and other odd jobs from the example set by his father, Jeremiah and together Jeremiah and Gerdie worked for Mr. Chambers all the way up into their eighties. Tiberius bought a little farm in Leonardtown, where Peaches grew up learning the tobacco trade. Then later on, Peaches cared for his folks until they passed away. Eventually Peaches's brothers and sisters moved to the big city of Washington so Peaches ran the farm with his wife, Betsy. They raised a wonderful family in that little farmhouse."

∾

"Was that a hard thing for a black family to get by back then?" I asked, gently interrupting Miss Biscoe's story. "I ask because it was about the time of the Great Depression, wasn't it?"

"Then…I mean, now what was I saying?" Miss Biscoe asked. "I often lose my place when telling a story," she apologized.

"I'm sorry that I interrupted your story," I said. "Please continue."

I looked up from my notes and noticed that Miss Biscoe was fading fast. Her head was tipping to the right, and her eyes were closing. I carefully got up from my chair and went to the kitchen, where Miss Ellen had finished washing the cups and cake plates.

"Miss Ellen, I think Miss Biscoe is tired. She seems to have fallen asleep."

"Oh, she's not sleeping; she's just taking a little rest. She does that frequently when guests are here."

"Now where was I?" came a little voice from the front room. I hurried back and took my seat.

"You were telling me how much Peaches liked to learn about things from his father and from books," I said. "Then you told me that eventually Peaches took over the farm when his parents passed on."

"Now Peaches Wilkes had a good friend living over at the farm next to him, and his name was Walter Graves," she continued. "Walter was an awkward boy and the only friend that Peaches had. Walter and

Peaches had a sort of understanding, or at least Walter had thought as much." Miss Biscoe continued her story.

∾

Peaches had to go quite a distance in order to attend the black school, while Walter's school was a short walk down the road. Peaches had to walk a mile or two to school, bringing him home just about time for afternoon chores and supper, whereas with his short walk home, Walter had already eaten his supper, done his chores, and was waiting by the gate in front of Peaches's home.

Walter's understanding was that Peaches was lollygagging all the way home, but Peaches knew that Walter just didn't get it. "Hey, Peaches," Walter said one day, "what in heck keeps you so long? Is your teacher keeping you after or something? It's getting too late to go swimming, and it's hot out here today."

"What do you think?" Peaches shot back. "You think I can walk a couple of miles in a couple of minutes? You only got to walk down the bottom of the hill. Why don't you ask your teacher if your Negro friend can come to your school? That way I'd have all the time there is to go swimming with you."

Walter thought about that for a minute, but it didn't make sense to him. Why did Peaches have to ask him questions like that? After all, Peaches knew the rules, and the rules were that you had to have different schools for the colored folks. Walter just never questioned things like that. That kind of thinking had always confused him.

"You know I can't ask my teacher if you can go to my school," said Walter. "You're a black boy, and black boys get to have their own schools. You know that. Why do you ask me stuff like that anyway? Don't you want your own school to go to?"

"Never mind," said Peaches, "you just will never get it, so I don't know why I bother with you."

"What do you mean by that?" Walter asked. "I only wanted to know if you want to go swimming or fishing in the creek for tadpoles."

"No," said Peaches, "I got chores to do, then I have to eat my supper, then I got to do some homework. It's the same every night, so why do you keep hanging around? You know I only have spare time on the weekend and after church on Sunday. I tell you the same thing over and over."

Walter put his hands in his overalls and put his head down like he was looking at his feet.

"Anyway," Peaches said, "I got to go in now."

With that, Peaches opened the gate to his walkway. "Maybe we'll swim Saturday if the weather's still nice," he said over his shoulder, "or after church on Sunday."

⁓

"Walter didn't know why there were so many churches or why the black people wanted to have their own social gathering places," Miss Biscoe explained. "Now, to his disappointment, his friend Peaches was always pushing him away." Miss Biscoe gave a little laugh and seemed to be thinking of something. "That was when, I mean…what was I saying just now?" she asked as she put her head back and closed her eyes. "Let me think a moment."

"Miss Biscoe, Miss Biscoe, can you hear me?" I spoke gently but decided that Miss Biscoe was probably very tired from storytelling. This time Miss Ellen came out from the kitchen.

"Well, Miss Rainey," she said, "I think she is down for the afternoon now. Perhaps you had better come another time?"

"Yes, absolutely," I agreed. "I was thinking the same thing, if Miss Biscoe doesn't mind."

"No, she wouldn't at all. I can tell that she likes you. You just call, and I'll tell her when you plan to come back. Do you know when that will be?"

"I hope in a couple of days, if that would be all right. I have to go and check on my place. I think I mentioned to you that my little cottage got hit pretty hard in the storm the other day," I said.

"Yes, yes you did. I am so sorry that you have had to go through that mess again. It seems that people on the water get those awful storms often these days. Was the damage very bad?"

"Yes, it was, but not as severe as it could have been. You know, the strange thing is that I was more upset about my two old trees going down then about the flood of debris that entered the house. That doesn't make much sense, does it?"

"Trees are living, breathing things," said Miss Ellen, "and I know just what you mean by being grieved over them. They are the only things that really explain history to us. To think that the age of a tree can be known just by the rings that they have. When they die or get cut down, there is no replacing them like a house, and all that history locked up behind that bark is just lost. Did you find out how old those trees were?"

"No, I didn't. I think that I can find out though because I'm having some of the larger pieces made into some little things, like picture frames. I might even get a table made from some of it. I'll ask the woodcarver how old he thinks my trees were."

"Oh, that would be so lovely to find out, wouldn't it?" Miss Ellen said.

"I just want to thank you again for your hospitality. Please thank Miss Biscoe for me, will you?"

"That I will do." Miss Ellen smiled as she took me to the front door. "Just call."

I went to my car and found enough room to back up and turn around. On the way out I wondered if Miss Biscoe would ever stay awake long enough to finish her story.

For now I had set in my mind to find out what had happened to Virgil and Jeremiah. For that information, I would have to go back to the Maryland State Archives in Annapolis. That was where I first found the letter from Virgil to his wife, and I hoped that I would find much more.

At the archives, I found a list of the black conscripts who had been guards at Point Lookout in 1864. Thumbing through the list, I came across the name Jeremiah Wilkes and an article that had been printed about the shooting of a prisoner of war. This article was partially derived from a doctor's report, along with some written documents from other prisoners giving their opinions, as well as hearsay about what had happened to the victim. The articles gave me more food for thought.

Chapter 18

A Dead Prisoner

J eremiah flinched as shots were fired in every direction. One of the guards had said to fire, and they all did. Maybe it was good news about the war that set them all off. That had happened many times before. Had the North won another victory?

Jeremiah didn't know this time any more then he had any other time because most of the guards never let him in on what was going on, even when they did know something. Jeremiah prayed that the shots were fired this time as a signal that the war had ended. He just didn't know.

He did know that he loathed being a guard at Point Lookout. Taken away from his young wife and children, he was given the oath, a blue uniform, and a Springfield rifle. With very little training, he was assigned guard duty above the prisoner tents. Now the rifles had been fired off again, he wondered what had happened.

There was stillness in the prison yard. Then after the momentary silence, prisoners slowly emerged from their tents, rummaging around from tent to tent to see if anyone had been hit by a stray minié ball.

"They got him bad!" called a prisoner from down below. "I think he's dead as dead can be. He's got blood coming out his nose, mouth and ears. Poor fellow."

With that announcement, others came out to see who the unfortunate victim was this time. "Oh man!" exclaimed another, "that bullet must have went straight through his head. Look at all the blood!" There was panic in their voices as the men hastily spread the gruesome details to one another.

"Isn't this Virgil's tent?" someone asked.

"'Bout time someone kilt that man," said another. "He was always trying to get something for nothing. Nobody ever liked Virgil."

"That isn't true," said another man. "He was good to anyone who deserved it." The prisoner held a candle up closer to Virgil's body. "I worked for him, and he always was good to me."

"Let me in there," said Gus Pruett as he pushed his way into the tent. Gus struck a match and held it in the crowded and dimly lit tent. A smile went across his face as he looked at the body of Virgil Cummings lying still on the bloody ground. "This here tent is mine now," he declared. "Virgil's dead, so there's no use to anyone else claiming what I'm taking."

"Who says this tent is yours now?" Another man stepped forward. "I was eyeing this tent for a long time, and I want it when the time is proper. I've worked for Virgil for the longest, and I should get it. Besides, his body is still here, and it wouldn't be right to just walk in here and take over his tent."

"Well now," replied Gus calmly, "I been in business with him too. I got information, and I got more then that. I even know who kilt him, and so that means this tent belongs to me now." Gus quickly struck another match and held it as he scanned the tent.

"You don't even know which guard shot Virgil," replied the other prisoner.

"Yes I do," Gus said, "but I'm going to make a deal with him, and then we'll see who gets the tent and who better watch his own back-side. The last thing a prisoner wants to do is report a guard. So I guess you know who's going to get this tent, and it ain't going to be you. That guard will be glad to pay for my silence."

The man looked at Gus and around Virgil's tent. "There's no guard up there who can be bribed. Those guards don't pay anyone for silence."

"What happened here?" a voice from behind interrupted. Gus looked to see a doctor from Hammond Hospital standing behind him, along with a Union officer and an enlisted man. The doctor held a lantern, which illuminated the bloody scene.

"I heard the shots from the hospital," said the doctor. "Who has done this to this man?"

"Don't know," Gus said sadly, "but it must have been one of them guards up on the walk. Nobody down here would do such a thing to a fellow prisoner. We ain't got guns down here."

The doctor put his lantern down on the dirt floor and looked at the body of the prisoner. "What is this man's name?"

"He would be Virgil Cummings of Northern Neck Virginia," answered Gus. "Everybody liked the man except for them guards up there standing around gawking like they didn't know what happened. One of them kilt my friend Virgil."

The doctor, not acknowledging Gus, ordered the enlisted man to get a stretcher and some help to carry Virgil's blood-soaked body back to the hospital compound. Then he looked at Gus and asked, "So you saw who did it, did you?"

"Well, I'm not exactly sure, but I have a good idea it was that local guard up there."

Jeremiah stood silent and still on the guard walk, looking down on the scene.

"Do you mean that guard standing alone up there?" the officer asked.

"Yeah, that's who I mean," said Gus.

"What makes you think it was him? From the hospital, I heard more than one shot going off."

"Well," Gus said, "I heard the two of them talking. I was minding my own business, and I heard them talking, so I went over to see what was going on."

"What did you hear?" asked the doctor.

Gus hesitated for a moment. "Not sure what they said, but I know that Virgil was plenty mad with the guard because he said so when he got back to his tent. They must have had words. You know Virgil was a man with a mean temper. Everyone knows that around here. Who knows what he said to that guard. He was probably trying to make some deal with him, and the guard didn't like it or something like that."

"So you were near the man's tent before he was shot?" the doctor asked. "It looks as though this body was dealt a beating as well as a bullet. Since you were near the dead man's tent, what else can you tell me?"

"I went back to my tent, and I just heard him mumbling something when he went past." Gus knew to say no more. Already the doctor was eyeing him suspiciously.

Up on the guard walk, Jeremiah turned and looked at the other guards, who were smiling and shaking their fingers at him. "What did you do now?" accused one of them.

"I didn't do anything," said Jeremiah. The guards mocked Jeremiah until the officer called for silence.

The doctor then asked Gus a question. "I thought you just said everyone liked him and that you were his friend? Now you're saying he wasn't liked because he had a mean temper? Are you sure you were friends with this man?"

The officer who was with the doctor didn't like questions being asked. "Go back to your tent, Pruett," the officer told Gus. "I'll get your statement later, though it sounds like the same old thing. You men should all learn to tell the truth—something you rebels just can't seem to do."

The doctor began to examine Virgil's body as Gus walked off with a smile on his face. The other prisoners stood nearby.

Two Union privates came to the tent, followed by another officer. Virgil's lifeless body was lifted up on the bloody blanket and placed on the stretcher to be taken away.

"Did any of you men see what happened here?" the new officer asked as he looked about the crowd of men.

"He was probably fighting with Gus again," said one of them. "They're always fighting about something."

"I know that Gus got himself fired from Virgil's crabbing enterprise and was hot under the collar about it," said another.

"Virgil deserves what he gets," said another man, "because he thinks he can order anyone around in here. I hated that man, and if a guard shot him, well…good riddance."

"I'll need reports on this," the doctor said to the first officer. "We need documentation when these things take place. I've seen for myself that paperwork has been totally disregarded here in this camp, and I mean to change that." The doctor followed behind the stretcher carrying Virgil's body for a short distance and then turned and listened as the second officer addressed the prisoners who had remained at the scene.

"Listen up," said the officer, "and do what I tell you. You are not going to disparage the Union army at this camp by reporting things that you didn't see. You will say that you don't know what happened because you didn't see what happened. Do you understand me?"

The men all either nodded yes or stared at the ground. The officer continued. "Winter will be setting in shortly, and we'll have to see about how many blankets and how much wood will be given out. It's going to be very cold very soon. Think about it."

The doctor took note of the officer's orders as he continued on with Virgil Cummings's body.

Sometime later, Gus reappeared to see what he could find in his newly acquired tent. He shoveled dirt over the blood on the floor with a piece of planking and began to rummage around the dead man's things. Lighting a match, he found a candle mounted on a flat piece of wood, which he lit. Gus intended to waste no time in establishing ownership of the vacated tent.

Beside the bushel of crabs that sat covered with wet beach grasses, he found some personal effects in a box with a lid underneath the cot. The box contained the few letters that Virgil had received from his parents as well as from his wife, Joanna, and Gus intended to read every one of them. In those letters there could be some good information about the South.

At the bottom of the box in a tattered envelope was a faded picture of a beautiful woman, probably Virgil's wife. As Gus sat on the writing crate, he thought of possibilities. He figured that soon the South would be defeated, and the war would end; every Confederate soldier knew that by now. If he played things right, he might survive to be released. But he could never go back to Georgia; things had gone bad for him there, even before the war.

Gus began to put together a plan for taking over Virgil's crabbing and fishing business. If he survived Point Lookout, maybe he could have a better life. And what if he could get to Virginia? The law wouldn't think to look for him there. What if he could personally deliver condolences to Virgil's wife? She was awful pretty. *What would Virgil think of me now?* He grinned. Then he left to retrieve his bedding from the crowded tent nearby and pushing the other prisoners out of his way made a nice little bed for himself in the dead man's tent. Once comfortable, Gus drifted off to sleep, not giving Virgil another thought, but he thought plenty about the pretty little woman in the picture, and what he would like to do to her.

Ten feet above the prison yard, Jeremiah Wilkes stood still. He had seen Gus point up to him after the shooting, but he couldn't hear what had been said. The other prison guards were pointing their guns down below now, ordering the prisoners to return to their tents, but Jeremiah couldn't move.

That man was supposed to bring him crabs for information. Now the man was dead, and some of the guards had accused Jeremiah of firing the fatal shot. Jeremiah realized that he might be in trouble. Up to this point, several shots had been fired at random by a guard or two on occasion, but only one prisoner had died. The guard who shot that first prisoner was never questioned. But now it had happened again.

∾

I was amazed with what I had found in the reports at the Maryland State Archives, especially Dr. Comstock's account of the dead prisoner. There were a few recorded testimonies from prisoners as well. Also, several of the guards gave reports of the incident saying that they witnessed Jeremiah Wilkes point his rifle in the direction of Virgil Cummings's tent, but this was not totally believable as another guard denied this, saying that he saw Jeremiah deliberately point his rifle into the air.

Whatever had happened, it seemed to me as if Jeremiah Wilkes had been implicated in the shooting of Virgil Cummings. But why, I asked myself, would he have done it, or how could he have been provoked to such an extreme? Had it been a careless accident or something else?

Chapter 19

Letters

The report by Dr. Comstock, as well as the assorted reports by some of the other prisoners about the shooting, confirmed my suspicions. The victim was Virgil Cummings, but I wondered why his name had been absent from all the other reports I had scanned, or why no one had been charged with his death. And where was the death certificate?

Upon finding this new information, I began to go from slide to slide on the microfiche, viewing the somewhat damaged and faded reports. After several hours of reading letters and bits and pieces of documents, I came upon one document that offered a piece of the puzzle.

There were various reports of death from disease and exposure and even reports about prisoners drowning while attempting to escape, but I found what I had been looking for in an unofficial report under the caption VIRGIL E. CUMMINGS OF WALNUT OAK, VIRGINIA, SHOOTING VICTIM. Evidently Dr. Comstock had much to say after the war and made sure his personal reports were printed in the public papers.

In one article the doctor had written that a minié ball fired from a Springfield percussion rifle had entered and exited the right hip of the victim. The report also gave details about the apparent head and neck wounds as well as the condition of the prisoner's kneecaps. One kneecap had been severely damaged by what appeared to be a blunt weapon of unknown origin.

The report made note of the fact that the minié ball had to have been fired from a raised elevation in order to have struck the victim at that angle and stated that the approximate location of the raised guard walk was likely the place where the projectile had been fired. Apparently the doctor had requested a check of the rifles issued to the guards on duty that night, but his request had been denied by the officer on duty, who cited that all of the rifles had been fired that night at precisely the same time and that the shooting had to have been an "unfortunate accident."

I read several accounts by prisoners who had discovered the body, stating that the victim had been shot in the head and that there was blood coming from the area of his nose or ears as well as behind his head. The doctor's report mentioned a concussion and fracture on the back of the skull, cuts and injured bones on the nose and face and knees, and a wound from a minié ball that had passed through the victim's hip. But nothing written by the doctor about a bullet wound to the head.

Dr. Comstock recalled a short conversation with a prisoner, Gus Pruett, a Confederate prisoner from Georgia and a friend of Virgil Cummings, as well as conversations with other witnesses on the scene. The doctor's comments stated that no one had actually seen who had fired the fatal shot that had hit Virgil Cummings and that in his opinion, "Most of the witnesses were blatantly unreliable."

Finally the doctor made note of having heard an officer warn the prisoners at the scene of the shooting that they were not to give any information concerning prison conditions or make remarks that would harm the reputation of the Union government. He finished his report by saying that he had personally witnessed neglect, harsh treatment, and unmonitored abuse by some of the prison guards as well as by one or two officers in the camp. However, most of the officers and guards seemed responsible in the carrying out of their duties, according to Dr. Comstock.

The doctor's report concluded, "It seemed clear to me that some of the prison officials were not interested in ascertaining the medical facts behind the shooting and had done what they could to silence the 'accident' as quickly as possible."

Another frustrating day had produced little about Virgil Cummings, other than the fact that the doctor had not stated the actual cause of his death. My mind was filled with questions that, as usual, would probably never be answered. I found that my eyes were getting weary, and I was hungry too, so I left the archives, bought a hamburger at McDonald's, then drove back to Southern Maryland to my cottage.

I was hoping that my place would look better then it had during my last visit and was pleasantly surprised with what I found. The usual number of pickup trucks, dump trucks, and carpenters could be seen, along with a Red Cross van and a few volunteers, who were busily handing out mops and buckets to help with the cleanup.

A Salvation Army van had been parked by the end of the road, and people were lined up to receive cold drinks and sandwiches provided by the organization. As I drove to my place, I waved to Mr. and Mrs. Manny, who were sitting out under the shade of a tree enjoying a cold drink of some kind. Then I parked my car and walked back to their yard.

"I see you have a little shade," I said to them.

"Hello there, young lady," said Mr. Manny as he stood up to greet me. Mrs. Manny stood up and gave me a hug.

"We were hoping to see you today," she said before sitting back down. "There are so many things going on here that we can't keep track of everyone."

Mr. Manny offered me his chair, but I told him that I needed to go check on my cottage. "It looks as though things are indeed getting cleaned up and you seem to have your electricity back on," I said.

"We lost our stove and refrigerator when the water got into the cottage, but the window air conditioners are operating because David hooked our cottage up to that little generator over there. The electric company says that the repairs will be finished soon, and we'll all be back online again," said Mr. Manny.

"Everything we need to visit for short spells is here. We have a cooler full of ice and food too. Please join us for a meal," said Mrs. Manny.

"Thank you," I said, "but I just ate, and I think I'll be good until late this evening."

"I'm sorry to report to you the sad news that several of the cottages will not be able to be repaired," Mrs. Manny said.

"Oh, that's not good news. Which cottages do you mean?" I asked.

"Mud Manor on the creek and the Carey cottage," she said. "The county won't let them repair their cottages, and it sounds like the state of Maryland may condemn both places. It doesn't make much sense to me."

"Well, can't they just rebuild?" I asked. I couldn't imagine the street without the Carey family or the folks at Mud Manor.

"There are new restrictions for building homes within so many feet of the Chesapeake, so they can't get permits to rebuild," Mrs. Manny said.

"That doesn't make sense to me," I said. "Why can't they get permits? There was a hurricane for Pete's sakes, and not as if they just let their cottages fall apart from neglect."

"I guess it depends on who you know at the permits office," said Mrs. Manny.

I could tell that Mrs. Manny was saddened for her neighbors as well as worried about her own little place.

"Say, young lady," said Mr. Manny, changing the subject, "did you ever find out about what happened to that prisoner you were telling us about?"

"Not a lot," I answered. "He was shot in the hip by a bullet that had been fired into his tent, apparently from the raised guard platform. I guess that sort of thing had happened several times at the Confederate prison, but I couldn't find an official death certificate, and his name isn't among the deaths listed at the monument site. The thing that intrigues me, though, is a doctor's report about the incident. Apparently it wasn't the gun wound that killed him but other wounds that had been found, such as head trauma, damaged kneecaps, and various other unusual wounds. Someone had to have beaten him before the minié ball passed through his hip. The beating may have been what killed him and not the bullet at all unless he bled to death from the rifle wound."

"You know," said Mrs. Manny, "I remember reading a little something about that. I don't know if an accurate count of the dead prisoners was ever compiled, and I've read about some of the violence that occurred there as well. I guess we'll never find out the full truth about what happened at that prisoner of war camp."

"There were investigations into the deaths there," I answered, "as well as several investigations for murder and neglect toward the prisoners, but I couldn't find a death notice or certificate for Virgil. It seems that after the war, records were sent to facilities where they were stored to be later compiled, but many men died in that camp without their names being mentioned anywhere, so finding actual death certificates seems an impossibility."

"That's a shame," said Mrs. Manny.

Just then we saw David drive his truck past us. He parked the truck near my cottage and walked back to greet us.

"How is everyone doing today?" David asked as he approached.

"Fine, we're doing just great," said Mr. Manny, standing to shake David's hand. I wondered how Mr. Manny could be so cordial despite what had happened to our neighbors. My mood was not so elevated.

"Would you like a nice glass of iced tea, David?" Mrs. Manny asked him.

"That sounds really good to me," he said. "Thank you."

Mrs. Manny opened up a large cooler and got out a paper cup, put some ice in it, and then poured iced tea from a plastic jug that had been cooling on the ice.

David accepted the iced tea with a smile and gulped it down. Then he looked at me in a sort of inquisitive way. "How are you?" he asked.

I wanted to ask him why he thought our neighbors were being denied rebuilding permits and why he couldn't use his influence to help them, but I thought that since Mr. Manny had changed the subject, I should try and cheer up as well.

"I want to thank you for all that you're doing for our little community," I said finally.

David looked at me and nodded. "It's the least I could do. After all, you people on this road have kept my great-uncle's homes up despite the bay eating away at them little by little."

"Your great-uncle?" I asked.

"Yes," he said, "I thought that you may have found that out since you've studied so much of the history in this area. I was going to tell you about it the day that I offered to meet you in Leonardtown. It was a bad time for you, so I thought I would save it for another time."

That's where my rudeness always comes back to kick me in the pants, I chided myself. "I thought that a man by the name of Lewis Chambers built this community?" I asked.

"Yes. That's him all right. He had big plans for this cluster of vacation cottages, but he hadn't figured that the bay wasn't going to cooperate. It still doesn't. Your cottages here on this street are all that's left of his carefully planned development."

"I wish you had let me in on that news, David," I said. "So your family goes back quite a ways in this area?"

"Yes, but then I don't want to claim that we go back as far as the *Ark* and the *Dove*. That would be pushing it." David laughed. "I would like to at least be the one person in the county not to claim that. However, my mother's side goes back quite a ways."

"Ms. Grant here has kept us captivated, along with the rest of the neighbors, with her stories of the prison and about the area during the years after the Civil War," said Mr. Manny. "Why don't the two of you kind folks share in the storytelling sometime soon?"

"I'd be happy to," David said. "Whenever Ms. Grant has the time. First though I need to get your OK on something, Ms. Grant. Could you step over to your cottage for a minute?"

"Sure," I said. "Mr. and Mrs. Manny, I'll tell you more about the information that I found at the archives later today, if there is time for that."

"I'm available to hear about that too whenever you all are," said David, a little too enthusiastically in my opinion.

"Yes," I said, "I enjoy listening to other people tell their history. We'll have to do that sometime."

"Just let me know when you find the time, *sometime*." David said.

Why hadn't I just left it alone? I seemed to always stress to others how busy I was. Why couldn't I just be gracious like everyone else around here? I felt my face flush again.

David thanked the Mannys for the iced tea and motioned for me to lead the way to my cottage. He said nothing as we avoided piles of debris on the roadside. A crew was still working on my roof, while another man was building a small step up to the side door; the hurricane had ripped it off, taking with it some of my siding.

"What did you want to ask me about?" I asked David.

"Take a look inside, and I'll tell you," he said.

Stepping inside the cottage, I saw several beams leaning up against the wall. "What do you think of those beams over there?" David asked.

"They look very old and rough," I answered. "Where did you get them?"

"Those beams were found under the flooring. I thought you might want to salvage them for use inside, maybe in the kitchen doorway. I was really surprised to see so much of it in such great shape. I think that most of the remaining cottages are sitting on newer lumber, which explains why your cottage held up foundationally much better than most of the others. This oak definitely has some history to it."

I could tell that carpentry was more than a job to this man. He touched the wood as though it were a living thing, pointing out the natural knots and rich colors bleeding through each piece. I saw that David's hands were rough and dotted with scars. Still they were strong hands, and I watched them as they tenderly touched the oak. David took my hand and put it on the wood.

"Just touch this wood," he said. "Can you feel how solid it is, practically petrified?"

"Yes," I said, taking my hand back. "Where do you think this wood was milled?" I put my hands into my pockets. David seemed not to notice my nervousness.

"Probably by some of the liberated black men after the Civil War. Lumber mills were one of the businesses that were open to them, and there were a number of mills owned by blacks after the Civil War that continued on up until the middle sixties. After the Civil Rights Act passed, some closed down their mills and moved up north to the factories where the wages were higher. I'm pretty certain that my great-uncle bought from the local mills here."

"David," I said, "I'm really looking forward to hearing more about this, and I apologize if I may have sounded uninterested in your history. I guess I just have a lot on my mind today."

He looked at me and smiled. "What if I have a motive behind my storytelling?"

"Motive? What motive?" I looked at David, who smiled and shook his head slightly.

"Nothing alarming," he answered. "I was just thinking that since we both like local history so much, you might want to spend some time doing a little research together. I realize that I may be overstepping my boundaries as a hired worker, but I guess I can't help myself. After all, we both helped to save the lives of the Carey family, so I felt that we had some type of friendship going on. Why not research together sometime? We are friends, right?" His brown eyes seemed to be searching for an answer and I hesitated.

"Yes, we're friends," I said.

"OK, see you later then," he said as he walked away satisfied with the little answer I gave him.

Later, in my room at the B&B, I sat on the bed wondering why I was so anxious over a normal conversation with a man. I didn't trust men, but at the same time I knew that all of them couldn't be bad. *What is wrong with me?* I asked myself. Then I started to berate myself—something I had become very proficient at.

After a few minutes, I decided that had beaten myself up enough for the day, so to shake it off, I left the B&B for a walk down Main Street in an effort to find a coffee shop. An ambulance rushed past me going to St. Mary's Hospital, and while I was watching the ambulance, I ran right into a woman who was in front of me, waiting for a seat at the Rumor Café. It was Miss Ellen.

"I'm so sorry," I said. "I was watching that ambulance and didn't see you."

"Oh, that's all right," said Miss Ellen, "I often find myself hurrying about. I guess we should all try to slow our lives down a little. Why, just look at Miss Biscoe. She's nearly one hundred years old, and she has often said in order to live life you've got to slow down and enjoy it."

"Well, I wouldn't question her authority on that subject. How is Miss Biscoe? I did want so much to come back and hear the rest of the history she was so kind to share with me."

"She is just fine as can be," said Miss Ellen. "In fact, that's why I'm here at the café. She just loves their shrimp salad sandwiches and often sends me over here to get one for her lunch to-go. When they are out of shrimp salad, she will settle for chicken salad. After she eats the shrimp salad, she will start in asking for her coconut cake. I figure, why lecture someone who has lived as long as she has?" Miss Ellen seemed truly fond of Miss Biscoe. "Should I tell her that you'll be returning for a visit soon?"

"Do you think that she would be available this afternoon, after lunch? If not, I can set something up for tomorrow morning. I know that she's a morning person." I was anxious to hear whatever stories Miss Biscoe would be willing to share with me and I wanted to get my mind off of David Woods. Realizing that I really didn't know how to be a friend to a man, I had been working out ways in my mind to avoid doing research with him, should he ask me again.

"Well, if you want to wait for me to get her sandwich, you are welcome to come back with me so that you can ask her yourself. She seems to have a lot of energy today."

I eagerly drove back to the little house, following Miss Ellen's old red truck, and after Miss Biscoe had finished her sandwich and had taken her catnap, I was able to see her. As usual, Miss Ellen served us fresh coffee and a big slab of coconut cake. "Miss Biscoe is betting that all this sugar is somehow not affecting her," said Miss Ellen. "She knows that the sugar is starting to take a toll, and yet still she insists on her coconut cake every single day. Now she's up to twice a day."

"Yes, and that isn't going to change much. I've been eating it every day for as long as I can remember, and I'm still here," Miss Biscoe said in her soft protesting way. "It's keeping me alive."

Miss Ellen smiled and excused herself while Miss Biscoe settled herself in her rocking chair. I placed her Indian blanket over her lap, covering her red toenails, and then I sat down.

"Now, I know that I was telling you about someone the last time that you came to visit. Who was that?"

"You were telling me a little about Peaches Wilkes the last time, and about his friend, Walter Graves. You told me about how hard it was for them farming and trying to make a living during the Depression."

"Oh yes, now I remember," she said. "I hope I don't repeat myself, but if I do, you just stop me."

I nodded, and Miss Briscoe continued her story.

Chapter 20

Guns and Oysters

"It hadn't taken Peaches a very long time to realize that he was running out of options for ways to support his family," said Miss Biscoe. "Tobacco wasn't bringing in much money back then. Farming vegetables and wheat helped for a while, but it wasn't enough to really get by on. Peaches always had big ideas for his family, and everyone who knew him admired the way he worked so hard. But hard work or not, things were not looking good for him.

"His best friend, Walter Graves, seemed to be doing much better after the still fiasco. It seems that the revenue agent, Cyrus Posey, had come up with a job for him, and the job involved oysters. Cyrus had himself a little oyster farm on the side and needed someone to take care of it for him. Walter was the man. He couldn't pay Walter much, but it was better then nothing, so Walter did that for many years while he did whatever he could to farm new seed crops with Peaches.

"It took a long time for the oyster beds to turn around, but they finally started to bring in a profit for Cyrus Posey and his partner, Walter. That was what was so hard for Peaches. He was going to lose the farm if he couldn't find a way to make a better living. Then came the oyster boom that Cyrus had hoped for.

"So Cyrus Posey was right about that?"

"Well yes," she continued, "and the big oyster boom was on the Potomac side of the bay and even way up the river. Anyway, it was around 1947 or so, the war was over, and men worked whatever jobs were available. A lot of men found work in the seafood industry. Now at that time the Maryland Tidewater Fisheries Commission put police boats in the Potomac River because oyster poachers were scooping the oysters up with dredging machines and robbing private oyster beds.

"So the fisheries people cleaned house. They let go of their lazy policemen and went about the business of hiring some new people to catch the oyster poachers. Cyrus Posey recommended Walter for the job."

I had questions about that. "Why would Cyrus want to do that for Walter?" I asked.

"I don't quite know the answer to that question," she said, "but I do know that Cyrus needed a friend, and he did have some history with Walter. Walter had tended oyster beds for Cyrus for many years, so Walter did know a lot about oysters by that time. Here is what I know about how Walter and Cyrus first got started with the oyster beds." Miss Biscoe continued her story.

∽

Walter couldn't believe his luck. Just when he thought he was going to go belly-up with the farm, and having somehow escaped jail when Cyrus and his agent found the still, he was hired to farm oysters for Cyrus.

"Walter, I want to do something to help out someone who used to be a friend," said Cyrus, sitting in Walter's kitchen the day after the fiasco with the still. "Remember how after school we would go behind the Wilkes farm and swim in the dammed-up creek? Those were days that I think about all the time, and more so lately. I'm just happy that

I didn't catch you and your neighbor down at your still. Those cows really did you a favor last night."

"So you know about what we were doing?" Walter was confused, and try as he might, he couldn't figure why Cyrus Posey had let them off the hook. Then he thought about Peaches. "It might be hard working for you when my other farmer friends find out about it. They might say I took up with a Judas."

Greta's mouth dropped open at her husband's statement.

"Walter, I know that not one person around here thinks that highly of what I've had to do for living, and I don't blame them for it. I hate my job, but as you know, it's the only job that allows me to care for my family. I had to take the agent job."

Walter put his hands in his overall pockets and sat back with his legs out in front of him.

"I'd like to help you and your family out for this very simple reason," Cyrus said. "I need friends, my children need friends, but most of all, my wife needs friends. Mrs. Graves, my wife speaks highly of you. She says that you do more for the temperance league than anyone, and I know that she would love to keep your friendship, though she realizes that we are not well thought of in the community. But Mrs. Graves, if it would be too uncomfortable for your family to befriend the Posey family, I would certainly understand it."

"I am quite sure that neither Walter nor I would have any problem at all with our two families being friendly. We temperance league ladies know how to influence our husbands. Why, any woman worth her salt can get by in that regard. We may not yet have won the battle, but we will continue to fight for women's rights, and we women will not tolerate drunken and abusive husbands running around in the woods like animals." Greta paused. "Mr. Posey, fate has put us together, and

Walter *will* take that job." Then Greta gave Walter a coy smile to beat all previous flirtations.

"Yes, dear, I *will*." Walter agreed.

Cyrus was relieved that Walter took the job, but in his mind he wondered if Greta Graves ever allowed Walter to speak for himself. "Thank you, Mrs. Graves," Cyrus said. "Walter, I'll put you to work in the oyster beds tomorrow, and we'll see how it goes from there." Cyrus stood and shook Walter's hand and then let himself out the back door.

"Wait," said Walter. "I just got to know one thing more. If it's such a good job, and you hate what you're doing, why don't you want the job?"

"If I could support my wife and children oystering full time, I would do it," Cyrus said. "Right now I have to keep my job. The government wants to control liquor now so that they can get that tax revenue, and these hold-out breweries all over the county are cheating the government out of some funds. Prohibition is really more about tax revenue shortfall then anything, you know, and I have some further still busting to do before my job is eventually phased out."

The explanation seemed reasonable to Walter, but he was still concerned about what his duties would be. "What am I supposed to do with the oysters?" Walter asked.

"The oysters are about to make a comeback after years of over-harvesting. The big oyster boom is coming, and I want to be in on it. That's why I need to get my beds full of seed oysters now. You can do that for me. Walter, my daddy had those beds producing good-quality oysters for twenty years before he died, and I've done all that I can do in my spare time to get the beds going again, but I can't do it alone. I need help your help. If the beds are a successful venture, then you and

I will have a business together, and I can give up this God-forsaken job of mine. Would you like to be my business partner, Walter?"

But the more Walter thought of what Peaches would think, working for a Judas and making money from it, the more he tried to figure a way out of the job offer. "From what I hear, there's not many oysters left out in the bay," declared Walter.

"On the contrary," said Cyrus, "people in town have been talking about the oysters coming back for some time, and many have put their oyster beds up the rivers."

"Well then," said Walter, "it's probably too late and too crowded to try and get started now."

Cyrus could tell that Walter wasn't buying what he was offering and decided to appeal to Walter's sensitive side.

"I'll give you one other simple reason for asking for your help, Walter. If you think my life is in danger catching moonshiners, just think about my life at the mercy of those oyster poachers and moonshine runners. There will eventually be plenty of business going up and down the Potomac, and if my name got out as an oysterman as well as a still buster, well, Walter, I'd be dead within a week. Some of the boys delivering moonshine on the river still have it out for me. I just need you to tend and safeguard my oysters. That's all I need for you to do."

"Cyrus was right about the boom. A few years later there were all kinds of activities over oysters. With that came poachers. By then Prohibition was over, and Cyrus had settled down to oyster farming and selling the succulent delicacy at a huge profit. That's why Cyrus put Walter in to become a Maryland Fisheries Commission policeman.

"Cyrus and his fellow oystermen were being robbed of their oysters. They called the oysters 'white gold.' Cyrus had made enough money to build a nice house for his family. His wife had recovered from her illness, and all seemed well, except for the fact that oyster poachers were about to change all of that.

"So, Cyrus was back at Walter's farm one day saying he had another job offer for him. Confident of their association by now, Walter sat up straight in his chair and asked what kind of job it was." Miss Biscoe shook her head.

"It's a job working for the Tidewater Fisheries Police," Cyrus told him. "I've put you in to be a Fisheries policeman so you can work out on the water protecting our investment."

"A policeman with a gun?" asked Greta. "Cyrus, you know that Walter has never owned a gun! Are you telling me that you want my husband to risk his life doing God knows what with guns for the sake of oysters?"

"It is dangerous," Cyrus replied, "but Walter can handle it. He'll be well trained, and he'll get an armed and trained pilot to assist him. Walter won't have to do a lot of shooting, and he won't have anyone after him because he's not a Judas, as they still refer to me."

"Well," said Miss Biscoe, "it wasn't long before Walter had been trained, tried, and equipped with a shotgun and an armed boat pilot. Then he was sent out on the new and much faster fisheries police boat. His life had become more than he ever thought it would be, and the pay wasn't bad either. Not only that, but Greta was advancing socially with the extra things that cash could buy, so no matter the danger, she was happy to send Walter out the door each night.

"Trouble was that Walter didn't like to work nights, leaving his beautiful wife, Greta, alone. But Walter couldn't think about those things while on duty. It was a dangerous job, and it called for absolute concentration on his part. But the other thing that bothered Walter was that he had no time to be able to see his friend Peaches Wilkes."

"So he loved his job?" I asked.

"You could say that," Miss Biscoe said, "but things went wrong for him. I often wondered how he could have taken that job in the first place. Everyone knew that he had a dreadful fear of guns or of killing anything. You just can't put a timid man in a position like that and expect for things to go right."

"What happened to him?" I asked.

"Poachers," she answered.

I settled in as Miss Biscoe continued her story.

Chapter 21

Potomac Poachers

Peaches watched Walter leaving for his patrol duty every night after supper. It made him anxious this night, knowing that Walter would soon be going off in the same direction that he would be going, but the Potomac was a big river, and Peaches was sure he could avoid his former friend. Lately he had taken to calling Walter "Judas II," and he had no intentions of allowing Judas II to catch him poaching oysters.

Peaches got into his old truck and waited for Walter to drive out of sight before starting up the Ford and heading out for the river. As Walter turned north toward Leonardtown, Peaches turned south where he kept a boat in a little cove just off of the St. Mary's River. From there he and two of his friends would head out in the evenings after dark to dredge oysters from the Potomac. This night he took his son, Reuben along with him.

More then once, Peaches thought about what he was doing and felt real shame for it too because he knew that if Walter ever found out what Peaches was up to, he would probably have to put him in jail. But then Peaches always figured that Walter was too softhearted to do that—either that or just plain chicken. He had also heard about the scant training that these water policemen received and figured that it would take a lot for someone so frightened of guns, like Walter had always been, to actually use one.

While Walter stood on the deck of the fisheries boat scanning the moonlit Potomac for movement, Peaches and his son quietly did the same. They could spot a Tidewater Fisheries Police boat a mile away and take measures to avoid it. The bow of a fisheries boat was capped with metal seams, and metal liked to shine in moonlight. Their motors were noisy too, unlike the special muffled motor that Peaches built for his boat.

Peaches and Reuben had been going up the Potomac slowly and quietly in the little boat for nearly an hour now, and not seeing anything shiny, Peaches ordered his son to prepare the dredge and then signaled him to put it over the side. Hearing nothing that sounded like a patrol boat, Peaches figured that Walter must be on the other side of the river and that he could easily pull in a load of oysters before the Tidewater Fisheries Police patrol boat could reach this side.

Reuben carefully swung the dredge arm over the side of the boat and began hand-cranking the scraper down into the Potomac waters without making a sound. He had recently oiled the winch and was proud of the fact that his father trusted in him and relied on him, and that was a good feeling.

Peaches was ready for the oyster beds he was sure to find and the money he would make, especially with oysters going for such a high price. He also figured that before the coldest of the weather started up, he had better take his chances, police or not, and try his luck before the hard-core poachers came out of the little creeks and inlets all along the Potomac. Cool weather was when the oyster season really got to going.

The recent demand for the white gold after World War II seemed to be making a big comeback. But Peaches didn't want to mess with any of those big poachers from the Virginia side of the river. They could be meaner than any fisheries policeman.

The small gas motor, specially refitted right in Peaches's barn, was made with a muffler encasement making the noise from the engine barely audible. It wasn't powerful enough to outrun a fisheries boat, but Peaches's boat also carried a second motor that could be quickly engaged to give a jolt of horsepower for escape, should a chase ensue. The escape motor gas tank was filled up and ready to run, but the little motor was all that was needed for now as it purred the boat slowly along, allowing the oyster scraper to hop along the bottom in the shallows near the riverbank.

Peaches, unlike some of the dredgers who crossed over the Potomac River from the Northern Neck of Virginia, actually feared being caught, though he hid this fear from his son. Reuben trusted his father and could find no reason to question his way of making a living for the family. But Peaches did some fearing nonetheless.

The first reason he was fearful was because of the shame that an arrest would bring to his family, and the second reason was that Walter would have to make a choice if he caught Peaches, and Peaches was not absolutely certain that Walter would be able to let him go. The third reason was that his beautiful wife, Betsy, would become the shamed wife of a jailbird, and she could never run the farm by herself in his absence. That reason alone was enough for him to make every effort to be careful.

Peaches and Reuben had already tried two locations, and having found no oysters to show for their effort, Peaches decided to rely on a conversation that he had overheard at the Hughesville Farmers' Market. He heard a farmer say that a little farther up the Potomac, near the Maryland side by the place where John Wilkes Booth had crossed the river, was where the mother lode could be found.

Though Peaches knew that he would be encroaching on some-one's oyster bed, he considered that his family was in need of winter clothes as well as some savings so he could one day send Reuben to college. "Necessity dictates decision," Peaches's father, Tiberius, once told him. So Peaches told Reuben to raise the dredge up again, and the two proceeded up the Potomac. The little boat finally stopped near the area of the Booth crossing. Every fisherman knew where that was.

Once again, Reuben swung the boom around and went about put-ting the dredge contraption over the side. Soon the scraper hit the bottom of the river, and it was time to start the little motor. Reuben gave a thumbs-up, and Peaches started the motor, which purred qui-etly to life. The boat moved along slowly, dragging the heavy scraper over the riverbed. Reuben manipulated the boom and watched the tension on the line as the scraper bounced along the bottom. Soon the boat was slowing as the scraper had caught on something.

About then Peaches shut the motor off and walked over to assist Reuben in turning the winch. "Well," said Peaches, "let's see what we've got."

The pulley struggled as the two turned the winch, using nearly all of their strength to get the scraper off the bottom of the river. Reuben gave a painful smile to his father as the two worked the winch. When the last of the cable line was pulled up, they saw, enclosed in the wire net, beautiful, barnacle-clad, colossal oysters.

The amount and size of the catch assured Peaches that he had indeed struck the right spot, and instantly he began calculating how many pounds and at what market price it would take to buy himself a better boat with a better winch. That way he could poach more oys-ters and send his son to the best black college available, maybe even Morehead College down in Georgia that he had heard so much about. His mind was racing as he continued to pull the boom around.

Reuben assisted as they opened the jaws of the scraper and let the load fall to the bottom of the boat. The weight was massive, and Peaches made up his mind right then to hide this load close to shore near Pope's Creek and then come back to the same spot for more. They would keep their catch in the creek until Peaches could get his friends to come back with their boats and help him haul the oysters to market. All of this was going through his mind

But Peaches had forgotten about Walter, who was now near the middle of the river, standing on the bow of the fisheries boat, looking up and down the Potomac with his binoculars. Walter had lately been feeling confident for the first time in his life. The training was quick and easy. The weapons he had, at least in his mind, were not designed for killing but only for sinking the boats of the runaway oyster pirates. He had fired the shotgun at the training yard, but remained sure that he would never have to use it to shoot at a person. He'd never liked violence of any kind.

As for his service revolver, it stayed nice and neat in a side holster, having also been fired only a few times at the shooting range. Hopefully it would stay in the holster, unused as well. He remembered the days when he and Peaches would go hunting possum and squirrel. It was always Peaches who did the killing and skinning of the poor old animals. For that he was grateful. Yet just having the guns in his possession seemed to make him stand a little taller.

"Hey, Walter," said his pilot, breaking Walter's dreaming, "I think I hear something." Walter turned his good ear in the direction that the boat pilot pointed to.

"I don't hear nothing," said Walter.

"Well, if you can't hear that noise, I don't know what to tell you," complained the pilot. "It sounds like one of them muffled small motors to me. You know, people been using them little motors around here to poach oysters from the river."

"Oyster pirates don't use muffled motors," said Walter, "because they can't get enough power out of them to escape the police boats. It's probably just a couple of night fishermen. This is the best part of the river for night fishing."

But his boat pilot had seen this attitude in Walter before and figured that Walter was afraid of confronting some of the poachers who had been running up and down the river causing trouble, stealing oysters, and even falling overboard and drowning after a few too many beers.

Most of them were the good old boys from the Northern Neck of Virginia, but not all. Lately some St. Mary's and Charles County men had been caught poaching too. One man from La Plata had died in the river after having his small fishing boat run over by a speeding poacher from Virginia. Tension was growing high between the two states as both claimed rights to the river and everything that moved in it.

"I'm going to set the boat in the direction of the noise and see what we can see," said the pilot.

"Well, I can't see frightening off some fishermen, but go ahead if you think you hear a poacher." Walter looked through his binoculars. The fisheries boat proceeded up the river, and Walter suggested that they go into the shallows of Pope's Creek and wait until they could both hear something.

Pulling the boat into the cove, the pilot turned on the spotlight so as to avoid the shallows. The pilot shone the light around, making sure the boat didn't run aground. As the light shone here and there,

Peaches and Reuben stood up, frozen in the brightness and covering their eyes from the glare of the spotlight.

Walter couldn't believe who he saw standing there. "That you, Peaches?" he asked. "And is that little Reuben there with you? What you two doing all the way up here in the Potomac?"

"You know those guys?" asked the boat pilot.

"Yeah, I know them. They're my old friends and neighbors," he answered. "Catching any perch or rockfish tonight?" asked Walter as he signaled the pilot to draw closer. "You fellows are sure up the river quite a ways."

"No, just going out now," Peaches lied. "We're in the cove here looking for some soft crabs. You know how the rockfish love soft crabs."

"Boy, if I wasn't on duty tonight, I'd sure be joining you two. How you doing, Reuben?"

Reuben made sure that the bow of the boat was facing the police boat and that he and his father were blocking the view of the dredging basket and the oysters scattered along the bottom of the bow. "I'm fine, Mr. Walter," said Reuben, "just fine."

"What's that behind them?" asked the pilot as he peered over the side of the boat. "Just fishing, huh? Looks to me like you're dredging for oysters!"

Walter looked and saw the oysters and the basket now lying on the bottom of the boat. "Peaches, what are you doing there?"

"Oh, Walter," Peaches said, "you can see what I'm doing. I'm trying to keep my family fed."

Walter looked at Peaches and wanted to cry. Cyrus Posey had found work for Walter, but Peaches had not been able to find a job anywhere. Tobacco had gone under, and the oyster business had been plunged into the hands of regulators and state agencies. Only a few in with the government of Maryland could rob the oyster beds. They'd been caught doing it a time or two, but nobody ever penalized them. They always said they were testing the oysters for size and quality, a sort of inventory as to the progress of the oyster comeback. The average man just trying to make a living was chased up and down the river and bay like a common criminal. Walter rubbed his forehead and stood thinking all of these things as the pilot waited for Walter to take some action.

"What are you going to do with these two?" the pilot finally asked.

"Make them put the oysters back in the river and skedaddle," Walter replied.

"OK," said the pilot, "but we got to write something up, don't we?" The pilot could see that Walter was not following regulations. "Don't we need a report?"

"No," said Walter, "we don't!"

Reuben lowered his head. "I'm sorry, Mr. Walter."

"Peaches," Walter said, clearly upset, "you and Reuben haul them oysters back right now to the oyster bed where you got them and dump them out. When you done that, you can get going back to St. Mary's and I don't want to see you up here in this part of the river again!"

Peaches knew he had caused damage to Walter's position and to his pride as well, but he was angry just the same. He thought about the day, years back, when Cyrus Posey had helped Walter get a job with the

Maryland Tidewater Commission Fisheries Police and about the way Walter drove off to work every night, not having to worry about Greta or their children being clothed and fed.

"Fine," Peaches hollered. "I'll put them back, but you can't tell me where I'm going to oyster or how I'm going to do it. I got people to feed and clothe, and if there's a way I can do that, I'm going to do it!"

Walter glared at his old friend. "Then use tongs to get your oysters," he reasoned. "You know you can tong oysters. Why you got to break the law by dredging?"

Peaches was irritated and wondered why Walter could never figure anything out. "It would take me three times the amount of time and labor to tong enough oysters to feed my family. Look at me! I'm getting old, and so are you. You're riding around in a big boat, and I got just this stinking little boat trying to make a living. Let me keep the oysters I caught," he pleaded.

"Can't," said Walter. "You get going back down the river and dump those oysters, and we're going to follow behind and make sure you do it." Walter turned his back and signaled the pilot to steer aside so that Peaches could go by. The pilot kept the light on Peaches and began to follow the little dredge boat out of the cove.

Peaches finally made his way back into the Potomac River, but before the fisheries boat was out of the cove, a large speedboat flew past them, sending up wake and a torrent of water over Peaches's boat, almost capsizing it.

"What the…?" shouted Walter.

"I think it's that Crazy Larry again," shouted the pilot. "You want to go get him this time, Walter?"

Walter could picture what would have happened to Peaches and Reuben if their boat had been rammed. "Yes!" Walter shouted. "Peaches, you get back in the cove and take cover. Crazy Larry is known for speeding up and down the river, and you aren't safe on the water as long as he's running it. You dump those oysters right here, and then you and Reuben hide, you hear?"

"OK," said Peaches, but he had no intention of dumping anything or hiding.

Walter gave the signal, and the pilot roared his two outboard motors full bore. The engines caught and nearly knocked Walter down. Off they sped in pursuit of Crazy Larry.

∾

"What happened next?" I asked.

"Dear," said Miss Biscoe, "I'm real tired all of a sudden. I think I need to rest a little. Would you mind if I just took a little nap?"

I took her hand in mine and patted it. "Miss Biscoe, I've kept you talking longer then I should have. Thank you so much for today." But before I could finish, Miss Biscoe's head was back in the corner of the rocker, and her face was relaxed in slumber. I wished that I could get sleep like that, suddenly and deeply. Why did my mind always race the moment my head hit the pillow?

Miss Ellen came out of the kitchen. "Oh, is she out again?" Miss Ellen put the Indian blanket up higher on Miss Biscoe's lap. "The dear thing can talk herself into a coma sometimes."

I nodded and quietly thanked Miss Ellen, letting myself out the door. The thought hit me that perhaps Linda Graves could fill in what Miss Biscoe had been relating, so I headed back to the B&B.

When I arrived, Linda was putting some fresh tea bags beside a silver platter loaded with assorted cookies and scones. "Hi there," said Linda. "There was a message for you, so I transferred it up to your room."

"Thanks," I said. "I've just had the opportunity to visit with Miss Biscoe again, and I have to thank you for putting me in touch with her. She has told me some fascinating things, as you have, and I'm very grateful."

"You are very welcome," said Linda. "I love to share my family history. Have you found out any new information about Walter and Peaches?"

"Yes, but I'm afraid that Miss Biscoe wore herself out telling me a story about them."

"Which story was she sharing?"

"It was about the day that Walter caught Peaches and Reuben dredging oysters near Pope's Creek."

"Yes, I remember that story very well. Daddy was very good about sharing and writing down family history, and Miss Biscoe has also been a source for what he didn't write down. Tell you what," Linda offered, "let me finish up in here, and after you've listened to your message, and I've checked in the guests who should be arriving any minute, we'll meet down here for tea and cookies, and I'll try to fill in the rest of the story for you."

"That would be wonderful," I said. "Thank you." Then turning to the stairs, I hurried up to my room and hit the message button on the phone. The message was from David Woods.

"Rainey, this is David Woods. Please give me a call when you get a chance."

He sounded a little upset, so I grabbed a pencil and recorded the phone number. The call was answered by a lady who said, "St. Mary's Hospital." She paged David for me, and soon he was on the phone.

"David, this is Rainey. What's going on, and why are you at the hospital?"

"I'm here at the hospital with Mrs. Manny," he answered. "Mr. Manny was just brought in by ambulance and may have suffered a heart attack or stroke. The doctor is talking with Mrs. Manny right now."

"Oh no," I cried, "not Mr. Manny! I'll be there in a few minutes."

"I thought that you'd want to come over," said David. "I'll be waiting in the emergency room lobby for you. I'm sure that Mrs. Manny will be grateful that you're taking the time to come over. She seems a little disoriented."

I thanked him and grabbed my purse and keys from the table and hurried down the stairs. "I'm on my way to the hospital," I said to Linda. "A good friend of mine is in the ER, and I'm going over now to see what's happened."

"Is there anything that we can do?" Linda asked, concerned.

"I don't know yet, but thank you." I said as I hurried out of the B&B.

The short drive took less then three minutes. Once inside the emergency area I saw Mrs. Manny speaking with David in the hallway. I went up to them and asked if Mr. Manny was all right.

"Yes," said Mrs. Manny, "I trusted the Lord to heal him, and the Lord answered my prayer. The doctor says that my husband's heart isn't damaged. They took a lot of pictures and gave him tests, but it appears that he has been overworking himself, helping with the cottage repairs, and became a little overheated. David tried to get him to sit and take it easy, but he wanted to help the neighbors pick up debris in their yards and didn't pay much attention to the heat. The doctor thinks that he suffered a heat stroke, but not a serious one."

My heart was pounding as I took Mrs. Manny's hands in mine. I had heard that heat strokes were very serious and sometimes deadly. "I am so relieved to hear that it wasn't more serious, and that Mr. Manny will be all right. How long will they keep him here in the hospital?"

"Well, I think they'll keep him overnight for observation. The doctor on duty said that they'll let him go home after he gets some IV fluids in him. He's very dehydrated. Hopefully we can go back down to the cottage tomorrow. We'll have to see what the doctor says." Mrs. Manny squeezed my hands and gave a sigh of relief. "It was so good of you to come, and we just can't thank you enough for your thoughtfulness."

"How did you get here?"

"David called the ambulance, and then I drove up with him. He has offered to stay here with me tonight and wait to see if Mr. Manny does well, and I told him that he should go back to all that work he has to do, but he wouldn't go, bless his heart."

"I have an idea," I said. "Why don't I take you over to the B&B where I'm staying? You could rest in my room, and I'll stay here with David to check on Mr. Manny. If anything happens, we'll call you or come and get you. It's only down the street a few minutes. You look so tired, and Mr. Manny will be sleeping all night. Why don't you try to get some sleep? That way you can care for him when he's released tomorrow." I wasn't going to take no for an answer, and I think Mrs. Manny realized that.

"Oh dear," she said, "I've never been away from him a single night in our marriage. What if he wakes up and finds that I'm not here with him?"

"Don't you worry about that," I said. "I'll come right over to get you and bring you back to the hospital if that happens. The B&B is just around the corner."

Mrs. Manny looked into my eyes and agreed. "I really could use a little nap," she said. "All right, if David wants to stay here while you take me to the B&B, I guess I could go rest for a few minutes, but I do hate to put you good folks to such bother."

David agreed to the plan and assured Mrs. Manny that he would stay. We left and drove straight to the B&B. Mrs. Manny was quiet, and I knew she was exhausted from the ordeal as well as apprehensive about leaving her husband. "I'll just take a little nap," she reminded me.

Linda graciously welcomed Mrs. Manny and offered any assistance that she could provide. I took Mrs. Manny up to my room and helped her get situated. Linda brought up some fresh sheets and towels, changed the bed linens, and left some cookies and milk on the night-stand. "Let me know if you need anything at all, Mrs. Manny," she said. "I remember that you stayed with us once before."

After reassuring Mrs. Manny again that I would call her, I thanked Linda and drove back to the emergency room. There I found David chatting away with Mr. Manny who was smiling from his prone position on the hospital bed.

"Rainey," said Mr. Manny, "thank you for taking the missus to your room. I'm feeling just great now that my veins are taking in a lot of fluid. Guess I did overdo it a bit today, but the doctor came in and said that they're putting me in a room with a television and a pretty nurse to watch over me, so I'm a lucky fellow from my point of view. He said I could go home tomorrow morning if my veins cooperate."

David laughed at the nurse joke and told Mr. Manny that we would be staying the night in the waiting room and that we would be taking turns sitting with him. Mr. Manny protested as a nurse and an attendant pushed his bed down the corridor. "You two don't need to stay here." He continued to protest until he was put in the elevator for the trip up to the third floor, and the elevator door had closed behind him.

"I wonder what Mrs. Manny would say about the pretty nurse comment," I said.

"She would probably let it go right over her head," David answered. "I would think that Mrs. Manny is pretty secure by now, don't you think so?"

"No woman is ever that secure," I said. "Did you get some dinner tonight?" I'm sure the cheeriness in my voice was due to absolute relief.

"Not really," he said, "but if Mr. Manny goes down for the night, I may run out and grab us a couple of burgers if you'd like one."

"Yes," I said. "Fries too, please."

"Ketchup?"

"Lots," I said. "Why don't you go now? I'm starving all of a sudden." I guess I was so relieved that Mr. Manny was all right that I forgot my manners. David didn't seem to mind.

"Can do," he said. "See you up in Mr. Manny's room then." I wanted so much to just hug David, but instead I took his hand and thanked him for what he had done for the Mannys. It seemed to me that David was always rescuing someone, and my relief that Mr. Manny would be alright caused me to babble on until David patted my shoulder and said, "Everything is going to be fine, Rainey."

The night passed without incident. Mr. Manny slept soundly while David and I took turns keeping an eye on him or sleeping on the waiting room sofa. I was tired and looked terrible, but I didn't care that my makeup was half off or that I needed a shower; Mr. Manny would be OK.

The next morning I brought Mrs. Manny back to the hospital. A doctor signed Mr. Manny out, and he was dressed and ready to go by nine thirty. David put the happy couple into his truck, and I waved good-bye as they departed for their cottage. It had been a long evening, and I was glad to get back to my room at the B&B.

Linda filled me in on Mrs. Manny. "She is a very sweet lady, and quite the talker. She told me that she hardly gets a word in edgewise when Mr. Manny is around. Is that true?"

"I guess it's true," I answered, "but she adores him above all others and laughs at his jokes. She's probably been hearing the same jokes for years."

"Rainey," said Linda, "I know that you're probably absolutely bushed about now, but I thought that I might fill you in and sort of give a conclusion to the story about Walter and Peaches, after you've had time to rest."

"I would really love that," I said. "In fact, I'm running on adrenaline now and probably couldn't sleep if I had to. Why not continue now?"

"Where did you say that Miss Biscoe left off? Was it about the time that Crazy Larry appeared on the scene?" Linda asked.

"Yes," I said. "What a name!"

Chapter 22

The Chase

Crazy Larry was famous in the Northern Neck of Virginia as well as in St. Mary's and Charles County, Maryland, each being situated on the Potomac River. He knew that river well, and some thought that he had some sort of ESP about where the oyster beds were. With the fastest boat on the Potomac to get him around, he could outmaneuver anything the Tidewater Fisheries Police could put in the water, and he enjoyed himself immensely when he could lure them into a chase.

He lived on a little cove somewhere on the Virginia side—nobody knew exactly where—but he knew every single cove from Dahlgren to Kilmarnock, and he made sure that he also knew the people who lived along those inlets. After all, he kept them supplied with the best oysters around for a reasonable price, and they in turn allowed him to hide in their coves whenever he had to run from the police boats. He also delivered home brew up and down the river for an additional fee.

This one particular night, Crazy Larry went out by himself—an unusual tactic and a dangerous one as well. But he had downed a few extra beers that night after his wife had kicked him out of the house again. Finding that his usual crew of poachers didn't want to go out with him—because he drove crazy even when sober—he told them all where they could go and went out by himself.

He headed straight for the grand oyster bed near Pope's Creek without bothering to slow his boat down once he got across the river. He must have made up his mind that it would be difficult to oyster by himself, so he might as well just harass the police. He waited to see who would give chase while he drank a few more beers, throwing the bottles into the river.

Walter had just about gotten back into the river when Crazy Larry saw the spotlight of the Fisheries boat. That's when Crazy Larry raced by, hollering a rebel yell at the policemen. He knew it would take them a few minutes to get out of the narrow and shallow inlet, and by that time he figured he could run up and down the river until the slower fisheries boat would eventually run out of gas. That had happened several times before.

Walter, on the other hand, had taken all he could from Crazy Larry. He had been teased by the other men on Potomac River patrol duty who said that even if Walter had the chance, he wouldn't fire his weapon at poachers. Several of those on duty had fired at poachers, resulting in a few Virginia men getting shot up pretty badly. But sadly, in return, a Tidewater Fisheries Policeman had been shot and killed. The police were out for vengeance, but the crew-short police seemed like sitting ducks as long as Crazy Larry ruled the Potomac River.

Walter realized that his friends were in danger as long as Crazy Larry was around, so this time Walter came up with an idea to fool him. After racing the boat out to the center of the Potomac, he ordered the pilot to cut the motor off and turn off the running lights.

"This is not a good plan," the pilot cautioned Walter, "and I'm not in the mood to get run over by a boat the size of a yacht! How's Crazy Larry going to know where we are? He's going to run over the top of us, you'll see!"

"He won't," said Walter. "Just grab your weapon and sit tight. This guy's toying with us, and we're goanna sink his big, beautiful boat right out from underneath him."

The pilot took a shotgun out of the gun box and loaded it along with two other weapons. Walter took his shotgun off of its rack and made sure that it was loaded and the safety was off. Soon they could hear the speedboat turning around and coming back in their direction.

About then, Peaches and Reuben had slowly made their way out of the inlet and along the shore as they headed back to the oyster bed. The oysters were still hidden in the bow of the boat, and Peaches was directing Reuben so that they wouldn't get too close to shore but near enough to the oyster bed. They could hear the fast boat out in the Potomac but not the police boat. "I think Mr. Walter has given up the chase," said Reuben.

"He never liked chasing anything, so it only makes sense that he won't chase that fool out there in the dark," said Peaches. "Pull up about another hundred yards and a little farther out in the river. I want to drop the jaws down one more time before we run for home."

"But we were told to stay in the cove and not touch another oyster out of that bed," protested Reuben. "Uncle Walter is goanna be cross with us."

"Yeah, I know, I know," said Peaches, "but since we can't ever come back here when Walter's around, we may as well get a few more oysters to tide us over."

Soon Peaches had the boom arm over the side of the boat and quickly lowered the dredge. "Start up the little motor and go in and out the river real slow like, so we can scoop up a load and get out of here," Peaches said.

Reuben did as he was told, but this time in a nervous state, he accidently started up the wrong motor. Instead of the muffled motor, the large motor jerked into forward motion. Over the side went Peaches. Before Reuben could straighten out the boat and slow it down, he heard the speedboat coming right for him. With its super loud motors roaring, and just before the boats collided, Reuben jumped overboard and swam in the direction where Peaches had been thrown.

The collision was more than terrifying. Smoke and flame went up so high in the dark that Peaches could see Reuben treading water while debris hit all around him. "Reuben, I'm over here!" Peaches hollered as he grabbed on to some debris. "Just keep swimming! I can see you, son."

Reuben swam until he reached his father, and the two of them each grabbed more boards from their destroyed boat and tried to float for the shore together. Parts of their boat flew up in the air and landed all around them, still in flames and lighting up the oil-slicked water.

Walter stood on the bow of the fisheries boat as the pilot raced toward the explosion. Panic-stricken, Walter could see that Peaches had not obeyed his orders. A plank from Peaches's boat shone in the glare of the searchlight as well as several life jackets, a bushel basket on fire, and a piece of the oyster dredge still attached to the side of what was left of the boat.

Walter gave orders to the pilot, and the police boat slowed carefully near the flames. "Peaches! Peaches!" Walter shouted. "Reuben! Peaches! Can you hear me?" Walter was in such a state that the pilot cut the motor and went up to the bow to help search for victims.

"Nobody could survive a crash like this," said the pilot. "We need to radio in for assistance." The pilot went into the pilothouse and called in.

Walter could see that debris from the speedboat and the debris from Peaches's boat were mingled together with oil and gasoline.

Plumes of flame lit up the area as spots of fire continued to burn pieces of the boats, which were now drifting south in the river's current. Walter knew then that his best friend, Peaches, and his son, Reuben, were dead.

Sobbing, Walter thought about all the times that Peaches had given Walter the better ideas in nearly every situation they had faced together. Why couldn't Peaches have listened to Walter just this once? Hadn't Walter given him the best and safest advice that he could this time? Walter put his face in his hands and let out a mournful cry. "I'm sorry my dear friends. What have I done?"

The boat pilot came out and tried to console him. "I'm pretty sure nobody suffered in a crash like this," he said. "I'm sorry about your neighbors, but you know they were poaching oysters, and they knew they were doing illegal dredging. You told them to stay put, and they didn't listen to you either." But Walter continued to sob, so the pilot left him there and went back to the radio room again.

"Stop that bellyaching, Walter," said Peaches from the water, "and give us a hand up!"

Walter looked down and saw two faces glowing in the residual light of the flames, both men hanging on to floating pieces of boat. In a state of disbelief, Walter stared over the side of the boat.

"How about giving us a hand up or something?" Peaches shouted as Walter stood gawking down at them. Then Walter quickly positioned a ladder over the side and put a hand out to help. Reuben first grabbed hold, followed by Peaches.

Once they were safely onboard, Walter and Peaches hugged each other and slapped one another's backs. Reuben couldn't stop thanking his Uncle Walter as Peaches shouted out, "I should have listened to you, Walter. I'm sorry. I risked your life and the life of my son tonight, but you saved us. Thank you, my friend!"

When the pilot saw the camaraderie between the two older men, one black and one white, one a policeman and the other a poacher, he shook his head. Now he had seen everything.

∾

"It was then that their friendship was solidified for life," said Linda. "They never did find the body of Crazy Larry, but some of his family and friends put some scathing editorials in the Virginia and Maryland papers, and there was some talk of the Northern Neck of Virginia seceding. Of course, as always, the talk was short-lived. People say that the ghost of Crazy Larry still haunts the Potomac to this day. But then, people tend to make heroes out of rebels." Linda gave a laugh and motioned with her hands that the story was over.

"What a story that was," I said. "I'm so glad that Walter and his friends survived! What happened to them after that?"

"Something pretty amazing," answered Linda. "Walter got Peaches a job with the Maryland Tidewater Fisheries Commission making his silent mufflers for their chase boats, and after that they both ran a little oyster and crab house together on the Potomac River, until they got too old to continue. If you've ever been to Crabby Sally's Crab Shack on the Potomac River, then you've been to the original site where they had their little business. I think there are three or four of those crab houses around the area now."

"Wow," I said, "how did they come up with that name?"

"Sally was Greta Graves's mother, and I guess she wasn't the loving mother-in-law Walter had wished for when he asked Greta to marry him, so Crabby Sally was the name he chose. Anyway, their crab cakes and oyster stew were legendary around here. They had customers coming down for their food from as far away as Baltimore."

"So they're a real life example of sticking together no matter what. True friendship," I said.

"Yes, and I'm proud to say that my grandfather made something of himself. People recalled at his funeral that he displayed many acts of kindness in his lifetime. They said that Walter was a kindhearted man who loved his neighbors as himself. He was truly a fine Christian man. He and Peaches had a friendship that survived all obstacles. My grandfather never stopped talking about their escapades until the day he died, and when he passed away, Peaches gave my grandfather the most heartwarming eulogy. Everyone laughed and cried over what Peaches had to say."

"Miss Biscoe said that Peaches lived a very long life?"

"Yes, he did. When they buried him, there was a procession of cars over a mile long. Miss Biscoe sat right up front at the service, and my father, Wesley Graves, gave the eulogy at his funeral, recalling events that grandfather had shared with him. Miss Biscoe sang some of Peaches's favorite gospel tunes. What a voice she had! You know, she is quite an interesting lady; in fact, it was her recipe that Walter and Peaches used to season their steamed crabs at the crab shack. She told me one time that the recipe came from a relative of hers and that it had been passed down for many years in her family. Something was said once about a prisoner of war at Point Lookout passing the recipe down, but I'm not sure about that. You would have to ask Miss Biscoe."

"How did the family get by after Walter passed away?"

"Well, my grandmother Greta was very lonely for her husband and never really got over his death. Somehow in their latter years she had come to love him and dote on him every chance she got. I remember the way she would always make his favorite cake when we children would visit. I can say that their love for one another was very strong toward the end of their lives. She survived grandfather a few years and then joined him in heaven.

My grandfather Walter made enough of a living off of his duties with the Tidewater Fisheries Commission Police, as well as the crab shack, to put my father, Wesley Graves, through college. He was the youngest of the Graves family and showed the best aptitude for studies. My father graduated with honors from St. Mary's College and went on to earn a law degree at Georgetown. I wish you could meet him sometime."

"That would be the icing on the cake for me," I said. "You've told me this story in a way that brings it all together, and I almost feel that I know these people. Thank you very much."

"You are very welcome," she answered.

"Do you know what happened to Peaches's son, Reuben?" I asked.

"Yes, I do. Reuben took over the crab shacks and became a successful businessman. He went to Morehead College and then on to business school at Emory University in Atlanta later on. He's still running the crab shacks, from what I hear. In fact, if you go to the original Crabby Sally's on Pope's Creek, you'll see pictures of Walter and Peaches all over the walls. He loved his father, but he also loved his 'Uncle Walter.'"

"I know one thing now," I said. "My next crab cake is going to come from that very crab shack. I can't wait to meet him, and I hope that he won't mind my interest in his family."

"I can tell you for sure that he won't mind at all. Reuben probably has so much more to tell about his family then I could tell you; things that you wouldn't think to ask. I'd be happy to go with you and intro-duce you to Reuben sometime if you'd like me to," she offered.

"Yes! I would love that," I said.

Having come to the end of the lives of Peaches and Walter, I had mixed emotions. I wanted to story to go on, but this story ended on a happy note. I had to let it go.

I knew that happy endings were rare. In fact, most of my research efforts so far had become dead ends.

I imagined that Virgil Cummings must have met an untimely death and that his descendants were among those who returned year after year to the Point Lookout monument, seeking answers about men who had vanished like the ruins of the prisoner of war camp had. In a way I felt sorry for Bennett Cummings and wondered if his search ever brought him the truth about his father's death.

Back in my room, I received a call from David Woods, and I was grateful that this time it wasn't about some other neighbor in trouble.

"Hey," David asked, "do you feel like joining me for lunch tomor-row at Rumor Café? I'll be in Leonardtown on business, and I wanted to share some information that you may be interested in."

I hesitated. "What information is that?" I asked. *I hope he isn't asking me for a date*, I thought.

"I'll tell you tomorrow," he said. "It's about history, and I think you'll be glad you came."

I told him that I would like to meet about his information. Meeting for a little lunch and some history lessons sounded fine with me, and I kind of looked forward to it.

❧

The next day I put a little lipstick on and my new jeans with a white blouse that I had bought in Leonardtown. *What am I doing?* I soon asked myself. Then I removed my lipstick with a tissue before driving to meet him.

We were served right away at Rumor Café and devoured the cornbread and crab bisque along with soft crab sandwiches.

"How is the research going?" David asked.

"It's going very well," I answered. "There are so very many wonderful people to learn about around this area. I've learned a little about your great-uncle, the developer of our cottages back in the 1920s. Linda, the B&B owner, has shared stories with me about her family and their lives in post–Civil War Maryland. She also put me in touch with an elderly woman who added more interesting facts. I've done a lot of research on the lives of the men who were prisoners at Point Lookout by searching the Maryland State Archives in Annapolis also, so I would say that I'm a very happy researcher about now. I just wish that I could find out more about Virgil Cummings. His story is such a mystery and I'm going to get to the bottom of it, hopefully."

"I hope you will," said David. "Point Lookout is a sad story. It was and still is a little bit of a pox on the county." He took a sip of iced tea. "As a prisoner of war camp, it's been compared to Andersonville. It was equally horrendous."

"Do you know a lot about what happened in that place?" I asked.

"I know some things. But there are many stories to that place that I'm sure I haven't heard. I've learned a lot by reading books, and from chatting with a few people around here who are descendants of some of the prisoners. I would like to learn more though. You know, there's a little reenactment that goes on at the monument and burial grounds near the cottages. Have you ever attended one?"

"Yes, I attended once and the controversy at that time was about the government not allowing the descendants of the dead prisoners to erect a Confederate flag next to the US flag that was being displayed there."

"Yes, that has always been a source of contention and always will be."

I finished my soft crab sandwich and asked a question. "After all of these years, the descendants still want answers about inaccurate totals for those who died and were buried at the monument, and also the manner in which they were all buried? The descendants have never given up, and I admire that."

"No, they haven't given up, but that's because the numbers have never added up," David said. "Many men who were registered as prisoners of war have never been accounted for, and neither do their names appear on the burial site monument. There are hundreds of missing men, but the government can't explain what happened to them, claiming that many records were either destroyed or lost."

"I was told that very thing, recently. I guess one of the hazards of that war, besides records being lost, is that their descendants have never received closure."

"Well," said David, "not only are some names missing from the monument, but I think that the way the dead prisoners were buried brought a lot of anger. Their bones were thrown together in a mass grave near the prison and then removed the same way and placed in the monument near your cottage; burial without dignity. There are plenty of other things that have upset the descendants, but that would take a long time to tell you about. Rainey, I hate to stop now but I have a lot of work to do tomorrow, and I may have to call it a day."

I looked at my watch and realized that we had been sitting there for nearly three hours. David was so easy to talk to. I thought about all that he had told me and wanted to ask more questions.

"David, thank you for sharing this information with me, and if you know more that you would want to share with me sometime, I'd be grateful."

"I would like that. How about we meet up again this weekend?"

"Would Sunday work for you?" *Did I sound too eager?*

"After church around two o'clock would be good," he said.

"After church?" It had started to occur to me that this guy, though very nice, was a little religious.

"Would you like me to stop by the B&B, or would the Old Town Coffee Shop be better for you?" he asked.

"There's a nice tearoom at the B&B. Come by and I'll ask Linda to join us."

"Linda?" David asked.

"Raley. Linda Graves-Raley. She and her husband own the B&B."

"St. Mary's County is a very small world." David laughed. "I know Linda. She attended Great Mills High School when I was there. I didn't know her well, but I knew of her."

"Well good," I said. "I'll tell her that you're coming by on Sunday. I'm sure that she'll welcome an old school acquaintance."

Back at the B&B, I told Linda that David Woods would be coming by on Sunday.

"David Woods was the best-looking guy in high school, and every girl there wanted to date him, including me. But alas," she said, sighing, "he only had eyes for one girl."

"Evelyn?" I asked.

"Yes. Did he tell you about her?"

"No, not really, but I saw that he had named his boat after her. We rescued the Carey family in that boat. Some of my neighbors told me about David's wife passing away, but I really don't know him all that well. He's willing to share some facts about Point Lookout, and we were supposed to get into a conversation about that over lunch, but we talked about other things too, and time got away from us."

"That happens when you enjoy a handsome man's company." I think Linda was trying to imply something, but I ignored it and continued.

"I came across some documents at the Maryland State Archives that listed some of the prisoners and guards who had been through that prison. David says that a lot of the records are wrong. I was hoping that he could help explain some things to me about prison life for the Confederates who were held there."

Linda agreed that the tearoom would be a great place for a history lesson, and I thanked her and made my way to my room for the night. But sleep escaped me for some reason. *Why does David seem so interested in what I'm interested in? Is he trying to make some kind of connection with me?* My thoughts made me nervous and I thought about calling and canceling with David, but I fell asleep instead, thinking again about his beautiful brown eyes.

❧

On Sunday David showed up at about two fifteen, entered the B&B, and joined Linda and me in the tearoom. He passed on the offer of tea, and then took a seat in the blue leather wing chair. "Do you remember me?" David asked Linda.

"Yes, I do remember you," she said. "You were on the football team and as I recall, earned a scholarship to Maryland?"

"Yes, but I never really made use of my education."

"What did you study there?" I asked him.

"I was a history major," he said. "I intended to become a high school teacher, but after a brief stint in the army, I took up carpentry instead. From there I eventually started my business. I don't have any regrets about my decision though."

"Rainey told me that you know about some events that took place at Point Lookout. I hope that you don't mind sharing with me as well?" Linda asked.

"No, I really enjoy sharing about that place. To this day it's still a point of contention, not so much with the younger people who are buying summer places down here, but definitely with the older folks. My father and mother were both history buffs and spoke with neighbors in the community, who were willing to share about their ancestors. My parents were always talking about it so I picked up an interest by association, I guess you could say."

"Rainey has been to the Maryland State Archives and has found some interesting facts too," said Linda.

"Yes," I said. "I located the diary of a woman who wrote to her husband while he was a prisoner at Point Lookout. It seems that he didn't get all of her letters, and she received only a few from him as well. It gets confusing though."

"That sounds interesting, but what is confusing about what you've found?" Linda asked.

"Well, it's as though his wife was conflicted about some of the things that her husband had written to her about his life as a prisoner. I brought several entries from her diary that I was allowed to photocopy while at the archives. Would you like me to read some of them to you?"

They both seemed interested, so I read out loud what I had copied.

Chapter 23

The Diary

July 1, 1865

*T*oday a stranger came to our home. I was seated on the front porch with Mama and Papa Cummings, enjoying the last of the cool spring breezes, when a man approached the house wearing threadbare Confederate army clothing and badly worn boots. We have seen many men in such condition lately, and have fed and even allowed some to bunk in the barn, as they make their way home to various towns in the Northern Neck. This man said that he had been released from Point Lookout. Oh dear God, will Virgil be home soon too?

The man seemed very tired and hungry, so Mama gave him a plate of food to eat, and Papa told him to rest in the barn. How Papa could refrain from asking the man if he knows Virgil I do not know. Oh, I am so anxious to learn more about what happened to my husband, but I am also afraid of the cruel information that I may hear. I will wait until the stranger has rested, and then I will try to find out when my dear husband will be home or at least when Virgil was released. But what if this poor man does not know my husband?

July 2, 1865

Oh dear God, to my horror Mr. Gus Pruett has told us that Virgil is dead. I could not contain myself after hearing this news. Grief has been poured out on us, and the room engulfed with moaning and tears. I feel that I do not wish to live *another day. And what of my dear son, who is now without a father? Why, dear God did this man wait until he had eaten our food and slept in our barn to tell us? It is cruel and beyond reason. He has given me a little box, which he claims was all that was left of Virgil's personal things. He found our address on the last letter that Virgil received from me, some six months before the end of the war.*

I cannot sleep and probably will never find rest again. Mama and Papa are both very silent, but I can hardly breathe a breath without shedding tears. Papa has asked us to go to our beds tonight believing that the Lord God is sovereign and that we must accept what God has allowed.

July 3, 1865

Mr. Pruett seems to be the only one who has slept through the night and he did not rise until noon. The humidity is settling in today, and there is hardly a breeze. Papa allowed him to wash up inside the house, and Mama provided him with some clean clothing. I wanted to protest when Mama handed this stranger some of Virgil's clothes, but I felt that Mama was somehow comforted by this act of kindness. I am embittered by it. He has asked that we just call him, Gus.

After he ate another plate of food, he said that he was feeling much stronger and was willing to tell us all he could, concerning Virgil. Mama and I were most anxious, but Papa was very silent as he held Bennett close to him.

The horrible stories of the atrocities at Point Lookout were overwhelming. I had to excuse myself several times as I could not control my tears. But later Mama told me as gently as she could that the Lord God had seen fit to take her dear son, my beloved husband, home to be with Him and that it would do no good for me to dwell on what was done. She said that we could never fully understand the will of the Lord, but that good always comes for those who trust in Him. She wiped my tears away with her soft hands and wrapped her arms around me, allowing me to cry once again. Who will comfort her?

Gus told us that Virgil died when a bullet was fired through his tent. He told us that the guards often fired random shots for no reason and that the guards were never held accountable if a prisoner was injured or killed. The shootings, Gus said, were usually done under cover of darkness.

I asked him if he had any idea why a guard would do such a thing to my husband, but he had no reply. I asked him if he knew who shot my husband, but again he only shook his head. Then he said that it was probably one of the local black guards from the area around Point Lookout, though he did not say why or how it happened.

I am far from forgiving whoever such guard may be. He has taken my beloved Virgil away. Why do men hate and kill, and who is this guard who has shattered our lives?

July 15, 1865

Gus has been with us for a while now. Papa has taken to him, though Mama and I are more reserved in his presence. It pains me very much to see another man wearing my dead husband's clothing, and I have said this to Mama, but she told me that we must be kind to those who have suffered. Today the men went down to the creek to check on Papa's oyster beds. Despite the war, some things have survived. Oysters are still selling at good prices, so Papa has asked Gus to stay on during oyster harvest season.

It seems as though Gus has no home to hurry off to. He was not married before the war, and he has not spoken of any living family. I feel sad for him. It must be awful to have been a prisoner and suffered so and then have no person on earth to help quell the memories of such misery. Yet at the same time I resent that he is here. I cannot explain my feelings.

August 20, 1865

It has been hard for me to write in my diary. Time has gone sadly by, and I am still sleepless most nights thinking of Virgil and of Bennett, who will never know his father. Gus has been most helpful to Papa. In fact, he has made himself so helpful that Papa has offered Gus a trial partnership in Papa's oyster business. Gus now goes out in the boat and plants the seed oysters in the various oyster beds. By the cooler months, we will be well supplied with oysters to eat and sell. Papa also has a crabbing business to help us survive as crabs are becoming popular with the folks in Washington and Baltimore. Nearly every week a buy boat comes from the Potomac or from the bay to purchase what we have harvested. The money has relieved our poverty.

I miss Virgil so very much, but I am sleeping a little better and have begun to accept what has befallen us. It has been nearly two months since learning of his death, but it seems that the good Lord is in the process of turning my mourning into acceptance. There are women all around these parts who have had to deal with the loss of husbands or sons. Some pitiful women have lost both. Black is the color that we wear.

September 20, 1865

I have gone down to the dock to see what prices Papa is getting, and I am so encouraged to know that we will have enough money to get us through the winter months. We are eating well as we have a steady supply of fish and oyster. Our farm crops are meager though, as many crops were pillaged by hungry men passing through this area after the war. We did manage to harvest some beans to dry and some corn to feed the livestock, but without money to buy necessities such as flour and sugar, we would have been going without many staples come the cold months, had it not been for the help of this man, Gus.

I am grateful that Gus has stayed on to help Papa. He is a different sort of man, one that I cannot quite understand. His desire to stay here with Virgil's family instead of going back to Georgia seems odd to me. I fear that he has lost everyone in Georgia, but I do not know for sure. I would like to ask him about his family, but he seems so content to be with us that I do not want to upset him should he have a reason to grieve. He rides into town daily to pick up our mail and to purchase supplies for Papa.

Why have I not received official word of my husband's death? I have waited for any word but nothing ever comes. Is this the punishment we widows must *endure? Our side has lost the war, and now we must wonder the fate of our husbands until the Union government sees fit to inform us? The cruelty of this is too much for any family to endure. I dream of Virgil every night and never want to wake up. It is too painful.*

September 30, 1865

Today Gus approached me and told me that he has a desire to speak to me privately. I am quite sure that he would like to speak with me about my husband, Virgil. It brings pain to my heart to think of Virgil, and most days I am so busy with Bennett and helping Mama with the farm that I sleep often from sheer exhaustion, a state I prefer to grief and tears all night, as I have often experienced. I will speak with Gus after church on Sunday. It is the only day of rest for us these days. I am preparing myself now to hear more about the prison camp at Point Lookout.

October 3, 1865

I could not be more distressed. Gus has asked if I would consider accompanying him to the Harvest Ball at the end of the month. Should I have had to tell him that I am still in mourning? Does he not know proper decorum? Have all customs been removed from general knowledge? My answer to him was that I could not accompany him. He seemed to understand and begged my forgiveness.

Have I been too hard on this man who has suffered so? Confusion has overwhelmed me. I shall speak to Mama and Papa about this tomorrow. I cannot believe the man to be so ignorant of proper behavior, although I know that he has had practically no education at all. His speech does not allow one to enjoy conversing with him, and he is awkward in his behavior, but perhaps he has never been taught to live in society. I must be more understanding of this.

October 4, 1865

Papa has been a great help to me. He told me that I must not mourn his beloved son forever and that Virgil would not want me to mourn, that I should think of little Bennett without a father to love him. Papa also said that I should help Bennett become the man that Virgil was, that I should think about the qualities Gus has displayed these past several months and to try to overlook his lack of propriety and lack of learning. I think that he is right, Gus has been a help to all of us, but how do I tell Papa that I do not feel comfortable being in the same room with Gus?

I am still missing Virgil and often dream of him coming home to me. Some nights I lie awake feeling his presence beside me. Is he truly gone forever? I could never love another man. I have chosen to remain in mourning until a year has passed. I could not do otherwise. Last night I dreamed that I had gone to the prisoner of war camp by boat to rescue Virgil. From the boat I could see him running to me, and I woke up screaming his name until Mama came into my room to calm me.

∾

I looked up to see if the diary had interested anyone besides me.

"This is so intriguing," Linda said, "and I am amazed that you found such a treasure in the Maryland State Archives."

"Yes, it is a treasure," I replied. "It took quite a bit of time to photocopy it, and some of the pages were missing, such as entries leading up to the time that Virgil's wife finally did speak to Gus. She mentions that she's going to speak to Gus about something, but then it appears that some pages had been torn from the diary."

"What do you make of that?" David asked.

"I don't know what to think. I mean, people write things that they don't mean sometimes," I said.

"You're right about that," said Linda. "I remember taking a few pages out of my diary because I was sure that my mother was reading it while I wasn't at home. She suspected that I was seeing a boy when I was supposed to be at a friend's house. She was right, of course, so I tore out the pages."

David laughed and asked, "Who was it?"

"Not telling," said Linda. "You were on the football team with him though."

"That could have been just about anybody. So he isn't the man you married, I guess?" David seemed amused.

"No, thank God!" Linda laughed and turned to me. "How about you, Rainey, did you have some torn pages in your diary?"

"I knew better then to keep a diary then. But I keep one now—in my head," I answered.

"Well, I'm glad that Mrs. Cummings kept one on paper," said David. "Do you have anything else from the diary?"

"Yes. I have some text telling about one other conversation that Joanna Cummings had with Gus. After that it gets even more confusing."

Linda excused herself and went into the kitchen to get a pot of coffee. She brought a mug out to David, along with a cream pitcher and some sugar. "I know you didn't want the tea, but how about some coffee?" David accepted the coffee, black, and I continued to read.

∾

December 25, 1865

Christmas is not the same without my beloved husband. Yet Bennett is a happy little boy and full of life. I see his father's ways in him already. He is a tender boy and also very ambitious. At nine months old he is pulling himself up on any piece of furniture that he can reach as he tries and tries to walk. He only gives up after exhaustion, but he does not cry with frustration. When I hold him in my arms, he touches my face with his little hands as if to say that everything is going to be all right. He has Virgil's eyes, and I pray to God that Bennett will become the man his father was.

Gus has become an even more important man in Bennett's life. I have resisted up to this point, but Papa was right; Bennett needs a man to give him attention, and I know that Papa is too busy most days to spend a lot of time with Bennett. As long as Gus has a little time to spend with Bennett, I will allow it. I have agreed to speak with Gus about the prisoner of war camp. He knows that I do not wish to accept an overture of any relationship other then friendship, but I have grown weary of protecting Bennett from a relationship with a man who truly seems to care for him.

The other day was very peculiar to me though. In speaking with Gus, he brought up some information that he had seemingly been holding back. He told me that Virgil had asked if he could join Gus's crabbing and trading business while at the prisoner of war camp. I distinctly remember a letter, one of the few I received, in which Virgil told me that he had a business of his own and that he had other prisoners working for him, mostly younger men not yet out of their teenage years. He never mentioned working for Gus or anyone else.

Gus also told me that Virgil had been suspected of reporting some of the other prisoners to the guards for stealing from one another! I remember also that Virgil had distinctly told me in a letter that he had taken pity on the men at the camp and that he had not made friends with any guards. He detested the treatment that they gave to the prisoners and therefore only traded with fellow prisoners.

Gus said that he personally stayed far from the guards as they could not be trusted with their rifles and that he repeatedly warned Virgil about dealing with them but that Virgil would not listen to him.

Why has Gus waited all this while to paint this different picture for me? I suspect that it is because he would like me to believe that my husband had been in the habit of betraying his fellow prisoners! I cannot believe such a thing of Virgil. Could Gus have a motive behind these sudden revelations? He has said things that make me feel very uncomfortable in his presence, such as asking me to consider that Bennett needs a father to help him grow to be a good man. Does he consider himself such a candidate? Has he been speaking to Papa about his? I am outraged at Gus's willingness to insert himself into my life, uninvited.

I need to find out the truth about my husband's life in prison, and I need to know the truth about how he was murdered and by whom, even if I have to travel to Washington to obtain the records from that miserable place. Will Papa help me, or will I go alone? I have further questions for Gus, and I plan to confront him with letters from Virgil that directly contradict what he has suddenly revealed to me.

∽

I paused because it was getting late, and Linda had to leave the room to take care of some arrivals. David sat across from me, looking at me without saying a word. I was uncomfortable with the silent look.

"Why do you look at me that way, and what are you thinking about?" I asked him.

"I'm thinking that you really pour yourself into your research."

"Yes, it keeps me going. Always has," I replied.

"So, past lives keep you going?"

"Well, yes, somewhat. That's what studying history is all about." I wondered where he was going with his questions. He was beginning to sound like my friend Jill.

"What about your life? Do you take time to live it?"

"What do you mean by that?" I was a little indignant.

"Never mind," he said. "I'm not trying to pry, just asking."

"Asking what?" I insisted.

"Well, I'd like to learn more about you sometime, but I have the feeling that unless you're rescuing stranded people, investigating the lives of others, or telling stories, which by the way I find very interesting, that you find life to be a little boring."

He wasn't accusing me. His look was not threatening. There was no condemnation of my life, yet I found myself defensive. "I guess I'm a little tired," I said, "and I didn't mean to sound unfriendly. I just enjoy what I do and see no reason to stop researching. Why should that bother anyone?"

David smiled. "You're something else," he said. "I've been with you on a boat in a hurricane, which was a life-threatening situation, and I saw a very brave woman help rescue the lives of a family. I have also seen you race to the hospital to help comfort and provide for your neighbors in distress, and yet you seemed to be bored with anything other than research and rescue. Do you ever go out on dates or anything close to a date or allow someone to rescue you once in a while?"

Not knowing how to respond, I sat staring at him. He seemed to want a reply.

"I guess some people would think that I've become too serious about my research. I tend to get that way. I admit too that I'm a bookaholic and that I like history, which seems more interesting then my life currently, but that doesn't mean that I'm bored," I defended. "After all, aren't we all just trying to make our way through somehow?"

David waited for me to finish my point and then simply said, "I was going to ask you the other day if you would go somewhere with me." *This man just ignored my little outburst,* I thought.

"How about it?" he asked.

"Go with you where?" I asked.

"To visit with a man who knows a lot of history and who also loves visitors. I told you that I may have some interesting information for you, and I have a friend I'd like you to meet."

"Can you tell me a little about him?"

"He's a man who washed up on a beach one day," he answered.

"Washed up on a beach? Are you kidding me?" I was perplexed and started to ask more questions. "What man and what beach?"

"That's all you get for now. I'll pick you up tomorrow, early—say nine. Sound OK with you?"

"OK, I guess so," I said, not really sure that I wanted to go with him at all.

When Linda returned to the room, David stood to leave.

"I should get going," David said as he got up off of the sofa. He walked his coffee cup to the coffee bar and turned back toward me. "You know, I love history as much as you do. I didn't mean to upset you by asking you about your life, but you do have a history. We all do, and every person has something interesting to share."

"I'm not upset," I said, "but my life isn't all that interesting. It's just a little unnerving to be asked about my life, you know?"

"No, I don't know," he said with a half-smile. "I'll see you in the morning?"

I nodded, and David left after thanking Linda for the coffee. I walked my cup to the kitchen too, wondering why David would want to know anything about me.

"May I ask what that was all about?" Linda asked.

"Nothing," I said. "David was just asking me a little bit about myself. I guess he wants to get to know me better, but I found the conversation to be a little too personal for my comfort zone."

"Rainey," she said with a laugh, "the man is clearly enchanted with you. It's very obvious to me, comfort zone or not."

Chapter 24

Water Baby

David arrived at the B&B before nine. I was still in my room, so he waited in the parlor while chatting with Linda's husband. When I came down the stairs David grinned as though we were going on a date or something, and I suddenly didn't want to go with him.

"Good morning, Rainey," said Linda's husband. "Are you doing more research today, or are you going down to your cottage?"

"Research it is," I said. "Though I haven't been told exactly what we're doing, I do know that it has to do with a man who once washed up on a beach."

"Come on, Rainey," said David. "You'll have to tell everyone about it later when you get back." David smiled at Linda's husband and then, taking my arm, led me out the door.

As I climbed into the truck, I could see that David had bought two cups of 7-Eleven coffee complete with stirrers, cream, and packets of sugar. "Fix some coffee for yourself," he said, as he settled in on the driver's side.

I prepared my cup and put the lid on. The coffee was hot and strong, just the way I like it, and I began to feel relaxed on the bench seat. I sipped the hot liquid and took in the scenery while David drove north.

"Thanks for the coffee, David. Where are we headed?" I asked.

"Not far, just up to Charlotte Hall."

"What's in Charlotte Hall?"

"The veterans' home," he said.

"I know that, but what's this about?"

"You'll see. I think you'll find that Melvin has led a very unusual life."

"Is that the name of the man who washed up on the beach?"

"Yes."

We drove to Charlotte Hall while David told me about the progress going on with the repair work on the cottages. He told me that the Wilderman home was nearly completed and that some of their grand-children had come back to visit their grandparents already.

The Carey family had been planning to raise their home up a little, but they and the owners of Mud Manor were still having some difficulty obtaining permits. It seemed that the permit people in the county were coming up with some strict new regulations that were holding the process up or were flat-out planning to deny those permits at all.

"What are the Careys and the owners of Mud Manor suppose to do now?"

"Since the hurricane destroyed so many smaller homes on the bay, the county decided to allow them a little time to repair. That's why we're working hard to shore up the foundations for as many cottages as we can get to. They'll inspect again and then decide on what they will allow after that. I don't know what will happen to their places," David answered, "but things *are* changing down there. It seems that some folks can build whatever they want on their lots and others can't. Look what those lawyers did when they bought the old house next to the Mannys."

"Yes," I said. "That was Patrick's family cottage."

"I guess Patrick is your ex-husband then?" David asked.

"Yes," I said, "but can we *not* talk about it right now?" I felt that questions about my failed marriage were too personal and would also ruin my mood.

"OK," said David. We drove the rest of the way listening to country music on the radio.

The grounds of Charlotte Hall Veterans' Home were beautiful with old brickwork, white freshly painted fences, and hedges and trees that looked as though they had been there for least a hundred years. A red brick walkway let up to the veterans' home. David parked the truck, and together we walked into the building, past the nurses' station, and all the way down to the room at the end of the hallway on the first floor, turning right into the last room.

"Hello there," said David as he walked over to greet an older gentleman.

"Oh, David," said the man, turning in his chair slightly, "I was hoping you would come by soon."

"You're looking good today," said David.

"Feeling old but good for my age," Melvin acknowledged.

"I've brought along a friend today. Her name is Rainey Grant. She's the lady I told you about." I walked over to Melvin, who put his hand out to shake mine, and I was surprised with the hearty grip. His eyes were a bright blue and friendly.

"Nice to meet you, sir," I said.

"Oh, you can call me Melvin," he said. "Everyone else does, you know. I don't have a last name. Never did. So they just call me Melvin or Mr. Melvin. Some of the nurses call me Mel, but I prefer Melvin. When you don't have a last name, you sure don't want to shorten the only name you've got!" Melvin chuckled and let go of my hand. David brought two chairs over and placed them near Melvin.

"Mr. Melvin, I'm just a little curious about the fact that you don't have a last name," I asked.

"It's a long story, but David tells me that you love a good long story, so I'd be glad to tell you mine." Mr. Melvin took a paper cup and poured himself a little water. His hands were shaking as he put the plastic pitcher back on the side table. "I don't know why they keep giving me a water pitcher that shakes so much," he said with a laugh. Taking a few sips of water from a bent purple straw, he began to tell his story.

"I was born sometime in 1897 or thereabouts. That's what the people told me. They found me on the beach and saw that I was a newborn baby. When I got old enough to understand a little about my life, I must have been about five or six.

"Back in those days, steamboats were the way to travel the bay waters. In fact, there were few bridges over the rivers, and taking a steamer to where you were trying to get to was the way to go. It would have been my first time on the water; I'm pretty sure, but not a good day for being in any kind of boat. I've never again put myself on a boat, and God willing, I don't plan to. I don't want my ashes scattered out on the water either. I use water for washing and drinking, and that's about it."

Melvin took another sip of water and cleared his throat. "It's a funny affair I've had with that bay. It took my mother and whatever other family I may have had away from me, but it also gave me life.

"From what I was told, the bay started out calmly that particular day. Why my mother was taking a steamer to Baltimore with a brand-new baby I just don't know, but the day started out nice enough. Just like other stories I've heard about the bay, a little wind stared to pick up, and soon a nor'easter started to show itself. Those things just whip up out of nowhere, and before a boat can get to safety, the storm is all over the waters and threatening to take a life.

"Well, we were on a steamer heading, as I said, to Baltimore. We'd just come down the Potomac, but I don't know where my mother boarded. It could have been in Virginia for all I know. All I do know is that when the steamer rounded the tip of Southern Maryland near Point Lookout, it was too late for the captain to turn around. The waves were reported by survivors to be twelve-foot swells and higher. That don't seem very high, but a boat caught in those kinds of waves is in danger when the rain starts pouring down like the flood of Noah.

"Before long, the steamer engines must have all cut out, and the boat was taking on water. The captain and passengers onboard soon realized that they would have to either sink or swim. All I know is what was reported. There were twenty-five men, women, and children on that steamer, and only five survived. The four who gave the only details that day were rescued right along with me. They had floated into shore on pieces of boat planks.

"They found me tied to a plank, and one or two of them managed to keep me afloat until we all washed up on the shore. I was by myself and didn't belong to the people who survived with me. How I lived, only the Good Lord knows.

"I did survive, but the trouble was that nobody claimed me. Nobody published that there was a missing woman with a baby. None of the survivors even knew mine or my mother's name. The boarding record went down with the steamer. To this day I don't know who I am. All I know is that one of the survivors said he saw a woman tie a baby to a board and set the baby down in the water, kind of like the story of Moses, I guess. Everyone was too frantic to take much more notice."

David looked over at me and could see that my eyes were filling up, but I shook it off and lowered my head to hide the tears. "You mean to tell me that you've lived all of these years with not one person claiming to know who you are?" I asked him.

Melvin shook his head. "Nobody ever did claim me, but I've lived a very full and interesting life. I've lived through a lot of good and bad, but I've lived just the same. I wouldn't trade my life in for anybody else's. As the Good Book says, God sends rain on the just and the unjust, and then he sends some sunshine to show us that the things we thought were important really don't matter that much. That's what life is about, letting go of things that don't matter."

I thought about my own life for a brief moment. The past year had been painful. I had been cheated on and left like a cast-off toy, but I had survived. Anxiety had taken me out of commission a few times, but somehow I always seemed to come back around. I had locked myself in my cottage, but friends still called me on the phone, and a hurricane had brought me out once again.

"How did you come to survive without a family? Were you raised in an orphanage?" I asked.

"Goodness no," he said. "I was raised by many nice folks. They didn't want to put me in an orphanage, so they just passed me around from house to house. I know it sounds awful to some, but I had more family than anybody else did back when I was little. I had at least three mothers to take care of me, black and white women, and several good fathers as well who taught me how to build things and how to read and write, but I always considered my real family to be Jeremiah and Gerdie Wilkes."

I almost fell over when I heard him mention the names of Jeremiah and Gerdie Wilkes.

"Melvin is a carpenter," said David, "and one of the best around. Jeremiah Wilkes taught him his trade."

"Yup, just like the Lord, I learned the carpentry trade and got by. When I grew older, I just continued to make things with my hands. Eventually all my folks died off, one by one. I miss them all to this day. But I don't feel sorry for myself. I got a lot of people out there who let me call them my brothers and sisters and nephews and nieces and grandchildren. They think of me as real family, and they come visit me when they're able. David here is one of them. He's what I call my grandnephew."

I looked over at David and asked, "Really?"

"It's true," said David. "My great-aunt was one of the women who cared for Melvin. I wanted to bring you here to meet Melvin so that you could ask him about Jeremiah Wilkes. I think you'll be happy with the answers to your questions."

"David, you have made my day! How could you have possibly known how much this would mean to me?"

"Mr. and Mrs. Manny filled me in on the story. They wanted to get to the bottom of what happened with Jeremiah as much as you did. I was here visiting Melvin, and we started talking about the old days. Melvin loves to talk about those days, and one day he mentioned a black family who had taken him in for a time. The names clicked, so here we are."

"Did you really know Jeremiah Wilkes?" I asked Melvin.

Melvin reached for his cup and took another long sip through a straw. "I did, and I've got a better long-term memory then a short one. Can't tell you what I had for breakfast this morning, but I can tell you what I know of Jeremiah."

Chapter 25

Adopted

66 I was picked up off of the beach on October 30, 1898. Like I say, I must have been a newborn, so I was given a birthday on the day I was found on the beach. It was Jeremiah's wife, Gerdie, who wanted to keep me though. Naturally, I was near death, but I must have had strong lungs because she said I was always squalling.

"When some folks came down to the shore to rescue the survivors, she grabbed that board and untied me, and then she carried me off to her home just like that and gave me the name Melvin, though I never did find out why. Times were hard then, and knowing what a hardship it was to feed their own family, some of the neighbors offered to help Gerdie and Jeremiah out by providing some food and clothing as I grew. I lived in many homes; some was nice and others meager, but I didn't know that it wasn't natural to have so many mothers and fathers.

"They all had compassion for me and helped to raise me. I guess Jeremiah and Gerdie must have been in their sixties or so when they picked me up off the beach. Later, when they got up in age, I was passed around to a few other folks in the area, and they took me in like one of their own, fed and clothed me, made sure I got to attend school, and taught me the Bible. Most of them were good, God-fearing folks, but I was closest in spirit with the Wilkes family. They had things

236

come up that brought them fear and grief, but they still kept their faith. I remember a few things that happened to them, and I wondered how they ever kept going." Melvin took a sip of water and continued.

"Jeremiah was forced into the Union army when he was just a boy. The Union knew that Maryland was not entirely pro-North and set about to occupy any area of the state that was near the borders of a Southern state. They wanted to prove a point about North/South loyalties. So down there at Point Lookout, the Union government placed black guards to watch over the Confederate prisoners. You know that act alone was going to make a bad situation worse.

"Many of them poor black guards had been former slaves, and they had every right to hate the Confederate prisoners they guarded. Some even guarded over their former masters. Well, the Union gave them a little training, but they forgot to tell them that they couldn't take vengeance on the prisoners. Several of those guards had been through hell, having their families sold out from under them and sent to plantations in the Deep South. Even their little children were sent away, never to be seen again. But Jeremiah told me that hatred never helped him get through life, and he wasn't about to join in with what was going on in that prisoner of war camp.

"It was a terrible war, and with it went all of the evil that men can do to one another. But I know, Ms. Grant that you didn't come for details about those atrocities."

"You can tell me whatever you'd like to share," I said, "and please call me Rainey."

"Well, the prisoner of war camp was just such a place. There was brutality going on in there, and it didn't come only from the guards. The prisoners were just trying to survive, and when you put some bad apples in any barrel, you're going to come out with some rotten apples. There were plenty of them in the camp, but men had to survive, and sometimes that meant doing things you wouldn't do if you weren't suffering so.

"Of course, being partly raised in a black family, I got to see both sides of the trouble that slavery brought. Everything bad starts from greed and ends with greed. It's been the bane of man since Adam and Eve. But you know, I loved my families and didn't care what color they were. I never understood the feelings going around back in those days, and I don't think I ever will.

"We all want more then the Good Lord thinks is best for us. Greed brought out the worst in some of the guards. They had been deprived as a people and wanted vengeance on their own terms. The prisoners were at their worst because it was one thing to get thrown in a Union prison but another altogether to have black guards over them. So they were deprived of their power over blacks, and to assuage that loss, some of them turned on one other. That's where Jeremiah comes in.

"But you know, I think that I may need a little time to rest up before I go on. Maybe the two of you young people could get a little lunch and come back? Sorry to act like such an old man, only being a young ninety-seven, but I guess I'm starting to put some age on me. I hope that you don't mind too terribly much."

"Oh no, certainly not, I think a nice rest is a good thing," I said.

"Thank you kindly," said Melvin. "I'll just take a little nap then."

Before David and I could close the door, Melvin had leaned back and closed his eyes. I wondered if there was any way at all that Melvin and Miss Biscoe knew each other. They both liked to nod off at the most interesting part of their stories.

"I can't believe this," I told David. "This man has such an incredible story to tell. Thank you again for thinking to introduce me to him."

"Glad to help," said David. "Melvin is very important to me. He treats me with respect, and I try to do the same for him."

"I noticed that. He's quite a lucky man to have survived with so many to care for him."

"Yes, God has really blessed him, and his faith keeps him going."

I was beginning to feel a little overwhelmed with David inserting God into so many of our conversations, but he had provided Melvin, who was turning out to be a link in my research, and for that I was grateful.

When we left the veterans' home, I fell silent while I thought about the people I had come to know so far. Mr. and Mrs. Manny had a wonderful quality about them. They were kind and caring. They overlooked my rude behavior and showed appreciation just to have me around them. The same was true of the Wilderman family, Mrs. Finch, the Carey family, Melvin, and especially David. I felt as though I had been in some sort of haze until now. Why had I never cared enough to know them before now?

"How about we drive up the road for a burger from Bert's for lunch?" David asked.

"Definitely!" I agreed.

"David," I said as we drove down Route 5, "I have never met so many wonderful people until lately. To tell you the truth, sometimes I wonder where I've been."

"I think you may have been someplace where I was once," he said. "After I lost my wife, I think that I lost myself. She was always so trusting. She trusted me, though I didn't deserve it."

"You didn't deserve her trust?" I was surprised to hear him say that.

"No, I didn't. I've changed, and I'd like to think that I've improved in some ways, but I never really deserved Evelyn or her trust."

I didn't know if I wanted to hear what he had to say, but I couldn't help myself. "Do you want to talk about it?" I asked.

"It doesn't bother me to talk about it if it doesn't bother you to listen."

Chapter 26

David Woods

"When I was young, I thought that I could do whatever I wanted, and because my mother was a widow with a lot of responsibility, I naturally took advantage of the situation. I started drinking before my fourteenth birthday and was probably a certifiable drunk by the time I graduated from high school. Even with that, I managed to get into college, but I was still unhappy. I had dated a girl, Evelyn, all the way through high school and college, but I felt like I needed to get away, so I broke up with her.

"I tried the military, but they soon found out that I was a drunk and let me go. The military took anyone then. Viet Nam was in full stage, but they kicked me out. I feel ashamed about that to this day. Once dishonorably discharged, I got a job in a lumber mill. That's when Melvin, an old boarder at my great aunt's house, set me straight. He didn't put up with my mouth, and I had a big one back then.

"I gave him sass exactly once. My mother liked him because he was such a character, but to me—that is after he straightened my attitude out—he was a man I could trust. He got me the job at the mill and taught me to appreciate hard work and how to make beautiful things with wood. I became a carpenter.

"I could never understand one thing about Melvin though. Even though he had no family and really didn't know who he was, he never reverted to pity or being self-centered. If things didn't work out for him, he would just try harder the next time. He always thanked God for everything in his life.

"I guess I wasn't interested in God at the time, but I was starting to think about Evelyn again. She was beautiful, intelligent, and a woman who shared Melvin's faith in God. We got together again and soon married.

"Melvin used to say, 'David, don't marry that young woman if you don't plan to share her faith with her. There's more to a lifetime with a woman then just getting your needs met.'

"He was always direct. I liked that about him later. I didn't listen to him that time though. I married Evelyn, and then I made her life hell."

"How did you do that?" I asked. David pulled into the parking lot at Bert's, and we sat in the truck with the AC still running.

"I went back to drinking and hanging out in bars with my buddies. I cheated on her every chance I got. She wanted children, and I didn't. When she did get pregnant, I told her that I would leave if she had the baby. I remember when she lost the baby that I was matter-of-fact about it. I even said to her, 'Well, you always say that everything happens according to God's will.' To this day I regret that statement more than anything else I've ever said in my lifetime."

David was beginning to sound like Patrick, and I began to feel uncomfortable with the conversation. How could men hate their own babies?

"She stayed with me even when I went downhill after the baby was lost. She said that she had forgiven me for what I had said to her about

God's will. I could see that she tried to be positive and loving, but I didn't feel like changing. Eventually I started staying out all night and getting myself thrown in jail for various misdemeanors. It wasn't long after that that Melvin bailed me out of jail. Then he took me to the woodshed."

"Took you to the woodshed?" I asked.

"Yes. He gave me something that I guess I had always been looking for. I got in his face and gave him some lip, even took a swing at him. The next thing I knew, he threw me down on the ground and beat some sense into me. I ended up with a few bruised ribs and a broken finger, but that was my fault for thinking I could make a move on that old man. These days what he did is something that a person could get locked up for, but I'll tell you one thing—that shed incident was the beginning of a big turnaround in my life. I was twenty-five."

"What happened with your life after that?" I asked. "Did your wife forgive you again?"

"She took me back. She loved me that much. Eventually I went to church with her and heard about what real forgiveness is about. I resisted for about five months before I finally accepted the fact that only Christ could forgive me and set me straight."

David stopped and looked over at me. But how was I to respond?

I didn't know what to think of David's story. My own husband had walked out on me just as David had walked out on his wife. But David's wife had let him come back. I was too hurt to even talk to my husband about what he'd done. Patrick left me and never once asked if he could come back. He never told me what I had done wrong or what I could do to make him happy. I had been abandoned and left feeling like a total failure.

"David, I tried to do everything to make my husband happy, even things that I didn't want to do, but no matter what, he just couldn't accept what I had to give. I don't know what I did wrong. To this day I don't understand it. It seems that a man has the ability to just turn a woman off like a light switch and never think of her again." I wanted to understand and was hoping David could explain.

"Has your husband remarried?"

"Yes."

"Then I think that it's probably harder for you to have peace about what happened or to think about forgiving your husband for what he did. I still deal with regrets and have to live with them, but I know that ultimately I have been forgiven. When Evelyn died of cancer, it was very hard for me. When you lose someone, sometimes the old guilt has a habit of coming back, and it can overwhelm a person. If I hadn't felt forgiven by God, I don't know what would have happened to me after I lost her."

I listened to David's story, but what he told me about God and forgiveness made no sense. How could a few confessions wipe away all of the pain that people inflict on one another? I was tired of hearing about God, and I couldn't believe that David's wife was so forgiving after the way he had treated her. The more I thought about it, the angrier I became.

"How am I supposed to forgive my ex-husband?" I blurted out. "He has a new wife, who must be everything to him that I was not. He has a beautiful home, a beautiful wife, and a beautiful baby. The man who told me that he never wanted children has a new baby. What kind of sense does that make? How on earth can you expect me to forgive him? I wasn't even good enough to have his children!" I turned and looked out the truck window. My anxiety level had not been this high since we'd rescued the Carey family.

David waited for me to calm down. "Well, for starters, you just mentioned some wonderful new friends that you have in your life. You have a beach cottage with a million-dollar view. You have a job that will start back up soon, and in the meantime, you can enjoy the summer doing all the research that you love to do. You know, the Wilderman and Manny families really like you, and they know that you care about them as well. And to tell you the truth, you're a bit of a celebrity after helping to save an entire family during that hurricane. You even tell them stories. What's not to like about you? But you do have something wrong."

"What?" I asked, afraid to hear the answer.

"It isn't me who expects you to forgive your husband."

"Well," I protested, "I'm glad to hear that. You may feel peace, but I'm not perfect because forgiving him is impossible, and so is having what you call, *peace.*"

"You're right." It does seem impossible to forgive sometimes."

"Then why have this conversation, David?"

"Because it's nice to be forgiven. I was, even though I didn't deserve it. And by the way, only one person has ever lived a perfect life."

Oh, here we go again, I thought, *I'm about ready to get hit over the head with religion.* I must have had a very perplexed look on my face. I had not asked for a sermon, and I resented the fact that there I was, trapped in a truck, with a sermon being shoved down my throat.

"I guess what I'm saying isn't making much sense to you right now, huh?"

"You are sounding very similar to the last car salesman that I dealt with," I said dryly.

"I'm sorry to hear that," he said with a laugh. Maybe we can talk about this another time?" David seemed to be searching for a comment or something.

"Can we please just change the subject?"

"Sure," he said. "I'm sorry if I shared more then I should have about my life. I just thought that we're possibly becoming friends; at least I hope so because I really like you, and I wanted you to know a little more about me. That's what friends do."

I didn't answer. Silence was what I wanted.

Finally David spoke. "If you want to talk to me about this again, I would be more then willing to answer anything that you want to know, but I've got to be honest with you: you will never feel true peace in your life until you learn to forgive yourself and others."

I reached for door and got out of the truck. "I'm a little hungry, David." At that moment I was thinking that friendship with him would be one long evangelical outreach program, and I was not interested in the least. I walked toward Bert's without another word.

We went inside and ordered burgers, which we ate without saying much. I found that I was caught somewhere deep inside with no way out. If what he said was true, then I had to ask forgiveness for myself for hating Patrick, but I had always tried so hard to be a good person, and I couldn't find much that I needed to be forgiven for. Patrick deserved my hatred, I reasoned. He even told me he would leave me if I didn't abort our babies. Where were my two babies now?

I grew silent as I thought about my two babies. In my mind, it had been Patrick's fault that I had the abortions. I wished I had never opened my mouth to David about my life, and was glad I had not told him anything else about myself. David hadn't wanted his wife to have children for him either. He was no better than Patrick as far as I was concerned. The distrust that I had for men began to engulf me, and again I wanted to run.

David left me alone, and I ate my lunch without a word. Music played in the background, and after some time went by, I finally pulled myself together. We finished our burgers, and I offered to pay for the lunch.

"Nope," was all he said, and then he took a napkin and wiped my chin. "Ketchup," he explained. I got up from the table, but David sat with a quizzical look on his face, and I hoped that he wouldn't talk about divorce or fault or forgiveness or God anymore.

"What?" I asked him. "I'm not really in the mood to have another religious conversation with you." I hoped that he would leave that subject alone.

"It was nothing like that," he said. "I know that I've already said too much. But, if you want to know the truth, I was thinking about how cute you are."

"Cute?" I was flabbergasted.

"I just call things as I see them. You're cute," he said again.

What is wrong with this guy? I thought to myself. *After a sermon on forgiveness he starts flirting?* He was ruining my day with this stuff and I wanted to leave.

"David, I think I'd like to go home. I'm not feeling all that well," I said.

"I'm sorry," he replied. "It's my fault for bringing up things you're uncomfortable talking about. I didn't mean to get into your personal life. It's just that I think I may have felt the way you do once, and I guess I messed up by talking about myself so much."

"Forget it," I said.

"Rainey, I think it would be better if we drive back to tell Melvin we'll come another day. I know he'll be waiting for us to come back, and I don't want to disappoint him."

"Alright." It was too far for me to walk back to the B&B, so I was stuck.

David nodded, and we got back into his truck and headed for the VA home. I was glad that the *God* conversation had ended, and I was feeling less anxious, hoping that seeing Melvin again could help me out of my mood.

This time Melvin was waiting for us in his wheelchair in the hallway and seemed pleased that we had come back.

"Thought I chased you away, Miss Rainey," Melvin said. "It isn't every day a pretty little thing comes to visit me, and I wanted to make sure that I could give a proper welcome just in case you did come back." Melvin put his hand up for me to shake and gave me a big smile. Then we followed his wheelchair back to his room, where he invited us to sit. *How can I leave now?* I asked myself.

"I tried to tell her she was cute," said David, "but she seemed to be in a big hurry to get back here to see you, so I guess she doesn't care what I think."

"If David says you're cute, then you'd best listen to him. He's never had trouble with women chasing after him, but he only goes for the ones worth keeping. I think he's decided that you're worth keeping," Melvin said.

"Ah, thank you," I said, embarrassed, "but we're just friends."

"Melvin, I think we should get back to your story about Jeremiah," David said. "Something tells me we're embarrassing our new friend here."

"Oh, yes," Melvin said, "I forgot where we were in the story though. Could you remind me?"

"You were telling us about how hard it was, both to be a prisoner of war as well as to be a black guard looking over Confederate prisoners. It seems that the job wasn't all that great for Jeremiah Wilkes," David said.

Melvin picked up where he had left off.

Chapter 27

Jeremiah

"I guess Jeremiah knew things weren't going to work out for him, the day the Union army sent an officer and a couple of black Union soldiers to the farm. They told him he was being freed from slavery because of the Emancipation Proclamation, but he didn't understand how that could be true, since they were practically forcing him to sign up by threatening him if he didn't.

"So he went with the men and soon found himself a guard at the camp for Confederate prisoners. He was just a young man when he was given a rifle and a blue uniform and told to shoot at will any prisoner crossing the dead zone.

"Trouble was that Jeremiah couldn't bring himself to shoot prisoners. But as in everything, like I said, it only takes a few bad apples to ruin the barrel. So one night some of the other guards got a little rowdy and fired off their rifles into the prisoner area, and a prisoner got himself killed. It wasn't the first time that very same thing had happened, but only this time, as Jeremiah told me, it was done on account of a feud between two prisoners.

"One of the prisoners was looking for a reason to kill off one of the other prisoners, so somehow the guards got involved in the thing, and that poor prisoner was shot right through his tent. But as I said,

Jeremiah thought it was done on purpose and that someone must have paid off a guard to do the job. But a lot of rifles were fired at the same time, so nobody knew exactly which bullet hit the man or which guard fired in that direction. Jeremiah had fired his rifle too; that's what they all did when they heard some good news about the war.

"Just the same, nothing was ever done about it. Jeremiah had not one friend up there on the guard walk, and talk was that he was the guard who fired the fatal shot. Well, since nothing could be proven one way or the other, the whole thing was dropped, and he got out of there as soon as the war was over. But that wasn't the end of the affair for Jeremiah."

"What became of Jeremiah then?" I asked.

"Well, that's where the rub comes in," said Melvin. "After the war, Jeremiah and Gerdie went to work rebuilding some of the old buildings that were left behind when they dismantled the prison. Mr. Lewis Chambers paid Jeremiah and his son, Tiberius, to help him restore the old house that once housed some Union officers. He had plans to build cottages along the water and sell them at a huge profit. Before the war there had been a little resort there, but most of those cottages had been torn down or had washed away by then. It was David's great-uncle that rebuilt the place."

"Yes, he did tell me that recently," I said.

"Well, Mr. Lewis Chambers didn't particularly have any leanings North or South, because he had seen a lot of cruelty on both sides. His father had a few freedmen working for his tobacco plantation. Jeremiah was one of them who worked for Mr. Lewis's father, Jacob Chambers. Poor Mr. Jacob Chambers died in the prison camp so Jeremiah and his wife eventually went to work for his son, Mr. Lewis Chambers, who had grown up to be a fine man. But there were some goings-on that made life real hard for Jeremiah."

"What kind of goings-on?" I asked.

"The kind of goings-on that could have led to getting Jeremiah hanged," Melvin replied.

"There was a lot of turmoil in this area after the war. People were blaming the North for atrocities at Point Lookout while others were blaming the South for atrocities at Andersonville. It all led to lawsuits and accusations after the war. The Fort Pillow massacre happened when Nathan Bedford Forrest took a group of Confederates with him to kill off the Union officers and the black regiment guarding the fort there. Some said that Forrest's actions were performed in revenge for the Union having armed the black troops.

"So with all of that going on, people just couldn't let that old war die out. In fact, we had a bunch of newspapermen writing up sensational and exaggerated stories about Point Lookout that led to a lot of pain. One of the ones who got hurt was Jeremiah Wilkes. A story was printed about a prison shooting, and he was named as a suspect along with some other guards.

"It was long after the war when things got stirred up against him. I remember there was this man from Virginia who came down to the Point Lookout Hotel, where Jeremiah and Gerdie Wilkes were working, and was asking questions about a prison guard. Said a prison guard killed his daddy during the war, and he meant to find him and take him back to Virginia for trial.

"The war didn't really end in 1865, you know. It continued on for both sides. I think that this man from Virginia, Mr. Bennett Cummings, was trying to find out who killed his daddy, and he had the guilty party narrowed down to just a few local boys who had been guards at the prison. So this Mr. Bennett tells Mr. Lewis that he was going to find the guard who killed his daddy."

"But if Bennett Cummings was a lawyer, what chance did anyone have to stand against him?" I asked. "Is there a possibility that Jeremiah could have been the one who killed Virgil Cummings?"

"Well, I'll tell you what I know and let you two folks put things together to work that out." Melvin began to tell us what he knew.

Chapter 28

Captive

Gerdie Wilkes was glad that the last of the hotel guests had hopped on the steamboat and gone merrily on their way. Soon the season would be over and the steamboats would come less frequently. As far as she knew, Mr. Chambers sold several lots, and already small summer cottages were being built by her husband, Jeremiah and son, Tiberius, who were hard at work earning money, and taking pride in what they were doing. But Gerdie wondered just how much longer Jeremiah, at his age, was going to be able to work so hard.

One day this Mr. Bennett Cummings showed up at Jeremiah's farm while Jeremiah and Tiberius were building the little cottages on the bay. So Mr. Cummings starts in asking questions of the young boy who was selling his grandfather's vegetables by the road in front of the farm.

"Hello, young man," said Mr. Bennett.

"Hello," said the boy. "What kind of vegetables do you want today, mister?

"I've been visiting the farms around here looking for some good produce, and a few of the locals told me that your grandpa has the best variety, so I just wanted to see what he has for sale. Is your grandfather around today?"

"No, he's up to the hotel building cottages with my daddy for Mr. Chambers. He's got lots of vegetables for sale right now though, and the tobacco is curing in the shed. The tobacco is for sale too. What do you want to buy?"

"Your grandpa works very hard for an older fellow."

"Yep, my grandpa has, all his life, my daddy says."

"That's just real nice. I hear that your grandpa is a war hero too. A lot of those old fellows work hard to this day."

"I know he was in the war. He didn't fight in any battles though, and nobody calls him a hero."

"No? What did he do in the war then?"

"He doesn't like to talk much about it, but he was a guard at the prison camp just down the road. Daddy says not to ask him any questions about it, but I've heard the old people talking about it a little. My grandpa is a meek man, and the Bible says that's a good thing, so we don't bother him about telling us how brave he was."

"That is right, young man. I see that you read your Bible."

"Yes, mister, I do. But you know, my grandpa reads his too, and so I guess that's why he won't gossip about the war. He says too many falsehoods go around from people who like to talk too much. Grandpa is more of a peacemaker."

"Well yes, I agree with your grandpa. In fact, I have heard rumors that there have been many people blamed for things that happened at that awful prison camp. Did you ever hear about those kinds of things? It just isn't right to blame anyone for things they didn't do, is it? You couldn't call those kinds of people peacemakers now could you?"

The boy thought he had better start selling the stranger some vegetables or his father would scold him. "Mister, what kind of vegetables were you looking for?"

Bennett Cummings smiled. "I'll take a small box of tomatoes if you have some ripe ones."

"Would you like to see what we have for sale out in the back?"

"Not necessary. I'll just take the tomatoes. How much would that cost me?"

"That'll cost you five cents."

"You're a good businessman." Bennett reached into his coin purse and took out a quarter. "Keep the change," he said. "You have been most helpful."

The boy looked over and saw two men standing by the car. "I can make a better deal if all three of you buy something, and we got some great cucumbers and kale."

"They didn't come for the produce," Bennett said. "They have some other business to do here in the county. You can go ahead and get my tomatoes though."

When the boy turned away to select the tomatoes, Bennett walked back to the car and gave the order. "Drive to the Point Lookout Hotel. We've found him."

When the Peaches turned back around he saw the car speeding away.

ॐ

Jeremiah stepped down from the ladder and seated himself in the shade of the cottage roof.

"Won't be long before we can start on the inside," said Tiberius to his father.

"Son, I think I need to go over to the hotel and rest up in the kitchen with your mama. She might even have something good to eat in there. I'm feeling a little weak today."

"It's awful hot out," said Tiberius, "and we're out of water. After you rest up, could you bring another jug of water back with you?"

Jeremiah told him he would, and then taking the empty jug in hand, he walked back to the hotel. Jeremiah entered the kitchen door and saw that Gerdie was busy cleaning up.

"Do you have anything I can eat in the icebox?" he asked. "I'm feeling a little weak, and I remember now that I didn't eat much for breakfast."

"I told you that you didn't eat enough this morning. When you going to listen to me?" Gerdie was worried. Jeremiah had not been himself lately. "And now here you are, and just after I finished cleaning the kitchen up. Sit yourself down, and I'll make you something. I think you eat too much sugar, and that can make you sick. You need to eat more of the vegetables we grow."

"Thank you, my dear young bride," Jeremiah said, winking at Gerdie, "but you know well enough that I don't like vegetables."

"That won't get you more sugary food," said Gerdie. She quickly put some leftover ham and greens on a plate and handed it to Jeremiah, who gave her a little kiss on the cheek.

"Jeremiah, you are just getting too old to do this heavy work. It's enough that you work the tobacco and produce. We're doing all right, so I want you to give up building those cottages. Tiberius can put some of his boys to work. They need some money too you know."

Before Jeremiah could say anything, they heard a car pull up in the back. "You better hurry up and finish that meal and get yourself back out with Tiberius. Mr. Chambers is back, and he won't like it if he sees we're not doing our chores."

"Now Gerdie, I thought you just told me I was too old to work, and besides that, Mr. Lewis knows its lunchtime. I'm only eighty, you know. Why do you pretend otherwise? I got many more years of labor left in me but I need fuel for my strong body." Jeremiah pinched Gerdie's bottom and she giggled and waved his hand away.

"Jeremiah, you're a foolish old man," she laughed.

"Hello," said a voice from the open back door. "We're experiencing a little radiator problem with our car out back here. Would you be so kind as to bring out a jug of water? We would be very grateful. Oh, I'm sorry. My name is Thomas. How do you do?"

"Just fine, Mr. Thomas. I'm Jeremiah Wilkes, and this is my wife, Gerdie."

Gerdie looked at the man and suddenly felt frightened. Wasn't this one of the men who had stayed at this hotel in the early springtime? It seemed to her that he and his friends had gotten into a conversation with Mr. Lewis that disturbed Mr. Lewis for a few days, according to what the maids told Gerdie.

"We don't have any jugs for water," Gerdie said.

"Yes, we do," said Jeremiah. "I got one right here beside me. Let me fill this up, and I'll bring it out to you."

The man thanked him and went back to the car, opening the hood. But before the hood was opened, Gerdie saw that there were two other men in the car. They had fancy hats on their heads and were dressed like proper gentlemen.

"Jeremiah," she said, "I believe those men have been here before. I think those are the men who upset Mr. Lewis when they stayed here once. You best keep inside here with me. If they're who I remember them to be, they was asking questions about the prison camp and other questions of the maids."

"Gerdie, if those men have been here before, they're probably going to check in again and stay here, and maybe buy a cottage from Mr. Lewis. Why you got to be so suspicious of everybody these days? You got to stop listening to the maids. They got nothing to do but gossip."

Jeremiah filled the jug with water and took it to the man, who was now leaning over the radiator. "Here's your water," said Jeremiah. But the man knocked the jug out of Jeremiah's hand. As it broke apart on the ground, another man bolted from the car, and together the two men tied a rope around Jeremiah's wrists and shoved him into the backseat of the car.

"Welcome," said Bennett Cummings. "I've got some papers with your name written all over them. Drive on," he said to the two men in the front seat.

Gerdie screamed and ran out toward the car, which was already being backed up. She pounded on the hood until the driver put the car in forward gear and knocked her to the ground. Then the car was backed up some more before being driven away. She didn't know if they ran into her on purpose or not, but she was hurt from it. Not long after, Mr. Lewis came driving up in his car and saw that Tiberius was holding Gerdie in his arms.

"Tiberius, you stay right here with your mother. I'm going inside to call for a doctor and some help."

"No," Gerdie said, "you got to go after those men who took my husband away." But Lewis Chambers ran into the house, called for help, and then came out with a wet cloth. He held her head up off of the ground and put the cloth on her head.

"Help will be here soon," Lewis said. What happened to you, Gerdie?"

"Some men came here. I think it was those men who were checked in here in the spring. They had that fancy car, and they took my husband away with them. I tried to stop them, but they run into me with their car. You got to go fast. I don't know where they're taking Jeremiah." Gerdie pulled on Lewis Chambers. "I'll be all right, just please go on!"

Tiberius took over for Lewis, holding the cold cloth to her head. "I heard what Mama told you. Please, Mr. Chambers, you got to help my daddy."

Lewis knew that Bennett Cummings had taken Jeremiah, and he knew that Jeremiah was in grave danger. Running back into the hotel, he called the sheriff of Leonardtown. Then he hurried into his car and sped after Bennett Cummings.

Chapter 29

Sheriff Joe-Joe

"**B**ut if the papers were legal, how would a sheriff be able to prevent them from taking Jeremiah?" I asked.

"Well," said Melvin, "Mr. Bennett Cummings may have had some papers in his pocket, but Mr. Lewis Chambers had Sherriff Joe-Joe, and nobody steals a man away or tries to run a woman down and gets away with it in his neck of the woods."

"Who was this Sheriff Joe-Joe?" I asked.

"He was a good man," said Melvin. "Sheriff Joe-Joe was of no particular rank or status. He hadn't had much of an education, and his family didn't claim any particular breeding either, but he got to be the sheriff of Leonardtown for one reason: he was fearless. Another thing was that he never liked anyone coming into his neck of the woods, especially from Virginia, and stirring up trouble." Melvin reached for his water and sipped some with a straw before continuing his story.

❧

People came from all over the South looking for answers about loved ones who had died at Point Lookout prison. Some of them got justice, but others never did. Some awful things happened at that prison, and there were plenty of missing prisoner records, so some of the dead prisoners were never accounted for by their families. Sheriff Joe-Joe had to put up with people from Virginia and all areas of the South who showed up looking for answers.

Joe-Joe was a big country boy, and everybody on the right side of the law loved him. He was a wrestler in high school and undefeated in his day. Folks said that when Joe-Joe took to the mat, he was an awesome sight to behold. He wore a leather cap over his huge head and dared any opponent to pull it off during a match. If it came off, that person would pay hell for it.

It was impossible to pin him in a match because he was so big nobody could get him on the ground. And if you can't pin someone by the shoulders, the next best move is to force him onto his belly so you can grab an arm and twist it. But Joe-Joe was too strong to turn, so nobody could do that either. That's why Joe-Joe never lost a match. There was no place for an opponent to grab him. Most the time all Joe-Joe had to do was just stand there while his opponent danced around him, looking for a place to grab. He was the hometown hero of Leonardtown and received training as a sheriff as soon as he was old enough to apply.

One day Joe-Joe got a call from his friend, Mr. Lewis Chambers. It seemed that Mr. Bennett Cummings of the Northern Neck of Virginia had taken Jeremiah from Mr. Chamber's hotel with the help of two men, after they'd nearly run down Gerdie Wilkes. Then off they sped for Virginia. The only way to Virginia was through Leonardtown proper and beyond, so Joe-Joe put up a roadblock in the center of town, and that's when the fun began.

Joe-Joe was a little annoyed because his phone kept ringing while he was trying to eat his lunch. He didn't like to be disturbed, so he ignored it. His soft-shell crab sandwich had been prepared specially for him by his mother, and he had just taken it from his lunch box and had only eaten one bite out of it before the phone started up again. The two-man office was really not equipped for much business as the crime in those days was practically zero, but the deputy was out and Joe-Joe, annoyed over the interruption, was forced to answered the phone.

"Sheriff Joe here," he said into the phone, "and don't you know this is my lunch hour?"

"Joe, it's me, Lewis Chambers," said the voice on the phone.

"Yeah, it's lunchtime," said Joe.

"Yes, I'm sorry to disturb you, but we've got a problem," said Mr. Lewis.

"What's going on down there?" Joe-Joe asked.

"One of our citizens has been run down by a car, and her husband was taken away by force. I need you to stop a car with Virginia plates on it as soon as it gets up there in Leonardtown. There will be three white men and a black man inside the car."

"Who's from Virginia, and who's being kidnapped?" Sheriff Joe-Joe dropped his sandwich onto his napkin.

"Mr. Bennett Cummings is the kidnapper, and Jeremiah Wilkes is the one being kidnapped," said Lewis, "and I need your help in a hurry. I think they mean to harm Jeremiah, and they injured Gerdie in the process."

"I know Gerdie and Jeremiah. Is Gerdie hurt badly? Did they run her over?"

"I don't know how bad her injuries are. A doctor is on the way, but I'm sure that Jeremiah won't be safe. We've got to stop those men from Virginia. Can you do something?"

Sheriff Joe-Joe was very protective of his people, and nobody was coming into his territory and kidnapping anybody. The thought of any woman, especially one as old as Gerdie, being run down made him angry, and everybody in Leonardtown knew better then to be around Joe-Joe when he was angry.

Joe-Joe ordered a few of the businessmen and some of the towns-people to go out onto Main Street with him and block it until some guards from the courthouse ran over to help, with their guns loaded. By the time the car arrived in Leonardtown, it was stopped and surrounded, and the captive was set free.

Sheriff Joe-Joe put Mr. Bennett Cummings and the insolent men with him into jail and left them there for a week, without outside contact. Eventually some lawyers came over from Virginia and got the three men released, but they never did come back.

Apparently those men must have decided it was best to let things go out of fear of being convicted of kidnapping and attempted murder for running down Gerdie Wilkes. I think Sheriff Joe-Joe may have put some fear in them too. Thank the good Lord, she was fine. She had some bad bruising, but they didn't hit her hard enough to do major injury.

Mr. Lewis Chambers took Jeremiah home in his car, and after that Jeremiah said some things that Mr. Lewis had never heard before. Jeremiah was in a kind of daze, so Mr. Lewis started asking about everything that went on.

"This is about the shooting at the prison camp, isn't it?" Mr. Lewis asked.

"Yes sir, it is," said Jeremiah. "This thing just won't die. It's been a chain around me most my life, and I'm tired now. I tried asking the

Lord long ago to make all this go away, but it seems I won't ever get peace."

"Was it you?" Mr. Chambers asked.

❧

"But Jeremiah wouldn't say a word, and Lewis never asked again," said Melvin. "I don't think those papers Mr. Bennett had were legal in Maryland at all. So anyhow, Jeremiah was left alone after that happened. Sheriff Joe-Joe was elected sheriff up until he was too old to carry out his duties any longer. But like I said, everybody loved the man."

"What happened to Jeremiah?" I asked.

"Well," said Melvin, "he did just fine after that. He continued to work at the hotel and tend his own farm. He and Mrs. Wilkes did real good for themselves, having raised a bunch of kids and grandchildren. Some of them have gone on to be real successful, and most still live around here. They're a quiet bunch and like to keep to themselves mostly.

"But you know it was never proven who shot that prisoner, though Jeremiah brought up a fellow named Gus a lot back in the day. I guess it's one of those mysteries that will never be solved. The Wilkes families don't do much talking about that incident to this very day. Can't really blame those good folks for silence over such a thing." Melvin took a long sip of water.

"Do you think that it was Gus who had that poor prisoner, Virgil Cummings, murdered?" I asked. "I mean, why else would Jeremiah have mentioned him?"

"Not sure myself, but men will turn on each other when they're suffering," Melvin said. "There is a certain shame to it all, but nobody knows what it would take to survive in a place like Point Lookout. It's best not to judge another, especially when it comes to survival."

Survival. I thought about that word for a minute as I heard the end of Melvin's story. Whatever had taken place at that prisoner of war camp there were still too many unanswered questions, and I wondered if the descendants of the prisoners who died there would ever get answers.

"I guess the one thing that people need to learn more them anything else," Melvin added, "is to survive their own shortcomings. That takes more courage than surviving the things of this world."

David reached over and patted Melvin's shoulder. "Thanks, my friend. I never get enough of your stories. You know, I've haven't heard this story before. I guess my mother's side of the family kept that unpleasant incident a secret."

"Yes," I said, "thank you so much for sharing what you know with me, Mr. Melvin. I have really enjoyed listening."

I thanked Melvin again and hugged him as he sat in his wheelchair. He seemed frail and tired, and I was feeling a little guilty for possibly taking up so much of his afternoon nap time, but he graciously thanked me for coming. After shaking hands with David, he waved good-bye to us with a smile.

"I have to hand it to you, Rainey," David said outside. "You have really devoted a lot of hours trying to find out the answers to this particular incident at the prison camp. I think that Melvin has just added to your research. Very impressive! In fact, between you and Melvin, I'm getting hooked on these stories. You know, I might just have to join you if you ever go to the National Archives in DC. You mentioned that you were thinking about it, and I'd like to be your research assistant or something like that."

"That would be fine," I said, "but I'm all business when it comes to records, and you may be very interested to know that it is rare to actually bring anything to conclusion. I will forever be indebted to you for introducing me to Melvin though. He has been so much help and so have you. Thank you for the offer." I didn't feel that I needed an assistant and hoped that he would just leave the subject alone.

As we walked back to the truck, I had a sinking feeling that I would never get to the bottom of who killed Virgil Cummings. I wondered if perhaps Jeremiah could be guilty. It wasn't a conclusion I wanted to consider. *Maybe I could use a little help*, I reasoned.

"Despite not getting to the bottom of a murder, I feel that I owe you for all you've done to help me," I said.

"You owe me nothing," said David. "However, I do want to apologize for overstepping my boundaries earlier. I shouldn't have pressed you on the forgiveness thing."

"Let's just forget about it, David."

Friend or not, I had no intention of sharing any more of my past with David. What good would that do? He would only try to evangelize me again. But...he did offer to help me, and my research could be done much faster with two shuffling through stacks of papers instead of one.

"I will think about your offer to help with my research," I said. David nodded but said nothing.

We walked back to the truck and began the drive back to the B&B. I realized that soon I would have to check out and return to my apartment. Leaving my cottage life for my dark apartment was not a pleasant thought. There was so much more to learn about the Civil War and post–Civil War years in this area where my little cottage stood. Thinking about all of the facts that I had crammed up inside of my head would have made most people crazy, but those facts helped keep me sane.

"What are you thinking about?" David asked as we drove.

"Oh, I don't know," I answered, "but I think that I'm actually becoming sad about the fact that I'll soon have to return to my apartment and resume my other life. I really am a little blue about that. I won't have as much time to research things."

"Where do you live uptown?" he asked. "It can't be that far away."

"No. I live about an hour and a half away in Annapolis. That's where my company has an office. I live near the Naval Academy stadium in an old apartment building. I think it was built in the 1940s, and isn't in the best of shape, but it's affordable and near my work, so I have no complaints. The one advantage to it is that the Maryland State Archives is a bike ride away, just down the street from me."

"You know," said David, "I was just thinking about something."

"What?"

"The Northern Neck of Virginia is only a short trip from here over the Harry Nice Bridge, so I was thinking that you may want to do a little investigating about Joanna Cummings before you head back to Annapolis. You shared with Linda and me that the Cummings family lived in Walnut Oak, Virginia. Wouldn't it be a good idea to look around over there to see what information there is about the Cummings family? You may find information there that Annapolis won't have."

Since I hadn't thought of that, I was surprised that David had. "Wow, I think that's a great idea. Maybe I'll look into that."

"Good," he said. "Let me know if you need any help." I could tell that he was not going to be put off any longer.

"Yes, I would like your help, but I know that you are up to your neck in repair work right now."

"That's true," he said, "I do have more work to finish, but if you are going back to your apartment, I'm sure that I could take a break now and then to help with your research. My crew is ahead of schedule too, and they are working hard. I don't need to be there twenty-four-seven. I'm the owner, you know."

I needed someone to show me the Northern Neck because I had never been to that area of Virginia before. "OK, I'd like to go as soon as I can get over there," I said. "Do you want to make arrangements to meet?"

"Just call," he said.

"Well instead of calling you, why don't we just plan to go next Saturday?"

"I can pick you up as early as eight thirty in the morning next Saturday. How would that be?"

"I'll be ready," I said.

When I entered the B&B, I went up to my room and thought about Melvin. How could a newborn baby who washed up on a beach and was never claimed by anyone turn out to be such a loving and secure gentleman? Could I ever hope to own those qualities? Not only that, but he was a walking history book of sorts. I wanted to visit him again sometime.

Chapter 30

Investigators

Early on Saturday morning David picked me up at the B&B. Before leaving with him, I told Linda that I would soon have to check out and return to my apartment. I was sad about it because I had come to think of Linda as a friend.

"I knew you would be leaving us soon," she said, "and I have to tell you that I'm really going to miss you. Will you be going up town or staying at your cottage?"

"I'm not sure," I said. "I guess it all depends on how far along the repairs to my cottage are, but I'll be going down soon to check the progress, so hopefully I'll be able to stay there. I only have four more weeks before I go back to work in Annapolis, so I would love to stay down this way if possible."

"We would love it if you could stay here with us," she said, "but if not with us, nearby is good too." There was something about Linda that made me wish I had a sister to share my life with.

When I got into David's truck, I asked him if we would have time to see my cottage before our journey to the Northern Neck.

"Not today," he said. "It's a little out of the way, and besides that, there are things being finished up down there today, with a lot of supplies being delivered and workers all over the street. How about you drive down tomorrow instead?"

"I guess I'll have to check out of the B&B soon, David, and head back to my apartment. When I say I'll have to leave soon, it's because staying at the B&B has done damage to my budget. I'll hate leaving though. I'd just like to see the cottage one more time before I go."

"I'm sorry to hear that. How about we try to enjoy today though?"

"So," I asked, "about how much of a drive is it to Walnut Oak?" But inside I was really wondering if he cared at all about the fact that I would soon be leaving.

"The drive is at least an hour, maybe two. We know that there should be information about the Cummings family in Walnut Oak, so why don't we start at the library and see what kind of records they have about the Civil War or other historical documents that may help in our search for answers? Hopefully we'll find what you're looking for," he said.

"Sounds good to me," I agreed, but I still wondered again why he did not respond to my comment about me leaving soon for Annapolis.

The drive over took about two hours as we meandered the back roads of the Virginia highway system. I found the area very beautiful and was surprised that it was still mostly a rural farm area.

We stopped for breakfast at a roadside restaurant, where we each ordered the special of scrapple, eggs, and biscuits. Then after gulping down our coffees, we shared the bill and got back into the truck.

Before we got started, David took a napkin from the truck console and wiped a spot off my chin. Then he sat looking at me. "You're still cute. Even with food running down your chin." He gently brushed a strand of hair out of my face and smiled down at me.

"Is my hair that messy?" I asked him as I pulled some strands behind my ears.

"No," he said. Then he pulled out of the parking lot and drove the truck in the direction of Walnut Oak. I wondered why he felt the need to touch me like that.

We found the public library at Walnut Oak and went right to work looking up the names of residents in the population index. Combing through names, we found that there were several people listed with the name Cummings, all residents of Walnut Oak or the surrounding small towns. I asked the librarian if she had any historical books about citizens from the time of the Civil War. She nodded, motioning for me to follow her to the reference area.

"I can't allow any of these books out of the library," she said, "but you're free to use the copy machine. We have microfiche with quite a number of Civil War articles and newspaper clippings available too."

I thanked the librarian, and together David and I looked through the dozens of recorded names in the population index as well as from other documents. From there we finally we came upon a book entitled *The Heroes of Walnut Oak.*

Some local historian had self-published a book for the people of Walnut Oak and the surrounding towns. In the book were some six names of men who had fought and died for Virginia; one of the names written in the book was Virgil E. Cummings. Beside the date of his birth was an entry: "Confined as a prisoner of war at Point Lookout.

No death certificate on record—missing prisoner of war." Of all the men from Walnut Oak listed, his was the only name entered without a death certificate recorded.

"I just don't get it," I said. "Did the War Department ever get their facts together?"

"According to what you've researched so far, I would have thought that one would have been produced by the time this book was written. Maybe there just isn't a death certificate," David said.

"What are you saying?" I asked.

"Maybe he didn't die in that camp."

"That's an odd notion," I said. "We know that he died because of his wounds."

"Do we know that for sure? Where's the proof?"

I thought about all of the records and microfiche and interviews I had conducted. I had read diaries and news clippings, but nothing that I had read ever officially referred to Virgil as deceased, not even Dr. Comstock's reports.

"I want to see if there are any historical records pertaining to Joanna Cummings," I said. "Maybe there will be some information in connection with her husband's death, like an official notice or something."

Again I went up to the librarian and asked her help. She led me to a section and handed me a book about the early prominent families of Walnut Oak. The name Joanna Baker Cummings was in the section along with her father and mother-in-law, Joseph Emmitt Cummings married to Julia Kemp, and Virgil E. Cummings married to Joanna Baker.

"David, there is something very strange here. Virgil was mentioned as the husband of Joanna Baker Cummings, but no notation was made of the cause of death for him, or the date of his death as it is listed for Joanna Cummings or Julia Cummings, her mother-in-law. But the shock is that this early newspaper article that I just scanned said that Virgil's father, Joseph E. Cummings, died of a drowning accident while attempting to save the life of his business partner, Gus Pruett."

"Was there anything in her diary that mentioned a marriage to Gus Pruett?" David asked.

"No, but we do know that she made a very brief trip to Washington, DC, to get an official death certificate for her husband, Virgil. Maybe she had to get that before she could marry Gus, legally? Look at this. The date that she traveled to Washington is the same date that her father-in-law drowned, according to this book." I was perplexed and wanted some clarity. "And according to Joanna's diary, she knew that Gus was in line to become her father-in-law's business partner, but only on the condition of marriage. I don't find a marriage certificate saying that she married Gus Pruett, so how did he become a partner?"

"I don't know, but what do you make of it, Rainey? It seems odd that two events like that happened on the same day." I could tell that David wanted answers too.

"I'm not sure what I make of it," I said. "But I will tell you, from what I've read in Joanna Cummings's journal, she didn't fully trust Gus, and of course neither had Virgil. Maybe after the death of Virgil's father, Joanna had no choice but to marry Gus, but why is their marriage not recorded? I began to think about what this could possibly mean, and the two of us talked about it for well over an hour, drawing some conclusions along the way.

Chapter 31

Joanna Baker Cummings

It had been nearly a year since Gus had arrived with the sad news of her dear husband's death, but even so, Joanna had become fixed on the idea that no matter how long she waited, Virgil would one day return to her. For all of her dreaming and all of the reports of errors being made in death records, she clung to the idea that Virgil was still alive. Just three months earlier, a neighbor had reported that her son, Travis, had made his own journey home after his mother had received a false report of his death.

Mama and Papa Cummings had accepted Virgil's death and had gone on with their lives, but Joanna had held out as long as she was capable. The thing that pressed on her mind more and more was the fact that her mourning period was nearly over, and by all accounts, she was expected to make Gus her husband and the father of her boy, Bennett. The idea of being wedded to Gus was unacceptable in her mind, yet her boy needed a father, and Papa Cummings was getting older. With so many thousands of war widows, she knew that her chances for remarriage were slim, and survival was paramount now.

The newspapers were finally reporting the atrocities on both sides. Reports about Andersonville and Point Lookout were frequently mentioned, fueling blame on both sides, but Joanna had come to the conclusion that no side had been totally right about the war. Lincoln had been assassinated, and Booth and his fellow conspirators were all dead now. There was so much death on both sides, but who to blame and what about the missing men?

Widows suffered in the South and in the North, and so did freed blacks as they wandered the country looking for work, clothing, food, and shelter. Freedom had not guaranteed their survival or safety. What mattered now was how to survive in a broken nation full of broken people living without hope.

With so many worries and concerns over her in-laws and her own concern about her little boy, Joanna knew that she must think logically, and so she did her best to keep from despair, and this brought about the decision to travel to Washington, DC.

Joanna prayed that the War Department in Washington, DC, had by now assembled the paperwork needed to give relief to the families of those men who had been missing since the war had ended. Since she had never received official notice of her husband's death, she had it in her mind to make the journey and find out the truth, no matter what the outcome might be.

When Gus found out that Joanna would be going to Washington and why, he did everything he could to stop her.

"I was thinking that your time of mourning is near to being over, and I got something I wanted to ask you," Gus said.

"My time is not entirely up," she replied.

"Well, it's getting to be close, and I was hoping that you would be willing to hold up on that trip to Washington long enough to hear what I got to say."

"This isn't a good time to discuss my trip."

"I've already spoke to Mr. and Mrs. Cummings, and they seemed grateful that little Bennett is thinking of me in a closer way."

"Yes, I've noticed that. You have been good to my boy, and I'm grateful for that as well."

"Well, it ain't your little boy that I want you to be grateful about."

"Gus, whatever you have to say to me will have to wait. I'm leaving tomorrow for Washington, and I won't be coming back until I have the answers that I need." Joanna stepped back away from Gus and turned to leave the room. Gus stepped closer to her.

"Just what kind of answers you looking for in Washington?"

"I want to know who murdered my husband."

"I know that, but I already told you what happened." Gus was becoming perturbed, and his voice was showing it.

"No. You told me what you thought had happened, which I appreciate, but there has to be official records, and I intend to read them for myself."

"It could be dangerous for you to travel alone. Why not travel there with a man who can protect you?"

"You are needed here. Papa is depending on you to help him with the crabbing and working the oysters. Besides, I'll be on a steamboat and not traveling by coach through the countryside alone. From there I will be perfectly safe at the home of my aunt. She will accompany me to where I need to go. Thank you just the same."

Gus gave Joanna a look that she had never seen before. His eyes were squinted and his mouth pursed. "You don't know what you're talking about. I been to Washington, and it's nothing but a city where women are mistreated and robbed. You better think again before you leave this farm. If I was you, I'd take a man along and not some old woman."

Joanna was taken aback by Gus's comment. "I appreciate your concern for me, Gus, I really do, but I will be perfectly safe. My uncle will be accompanying my aunt and me."

"You aren't hearing what I'm trying to tell you," said Gus. "I want to go with you. Don't you want your aunt and uncle to meet your future husband?"

"Husband?" Joanna turned away from Gus. "Thank you for your concern, but if I feel the least bit threatened, I will wire you to come." Joanna felt uneasy and moved farther away from Gus.

Gus, sensing that he had said too much, straightened himself up and changed his mood. "All right then, but I want you to know that I'll be worried about you in that awful place. But like you said, you can wire me a message, and I'll come and look after you."

Joanna couldn't figure out if she was revolted by Gus, but more than ever there was something about him that seemed to threaten her peace. She thought to tell Papa about Gus's demeanor, but then she changed her mind several times, thinking it best not to frighten Papa with Gus's words of warning about her trip to Washington.

Papa had enough worries and had not been supportive of her trip to see her aunt at all. When she told him that her main reason was to investigate Virgil's death and to obtain a legal death notice, Papa had softened. The thought of actual accounts of what happened to his son seemed a good thing to him as well. Joanna was relieved by the fact that Gus would just have to wait—maybe forever—for her to say yes.

Eventually our ideas started to merge together and the conclusion we had come up with seemed to make sense to us both, so I asked David how much more time he had to investigate with me.

"I've taken the whole day off. Why?"

"Could we drive to the National Archives and see what we can find about Virgil? There has to be something like hospital records or a muster roll or duty roster of some kind. I've always wanted to visit the National Archives, but for some reason I've never taken the time to do so. It would mean a lot to me if you could take me there today." I realized that I was asking a lot of David, but I couldn't hide my excitement.

"It's still early enough to get in. Let's go," he said. "I know a short-cut into the city, and it is Saturday, so we should get there within a couple of hours."

I was grateful to David for doing this for me, and for once I was relaxed and dead set on getting to the bottom of my final question. What had happened to Virgil Cummings? Was there no death certificate, because he had not died at the prison? Had the prison messed the records up, as had been the case at most every Civil War prison camp? Had his bones been thrown in a common grave along with the bones of thousands of other dead men? Had he deserted or died after being released at the end of the war, or had Virgil simply not gone home because he was maimed or mentally impaired for some reason? Also, if he had died in the prison, was there a record of who may have killed him? My mind was floating in a hundred directions.

David drove the truck into the city, and I marveled as he found his way to the National Archives. "How did you know how to get here so quickly?" I asked him.

"I've been here before," he said. "I think I told you that I was a history major in college, but it didn't pan out for me. I guess God had other plans for my life. I've been here many times just digging into records and thinking about things. I've studied World War II more than any other subject, but I've taken a look at the Civil War records as well. I'll lead you right to them."

There again I had to hear about God and God's perfect little "plans." I wanted to say something to David, but I decided not to stir that subject up again, and just let it go. I appreciated his help more than being annoyed with his spirituality, at least for today.

Once inside the National Archives, I was awestruck with the building and the vastness of the important documents on display. But I would have to save the tour for another day. David helped me find the Civil War documents and microfiche, and together we pored through the records of those who had been imprisoned at Point Lookout. We found a few books written about the camp and scanned information until we were fatigued and our eyes were blurry.

"I think we've been looking at records for too many hours," I whispered. "There isn't one section or index that I've scanned that's given me any new information about Virgil Cummings. It makes no sense to me that the man simply vanished. Have you found anything interesting?"

David smiled. "I think so. I'm in the middle of scanning a report written by a Lieutenant Arnold Brown about some Confederate prisoners, at various Union prisons, who took the Union oath right before the war ended. It seems that the men were considered traitors by their fellow prisoners. Some of the oath-takers were sent home, but others were sent elsewhere, even injured soldiers, according to this report."

"That's interesting," I said, "but where are we going to get the names of those men?"

"Well," David said, "I'm reading something now about some regiments that were sent out west to work at the outposts and forts created to protect the settlers from the Indians. It seems that they had multiple duties out west, and this report states that the men who had taken the oath of the First US Volunteers were called 'galvanized Yankees' by their fellow Confederate prisoners and were considered traitors."

I had never heard of that term and wanted to learn more about it. I searched until I found more information about Confederate soldiers on the frontier and together with David looked for an answer to our question. Had Virgil Cummings taken the Union oath to become a "galvanized Yankee"?

David and I began to hypothesize, taking into account all of the information that we had collected.

Chapter 32

Galvanized Yankees

Virgil opened his eyes and immediately felt a sharp, burning pain in his lower right side, and his head hurt so badly that he could hear himself moaning. "Where am I?" He tried to see who was standing next to him as he felt a presence, but he couldn't turn his head.

"Settle down, young man. You are in Hammond Hospital, Point Lookout." The doctor walked close enough to the cot for Virgil to see him.

"Who are you?" Virgil asked.

"I'm Dr. Comstock, one of the doctors here at the camp. You were shot, but the bullet passed through and out the right side of your hip, with the minié ball missing any vital organs. I've dressed your wound, and I think that you'll heal. You are a very fortunate young man, but it looks like you took a few severe blows to the back and front of the head as well as the bullet wound. You have a bad concussion and slight fracture. Your head was a mess of blood when you were brought in. I have no explanation for the head wounds or the damage to your knees. Do have any idea how you got them?"

"Gus," Virgil muttered.

"Your friend?" asked the doctor. "He thinks you're dead and seemed quite sad about it, so why do you think he had something to do with this? How would a fellow prisoner get a gun?"

"I know only one thing doctor, Gus did this to me. He beat me and then threatened my life, and now here I am with a hole in me and a banged-up head. What would you think if you were me?" Virgil put both hands on his bandaged head. "I'm in a lot of pain. I need you to give me something for the pain."

"You need to lie still and try not to talk," said the doctor. "I'm afraid that I have nothing I can give you for pain right now, but if what you just said is true, I wouldn't want to go back to my tent if I were you. You would be safer right here. A guard had to have shot you, but someone else beat you almost to death. It seems that the one who beat you was hoping to take your life. But what would have provoked a guard to murder you?"

"Does a guard have to have a reason? They do it for fun," he said. "Why do you care? You're a Union doctor, and I'm a Confederate prisoner. What do you have to lose if I just conveniently die of a gunshot wound?"

"I may be a Union physician, but I have also taken an oath to save lives. It wasn't that long ago when I was your age, though time has a habit of putting years on a person. Nevertheless, you are not going to die if you take my advice and save yourself so that when the war is over you can return to your family."

"Advice? What advice?" Virgil tried to control his pain by speaking in a more controlled tone. "How can I save myself? As soon as I'm out of here, someone will try to kill me again."

"My advice to you is to take the Union oath. There's word going around that a guard fired down toward your tent, but it's impossible to ascertain which one because all of the guards shot at once. You had better be concerned about that guard, or for that matter the fellow prisoner who beat you. Taking the oath may save your life."

"Take the oath? I would never do that!" said Virgil. "I'm no deserter or turncoat, and I don't plan to be!" Virgil held his head again and sucked in a deep breath.

"Even if taking the oath means that you will see your family again? Do you have a wife or children?"

Virgil's heart began to tighten as he thought of Joanna. He hadn't heard from her in months, and he feared that something had happened to her. "I have a wife, but taking the oath would ban me from my family forever. My family would never forgive me for doing that."

"You know, many injured young men have taken the oath just so they could go home. If your home isn't beyond the Union lines, you could be released if you take the oath."

"I'm from the Northern Neck just across the Potomac from here."

"Oh, I see," said the doctor. "Well there *are* a couple of options. One option is that by taking the oath you could be exchanged for a Union prisoner, but the North isn't doing many exchanges now that the war is drawing down. Another option is to be sent up north somewhere to do labor for the government, but I've heard tell that they may send some of those boys to the front lines to fight for the Union." The doctor looked at the wound on Virgil's hip.

"The option that may be best for you is to join one of the regiments that will be sent west to help with the Indian uprisings. They will be used to help keep the peace there. As soon as the time of your enlistment is over, you would be given pay for your service to the government and sent home, or if you wanted to stay out there, you would be able to do that. What I'm saying is that there are options for you should you take the oath."

"None of those options sound good to me," Virgil said. "They'll have to send me home after the war anyhow, so why should I take the oath? What's the use? I told you that if I take the oath, there will be no welcome home for me. There is really nothing I can do but sit it out."

"Except, young man," said Dr. Comstock, "from what you've told me, someone wants you dead. If you aren't concerned about that and you want to wait out the war, then I'll release you back to your tent when your wounds have healed. It's up to you, but I will tell you this—the South is indeed going to lose this war, and in the interim this prison camp will be a torturous place to live."

"It can't be any worse of a place then it is now," Virgil said with a grimace.

"Another several boatloads of wounded and dying Confederate prisoners are expected within a day or two. Those prisoners, added to the current overcrowding, will quickly deplete food rations and winter fuel and blankets. While you still have an opportunity to get out of this place, you should think long and hard about what I've told you."

Virgil could hear moaning coming from the other hospital beds. He estimated that there were at least thirty or forty beds in the tent. "I hate this place. Why don't you get more doctors out here to care for these poor suffering men? Why don't you give us something for our pain?"

"Those men were brought in this morning, and I can tell you that most of them will be dead within twenty-four hours."

"I try to ignore statistics. I'm trying to survive, and I don't want to hear bad news," Virgil said through clenched teeth.

"Well, there have been some major defeats for the South. The hospitals on both sides are full to the brim with the dead and dying. Only a handful of the men in here are in the kind of shape that you're in, and some of them have already taken the oath and volunteered to go out west. The South has no chance of winning now."

"How do you know that? General Lee isn't a quitter. He will prevail, and so will the South."

"Now, just take a look around you," Dr. Comstock reasoned. "This camp was never intended to house the thousands of men who are crowded in here. These are men from your side. Most of them just want the war to be over so that they can go home. The North has the manpower, the weapons, the food, and the railroads under their control. It doesn't look good for the South right now, and medicine is scarce. Men die under conditions like these."

"You didn't mention our noble cause, Dr. Comstock; we have a cause as noble as your side." Virgil felt a jab in his side as sharp pain seized him. "You got to give me something for this pain. I can usually tolerate it, but I think I need something."

"I told you that I can't give you anything. I have only a small supply left, and as you can hear all around, I can't spare any for you. You will feel worse by tomorrow and for several weeks or so, but after that you will begin to feel better. As I told you, you are in better condition then most of these poor souls."

"What about finding the guard who tried to kill me?" Virgil asked. "What if he shoots another prisoner? Who is going to find out who did this to me?"

"In your case, an inquiry will be made in an effort to find the shooter. However, there is little justice in times of war. What's more important for you right now is to realize that someone wants you dead, and you're lucky that you're not." The doctor skillfully and quickly removed the old bandages from Virgil's side and began to redress the wound. He placed a fresh bandage on his head wound as well.

"Think about my advice to you, young man," said the doctor. "Those new regiments being formed will be heading west in two months. Your wounds should be healed enough by then. And by the way, the names of the men going out are being kept from the other prisoners for now. They will be called a work detail that is being sent out of the camp to do labor for the Union. This is so they don't have to face their fellow prisoners after taking the oath. I'd like to see you go with them."

"I don't know why you would care one way or the other." Virgil grimaced as more pain shot through his hip.

"As I said, I took an oath to be a doctor, and I do not discriminate concerning who my patients are. This prison has made it very hard for me to practice my profession. I've seen a lot of abuse and a lot of needless disease and sickness. I'm tired of death, and I want this war to end. I too have a family waiting for me after the war is over. And as far as justice goes, I plan to write a report exposing the treatment of some of the prisoners here at this camp. I hope that my words will bring about justice someday. There will be plenty of doctors on both sides of this war who will make similar reports. I'm sure the prison camps in the South are equally horrendous to those in the North. History will tell the tale."

Virgil watched as the doctor put his instruments in his bag and walk out of the sweltering tent. He could hear moaning and crying all around him. The smell of death and oozing wounds made its way into his nostrils. He turned his head to the side and began to heave, but he had nothing in his stomach to give up.

The moaning and screaming went on into the night and did not stop, even in the morning. Virgil's own pain had grown more intense, but he bit his lip rather them cry out. Hours and hours went by, and finally the next day the doctor came back to check on him and change his bandages, saying nothing to Virgil.

"I want out of here in the worst kind of way," Virgil whispered to the doctor. "I figure if I go out west and the war ends soon, at least I'll still be fighting, and it won't be against my own side. That doesn't make me a deserter or a coward. But what about everyone in the prison yard still thinking I'm a dead man?"

"As far as I know, word hasn't gotten out to the contrary," the doctor said. "Everyone thinks you're a dead man, so why don't we just leave it like that? Several of the prisoners have done the same thing. We won't issue a death certificate, but we won't deny that you've died either. Paperwork mistakes are common in wartime and always will be." The doctor turned to leave but paused first.

"If you're serious about this, I'll send an officer in to read the terms of the oath to you. No one will know that you're alive except me, the officer, and the others who will be taking the oath. When you get to your station out west, no one will care who you are, and your fears about being a traitor will wear off one day, just as your pain and this terrible, senseless war will. Once some time goes by, you *will* be able to go home. People are forgiving. Things will be forgotten, and understanding will prevail. I'll send an officer in, and I'll be back to change your bandages tomorrow, provided that there will be bandages left."

The officer arrived at the medical tent that evening. Virgil noticed that he had stopped at other beds before making his way over to explain the oath of allegiance. The officer held the written oath up and allowed Virgil to read it. He explained to Virgil that after his release from the hospital, he would be put in a private area of the camp with others who would take the oath with him, and then they would be sworn in. From there they would be formed into the First US

Volunteer Regiment, trained, and sent out for duty. The officer put the oath papers into his leather pouch and left the tent as quietly as he had entered it.

A feeling of dread came over Virgil. What had he done? He had never before imagined that he could commit a traitorous thing such as this. Had he really made up his mind to swear off his own country? But no matter what reasoning he could think of to justify his actions, he was filled with remorse and self-hatred just thinking about taking the oath to the Union.

When he tried to think of Joanna, he could no longer picture her. When he thought of his beloved mama and papa, he imagined the pain that his actions would cause them, and he remembered something that his papa had always told him. He had said that a traitor in the family makes traitors of the whole family, and that it would be better had the traitor died a good death then to have put a good family to shame.

Never one to make excuses for himself, Virgil thought of the only thing that gave him a reason to live; he would go out west, along with other Confederate soldiers who took the oath. He would fight for and protect settlers heading to the frontier. This was something that he could do. But could he ever go home?

As we speculated about Virgil Cummings, David and I scanned for names of those who had taken the oath to the Union and had gone out west. There we found the name we had been looking for:

Virgil E. Cummings, Pvt.
Company G, Fifty-Ninth Virginia
Point Lookout Camp for Confederate Prisoners

"Do you think that any of the other prisoners could have found out about the First Volunteer Regiment?" I asked David.

"I think it would almost be impossible for them not to find out," he replied. "Men hate other men who betray their country. Traitors are always found out."

"So somehow you think that Gus found out? If so, what do you think he did about it? After all, he was safe as long as Virgil was dead."

"I guess we'll never know," said David, "but I have an idea that Gus could find a way to survive whether Virgil was dead or alive. He was mentioned as a partner to Virgil's father."

"Maybe we should do a search on Gus next," I said. "Everyone has a past. Joanna's diary said that he was from Georgia."

After another hour of combing records, we discovered that the record of release for Gus Pruett from Point Lookout was dated shortly after the war had ended. It stated that his hometown was Atlanta. From there we searched for any facts that may have been printed in the Atlanta papers about him or his family. What we found disturbed us both.

Chapter 33

Gus Pruett

In his mind, Gus figured he had done things no other man would have done for the family of Virgil Cummings. Hadn't he brought the farm back to life? But with all he had done, especially for Virgil's wife and son, he had come to the conclusion that things were about to go bad for him.

Joanna had taken herself to Washington and away from him. If she should find out anything about Virgil in Washington, Gus would be forced out of his rightful due, for he figured that the farm at Walnut Oak would be his one day. How could he get Joanna back to the farm before she found out about Virgil? Up to now no mail had come through about Virgil, he had made sure of that, but what if she found out something snooping around the war records?

Mr. Cummings had signed a paper saying that as a condition of partnership, Joanna must agree to marry Gus. If they married, a portion of ownership would belong to Gus and Joanna, but Bennett would be the majority owner when he came of age. Gus would always be just a minority partner. The thought of that spoiled brat of Virgil's giving him orders was more then he could stand.

Joanna had left on the morning steamer to ride up the Potomac to Washington, but Gus knew that even if he tried he couldn't get to

Washington for another day. Mr. Cummings had given him his blessing when Gus asked about marrying Joanna, but she wouldn't even let
him propose. And now she was up to something that could possibly
force him to take drastic measures. Gus went to find Mrs. Cummings.

"I was hoping to take little Bennett out in the boat fishing today,"
he said.

"Oh, Gus, I know he would love that, but he is very upset about his
mama leaving, so I think I'll keep him close to home today. Joanna
wouldn't approve of him going out today as he seems to be running
a little fever, and he keeps rubbing his ears too. Just to be on the safe
side, I'm going to keep a close eye on him today. You have been so good
to him, and he just adores you, you know. I'll see how he is tomorrow,
and if he's better, I'll let you take him down to the dock with you, but
he really is still too young yet to go out in the boat."

"I was just thinking the boy needs to learn manly things and grow
up a little. He don't look too sick for a little boat ride."

"Gus," said the surprised grandmother, "he is still just a toddler.
We don't have to worry about all of that just now. He'll be the man that
Virgil would have been proud of someday. We'll see to that, but today
is just not a good day for him. He may be teething again."

Gus put on his friendly smile and tried to calm himself down.
"Maybe you're right. I guess men are always trying to grow the boys
up fast."

But he had to walk away. Virgil's name made him furious, and he
didn't want Mrs. Cummings to suspect just how much he hated that
name. He walked off with the notion that Virgil would always ruin
things for him. Soon he was so worked up that he hardly noticed Mr.
Cummings.

"Gus," said Mr. Cummings, "I was just about to go look for you. I was going to check the oyster beds, but I'm feeling a little stiff today, so I was hoping you'd come along. I'm afraid the gout is getting the better of my back." Mr. Cummings could see that the look on Gus's face was not a happy one.

"I know you're upset about Joanna leaving for Washington this morning, Gus, but I wouldn't give up hope. She knows how good you are to the missus and me, and you certainly have been wonderful to little Bennett. Give her some time. She'll come around."

"Yes sir, I know it," said Gus, "but I guess you can't blame her for wanting to get that death certificate in her hands. It seems a woman has to have proof before she can settle down with another man."

"Oftentimes that is the case with women," agreed Mr. Cummings. "Mrs. Cummings is the same way about proof and wants to get to the bottom of everything I say to her, so I have to mind what I say. There is really nothing weak about the weaker sex you know." Mr. Cummings patted Gus on the back. "Come on now, let's go check the oyster beds and see how our seedlings have done over these long months."

Gus looked over at the small wooden boat tucked up on the shore under a tree. "I'll get the boat," he offered. Then Gus pushed the boat out and down the hillside until it slid into the creek just off of the Potomac River. The two men climbed into the boat, and Gus rowed them out into the cove to a shallow area near the riverbank. Mr. Cummings pushed the tongs down into the murky water, opening and closing them until he could feel the resistance of an oyster shell. He then pulled the tongs up and dropped a large oyster into the boat.

"Let's crack this big oyster open and see what we have here," he said.

Gus took the oyster knife from the bow of the boat and handed it to Mr. Cummings, who with great skill opened the oyster in seconds. Then handing the knife back to Gus, Mr. Cummings offered Gus the colossal white oyster. "Give it a taste and see what you think, Gus."

Gus tasted the oyster and then swallowed it down. "I think the beds are going to make us rich!" he said enthusiastically. But Mr. Cummings looked at Gus.

"Well, I appreciate that, but Joanna needs to give you her hand in marriage before the partnership is final. I do hope that she says yes, and it would be nice to have you in the family, but don't worry, I'll be willing to make you a business partner as soon as Joanna says she will marry you." Mr. Cummings hoped that Gus would understand. "Joanna has a mind of her own, you know, and we are only her in-laws. We can advise her, but we don't have authority over her."

Gus cleared his throat and tried to think of something to say but couldn't. He began to realize that he didn't have things as sewed up as he once figured. Mr. Cummings couldn't have made these oyster beds into anything without him, he reasoned, and besides that, he couldn't have kept the farm up or made the crab harvest profitable by himself either. Everything he had done to win Mr. Cummings over was for nothing, for now everything depended upon the feelings of a woman, and not on the help he had been to this whole family. Women were always trouble, and they'd ruin everything if a man let them.

Gus thought about the woman in Atlanta who wouldn't marry him. She'd caused him trouble too, always insisting that he wait. But then she turned around and married someone else. Gus remembered the last time he saw them, husband and wife together. They were walking through the park in the center of town. It was nighttime, and Gus was there waiting for them. Gus had beaten them to death with a club. Their bloody bodies were found and buried, and their families mourned and prayed for justice to no avail, but then a witness showed up. That made for a total of three dead bodies. Gus knew then that he had to get away from Atlanta. The South was desperate to recruit men, and Gus was desperate to escape the law. Joining up was a life-saving move.

"Gus, are you all right?" Mr. Cummings broke into Gus's thoughts. "I don't want you to be upset with what I've said. I'm only speaking the facts as they are. But have heart, Joanna will only be away a short while, and she may come around to your offer in a positive way yet. I'm hoping that she does."

"Yeah," said Gus, "she probably will once she sees the light." He smiled and tried to rid himself of the downcast anger that had become apparent to Mr. Cummings. "What do you say we go out a little more into the river and check some of those crab pots again? I bet them crabs are eating away at that fish we cut up this morning."

"But we just put the fish in the crab pots a few hours ago." Then, not wanting Gus to think him disagreeable, he relented. "But if you think the pots are ready, I guess we should give them a little check."

With that, Gus grabbed the oars, and the two men sat down for a short trip out into the Potomac. Morning mist was rising off of the river as the red crab pot buoys mystically came into view.

"Bet these crab pots are full already," said Gus. "They fill up early when the weather's like this."

When they got to the first crab pot, Gus bent over to bring the pot up, but there wasn't a single crab it in. He tossed the pot back over. "Let's try another one," he said.

"I don't think the crabs have had time to smell the bait," said Mr. Cummings, "but we can certainly look while we're out here."

The next crab pot was out farther into the river and down deeper, so Gus grabbed the buoy and started to pull the rope up. "I think we got something in this pot," he said. "Look how hard it is to pull the pot up." But Gus was standing too close to the side of the shallow boat, and fell overboard still clinging to the crab pot. The pot went back down toward the bottom of the river, and so did Gus.

When Gus didn't come up immediately, Mr. Cummings quickly grabbed the rope and stopped the pot and Gus from continuing down into the deepest part of the river. Bending over, Mr. Cummings could hardly pull the weight of the pot toward him. His back was weak and the load too heavy, but he continued to pull the rope while looking overboard for signs of Gus. Then the rope stopped altogether, and Mr. Cummings felt a hard pull, causing him to go over the side and into the river.

Once under the water, he felt something around his neck pulling him down and under. He struggled to get to the surface of the water, but he couldn't free himself from the death grip of the rope. The rope was tight as he struggled to free his neck, but he soon became too weak to continue. As he sank lower into the cool water, his thoughts soon became peaceful, and his arms went limp. The last thing he saw was the empty crab pot.

When the telegram came, Joanna screamed and fell to her knees. The telegram read:

> *Papa has had an accident, and we have lost him forever. Come home quickly. I need you. Please hurry. Mama Cummings*

Joanna had not had time to settle into her aunt's house before the telegram from her mother-in-law arrived that afternoon. Overcome with disbelief, Joanna clung to the telegram and refused her aunt's comforting arms.

"Joanna, dear, please let me help you up. I need to help you get yourself together so that you can go home on the morning steamer. Your uncle and I will accompany you if you would like us to, but please, dear, please let us help you."

But Joanna stayed where she was. With her husband missing or dead, and now her father-in-law gone as well, she realized that Bennett would be devastated and her mother-in-law would be alone, a widow with no means of support. She and Bennett would be all that she had to help her in her old age. But how could she be of any benefit to her mother-in-law? The thoughts overwhelmed her, but she got up and readied herself for the grief to come, accepting her aunt and uncle's comforting embraces.

Early the next morning, the steamer docked at the farm. Holding little Bennett by the hand, Gus helped Joanna onto the dock. Dressed in one of Virgil's suits and looking very sad, Gus said, "Joanna, I don't know what to say, excepting that I'm glad you got yourself home when you did. Your mother-in-law is up at the house and is very much in a mournful state."

"Thank you, Gus," Joanna said as she looked down at her little boy, "for being here for Mama and little Bennett. I don't know what Mama would have done without you." Then Joanna took Bennett's hand and walked slowly toward the farmhouse.

Following close behind them, Gus gave an awkward tilt of his head and said, "Welcome home." As he watched Joanna walk to the house, thoughts of being married to her caused him to grin from ear to ear. But as far as Bennett went—well, he would cross that bridge when he came to it.

$\sim$

"But what about being a galvanized Yankee?" I asked David. "Do you suppose that Virgil's letters ever got through to Joanna? After all, he would have been free to write letters as a Union private, wouldn't he?"

"I don't know, but there are possibilities," said David. "Let's look for some information about The First Volunteer Regiment and what could have happened to the men who signed up to go out west."

We scanned more documents and tried to imagine what it must have been like for Virgil. There were many interesting accounts by those who had taken the oath as well as correspondences donated to various museums that had ended up at the National Archives. These letters contained valuable information, so we read as much as we could.

Chapter 34

The First US Volunteer Regiment

Virgil was having second thoughts about what he had done on the day that the oath-takers were gathered together. He had been discharged from the hospital after several weeks in recovery, but his pain was still fierce and standing straight nearly impossible. Some of the men were talking among themselves while others stood perfectly still. Silent, Virgil kept picturing his father. Could his father forgive him one day? Would he welcome Virgil home? Standing in the large tent with approximately twenty other Confederate prisoners, Virgil recognized a few faces. One of them had worked for Virgil's crabbing business. Most of these men were good and honorable, and a few were worthless fellows, but most seemed as deeply concerned as Virgil about what they were about to do.

"I was against this war from the first," said a young Confederate standing next to Virgil. "We never owned a slave and had no thought to do so. I only wanted to fight for the sovereignty of the South, not to keep slaves. To me this war goes against everything the Lord intended for our great country. I only pray that the Union will one day be restored."

Virgil looked over at the man. "Aren't you worried about what the folks back home will think?" Virgil asked.

"Not at all," replied the young man. "My family doesn't believe in war or slavery. We're Quakers, probably some of the few in South Carolina, and my father is an elder in the church. He begged me not to join up, but I was determined to be a man and fight. I guess I made a bad decision. I know that my family already finds me a traitor to our beliefs, and now I'm a traitor to the South. Guess I won't be going home once we're out of our duty time. Maybe someday I will go home, but not until I get a letter saying I'm welcome back."

"How do you know they won't be sending us to the front lines?" Virgil asked. "We could get out of here and still be sent to the front lines where we could die fighting against our own people. It could all be a lie about the regiment going out to fight Indians."

"I heard that they tried to send some up on the line, but I guess Grant sent them all back, saying that we were to go west and support and protect the forts out there. I heard that Grant thought it was a bad idea to make Confederates kill other Confederates. Who came up with an idea like that in the first place?"

"Maybe Old Abe did," replied Virgil. "We didn't want this war in the first place, but Old Abe just wouldn't leave us alone."

"Well, I just want to be a peacemaker and not fight in anymore wars." said the Quaker. "I heard that they want us in a peace-keeping type of mission out west because many of the Indians can see their own futures, and are beginning to realize that peace is superior to total conquest by the white man. Some of the Indians would still rather kill then make peace, but it makes sense to me to go out and help those new settlers. I would rather be out west then where I am now. A fellow could lose his mind in this prison camp. Besides, I know that a lot of men are going to die in this place, and I don't intend to be one of them. Of course, I don't want an arrow in my back either."

Virgil nodded his head in agreement.

"Seems it isn't safe in or out of here," said the Quaker, "but this prison camp is too crowded, and the men are getting so sick and fretful that you can hardly breathe. I'm not cut out for this kind of suffering. Better for me to try to help out west or somewhere I can see results."

"So you think that what we'll be sent to do is nobler then defending the South?" Virgil asked.

"The South is going to fall. I'm afraid that the South won't be able to sustain itself against such a powerful Union force. We are as good as done for."

The officer in charge called the prisoners to stand at attention and had them recite the oath of allegiance to the United States of America. After each man signed the oath declaration, they were told to pick up whatever provisions that they had brought with them and follow another officer. There at the outer edge of the camp, a special area was reserved for the oath-takers, and that was it. It was done. In pain and with the Quaker helping him along, Virgil followed behind the other men.

As the line of men walked to their destination, Virgil could see that it would be impossible for the other prisoners not to know what was going on. He could see prisoners behind the fence gazing between cracks in the boards. He could hear them talking and shouting cuss words at them.

"Galvanized Yankees is what you are, you traitors! Rot in hell, you cowards! You ain't any work detail, and we know what you boys are up to."

Virgil hung his head hoping that his bandages would hide his face from them. The last thing he wanted was for Gus Pruett, or whoever *his* guard was, to take another shot at him. The walk seemed to take forever and his hip and knees were still giving him pain, but once he was at the new quarters, Virgil decided to pull himself up and act like the man that he was. He may be a galvanized Yankee, but he would be the best one that he could be.

∾

Before the day was over, word had spread quickly around the prison compound that twenty more men had taken the shameful Union oath. Names were named, and talk was heavy. Some men threatened to find their way over to the traitors' compound and murder them in the night. Most couldn't believe that Virgil Cummings was among them.

"That man was supposed to be dead and rotting by now," said Gus. "I guess he thought that he could keep it secret in here that he ain't dead, but that is sure not the case. He's a traitor and a worthless deserter, and his family won't ever take him back. Somebody better write and tell his family about what he done."

"Not one of them men is going to be able to go home," said another prisoner. "If they try to go home and we see them on the road after we get out, they may as well pray to God for mercy."

Gus thought about that for a moment. The thought of Virgil getting to go home overwhelmed him with fear. Virgil could claim that Gus had nearly beaten him to death and then had a guard shoot into his tent. Though this indeed was true, he feared that the guards would talk. He would have to bribe them with seafood or whatever he could lay his hands on to keep them quiet. If anyone talked, his plans would be ruined.

It seemed to Gus that Virgil was always coming out on top of things and always thwarting Gus's plans. "Why didn't that man die when he should have?" Gus said.

"I hear tell that the Union is going to send those boys out west to fight Indians. Hope they get their heads scalped," said another prisoner.

Now there was a possibility that Gus hadn't thought of. If Virgil wouldn't die with a bullet in him, maybe some Indian would kill him. But then, Gus thought, with Virgil's luck he might live. Not only that, but now that Virgil had joined the Union, he would probably write a letter home and tell his family what he was doing, what had been done to him, and who did it. They weren't holding up the mail for Union soldiers, and the Union might even consider Virgil a hero and send all of his letters off to Virginia, now that he was a traitor to the South. They could also go after Gus for the crime. Then his name would be in print, and he might be found out for what he did in Atlanta.

Gus's mood grew dark as he walked away from the other men and went into his tent to be alone. The place smelled of Virgil, and Gus's thoughts continually went to what could have gone wrong with the guard. He'd told the guard to fire more than one bullet into the tent, and he paid the guard to do the job with the bushel of crabs that Gus had taken from Virgil's tent. Now nothing was going according to his plans.

Gus thought about the letters that Virgil could write home. There was only one thing he could think of, and that was to intercept Virgil's letters, both coming in and going out. But who could help him with getting the letters? He carefully approached his guard that very night.

"Nobody gets into that mailroom except the civilian who's been put in charge. He gets a little extra food for his effort and is treated nice by the officers," said the guard. "I don't know for sure, but I heard that the civilian and Jeremiah knew each other from before the war. I'll threaten Jeremiah to tell the mailman that he better cooperate. But for this I expect another bushel of crabs by tomorrow night."

"I can't get a whole bushel of crabs for you by then," protested Gus.

"Well you wanted to get Virgil out of the way, so now you better do as I say or else I guess you won't be getting those letters." The guard laughed at Gus. "You don't even know what you're doing, do you? You're probably scared to death you're going to be found out." He laughed again and shoved his rifle into Gus's stomach. "You get me those crabs or you might get more then Virgil got."

"I'll get the crabs if I have to work all night and day, but you need to get going right away with stopping that mail. I can't let any mail get out from Virgil Cummings, and I need the ones coming in here for him too." But Gus wasn't sure that the guard would even cooperate.

∾

When the other guard told Jeremiah what he had to do, Jeremiah refused to do it.

"You better think twice," said the guard. "Me and the rest of the guards are going to say you shot at that man. We'll all say we saw you do it too. You better just do as you're told before more officers come to get statements from us."

Jeremiah tried to reason with the guard again. "We're both black men fighting a war that's going to change things for us and make our lives better. Why do you want to make my life worse then this guard duty has already made it?"

"You know what will happen to you if we tell them you shot at that man on purpose? They'll put you on trial, and you'll be in prison for the rest of your life, or maybe even hung. You're black, you know, and you killed a white man. Somebody will come after you someday; they always do."

Jeremiah didn't take the threat lightly. "I'll get the letters," he said finally.

"Now," ordered the guard. "You go now, and you tell that civilian prisoner who's in charge of mail that you got special permission to collect all things pertaining to Virgil Cummings. You tell him whatever you got to tell him, but there better not be one letter going out or coming in for Virgil Cummings or you're goanna end up in a bad place after this war is over."

The mailman didn't want to turn over letters to anyone. The Union had held up the mail for months, and now he was being asked to give mail out to someone other than an official.

"I can't," the mailman said, "or else I could lose this job in here, and then I'd be starving like everyone else. I'm a civilian, as you know, and I shouldn't be here in the first place. All I do is sort the mail and put it in bags. I don't know if the prisoners will ever get their mail, but that's what the Union has ordered me to do for now, and I'm going to keep doing it."

"Nobody is going to know," said Jeremiah, "and if you don't turn those letters over to me, I'm going to get myself hung. Don't I give you information about goings-on in the prison yard so you can get it out to the families? We got to help each other. I never wanted in this army, but I'm stuck, just like you. We both want out of this place, but we need to keep ourselves alive in the meantime. Please help me."

The mailman thought about what all of this would mean. He had been taken as a civilian prisoner only because his father had hidden his black farmhands from the Union while they road from farm to farm, separating families and hauling off freed slaves. As punishment for harboring a would-be enlistee, Jacob was taken away from his wife and children and given a year's duty tending the camp mail. He was allowed visitors and knew that his family was doing everything they could to get him released, but now he was faced with more punishment if he were caught helping Jeremiah.

"I'll try to see what I can find," said the mailman, "but it won't be good for me or my family if I'm caught."

"Yes, I know it," said Jeremiah. "Soon, I hope, we'll both be getting out of here and heading back home, but until then we've got to help one another. You'll find mail to and from Virgil Cummings in those letters over there in that Virginia bag. Take them out and give them to me. You'll have to do this for the whole time you're in here. We're both putting our lives at risk, but we have to do it."

The mailman looked at Jeremiah. "I know, I'll do it, but what are you going to do with the letters?"

"I don't know, but I'll think of something," Jeremiah said. "I might not turn all of them over because I think someone's out to do harm with them, but I still need you to get every last one of them to me." Then changing the subject he asked, "How's that baby boy of yours doing, Mr. Chambers?"

"Lewis is doing just fine, Jeremiah. My wife was going to bring him to visit, but I told her that I didn't want her to see this horrible place. It's no place to bring a baby, even though I want so much to see him."

"I'm sure you'll be seeing him soon," said Jeremiah. "This war isn't going to last much longer."

"I hope you're right about that, Jeremiah."

Mail had been stacked in bags according to the states, and Jacob went through the bags of letters to and from Virginia. After sifting through the mail, he found some letters from the family of Virgil Cummings of Walnut Oak, Virginia, and soon he had a small pile of letters to give to Jeremiah, both incoming and outgoing mail. He put the letters into a sack and pulled the cords tight. When Jeremiah came back for the mail, he would be surprised by how many letters there were.

∾

"So who on earth ever received those letters?" I asked David.

"I don't have a clue, but mail was a problem during the war with all of the fighting and railroad disruptions. If Virgil did go out west, he may not have had access to the telegraph, if they even had a station where he was. I just don't know."

"David, do you think that Jeremiah may have turned some of the letters over to newspapers or museums, even historical societies?"

"Well, the letters and journals that we've gone through had to come from somewhere. After all, look what we've found out in one day. If we found some of Dr. Comstock's writings as well as from former Confederate prisoners, even oath-takers, just think what we might uncover."

"That's true," I said, "but there is one thing on my mind. Virgil's letters were confiscated while he was a prisoner, but that doesn't explain why he didn't write to Joanna after he left to go out west. Surely he could have sent letters to her then."

"Maybe the mail was kept from her by someone, maybe even by someone who had an interest in Virgil's family."

"Do you mean, Gus Pruett?"

"There are a few letters here from the various forts that were built around the end of the Civil War. From what I've read, Fort Rice was a pretty active place. I've read several letters from men who were attached to the First Volunteer Regiment formed at Point Lookout and discharged around 1866. I'm pretty sure that they had mail delivery to and from Fort Rice. So if Joanna Cummings was in mourning, she probably avoided any public places and maybe didn't pick up her own mail.

"I can live with scenarios," I said. "Go ahead and tell me what you're thinking."

Chapter 35

The Post Office at Walnut Oak

Joanna took her mother-in-law into her arms and held her. "Mama, please don't worry. Papa would want you to know that he is in a better place. He loved you and all of us as much as he could on this earth, and he still loves us from heaven, even now."

"Joanna, I know that what you say is true, but how will we ever survive without him? What will we do?"

"Mama, I don't even know what happened to Papa yet. Do you think that you could sit and tell me? I need to know what happened."

"Yes, dear," said Mrs. Cummings. "I suppose I need to tell you, but Gus was there, and I think you should hear it from him. Gus, would you please come over and tell Joanna how the accident happened? I just can't."

Gus came from his standing position and sat down. After placing himself on the settee and putting on a grim face, he looked over at the two women and began to tell what had happened to Mr. Cummings.

"But he was such a strong swimmer," said Joanna.

"Yes, he surely was," said Gus. "But with me overboard and all tangled around with that crab pot rope, it must have took everything he had to get the rope off me. In the process, I guess he got tangled up himself. By the time I got up for a breath of air and dove down to get him, he was already gone. The rope that he took off of me must have gotten tangled up around him too. I feel so awful about it. That man saved my life." Gus hung his head down and put his hands to his face. Little Bennett toddled up to him and put his hands up for Gus to pick him up. Gus picked the little boy up and put him on his knee.

"Please, Gus," said Joanna. "This wasn't your fault. Papa would have tried to save anyone in trouble. That was the kind of man he was, and there is always a reason behind anything that the Lord allows. Please know that we do not blame you in any way."

Joanna gave him a consoling look, and Gus knew that he had just won an incredible victory. Joanna would be his, and so would the farm. Everything he had worked for had just been handed to him. He looked at Joanna and thought about how long it had been since he'd been with a woman, and then he lifted Bennett up and held him high above his head with his two strong arms. He thought how nice it would be if he could seal the victory with a wedding. Anything was possible now, he thought, even another accident.

"Thank you for saying that, Joanna," said Gus. "Mr. Cummings was the bravest man I ever seen. He tried to save my life, and he lost his for it, sort of like in the Bible and what it says about, Jesus. I'm sorry. I guess little Bennett here is the one who's going to have to get by without a daddy or a granddaddy now. I feel real awful about it all." Gus put Bennett on his knee again and allowed his mind to think of even bigger possibilities.

The war had been over for almost a year now, and that meant that Joanna's mourning period was nearly over. Gus knew enough to lie low and not make any advances toward Joanna after the drowning.

He didn't want to push her to go back to Washington looking for a death certificate, only to find out that her beloved was still alive. But Gus didn't want to give that too much thought. To his knowledge, any letters that had not been confiscated in the prison were probably as lost as they could be somewhere in the confusion of postwar record sorting. He had taken care of the rest.

Already there had been uproars going on about the lack of information on former prisoners, such as their date of release or status. Prisoner of war camps had incomplete records of prisoners who had passed through their gates. Were these men dead or alive? Gus was sure that the government would never get to the bottom of everything. The information barely trickled out now, and with luck some of it would never be found out.

Even still, Gus had no peace of mind when he thought about the possibility of Virgil just showing up one day. But try as he might, he couldn't think of anything else he could do. If a letter showed up, it would be of equal calamity, so Gus had made sure all along that he and he alone collected the mail coming in to Walnut Oak. In the process, he had retrieved several letters that were mailed from Fort Rice, Dakota Territory. The post office clerk gave all the letters to Gus, knowing that the family was in deep mourning and that Gus had come to help Virgil's family survive.

"Morning, Gus," greeted the postmaster the next day. "I got another letter here for Mrs. Cummings from out west. I'm just so awfully sorry to hear about Mr. Cummings passing away by drowning like he did. It's just awful."

Gus gave a slight nod. "Thanks. Could I have the letter now?"

The postmaster started to hand the letter to Gus. "This letter is just like the other ones," he said, still holding the letter. "No return address is listed on this one either. Does the younger Mrs. Cummings have family out west or something?" The clerk always made sure that he knew who was getting what mail, as well as where the mail came from, and who had sent it. He figured it was his job, and he paid no attention when told to mind his own business. These letters had him intrigued.

"It's just some old friend of hers," said Gus. "Women who move out there get lonely for friends, you know."

"Yeah, I know how the womenfolk are by now," the postman agreed. "Been married twenty years now, and—"

Gus snatched the letter from the postman and left in a hurry, galloping his horse down the road and away from town before stopping the horse under a tree. Allowing the reins to drop from his hands, he tore the envelope open and read. He knew who had written the letter. Would Virgil never die?

November 15, 1866
My dearest Joanna,

I have been sending letters to you explaining about why I took the oath for the Union, but still I get no reply. My only way of reaching you is through the mail as telegraph offices are far from the fort and have often been interrupted severely by the Indian conflicts. Our duty here is to make and keep the peace with the Indians, but even though the lines have been disrupted, I have no reason to believe that you have not received my letters, or at least some of them.

When I took the oath, I feared that you would all be disgraced by my actions, and now I know that not only have I disgraced you, but believe my actions have caused you much suffering. I long to know how you all are, but in my heart I feel that you have all turned your affections away from me because of what I have done. I know that the war has left many scars, and I know too that if the citizens of Walnut Oak have found out about me, that they have probably abandoned any connection with you. But can you not find room in your heart to forgive me?

I do not know what to say. Having fought Indians and suffered many hardships, including lack of food and freezing temperatures, I have come to the conclusion that I would have been home now had it not been for my near-death experience while a prisoner. Did you not have sympathy for me when I was shot at through my tent? Why did you not answer my letters? I know that the mail was held up, but after the war you should have received my letters. If you had read them, you would know just how much danger I was in. That is why I took the oath. I took it so that one day I would see you again. It is all that I have lived for.

A fellow prisoner threatened to kill me on that same day that I was shot. His name is Gus Pruett, and he is a worthless fellow who was bent on taking revenge on me. I joined the Union so that I could come home to you after the war, as a soldier and not as a traitor and oath-taker. Now I doubt that I can ever come home. You will not forgive me. My letters to you have not been answered, nor have I received any letters from my dear parents.

We men are being released in a few weeks, after having served as the First US Volunteers, a regiment that has performed many honorable acts of bravery. We have fought to keep the West safe for all who would come to settle here. That is why I am writing to you now and why this will be my last letter. I will hold out hope that you will reply favorably as soon as you can.

I have never stopped loving you nor yearning to see my home again or my dear mama and papa. But now I know that I can never come home. It would only be a further disgrace to all of you. I am asking that if you have any love for me now, if you want to see me again and be my wife, please come out west to join me. Here we can begin our lives together again, free of insult from those who may only look at me as a deserter. We can finally start a family too. Remember how we always spoke of having a houseful of children? Do you ever think of those plans that we made together?

Things are peaceful here now and I hope to buy a little piece of land in the territory and to build a beautiful home for you. I think you could grow too love it here. There is a river that is full of fish, and around here there is plenty of game for food. Several of the other men have done the same and have asked their wives and families to come. Others have given up on their families and have moved farther west to the new gold fields. If you do not come, I may have no choice but to join them. What use would it do to wait for a woman who has lost her love for me? Have you found another to love?

I love you more than my life, but you must write to me telling me that you will come. I need you so. Please forgive me. If I don't hear from you soon, I will understand that you no longer want me as your husband. I will not hold that against you, but I will never forget how I have loved you, and always will.

Your loving husband,
Virgil E. Cummings, Pvt.
US First Volunteer Regiment
Fort Rice
Dakota Territory

When Gus finished reading the letter, he couldn't believe his fortunate situation. He also realized that Virgil had no knowledge of his little son, Bennett. Joanna would never get another letter from him, and that would be the end of it. Virgil would not be coming home.

Gus took the letter and tore it into pieces, and then he found a soft spot in the ground by an oak tree where he had buried the other letters. He dug a hole with a flat rock and buried the new pieces. Then mounting his horse, Gus galloped toward the farm and into his new life.

∞

We had reached the end of another scenario, at least for this day, but the scenario that David and I had pieced together gave me little hope for the favorable ending I had sought.

"This just can't really be what happened," I said. "There has got to be a future for Virgil and Joanna, some truth about what happened to them. What about Gus and Bennett? We're missing all kinds of facts about them, and if we keep looking, I'm sure we will find more reports or letters, maybe even the ones that Jeremiah retrieved. Do you think that Gus got hold of those letters, or did the guards destroy them? Maybe Jeremiah kept them himself?" I began to feel as though many lives were still being held in some sort of limbo, and the prospect of no conclusions was weighing on me.

David looked at me and let his eyes and voice say something that I needed to hear. Did he have to say it?

"What we have been looking at here is history, past history. Rainey, history doesn't always have a conclusion or finality to it. That's life as it was, and this is life as it is. We can't fix or change past history. History is done. I don't think you should stop looking for answers about these people, I'm not saying that, but you may want to spend equal time looking and thinking about your own future. It may actually be more interesting." David lifted my chin up and smiled. "Only the future can be changed, and I think that your future may have some great possibilities."

Chapter 36

Great Possibilities

I thought about what David said for the entire drive back to the B&B. The day had been somewhat disappointing, but somehow satisfying also. The night air was still very warm, but a cool breeze found its way to the porch as David walked me to the door.

"David, I've been thinking a lot about what you said. You said that we can't change the past but we can change our future. What did you mean by that? I know that the past can't be changed, but I also believe that the future is just about what randomly happens in life. We can't change that either. The future just happens, random and changeless."

David leaned against the porch column. "I'll be working down on your road again late tomorrow afternoon. Why don't I come by your cottage after I finish, and we'll talk more about that? For now I'm going to just say goodnight. It seems that I'm going to have to come up with some answers to your questions about the future, and that will take a lot of thought." He put his arms around my waist and gently drew me close to him. "I'll look forward to seeing you again tomorrow. I kind of like you, but then I told you that once before, didn't I?"

"Did you?" I asked him.

"Goodnight," he said, letting go of my waist. Then he was gone, leaving me standing alone on the porch.

Please don't go, I thought. But instead I watched him drive away.

Sleep escaped me as I sat on my bed thinking about my future. Somehow I had not envisioned myself doing anything but what I had been doing. Bookkeeping was a way to survive, but how could I go back to just existing after the life I had been living, doing what I loved to do? Getting to the bottom of the lives and deaths and legacies of people had kept me going for these many weeks, but so had getting to know the people around me. Now what was I to do, and what made David think that a future of bookkeeping could be interesting, or did he mean something else?

∽

The next day I ate my last breakfast with Linda and her husband. We chatted for a while. It was hard to finally say good-bye, knowing that I would be leaving them as well as my cottage neighbors, and returning to my old life in Annapolis. Linda gave me a hug and reminded me to visit her from time to time.

"If I have to bribe you by breaking into my father's journal to get you back here, I will. I told you that I've read things that may be shocking to sensitive eyes in those journals, and I might be willing to share." She hugged me again and said, "I'll always have that little room ready for you should another hurricane crop up."

"I would drive down here just for your cooking," I said, "but please, don't mention hurricanes! Thank you for everything, Linda." I quickly got into my car and drove away, practicing how I would tell my cottage neighbors goodbye without getting emotional. I planned to make it short and sweet, but I was already dropping a few tears just thinking about how much I would miss Linda.

After I entered my road, I could still see that much more needed to be done to restore our cottages to what they had once been. Many roofs were covered with green and blue tarps. There were gutters and downspouts lining the road and bushes and trees still needing to be cut up and carried off. As I approached my cottage and parked, I was sad to see stumps where my two old trees had been, but when I looked out over the bay and saw the pelicans diving, the white puffy clouds hanging as if suspended in the air, and even a stray cat taking up residence in my old, ruined chair in the yard, I was somehow pleased with the way things looked.

My key was not operating in the lock as smoothly as it once had, and I figured that water must have gotten into the keyhole, rusting it out. But with some effort I was finally able to get it open. Then I pushed the door in and stood suspended and unable to move as I looked inside.

There in the middle of the room was my antique bamboo rocking chair, cleaned and sitting proudly as if to welcome me. On my surviving bookshelf my periwinkle shells that I had collected over the years sat in an old blue Mason jar. Mounted on the wall were my wooden beams and a beautifully carved frame made, I was sure, from one of my fallen trees. My oak table had also been cleaned and repainted a soft ocean blue color, and the two chairs at the table had been covered with blue and white gingham seat cushions. A note on the table from David said, "The neighbors got together and painted your furniture, and Mrs. Manny made the chair covers for you. Look in the refrigerator."

Sitting in the middle of the table behind the note was a handmade birdhouse, white with a red roof. I thought about Miss Biscoe's birdhouses and how much I had loved them. I didn't know who had made the birdhouse for me—there was no note—but I suspected that David had made it.

My electricity had been restored, and my small refrigerator was purring away. When I opened it, I found drinks, some lunch meat and bread, a jar of homemade pickles, some cheese slices, and a cold noodle salad. A note on top of the salad said, "Enjoy this little meal," and it was signed, "Love, Mrs. Wilderman." I started to cry. Like I said, I cry at the oddest times.

As I surveyed my cottage, I could see that someone had cleaned and sprayed my walls and that the damaged areas of drywall had been replaced and painted over as well. My bedroom was in good shape, and my linens had been washed and put at the foot of the bed. In short, my cottage looked well enough to inhabit. My tears continued to flow as I walked around in silence. Then I walked outside into the bright afternoon sun.

I could see the waves as they beat upon the rocks, white foam leaving their mark behind. It was the changing of the tide, and seagulls were swooping down and the ospreys were beating their wings high overhead, waiting for an opportune time to dive.

I felt as though I had become their guardian as I checked the sky for any possible storm clouds. That was becoming a habit with me now since learning from my neighbors that some things could be predicted by observing even the smallest of obscure signs. But the birds didn't need me to guard their lives. They had that knowledge somewhere deep inside of them.

There was something stirring deep within me as well. I had never experienced it before, but it was so deep that I could hardly express my feelings. From somewhere came a feeling of belonging and purpose, as though the hurricane had brought about a declaration in me or a validation that I was loved and respected and appreciated. In my fifteen years of marriage, I had hardly felt more than average or ordinary, and those feelings were on a good day.

I looked around my debris-covered yard again, feeling more grateful then ever before. Out front a crab boat crew was busy working their pots with the boat's diesel engines idling and sputtering, sending up a plume of black smoke. My hot-pink hibiscus plants, those that had survived the hurricane, were bending low in the soft breeze. A few pelicans were dive-bombing in the water in front of the rock wall, and I could hear an occasional jet flying high overhead from the Patuxent River Naval Air Base. I felt safe and at home.

I looked back up the road and could see that Mr. and Mrs. Carey were walking along with their daughter, Billie. They waved and walked toward me as I stood in my front yard.

"There is one of our heroes now, Billie," said Mr. Carey. Billie came to me and hugged me.

"Mr. Carey, believe me when I say that I am no hero," I said, hugging Billie and enjoying her arms around me. "I wasn't brave at all. David did all of the work, not me. But thank you for the compliment."

"Well we are ever so grateful, and so Mrs. Carey, Billie, and I would like for you to come over for some blue crabs tonight. We've bought a large new picnic table and a nice large steamer, and we're going to buy some number ones and cook them to perfection with plenty of Old Bay. We've invited the whole neighborhood to come so that we could all thank you for saving my family and for the kind things you've done. Even the Mannys are going to drive down just for this event."

"I can't believe the way my cottage looks," I said. "And my refrigerator is stocked, and my furniture has been repaired and painted. You all have done so much for me that I'm overwhelmed. I just don't know how to thank you. But I would love to come and enjoy some crabs. Just let me know what time."

Cottages

"I think we'll have the crabs ready and on the picnic table at about six or so," said Mrs. Carey.

"I'll be there," I said. "What can I bring?"

"Bring that nice man, David, with you," said Mrs. Carey with a smile. I could tell by her tone that she meant it in a neighborly sort of way. Or did she?

I accepted their offer graciously before they took Billie for a walk on the beach, and then I called David.

"David, here," he said in his business voice.

"David," I said, "this is Rainey, and I want to say something to you. There are so many things that I need to say, but I don't exactly know where to begin. I just don't deserve this life, and these neighbors, and you..."

"Whoa," he said, laughing, "slow down and tell me what this is all about."

"David, I've just been inside my cottage. I think you know why I'm so excited, humbled, and thankful. I can't believe what you have all done for me. I've been rude to you, and yet you have been so kind in return. It must be that religion of yours," I teased, "and I want you to tell me all about that when you get a chance."

"OK. But first," he answered, "yes, you do deserve to be thanked by those in the community. You have been brave, caring, and kind to everyone. People down here don't take those things for granted. Second, I don't have a religion. I have a *faith*. Maybe I should have explained that to you so that you would understand. In fact, I botched that whole conversation up so badly I was hoping that you would give me another try at it this evening."

"How about you try again after the crab feast tonight?" I asked. "Mrs. Carey specifically asked me to make sure that you would be here at around six o'clock, and Mr. Carey has invited the whole neighborhood. I think they feel the need to thank us again for the rescue."

"I wouldn't miss it," he said. "In fact, I knew all about it and was planning to be there. Mrs. Carey called me."

"Oh she did, did she? I didn't know that."

"You weren't supposed to know about it. Would you mind if I park the truck at your place?"

"No, in fact, I want you to come in for a minute when you get here."

"OK, sounds good to me," he said.

Before David arrived, I changed into my Capri jeans and my worn Baltimore Orioles T-shirt, suitable for picking crabs, then dabbed on a little lipstick. My hair was tied back in a ponytail, which I pulled through the back of my old Seattle Mariners baseball cap, and I had just put my flip-flops on when I heard the sound of a tap on the door.

I went quickly to the door and opened it. A cool breeze blew past David, and I breathed in his aftershave mingled with the salty smells of the bay. He was clean-shaven, and his black hair still looked wet from a shower. I gave a welcoming smile, and his brown eyes smiled back at me as he stood in the doorway. But I couldn't stand still. I put my arms around his neck and said a simple, "Thank you, David." Then I hugged him tightly.

"I hope this is a trend," he said hopefully, "but why the thank you?"

I let him loose from the hug. "I am so thankful to have a dear friend like you," I said.

"So we're finally friends then?"

"Yes. I'm grateful for you and everyone here. Because of all that everyone has done, I'll be able to stay at my place for a few weeks before returning to Annapolis. I'm so very thankful, especially to you, David."

He put his arms around my shoulders, and then drawing me slowly to him, whispered in my ear, "I can deal with this kind of thankfulness any day." Then he stood looking down at me and asked, "Is this a perk for being your research assistant or something?"

"Absolutely, this is a perk," I answered.

We could hear the Chesapeake churning up again, but this time it was just a change in the tide, that wonderful tide that signaled the ending of another day. David took my hand firmly in his and closed the door behind us. We walked in the direction of the cookout, enjoying the breeze that brought the smell of fresh steaming crabs seasoned with Old Bay. I looked up the road and saw that some neighbors had arrived and were walking toward Mr. Carey's place, coolers and picnic baskets in tow.

Mrs. Finch had put her Four Tops tunes on, and some of the children were dancing to the music. Her POW flag was waving gently, and her pier was full of people overflowing from the adjoining yards. I squeezed David's hand as we approached the Carey cottage wishing so much that everyone and everything could stay just this way, and that all the cottages could be repaired. I wanted to start believing too that my future would hold those "great possibilities" that David had mentioned. And you know, I think I just might have *faith* that it will.

A note from the author:

Thank you for reading Cottages. I hope you enjoyed Rainey's stories and that you'll look forward to reading more of her "historical gossip" in the next, Chesapeake Bay Stories, novel. Though many of the characters in my novel have names similar to persons located in the St. Mary's County area, each of my characters is a complete creation of my own imagination, and not intended to possess any similarity to anyone living or deceased. You may view the actual names of Confederate prisoners who suffered and died while imprisoned at Point Lookout Camp for Confederate Prisoners, inscribed on the monuments located beside the road, on the way to Point Lookout, Maryland.

36054876R00185

Made in the USA
Charleston, SC
21 November 2014